DON'T TURN AROUND

...manda Brooke is a single mum who lives in Liverpool ...h her daughter, Jessica, a cat called Spider, a dog ...ed Mouse, and a laptop within easy reach. Her ...r novel, *Yesterday's Sun*, was a Richard and Judy ...k Club pick. *Don't Turn Around* is her ninth novel.

...amanda-brooke.com
...nandaBrookeAB
...w.facebook.com/AmandaBrookeAuthor

Also by Amanda Brooke

Yesterday's Sun
Another Way to Fall
Where I Found You
The Missing Husband
The Child's Secret
The Goodbye Gift
The Affair
The Bad Mother
Don't Turn Around

Ebook-only short story
The Keeper of Secrets
If I Should Go

AMANDA BROOKE

Don't Turn Around

HarperCollins*Publishers*

HarperCollins*Publishers* Ltd
1 London Bridge Street
London SE1 9FG

www.harpercollins.co.uk

A Paperback Original 2019
1

A catalogue record for this book
is available from the British Library

ISBN: 978-0-00-821918-5

Set in Sabon LT Std by Palimpsest Book Production Ltd, Falkirk, Stirlingshire

Printed and bound in Great Britain by CPI Group (UK) Ltd, Croydon CR0 4YY

For my children, Jessica and Nathan

Prologue

The Confession

The rhythmic slap of my ballet shoes against the linoleum-covered steps echoes down the stairwell. As my pace slows, my head droops and my gaze falls onto the worn and familiar treads that lead to the seventh floor and home. I know each and every scuff mark, every chip of paint, and even the crumpled tissues and sweet wrappers discarded by my thoughtless neighbours are familiar to me. Unlike my apartment block's gleaming city-centre exterior, its spine has an air of abandonment. The stairwell is rarely used and less frequently cleaned, and there have been times when I've taken it upon myself to return with rubber gloves and a bin bag, but no more. Believe me, I've tried, but nothing I do ever makes a difference.

My legs are trembling by the time I reach my floor and I take a moment to catch my breath. Drawn to the window with its view of the Liverpool waterfront, I follow the line of docks until they're rudely interrupted by the modern edifice of a thirteen-storey office block that sits awkwardly

1

between Canning Dock and the Pier Head. This is Mann Island, and although it hasn't been an island for centuries, the place where I work certainly looks stranded next to the iconic outlines of the Port of Liverpool, Cunard and Liver Buildings. The Three Graces had been basking in the after-glow of a crisp autumn day when I'd set off on the short trek home along the Strand, but the world has darkened since, and the Graces have been reduced to silhouettes, pockmarked with yellow, fluorescent lights. As I step back from the window, my eyes refocus and I catch my reflection.

The apparition floating beyond the sheet of glass is weighed down by the heavy houndstooth woollen jacket hanging off her shoulders. Her round face is framed by straggly mouse-brown hair and a severe fringe that's become frayed from her exertions. Her complexion is pale against the starless night and there's no spark in her eyes. The fight has left her.

I don't recognise this woman captured by the failing light, or perhaps I do. There's something about her that reminds me of Meg. My cousin's hair was a similar shade although you would describe hers as golden, and she never hid behind a fringe. Meg was bold, and yet the hopelessness in the face that stares back at me immediately brings her to mind.

I retreat to the exit door only to stop when I hear a noise. The soft squeak of a rubber sole on linoleum came from the floor above, or I think it did. The world falls silent again and I'm about to dismiss the crawling sensation that I'm being watched when—

'Hello, Jen.'

Instinctively, I grab the safety bar but I don't open the door because I've already recognised the deep voice that sent a jolt of terror down my spine. The fact that he's here shouldn't surprise me, and I know it won't matter if I run away, or stand and fight. He's already won.

I turn my head slowly but he stops me.

'Don't turn around.'

Keeping my head to the side, I stare at the window with its mirror image of the landing behind me. No figure appears from the shadows, no hand reaches out to wrap around my neck.

'What is this? Don't you have the guts to face me?' I ask, my voice surprisingly calm.

There's a pause and when he replies, he sounds closer. 'If I thought it was going to be easy, we would have had this conversation ten years ago.'

'This conversation?' I ask. 'If it's a confession you're planning, I'm not the one you should be talking to. It's Meg's parents who deserve answers.'

'Ruth and Geoff don't need to hear what I have to say.'

'I suppose you're going to tell me you've been protecting them all these years.'

'Not only them.'

My laugh catches in my dry throat. 'Oh, I see. You've been protecting me too.'

'If Meg had wanted you to know everything, she'd have told you *everything*.'

'Maybe she tried,' I reply as I picture a torn scrap of yellow lined paper. Meg's suicide note, or at least a remnant of it.

'No, she didn't,' he says with finality. 'Christ, Jen, didn't you know her at all?'

'She was my best friend. Of course I knew her!' I tell him, raising my voice to camouflage the doubt.

'Not like I did,' he says in a whisper.

A door swings open three flights down and shrieks of laughter ricochet off the walls as a group of raucous, and possibly drunken friends race to the ground floor. Their giddiness reminds me of times lost, but I can't trust my memories. How many of Meg's smiles were a disguise for unfathomable pain?

When another door slams shut and stillness returns, I hear the whisper of stealthy footfalls. I scan the reflection of the empty landing and glimpse movement on the small section of the stairs that are visible to me. I spy a pair of black boots and legs clad in dark jeans. I twist my body towards him.

'I said, don't turn around.'

'Why?'

'Because I can't . . .' He curses under his breath. 'I won't do this if you're looking at me.'

1

Jen

Two months earlier . . .

As I watch the TV crew setting up the interview, I stand as close as I dare to the floor-to-ceiling windows to give myself the best view across the office. The intensity of the summer sun reflecting off the white Portland stone of the neighbouring Port of Liverpool Building forces me to shield my eyes as I follow what the camera sees.

A banner for the Megan McCoy Foundation, set up by Ruth and Geoff set up in their daughter's name three years after her death has been strategically placed to obscure the logo of McCoy and Pace Architects. It looks a little worn but better than it did this morning when I unearthed it from the bottom of the stationery cupboard. I used a Sharpie to cover up the scratches and I'm hoping the camera won't pick up where I went outside the lines on the telephone number for the Lean On Me helpline. There's half a roll of duct tape holding it all together on the back, but if the relaunch goes as well as we're hoping, I can order new banners.

The cameraman points his lens over the reporter's left shoulder while she asks, 'Perhaps you could start by telling us a little about Megan.' The camera zooms in on the middle-aged woman sitting at one of the two helpline pods that represent the sum total of the foundation's resources.

Ruth's long, slender body is tense but I see the lines creasing her brow soften as she begins to build a picture of her daughter in her mind. 'She was my youngest – I have a son, Sean, who's two years older – but Megan was the baby of the family. I know we spoiled her but that didn't *spoil* her, if you know what I mean. She was no trouble, always did as she was told and she couldn't have been more thoughtful and caring. Not a day went by without her doing something that was sweet, or funny, or just made my heart clench with love.' Ruth's smile broadens as she adds flesh to her daughter's memory.

The spider's web of wrinkles around her eyes that mark the ten years Ruth has lived with her heartache cut a little deeper and her smile falters. Her short, dark brown hair emphasises her paling complexion.

'What went wrong?' asks the reporter.

Ruth's eyes flick towards me. 'She fell in with the wrong crowd.'

I know my aunt better than I know my own mother. The look she gives me is not one of reproach. I'm no more responsible for Meg being led astray than she, but we carry our own guilt. I shift uncomfortably, aware of the wall of glass next to me that seems suddenly fragile.

'Megan had been doing extremely well at school. Eleven

A star GCSEs,' Ruth continues. 'Sean had gone off to university and we expected her to follow suit, but when she went into sixth form, everything changed. In those last two years, she went from being able to talk to us about anything, to not wanting to be in the same room as me or her father. I thought our relationship with our daughter was unbreakable but it was as if someone had hacked into her mind and completely rewired it. Geoff and I tried everything to get her back on track, from cajoling, to bribery, to threats, but nothing worked. As a last resort, we grounded her, something we'd never had to do before, but when she wasn't barricading herself in her room, she would sneak out as soon as our backs were turned. We could see what was happening and were helpless to stop it.'

Ruth pulls at her polished fingernails and I find myself looking through her and into the past. I spent more time with Meg than I did my own sisters and of all the memories I have, the one that rises quickest to the surface is our last trip to school to pick up our A Level results. I have a vivid picture of standing with a cluster of friends as we tore open our envelopes. I had the grades I needed for my first choice uni, but my joy was short-lived as I became aware of other people's reactions, and Meg's in particular. She was deathly pale but her cheeks were pinched crimson as she watched Lewis Rimmer punch the air. She screwed up her envelope and flung it at his smug face.

'What did I do?' he asked as she stormed off.

It's a question I still ask myself.

I wonder if Ruth is thinking of him too as she curls her fingers into fists. 'Meg was devastated when she failed her exams. Uni had been her escape route, I think. It would

7

have given her the chance to distance herself from the bad influences in her life.'

'Was there substance abuse?'

'No, but there *was* abuse,' Ruth says carefully.

Shock forces me back a step and my shoulder thumps against the window before I can right myself. What is Ruth doing?

'When Meg died,' Ruth continues, her gaze remaining fixed on the reporter, 'there was evidence of self-harm and a previous attempt to take her life that we knew nothing about. She hurt herself and I believe that was because someone was hurting her more, emotionally if not physically. Through my years on the Lean On Me helpline, I've learnt that an abuser's greatest weapon can be the mind of his victim.'

A frown forms as the reporter checks her notes. She's done her research and knows there was no mention of abuse in the coroner's verdict. The foundation's website simply states that Meg took her own life less than two weeks after failing her exams and that it was a senseless loss. That's always been the official line and the abuse that we as a family know Meg endured has gone unrecorded and unpunished. Up until today, Ruth has kept to a carefully edited version of her daughter's death to avoid litigation, and I don't understand why she's chosen now to speak up. Or perhaps I do.

Despite our best efforts, there has been little interest from the media in our cause. Press releases have gone unread and the handful of press interviews we've been able to secure have resulted in minimal column inches. This pre-recorded interview is our last-ditch attempt to draw in new callers and keep the helpline open, but there's no guarantee that it will air this evening. It's been a slow news week after the August bank holiday weekend but if something more newsworthy comes along, our story will be shelved. Ruth wants to make sure that doesn't happen, and she certainly has the reporter transfixed.

'It's no coincidence that one of the foundation's principal aims is to give young people the tools to recognise when they're in toxic relationships,' she continues. 'Tools that could have saved Meg's life.'

The reporter leans in closer to ask the question Ruth shouldn't answer. 'And who was it that hurt your daughter, Mrs McCoy?'

My fingers dig into the flesh of my arms – surely she won't do it. Naming the man we all loathe might grab the headlines, but a lawsuit would follow and my next press release won't be to promote the helpline, it'll be to announce its closure.

'There was a boyfriend,' Ruth explains, skirting dangerously close to the truth. 'I'm sure part of the attraction for Meg was that she knew we wouldn't approve, but I'd been willing to give him the benefit of the doubt. Geoff was less accommodating and, as it turned out, his instincts were better than mine. To understand what this man took from us, you would need to have known the person Meg was before she met him. When she was at her best, my daughter could light up a room. Pick a memory, any memory, and there was Meg right at the centre of it all, bright and beautiful.' Ruth's eyes light up, only to dim when she adds, 'But in the space of two short years, he took every last spark of life she had and stamped it out. It was as if my sweet girl had been hollowed out. I lost her long before the day she died.'

I close my eyes, feeling a tension headache creeping up my temples. Even without a name, there are plenty of viewers who will know exactly who Ruth is talking about. I have to hope that Lewis won't be one of them.

'And that was three days before her eighteenth birthday,' the reporter adds.

'Ten years ago this coming Thursday.'

'And the note Megan left. Did it mention anything about what she had been through?' the reporter asks as she refers back to her notes.

'The scrap of a note we were left with explained nothing,' Ruth replies, choosing her words carefully.

When she looks at me, I shake my head urgently. The police investigation had found no evidence that someone else had been there when Meg hung herself, or that the note she had left had been tampered with, despite never finding the missing half to the page taken from her notepad. No matter what we might think privately, our suspicions can't be made public. Acid burns in my stomach as I watch Ruth return her gaze to the camera, her eyes blazing with fury.

'Meg told us she wanted her shame to be buried with her, but no child should be buried in shame. She was seventeen years old. If there's any shame, it's mine. I didn't see what was in front of me, and I can never change that.'

'You have nothing to be ashamed of,' the reporter tells her.

'Tell that to the people who go to extraordinary lengths to avoid mentioning how I lost my daughter,' Ruth hits back. Her voice softens when she adds, 'But if we don't talk about suicide and the pain it causes families like mine, how can we open up the conversation and reach out to those struggling with suicidal thoughts? Meg thought she was sparing us. I wish I could have told her that whatever she was going through, or whatever she thought she was putting us through, it wouldn't last. It's the grief that goes on forever. I didn't simply lose her that day, I lost an entire future. I've recently become a grandmother but I'll never see the children Meg might have had, or celebrate countless other milestones in her life.'

'You've created a wonderful legacy in her memory. She would be very proud of you,' the reporter says gently.

'As I am of her. The Megan McCoy Foundation wouldn't exist without her. Our daughter thought she had run out of options and our job is to make sure that young women, and men too, realise there are *always* options. I'll never know what Meg would have made of her life if things had been different, but thanks to the Lean On Me helpline, I know quite a few young people who were on a similar path and are now enjoying lives they never thought possible. It's a lovely feeling when they get back in touch to share good news.'

'Perhaps you could tell me about some of the people you've helped.'

'I didn't do it alone. It's been a group effort,' Ruth says as she catches my eye. There's a hint of a smile. She's back on script.

Pressing my chin to my chest as Ruth recounts the foundation's successes, I allow the relief flooding my chest to ease away my tension.

I'm not sure Ruth realises it, but the first person she saved was me. Meg's death didn't only rewrite her parents' future, it rewrote mine too. I was always the shy one, hiding behind Meg's armour of overconfidence. She could jump from a stage and never doubt that someone would catch her, while to this day I refuse to step into a lift because I'm convinced a cable will snap. Unlike Meg, I've never put my fears to the test but then I don't need to. Bad things do happen – Meg proved that.

It would have been nice if my response to my cousin's premature death had been to grab every opportunity that life had to offer, but I didn't see the point. Not all leaps of faith ended well, so why take the risk? Much to my mother's chagrin, I turned down my place at university and denied her a full complement of four daughters with degrees, husbands and successful careers. In her eyes, I've failed on all counts.

I spent the years I should have been at uni flitting from one casual job to another until Ruth asked for my help setting up the foundation. She had commandeered a corner of the new offices of McCoy and Pace Architects and she wanted my help to launch the Lean On Me helpline. The role was voluntary, the charity couldn't afford paid staff or much else for that matter, but Ruth found a way around that by employing me as an admin assistant and allowing me to split my time between the firm and the foundation.

I was reluctant at first, and Mum wasn't too pleased that I was being offered such a lowly position in her brother's firm, but I wasn't looking for favours from Auntie Ruth and Uncle Geoff. They became simply Ruth and Geoff as we adjusted to our new roles in each other's lives, and although certain aspects of the work can be a challenge, I've been surprised by how much satisfaction I've gained from helping others through the charity. I'm less keen on my admin duties but, if the relaunch of the helpline is a success, if we secure more funding and reach out to more people, then I plan to start training to be a counsellor. It's by no means guaranteed and I share Ruth's desperation, but I'd like to believe that Meg is steering me towards a career I never knew I wanted. This relaunch has to work.

When I lift my head, Ruth is beaming a smile at the reporter. She's in full flow, talking about the helpline. It might not be on the grand scale of some of the national charities we work with like the Samaritans, Women's Aid and Refuge who can offer twenty-four-hour support but, for three evenings a week, we are there for young people who often have nothing more than a growing sense of unease about a relationship and want to talk it through. A listening ear might not sound like much, but we've had enough successes to make the last seven years worthwhile, and long may it continue.

A shadow appears in my periphery and I turn to find Geoff with his shoulder pressed against the window.

'I wish you wouldn't do that,' I whisper, my pulse racing as I imagine a creak as the window frame loosens, followed by the sound of glass and bone shattering on the concourse below.

Geoff straightens up. 'Sorry.'

Like Ruth, my uncle's tailored appearance gives no hint of the trauma he's suffered. He was the one who found Meg in the garage but if the shadow of that memory persists, it's hidden behind the twinkle in his grey eyes. The only marked difference I've noticed in the past decade is a receding hairline and the slight paunch he carries as a result of too many whiskeys.

'How's it going?' he asks, tipping his head towards Ruth.
I attempt a smile but my eyes give something away.

'What's happened?'

'Ruth might have suggested Meg was being abused,' I say with a wince. 'She didn't mention *him* by name but she said enough for anyone who knew Meg to join the dots.'

'Including Lewis,' Geoff replies, his mouth twisting into a snarl. 'I wish we could name that bastard and prick his conscience, but I doubt he has one. He's not the one who suffers when old wounds are reopened.'

I want to give my uncle a hug but that would simply acknowledge the pain he tries so hard to hide. 'It'll be worth it if just one person sees the interview and reaches out,' I tell him.

'It's a lot of effort to go to for one person, Jennifer,' he warns.

Despite being a trustee of the foundation, Geoff has always taken a pragmatic view of our work. He was the first to challenge the effectiveness of the helpline in light of the sharp decline in callers, and his initial suggestion was to wind things up as a precursor to retirement, which he's mentioned an awful lot since turning sixty. The relaunch isn't only about convincing new clients to believe in us.

'We'll get plenty of new callers after this,' I promise, with enough conviction in my voice to make the cameraman on the other side of the office raise an eyebrow. I mouth an apology and for the remainder of the interview remain tight-lipped. It's not as if there's anything else I can say to Geoff that Ruth hasn't already tried. Results are what we need and I pray that Ruth's interview will draw the right kind of attention.

2

Jen

'Did you see the interview?' I ask Mum as I pour a layer of béchamel sauce over lasagne sheets.

'Ruth didn't look at all well. Her eyes were sunken and I bet her fingers have been chewed to the quick beneath those false nails.'

I pull a face, which fortunately Mum can't see because she's on speakerphone. 'Ruth's fine,' I say. 'If she looks tired, it's because we've been working so hard on the relaunch. I thought she came across really well, and we got the message across that we needed.'

'It's a good cause, we all know that, but was it wise to name Lewis?'

'She *didn't* name him.'

'As good as,' Mum says, filling my heart with dread. If she thinks that, so will everyone else.

In the hours since the interview I've tried to remain positive but there's no running away from the fact that Ruth has taken a huge risk. She's made the first strike, and if I know anything about Lewis, it's that he will hit back.

'I can understand why she's so determined to blame him,' Mum continues. 'It's got to be better than facing the truth.'

'Oh, and what exactly is the truth?'

I hear her sigh. 'She blames herself, like any mother would. And I know she'd love to go back and do things differently but that's never going to happen, is it?'

'And what would you do differently?' I ask through gritted teeth. If my mother wants to start apportioning blame, a chat about the role she played is long overdue.

'I loved Meg, you know I did,' she says firmly, 'but it's time to stop dwelling in the past. That video montage they showed – poor Meg, all smiles and full of life – it broke my heart. Goodness knows what it did to Ruth and Geoff.'

It broke my heart too, I want to tell her. But I shouldn't have to. 'Ruth wanted to share it, Mum,' I continue. 'It was her idea. The helpline wouldn't exist without Meg and that's how she keeps her memory alive.'

'That, and having you around,' Mum mutters, edging closer to the subject neither of us dare raise.

I'm the youngest of Mum's brood and it's fair to say that the novelty had worn off when she got to daughter number four. I gravitated to Meg because we were the same age and, well, because she was Meg. It wasn't because my aunt and uncle had the posh house and the spare room I could have to myself whenever I stayed over, although Mum always insisted that was the draw. I loved being somewhere where I wasn't lost in the melee of family life, and there were times when I wished Ruth had been my mum. Occasionally, I still do.

As I drop globs of bolognese sauce into the oven dish, it splatters across my white cotton shirt. I want to swear but I don't. 'Ruth and I share a passion for what we do,' I explain. 'Look at what we've achieved, Mum. There's a lot we can be proud of.'

'Of course there is,' Mum says in a placating tone that riles me. 'Your father and I *are* proud of you, as we are of all our daughters.'

'Where is Dad?' I ask, to steer her away from what I know is coming next. My sisters are her favourite topic of conversation.

'He's still watching the news. He says hi.'

I doubt Dad has peeled his eyes from the TV screen. Having brought up four daughters in a compact terraced house, he learnt long ago to tune out of the conversations going on around him.

'Have you heard Hayley's news?' Mum continues. 'She's only been back from maternity leave two months and they've promoted her already.'

'Yes, you told me.'

Mum hears the sharpness of my reply. 'You'll get there too, Jennifer. You have as much potential as your sisters and you're still young-ish.' There's a telling pause before she adds, 'Although I was looking at how long it takes to become a certified counsellor. You really should start training sooner rather than later.'

I regret ever mentioning my musings to Mum, but I'd been in the middle of planning the relaunch and Ruth had me all enthused about how the foundation might actually expand its services beyond the helpline, despite Geoff's calls for caution. But Mum's right. It will take years to become qualified and there would be sacrifices I'd have to make along the way.

I glance across the open plan apartment, with its polished timber floor and gleaming surfaces. There are no sticky finger marks on the glass dining table, no Lego bricks gathering dust beneath the pale grey sofa, and the corner desk has no teetering tower of files brought home from a demanding job. I'm unlike any of my sisters.

It's as if Mum is looking over my shoulder when she adds, 'And it's not the only thing you need to start planning.'

I don't know why I bothered answering the phone when I saw Mum's name appear. On a day when I'm desperate for a hug, my mother puts me in a stranglehold. Can't she see that I'm happy as I am?

'It's ten years since – you know,' Mum continues. 'It's time to move on and start building a life for yourself.'

As Mum's voice drones on from the speakerphone, I carry the lasagne to the oven. The dish makes a clatter as I drop it onto a baking shelf and I don't hear the front door opening. When I straighten up, Charlie catches me pulling faces at the phone.

'You're twenty-eight years old, Jennifer,' Mum continues, having given up pretending I'm still young-ish. 'You need to think about settling down properly, and Charlie's business is doing well. Isn't it time he popped the question?'

Charlie's eyebrows lift as his mouth pulls into a smirk. Mum would have a fit if she knew that in almost eight years of living together, Charlie has asked me to marry him a total of five times and my answer has always been the same – what we have works.

'I'm waiting for Jen to ask me, Eve,' Charlie calls out.

There's a long pause and I can't tell if Mum has been struck dumb because she's realised Charlie was listening, or she's simply horrified at the idea that one of her daughters should have to do the asking.

'Don't worry about us, Mum,' I say to break the silence. 'We're happy enough as we are. Shouldn't that be what matters?'

'I'm only looking out for you— for both of you,' she adds. 'You don't have to settle for *happy enough*. That's all I'm saying.'

This time when I pull a face, Charlie does too and we have to stifle our giggles as we say our goodbyes to Mum and I cut the call.

'That's *never* all Mum was saying,' I mutter.

'It's your fault for not fitting into her standardised daughter mould.'

'And she won't stop until she's hammered me into place.'

'I like a woman who knows her own mind,' Charlie says before adding quickly, 'You do know I'm talking about you, right? Not your mum?'

'I know,' I reply although I'm not sure I do know my own mind. My refusal to conform could be because Meg passed on her rebellious streak to me as a parting gift, but I suspect what she actually left me with was fear – fear of opening new doors when the one behind was torn off its hinges and will never close. I doubt I could look to the future at all without Charlie. He knows what we left behind. He was there too. 'Thank you for saving me from my mother's designs.'

'As I recall, we saved each other,' he replies.

Moving closer, Charlie circles the kitchen island that divides the kitchen and living space. He's a foot taller, some might say lanky, with curly brown hair and hazel eyes pinched into a permanent squint because he refuses to wear glasses except for driving. He says they make him look like a geek and I'm inclined to agree but it was his geekiness that attracted me to him, and that was long before he ever noticed me.

We met in high school and were part of the same circle of friends with Meg at its core. There was an unspoken rule that none of us could fancy each other, and no one had an issue with that until we started sixth form and Lewis infiltrated the group. That was when the rules of engagement were rewritten and Charlie and I were one of the last to pair off. The fact that Lewis was the catalyst might suggest his influence was a good thing. It wasn't.

His arrival heralded the end of all our teenage dreams, and Meg wasn't the only one who would fail her A Levels. Charlie did too, and if I'm honest, I was more worried about him at the time than I was Meg. I was no longer the person she turned to in a crisis, and I proved to be no help to Charlie either. After Meg's funeral, he disappeared for a while. He went to work for his uncle in Warrington and when he returned a year or so later, he found me where he'd left me; still at Mum and Dad's, still grieving, still scared to look to the future. Thank God for Charlie.

A smile creeps across my face as I watch him pick up a damp dish cloth and begin treating the red spatters on my shirt as if they're war wounds. He has the presence of a paramedic although his area of expertise lies closer to stain removal.

Taking advice from his uncle, Charlie had come back to Liverpool with a plan. He set up his own cleaning business and I'd been helping him when Ruth stole me away to work for her. It was probably a good thing that I left when I did. As is apparent from the mess I've made in the kitchen, cleaning is not my forte, whereas Charlie has found his vocation. Despite what my mum might think, you don't need qualifications to be a success.

'What on earth's got your mum riled up this time?' he asks.

'The interview. Meg's anniversary. Hayley's promotion. The full moon,' I say, counting them off on my fingers.

Charlie's quiet for a moment. Meg has that effect on us. 'How did the interview go?'

'I imagine that depends on who you ask.'

'Forget whatever your mum's said.' He puts the cloth down and wraps his arms around me.

Resting my head on his chest, I say, 'I'm not talking about Mum, and the interview itself went well. It might only be the local news but our services are targeted to the North West anyway, and it's just what we need to raise awareness.'

'But?'

'Ruth . . . She all but named Lewis as Meg's murderer.' I'm forced to raise my head as Charlie pulls back from me in shock. 'I know, I know. You don't have to give me that look.'

'Does she realise what she's done?' Charlie asks, as if the retribution I've been fearing is all but guaranteed.

'I think Geoff will have driven home that message. I saw them having words after the TV crew had wrapped up,' I tell him. I'd watched them in their glass-fronted corner office and I didn't need to hear what was said to know it was a heated discussion. 'She's been so careful in the past, wording everything perfectly in case Lewis decided to sue

21

us for slander and close us down. But we're so close to closing down anyway and Ruth let her frustration get the better of her. It could have been worse. There was a moment when I thought she was going to mention the note.'

Charlie backs away. 'But she didn't?'

The loss of Charlie's warm embrace sends a shiver down my spine. 'No, but she did mention abuse and she did mention a boyfriend,' I reply as a knot of anxiety tightens in my chest.

I don't want to be scared of Lewis; he doesn't deserve one drop of my emotions but it's difficult when you don't know, and have never known, exactly who you're dealing with. As a newcomer to our school, we knew only the rumours about Lewis's past. He played up his tough, macho image to assert his position in our group but there were times when it was impossible not to feel sorry for what he and his mum had been through. In hindsight, that vulnerability was an artifice, and the only thing about Lewis that was indisputable was the terrible effect he had on Meg.

'I don't blame Ruth. People deserve to know what he did,' I continue. 'It doesn't matter what the police found or didn't find, Lewis was there that day, the missing note proves it. Meg could have been alive when he got there for all we know. He might have bullied her into doing it. What gets me most is that he was callous enough to just leave her hanging there. Can you imagine?'

'Don't,' Charlie says, his hand trembling as he wipes away a fat tear slipping down my cheek.

'He's a monster, Charlie.'

'I know, but he's a monster I'd rather you kept away from.'

'If he's still in Newcastle, he won't see the report and, with any luck, no one will bother to tell him.'

Charlie holds my gaze a second too long. I want him to pull me close again so I can ignore the shadow that passed over his face, but he doesn't move. I fall back against the kitchen counter. 'What is it?'

Mirroring my movements, Charlie leans against the kitchen island, pushing his hands deep into his pockets. 'He's back in Liverpool, Jen. He has been for a few months.'

'And you didn't think to tell me?' It's not quite a screech but it's close.

'I didn't think— I *hoped* I wouldn't need to. It's not like he kept in touch with any of our friends.'

I clench my jaw and make a concerted effort to match Charlie's supplicant tone. 'I was hoping he'd be in prison by now, or killed in a gang war like that cousin of his.'

Lewis was a magnet when it came to trouble. The only reason he had appeared in our lives was to escape the mess he'd left somewhere else. He was fifteen when his cousin was stabbed to death near their home in Huyton and Lewis's mum hadn't wanted her only child to suffer the same fate. She had packed up and moved with her son to South Liverpool, cutting off all ties with the family who accepted violence as the norm. When I heard their story, I was full of admiration, and despite what's happened since, I do have respect for what his mum had wanted to achieve. I've spoken to many women who have walked away from abusive relationships with nothing except the determination to find a better life for their children, and although Lewis's mum fled under different circumstances, she had given her son the best chance possible. Lewis was the one who squandered it.

Charlie sighs. 'He's back because his mum's ill. I think it's cancer or something. I don't know much.'

'You know a lot more than I'd expect considering he *doesn't* keep in touch with anyone we know. Have you actually seen him?'

He flinches. 'He's the last person I'd want to see, Jen. I don't want him in our lives any more than you do. It was Jay and Meathead who bumped into him, and no, they weren't stupid enough to suggest a school reunion. They hooked up on Facebook, that's all.'

'And you say they're not stupid?' I'm managing to hold back my anger but it's not easy. I take deep breaths as I process the news. My skin crawls at the idea that Lewis is nearer than we thought, and if Charlie's idiot friends can bump into him then how long before I do, or God forbid, Ruth or Geoff? 'Is he back in that flat over the off-licence on Allerton Road?'

'No, it was the first thing I asked. His mum moved to Bootle and he's living there with her. I don't know where exactly,' he answers before I can ask.

I'm relieved that Lewis is living north of the city but it's still too close. 'What else have they found out?'

'Nothing really,' Charlie tries, only to squirm under my gaze. 'He's a personal trainer.'

'Successful?'

Charlie shrugs. 'No idea. He works freelance at a hotel.'

It's like pulling teeth. 'Which one?'

'I don't know, Jen. Honestly, I haven't taken that much notice. Does it matter?'

I push past Charlie and cross the living room towards the window. Across the sprawling city, lights are flickering on as the summer's day draws to a close. My eyes travel the route I take to work along the Strand to Mann Island

24

and I'm struck by how many hotels I can see. 'What if it's one of those? What if I walk past him every day?'

Charlie keeps his hands in his pockets as he approaches. He's heard the tremble in my voice and when he realises it's my entire body shaking, he pulls me back into his arms. 'He's not interested in us, Jen. If I thought he was a threat, I would have done something about it,' he tells me.

It's a nice thought but what Charlie gains in height, Lewis always made up for in muscle, and if he's working as a personal trainer, I imagine he's more than a match for my would-be hero. 'The only reason you don't think he's a threat is because that's what Lewis wants you to believe. He's bad news, Charlie. He always was. Why can't you see that?'

'I do,' he says, kissing the top of my head. 'But none of us are teenagers any more. What happened with Meg changed us and I bet it changed Lewis too. He'll have enough on his plate looking after his mum. It's time for us all to get on with our lives.'

'Unless you're Meg,' I remind him.

As I close my eyes, I replay the snatches of video included in this evening's news report; Meg blowing out candles on her tenth birthday, playing football on the beach with me and Sean, taking centre stage in a school play. But then my thoughts turn to Ruth, her voice breaking as she told the reporter how Meg's death was a slow and painful process that began when Lewis invaded our lives.

'It's not fair. He can't come back here and expect us all to forget what he did,' I say, only to realise that Ruth has made sure he knows that we haven't. 'It's not over. It was stupid to believe it ever was.'

3

Ruth

The build up to Meg's tenth anniversary has followed a familiar pattern of emotions: the growing sense of impending doom; the tension during the day itself as I relive Meg's last hours and imagine her torment; the brief respite that I allow myself when I go to bed having survived another year without her; waking up this morning to begin the countdown to what should be Meg's twenty-eighth birthday on Sunday.

When Geoff decided to go into work today, leaving me home alone, I felt nothing but relief. Yesterday had exhausted us both and the only reason we managed to get through the anniversary without a cross word was that we didn't talk that much at all. I'm all talked out.

Luckily, the TV report was the last in a series of interviews I've given in recent weeks – my last desperate attempt to get people to take notice of our work before Geoff has his way and we wind up the foundation. I knew it wouldn't be easy. The press had grown weary of the retelling of the version of Meg's life that satisfied the coroner but has never satisfied me.

Don't get me wrong, I accept that Meg had suicidal thoughts but on that last morning, I thought she'd turned a corner. She said she had plans. I never thought . . . Something else had to have happened. The note we were left with didn't explain it. She had written just twenty-two words, twenty-three including her name, and I can recall each one by heart.

I'm doing this because of you.
    I don't expect anyone to understand why I chose this way. Bury my shame with me.
    Megan x

It's not enough. My Meg had more to say and it was about Lewis. In her final texts to him, she demanded that he answer her messages and, when that failed, she asked him not to hate her. He would have known she was about to expose him and despite an alibi that placed him in the gym all afternoon, he was there. Witnesses can be bought, or threatened. They can also be silenced and that was what he did to Meg when he tore the note in two.

I've been quiet for too long, and I could tell Geoff wasn't happy with me as we wrapped up the interview. He'd been skulking in the background and I thought I was prepared for the argument, but after thirty-two years of marriage, I still can't predict my husband's reactions. It had never crossed my mind that it wasn't what I said about Lewis that had upset him as much as the fact that I had shared our home videos of Meg.

27

After she died, Geoff had spent an age collating and digitising every image and recording he could find of her. The painstaking task had occupied his mind for a while, bringing light relief to our darkened world, and when it was complete he'd presumed we would sit down and watch them together, but I couldn't do it. I didn't want to see our beautiful girl shine, only to watch her light dim before my eyes, or face the finality of the blank screen when the recordings came to an abrupt end.

Tipping back my head, I stretch my spine and listen to a low whine coming from the floor above. I'm sitting alone at the breakfast bar in the cavernous kitchen I designed myself. We had the house remodelled the year after losing Meg, extending out to the side by knocking down the garage with its indelible memories, repositioning the kitchen, and adding a fifth bedroom upstairs. Not that we needed another bedroom. Sean had decided to stay in Stratford after completing his degree and our nest had been well and truly emptied. Geoff wasn't the only one who needed to find a way to stay connected to our daughter, and while he has his library of videos, I have my kitchen.

Resting my hands on the cold granite counter, I stare up at the ceiling until my focus adjusts to the middle distance. I don't generally tell visitors this is where Meg died. I expect most would think it ghoulish but after ten years, her death no longer holds the power to shock me. I'm aware of her absence constantly and there's something comforting about being this close to the spot where my daughter's soul left her body.

It's one of the few aspects of my grief that I don't share during my campaigning, that and how I chat to Meg whenever I'm home alone. Lately, I've been telling her my worries about the future and how Geoff's plans are diverging from my own. I promise her I won't forsake her memory and give up on the helpline because the two are inextricably linked. I know there are national charities that have the resources to do our job and more, which is why the demand for our services has been in decline, but I can't let it fail.

'God, Meg, I hope this relaunch works,' I whisper.

As always, the returning silence is deafening. The high-pitched whine I'd heard earlier has stopped too, replaced by light footsteps moving about upstairs. The palm of my hand is ice cold as I place it over my fluttering heart. For the briefest moment, I let myself imagine it's Meg. How I'd love to hear her giggling, or the creak of the bed as she and Jen use it as a trampoline until I have to yell at them to stop.

My breath catches in my throat. I wish I'd never shouted at her. If I had my time again, I wouldn't worry about them breaking the bed, I'd run up and join them. But it's not Meg's footsteps I hear and no amount of wishful thinking will make it so.

Hiring a cleaner was a spur of the moment decision. Jen had been telling me how well Charlie's business was doing and how he might be expanding from domestic to commercial services. I suspect she was sounding me out about taking on our office cleaning but we have years to run on the current contract and it was at home where help was needed.

Geoff and I are at the office five days a week and we often bring work home at the weekend. What free time we have is usually spent wining and dining potential clients or, in Geoff's case, meeting them on the golf course. Hiring help made sense but I never expected to be sitting here imagining that it's Meg upstairs. It's no good, I can't bear it any longer, I simply can't.

My heart is thumping and I'm about to shout up to Helena and ask her to leave when I hear the growl of Geoff's Audi pulling onto the drive. I check the time. It's not yet four but for once I'm glad to have him home. I'm filling the kettle when he appears at the doorway and hesitates. Whereas I can spend hours in the kitchen, tucked away in the quiet corner I created with an overstuffed sofa and well-stocked bookcase, Geoff finds no comfort in this room and steels himself before stepping across the threshold.

I often wonder why he didn't raise an objection when I drafted the new plans. We had agreed we didn't want the garage left as a mausoleum, and moving out of the last home we shared with Meg was never an option, but he could have offered an alternative suggestion. He didn't because my husband is generally happy to go along with whatever I want – or at least he was.

'Did you let everyone have an early finish?' I ask.

'Everyone except Jen. She insisted on hanging around till whoever's on the helpline arrives.'

'It'll be Alison tonight,' I tell him.

The helpline is open from five until eight on Monday, Wednesday and Friday evenings. It used to be open five days but we had to cut back when the calls dwindled and it became increasingly difficult to expect what had been a merry band of volunteers to give up their evenings when there were so few calls, or occasionally none at all. There are only five of us now, including me and Jen.

'I was thinking,' Geoff says as he sidesteps the breakfast bar to join me. 'It's not too late to take Sean up on his offer. We could be in Stratford in a couple of hours.'

I suppress a sigh. 'But we've already told them no and they'll have made alternative plans.'

'We could book into a hotel,' he replies as he takes a whiskey bottle from the cupboard. 'It's all very well seeing the twins on FaceTime but that's no way to get to know their Nanna and Gramps properly.'

My shoulders sag. We've had this conversation before. 'It's not that I don't want to see our little babies, but I have to be here for Meg's birthday.'

Geoff's head hangs down for a moment. 'It was just an idea.'

I watch as he pours two fingers of whiskey into a glass. We grieve in our own ways. 'We'll do it another weekend,' I promise.

There's a thump above our heads as Geoff reaches for his glass. He pauses as a brief look of pain crosses his face.

'I think we should let Helena go,' I say, drawing his attention back to me. 'I don't like having someone else in the house.'

Geoff needs no further explanation but still he hesitates. 'You might feel differently in a few days,' he says. 'You know how this time of year affects you.'

He makes it sound as if it's only me who's aware of the melancholy haze that descends during the last week of August but I know he feels it too. That's why he reacted as he did to the videos being shown. That's why his heart skipped a beat when he heard someone moving about upstairs. Just once, I wish he'd remember we're not in this alone.

'Putting it off won't make any difference. I'll speak to her today,' I say.

'If you're sure,' he replies before savouring the first mouthful of amber liquid.

'Have I missed anything at work?' I ask as I race to make our coffees before he can finish his drink and refill his glass.

'Nothing much. The city planners are being difficult over the Whitespace project but I've asked the team to mull over possible solutions for next week.'

The Whitespace project is a major inner city redevelopment and one of the biggest schemes we've ever worked on. 'I saw the emails this morning,' I tell him. 'Oh God, that reminds me, there was one from Selina asking if we'd sponsor a whole table for her fundraiser.'

'Yeah, I had that one too.'

Selina Raymond is a force to be reckoned with despite her advancing years. Our paths had crossed a few years ago after her lodger had moved out of her large Victorian house and she decided to convert her home into a refuge. She had heard about the helpline, which was going strong back then, and when she discovered it had been set up by two architects, it didn't take long for her to convince Geoff and me to design the refuge at cost, and now she's looking to expand.

'She's going to struggle for the extra funding this year,' I continue.

'As are we all,' Geoff replies, swirling the dregs in his glass as he speaks.

The black hole in the foundation's budget is another argument Geoff has used for closing the helpline. In the early years, when Meg's loss was raw, it had been relatively easy to pull on our clients' heartstrings, but donations have dried up of late. I'm hoping our recent publicity will make all the difference.

'Things will get better,' I promise.

'They already have for Selina,' he replies brightly. 'I made some phone calls and our clients didn't need much persuading. They're aware of how much these projects mean to us and our Whitespace partners have been particularly generous. I've already confirmed our table.'

'You've done what?'

'I thought you'd be pleased, my love. Surely we owe her after all the times she's offered refuge to our callers.'

'I'm not disputing it's a good cause, but if we're asking for donations, it should be for the foundation.'

'And that can still happen, but for now, I'd rather see the money being put to better use.'

'Better use?' I ask as Geoff drains his glass. 'What *we* do should take priority. Or –' my eyes narrow, '– have you already made up your mind that the relaunch is going to fail? Is that what you want?'

'I want what you want, my love,' he says, looking hurt by the suggestion. 'Haven't I always supported you? The helpline is Megan's legacy, I know that, but one TV interview isn't going to be enough to turn around our fortunes, no matter how controversial you tried to make it.'

My jaw twitches. 'Lewis deserves to be named, and I hope someone has told him what I said. I hope he looks it up online.'

Geoff puts his tumbler down with a loud crack. 'So he can see the videos of Megan?' he asks, his face twisting. 'That's precisely why I didn't want you sharing her with the world, Ruth. She's my daughter and I don't want *him* looking at her.'

His eyes are glistening but Geoff won't cry. He never has, and as much as I appreciate the times he's needed to be strong for both of us, right now it would be nice to know that the pain that never leaves me has stayed with him too.

'Sorry,' I try but Geoff shakes his head.

'What's done is done,' he says. 'But I do think you need to look at our situation objectively. It's going to take more than the cost of a table at Selina's fundraiser to keep the foundation afloat and, as a trustee, I believe a managed closure should remain on the table.' Geoff gives me an imploring look he hopes will sway me. 'Come on, my love. How old do the twins have to be before we've missed out on them growing up? I'm sixty, and you're not that far behind. We should sell the business, move closer to Sean. This is the point in our lives when we should be winding down.'

And there it is, the plan he's been alluding to ever since he first raised the possibility of closing the helpline. I knew it was coming and that's why I didn't only fight harder with the relaunch, I fought dirty. Meg's foundation has never been as important to Geoff as it is to me. It was just another of my plans that he simply went along with while I worked tirelessly to rebuild our lives in a way that kept our daughter at the centre of us all. Now is not the time for objectivity. I can't let go of her, not even for my two-year-old grand-daughters.

My expression alone tells Geoff what I think of his idea, and when he turns away, his hand reaches instinctively for the bottle of whiskey.

'Geoff, you'd hate giving up work . . .' I start but my words trail off as I hear Helena making her way downstairs. I feel an ache in my heart, quickly followed by a flutter of nerves. 'Can we talk later? I need to get this over and done with first.'

'I'll do it,' he says as he refills his glass. Taking his drink with him, he heads to the door but looks back. 'I know walking away isn't something you want to consider, but retirement could give us fresh challenges. Is it such a terrible idea?' Before I can answer, he shakes his head in defeat. 'I know, my timing's awful – the helpline – the relaunch. I should have worked out by now that you're hard to stop once you've set your mind on something.'

'*Impossible* is the word I'd use,' I say with a wan smile.

'Yes, I would too,' he replies before leaving the kitchen and closing the door behind him so I don't have to listen to the awkward conversation he's about to have.

4

Ruth

After reliving the worst week of our lives, the world has tilted back on its axis and it's time to begin a new year without Meg. The flowers have been placed on her grave, the candles lit in the church and when I awoke this morning, the feeling of dread that had plagued me for weeks had lifted. As I'd put on my linen suit and picked up my brief-case, I was ready to rejoin civilisation and tackle any problems life could throw at me because almost everything has a solution – only death takes away our options. Which makes me wonder how I should respond to this latest dilemma.

I prod the envelope Geoff had dropped back onto my desk after reading the contents. The cream paper is good quality, as you would expect from a solicitor's office, but if it's meant to intimidate, it doesn't. It's no more than paper and ink, I tell myself as I wait for Jen to step into the office.

'Geoff said you wanted a word?'

'You'd better sit down.'

Jen keeps her back straight as she slides into the visitor's chair. She plays with her fringe which isn't long enough to hide the furrows on her brow that deepen as her eyes dart from the envelope caught beneath my red lacquered fingernail, across my pristine silk blouse and up to my face. I try to give her a look of reassurance but I can't quite pull it off.

'Geoff looks awful,' she says. 'Is he OK?'

'He's gone in search of some paracetamol.'

Jen makes a move to stand. 'I have some in my desk. Do you want me to get them?'

'No, he needs some fresh air anyway. I'd told him not to come into work today but he has to learn his lesson. He can't drink his way through an entire weekend without facing the consequences. That's not why I asked you in.' I pick up the envelope stamped with a large red confidential mark, and prise out a single sheet of paper between a finger and thumb. 'This is why you're here.'

I let Jen take the letter but I don't give her time to read it. 'It's some trumped-up solicitor's clerk representing a certain Lewis Steven Rimmer,' I tell her, tasting bile as I speak his name. 'I've checked out the firm and they deal mostly with conveyancing so I don't think we have much to worry about. I presume it's a friend of Lewis trying to scare us. He's asking us to cease and desist disparaging his client or they'll take us to court.'

The letter trembles in Jen's hand as she scans the contents. 'He wouldn't dare.'

'Of course he wouldn't,' I tell her, my voice strong. Lewis Rimmer has taken all he's going to from my family, and I won't as much as flinch from this latest attack. 'To make a case, he would first need to crawl from beneath whatever rock he's hiding under and admit that he recognised himself in the person I described in the interview.'

'What are you going to do?'

'Carry on with more of the same,' I say simply. The corners of my lips pull into a smile. 'I like that we've made him uncomfortable. Don't you?'

'Of course, but he's not going to stop at a solicitor's letter if you upset him again,' she replies as the letter slips from her grasp. We watch it float onto the desk and Jen gulps down her next breath. 'Look, Ruth—'

'This doesn't change a thing, Jen,' I tell her. 'You've worked so hard on the relaunch and we've got people's attention again. I don't care that Lewis is one of them. This letter is another of his games, just like Meg's note. He could have destroyed all of it but he left enough to make us question ourselves. He could have gone anywhere to escape the backlash but he went to Newcastle, deliberately choosing the university Meg had planned to go to escape him. After messing with her mind, he thought he could mess with ours too.'

Jen chews her lip. 'Do you think it's possible he's changed? Charlie thinks there's a chance and maybe this letter is Lewis's way of saying if we leave him alone, he'll leave us alone.'

'It's possible,' I say, sounding no more convinced than Jen. 'We both know there are some men who can learn to control their behaviour, but first they have to be willing to acknowledge the damage they've done. This isn't a letter from someone who's ready to confess his sins. Lewis is still pleading his innocence. He sees himself as the victim, not Meg. He hasn't changed.'

'What does Geoff think we should do?'

'I don't need to tell you that he hates Lewis as much as I do.'

'But?'

Although the solicitor's letter isn't entirely unexpected, it's visibly shaken Jen. I doubt she wants to hear what I have to say next, but it won't come as any more of a surprise to her than it did to me. 'Geoff mentioned retirement again at the weekend. He wants us to not only close the helpline but sell the business and move to Stratford so we can spend more time with Sean and the girls. It's a happy picture he paints but I can't do it.'

'Is that why you went all out with the interview? You think this is our last chance to save the helpline?'

I swallow the lump in my throat. 'If it hadn't aired, I suspect we'd be having an entirely different conversation. I had to do something, Jen. I won't let Meg go, not without a fight.'

Jen follows my gaze to the photo on the bookcase next to my desk. It was taken many summers ago on a beach in Cornwall and captures a treasured moment of completeness with all four members of the McCoy family. Sean has his arms around my neck while Meg was meant to be propped up on her dad's knee but she'd decided to dive across the three of us just as the photo was taken. We're all laughing at her, as was the girl behind the camera.

'Do you want me to take another photo, Auntie Ruth?' Jen had asked, eager to get things right.

My niece was only seven and it was her first holiday with us. She had refused to go away with her family to Spain that summer because there had been turbulence during the flight home the year before and she had become hysterical. The intention was to leave her behind with her grandmother, but I wouldn't have trusted my mother-in-law, God rest her soul, to look after a goldfish, so I'd offered to take Jen with us. The two girls were thrilled, Sean less so.

Jen and I smile at the memories of that holiday and the ones that followed. There were times when it felt like we were a family of five, with Jen and Meg more like sisters. 'I didn't know how lucky we were back then,' I whisper.

'You can always make new memories with the twins,' Jen offers.

My smile twists. 'I know, but Geoff called it walking away. Why would I abandon Meg's legacy when there are so many questions left unanswered? I have Lewis's attention now. Maybe that's not such a bad thing.'

Jen doesn't answer straight away. I can only assume that the threat of legal action continues to play on her mind. 'Whatever happens, we can't give up on the helpline,' she says at last. 'I won't walk away either.'

My smile reaches my eyes. 'And that is the right answer, Jennifer. We might not get as many calls as we'd like but every one we do receive is important. Did you see Alison's call sheets from Friday? Gemma phoned. Ryan's been bombarding her with messages.'

Gemma is a very unhappy young woman, and although our main role is simply to listen, all our volunteers have been trained to help our callers recognise a partner's manipulative behaviours. In the last month, we've been working with Gemma on some strategies to end her relationship as painlessly as possible.

She still lives at home with her mum and whenever I've taken one of her calls, it feels like a second chance to say the things I should have said to Meg, if only I'd known to recognise the signs of abuse for what they were. There's even an inflection in Gemma's voice – a slushiness to her 's' sounds – that helps me imagine it is my daughter, and I'm determined to win this one.

'She hasn't replied to him, has she?' Jen asks hopefully.

'No. But she has read them. Ryan won't let her go unless it's on his terms. He's from the same mould as someone else we know and if Lewis wasn't up in Newcastle, I could believe it *was* him, simply going by a new name,' I say. It's one of my worst fears: that Lewis will do to another poor girl what he did to Meg.

'You don't really think it's him, do you?' Jen gasps, her face draining of colour.

I want to shrug it off but her shock twists my insides. 'If I'm honest, I think the same about most callers but Lewis isn't unique.' I bite my lip. 'We have to keep the helpline going, Jen, although right now that might have to be on a shoestring. Geoff has persuaded our lovely clients to donate to Selina's fundraiser so we'll have to hold off asking them to put their hands in their pockets again so soon.'

'Don't worry,' Jen tells me earnestly. 'I know how to drive a hard bargain. I've already had the flyers we need for Fresher's Week printed for next to nothing.'

Next to nothing is about all we have, but Jen doesn't need to know how bad it is yet. 'I knew I could count on you.'

When Jen grips the armrests, I'm expecting her to stand but she doesn't move. I think I can guess what she's too polite to say. 'Sorry, I'd completely forgotten to apologise about the fiasco with the cleaner. I hope Charlie doesn't mind us letting her go?'

Jen bats away the apology with her hand, although the frown doesn't leave her face. 'He was worried there might be a problem with her, that's all.'

I shake my head. 'No, if there was a problem, it was with me,' I assure her. 'I could hear her moving about upstairs and I got it into my head that it was Meg.' I try to laugh as I blink away unexpected tears. 'Not that I ever heard my daughter vacuuming.'

'No, it was always Meg creating the mess.'

'Not the worst ones,' I mutter as I make a point of picking up Lewis's letter, screwing it into a ball and throwing it at the bin. When I miss, I refuse to view it as a bad omen.

5

Jen

The automatic lights that react to movement have switched themselves off in all but one section of the office above the helpline pods. I've been sitting here for over an hour but the only person I've spoken to since the helpline opened has been Charlie. It's his turn to cook dinner and he wants me to pick up some sour cream on my way home. It's chilli night.

With one ear trained on the silent phone, I look out of the window and watch the shadows lengthen. I always cover the Wednesday shift and it doesn't bother me working alone. The office is secure enough, with electronic passes to control access to each floor, barriers on the ground level and security guards who replace the concierge staff on the front desk until the last person leaves. Tonight, that will be me when the helpline closes at eight, by which point the September sun will have set.

So if I'm not bothered, why does my stomach twist at the thought of leaving?

It's the same reason I regret not telling Ruth about Lewis being back in Liverpool. We all need to be on our guard and I was going to warn her on Monday, but then she mentioned Geoff's push for retirement. If he knew Lewis was back, he'd use it as another argument to 'walk away'. Ruth's made it clear she's not going to do that, in which case, does she really need to be looking over her shoulder every time she steps out the door? It's not like she'd bump into him on the way to work since she drives in with Geoff. My silence on the matter is saving her from unnecessary worry, I tell myself.

With a smile, I realise that was precisely what Charlie had been doing for me. I shouldn't have been so angry with him. He knew how stressed I'd been over the relaunch.

My insides twist again. It's the future of the helpline I should be worrying about. The spike in calls we were hoping for after last week's publicity is yet to materialise – discounting all the put-down calls Gill had on Monday. As I wait in vain for the phone to ring and hope sinks, my thoughts return to Lewis.

At the moment, he knows more about me than I do about him and I need to redress that balance – to hell with Charlie's mantra of live and let live. I turn from the window and retreat inside the cocoon of the helpline pod. It's essentially one of two workstations that face each other with a privacy screen in the middle and two more on each side to prevent conversations from carrying. It's not particularly effective at cancelling out noise when both pods are in use, but that hasn't been a problem since we cut back to just one volunteer per shift.

Closing the call log on my screen, I open up Facebook

and check to see if any of my friends list Lewis as one of theirs. There are only a handful of people I've remained in touch with who would have known him and I'm pleased, if not a little frustrated, that none have been gullible enough to reconnect with him, and that includes Charlie.

With no other choice, I set aside my dignity and send friend requests to Jay and Meathead. I haven't seen either of them in years but, from their profile pictures, they don't appear to have matured with age. I hope they don't think I'm trying to hit on them but I'll be more offended if they refuse my requests.

Next, I turn my attention to Google. My first search of Lewis Rimmer produces global results so I add Newcastle to the search bar, my body tensing as I press the enter key. The screen updates and halfway down the page a selection of photos appear. Most are close ups of men I don't recognise and group photos too small to discern one face from another. The photo that raises my hackles is on the right-hand edge of the screen. I stab the cursor over Lewis's face and a new page opens.

It's an old student union press release heralding a twenty-year-old Lewis as their star rugby player, on track for a first class honours sports degree. In the post-match photo, his straw-blond hair is scraped back from his sweaty brow and his cheeks are ruddy. His steel-blue eyes are all the more piercing without the wire-rimmed glasses he used to wear. Unlike Charlie, Lewis made eyewear look seductive but I suppose contact lenses would be more practical for someone with such an active life.

I haven't seen that face for ten years and I'm struck by how normal Lewis looks. It would be nice to think that remorse changed him for the better, but Ruth isn't the only one who can imagine history repeating itself. More determined than ever, I return to my original search and change the city from Newcastle to Liverpool. There's nothing new and that bothers me. If Lewis is freelancing as a personal trainer, why isn't he advertising himself more prominently?

I'm wondering what he's hiding when the phone rings, and I let out a yelp as if he's caught me spying. The helpline doesn't use caller display so I have no clue who is ringing and from where, which can be frustrating at times, but it's a matter of trust. Ruth was very clear about how the helpline should operate and all volunteers are trained to listen and encourage, not to dictate how someone should live their life. We don't record any information that the caller doesn't want to give willingly.

As I pick up the phone, I hope it's not going to be another put-down call. I want it to be someone who will make me work harder than ever to keep the helpline open, but there's a part of me that would rather we weren't needed. I wish there were more Charlies and fewer Lewises in the world.

'You're through to the Lean On Me helpline. How can I help?'

'Jen, is that you?' the girl says.

I recognise Gemma's voice as quickly as she's recognised mine. We've never met but during our previous calls, I've conjured an image of a young woman not dissimilar to Meg. Her gentle lisp is achingly familiar. 'Hi, Gemma. How have you been?' I ask as I bring the call log back up on screen.

Our information system isn't particularly sophisticated

but we do log every call; from the simple requests for information, the put-downs when the caller loses their nerve to speak, to the calls where we can and do make a difference in someone's life. Some of those calls are straightforward, often young women in first relationships who want advice on how to dump boyfriends whose only crime is not meeting their expectations. And then there are the callers like Gemma, who are in toxic relationships but aren't able to recognise or accept that they are being abused. Except we all thought Gemma had seen Ryan for what he was. When she broke up with him two weeks ago, I was hoping she wouldn't need us any more.

'I've been so busy at work lately and I'm exhausted,' she says. 'I could have gone to an Arctic Monkeys gig tonight but I'm giving it a miss.'

As she talks, I tap through the call sheets as quietly as I can. All our information is anonymised unless our callers need us to act on their behalf with other agencies, and only then will we create a case file. Gemma's calls don't fall under that category and haven't been cross-referenced. Discounting the cluster of five put-down calls on Monday, there have been only seven calls since my last shift and I quickly dismiss the ones from previous callers who had seen Ruth on TV and wanted to thank us for our help, and another from a young man.

The two remaining sheets clearly relate to Gemma; one is the call Ruth mentioned Alison taking last Friday and the other is a call Gill took on Monday evening. The details in each are scant but the message is clear. Ryan wants back into Gemma's life.

'I should have given you the tickets,' Gemma continues.

'I'm more of a Harry Styles girl myself,' I tell her.

Gemma laughs. 'Eugh, I forgot you liked him. Well, if ever I get tickets for Harry, they're yours,' she says, making me smile. We don't give out personal details to our callers beyond our first names, and any contact outside of the scope of the helpline, even to pick up concert tickets, wouldn't be condoned, but despite these limitations, Gemma and I have formed a friendships of sorts.

'So why didn't you want to go to the gig?' I ask. 'Were you just tired or was there another reason?'

'Did you know Ryan's been messaging me?'

'I was just checking the note of your last call. Are you still ignoring him?' Please say yes, I silently pray as I wait for her reply, which isn't immediately forthcoming.

'I keep looking at the checklist on your website about how to spot dating abuse and it's not like Ryan did anything particularly bad. OK, it was a bit overwhelming sometimes but that's only because I'm not used to people paying me that much attention. I'm not saying Mum doesn't do her best, and she made all these promises about us doing more stuff together after I split up with him, but it turned out that meant joining Tinder, so if anything, she's the one taking risks by going out on actual dates and I should be getting *her* to phone you.'

I wait until Gemma takes a breath. 'Have you replied to him?'

'He was the one who sent me the tickets. He said they were for me and Mum but I'd told him ages ago that she hates music gigs. I know what he's like,' she says with not nearly enough alarm in her voice. 'He would have bought an extra ticket and been there waiting for me.'

48

'What do you think would have happened if you had gone?'

'I'll never know,' Gemma says softly. 'I told him I wasn't going. It was only fair. I said I'd leave the tickets at the box office if he wanted someone else to use them.'

So she has replied to him, I realise. 'How did he react?'

'He was fine about it, and said he didn't want anyone else to have them. He said, if I was too tired to go, he'd pay to have the Arctic Monkeys come to the house for a private performance.'

I try to form an image of the man who loves Gemma too much, but it's Lewis's leering face that springs to mind. 'How old is Ryan?' I ask. 'I can't quite picture him.'

'He's in his late twenties, and he's really fit. You should see him, Jen. He has a six-pack and everything,' Gemma says, making my heart clench. 'It's not like he tries either. It's because of his job.'

I don't want to ask. I really don't want to ask. 'What does he do?'

'He's a builder, so he doesn't earn enough to pay a busker off Church Street to serenade me, let alone the Arctic Monkeys.'

With some relief, I let go of my paranoia and concentrate on picking up where Gill left off on Monday, by reminding Gemma of the behaviours that made her call us in the first place. 'How often is Ryan texting you?'

'Well, I've had two messages since I've been on the phone to you,' she says by way of an answer.

'That sounds familiar. I remember how often he'd interrupt our calls when you were actually dating, and back then he'd expect an immediate reply.'

She makes a non-committal noise. 'Or he'd start panicking because he was scared something had happened to me. I know he has insecurities, Jen, and I've told him if he wants me back, things have to change.'

I'm shaking my head as I see where this is leading. 'And how do you imagine things changing if you did get back together?'

'For a start, I've told him he can't interrogate me every time I go out with friends.'

'And do you think he would be comfortable with that? I wonder how he'd react to you going out for a pub lunch with your work mates,' I ask, knowing this was something he had put a stop to early on in their relationship.

'He knows his jealousy was part of the problem,' Gemma says. 'I'm not daft, Jen. You must hear the most awful stories about women who get fooled into thinking their boyfriends will change, only they don't and the abuse gets worse. But that isn't me. I'm not rushing into anything. I promise.'

'Just remember that he'll be on his best behaviour until he has you back under his control.'

'I know,' Gemma says, but there's a note of resignation in her voice that I don't like. 'Sorry, I'd better go.'

I want to ask how many more messages she's received, but I don't. Gemma can recognise the familiar patterns of obsession for herself.

'You will call again, won't you? Before you make any drastic decisions.'

'You've all been so good to me. Of course I will.'

The phone cuts off and as I replace it gently on the receiver, I'm replaying our conversation in my head. Did I say too much, or should I have said more? We'd built up a good relationship over the last month or so but that doesn't mean I can tell her what to do. She has to decide for herself.

As I write up the call sheet, I notice a message flash up on my muted phone. It's from Mum, inviting me and Charlie over for Sunday dinner. I'm still annoyed with her for what she said about Ruth and if I go over there, one of us is bound to say something we'll regret and it will probably be me.

I send a swift excuse before returning to my computer to check my Facebook page. Meathead has accepted my friend request so I go straight to his list of friends. Lewis's name isn't amongst them and none of the thumbnail photos jump out at me. I go through the list again, line by line until I come across someone called Lewis McQueen whose profile picture is a team photo – very sporty. I click on the name to reveal a small collection of public photos and my heart leaps in my throat. Lewis has aged, unlike my Meg.

I click on a photo of Lewis standing on a beach. His sea-salty hair is long enough to tie back and his pale complexion concealed by a glowing tan. Of more interest to me is the woman he has his arm around in a proprietorial pose. She doesn't look much older than Meg.

When the phone rings again, I snatch it up.

'Hello?' I ask.

There's silence on the other end of the phone and I calm myself. 'You're through to the Lean On Me helpline. How can I help?'

There's another pause and I'm expecting a put-down, but then, 'Who are you?'

'My name is Jen. Can I take—'

There's a small intake of breath. 'You are Megan's cousin?'

The next pause is of my making. The caller is another young woman, possibly around Gemma's age but with an Eastern European accent. I think she might be Polish but I'm less concerned with her nationality than the question she just posed. I decide to stay professional but cautious. 'Could you tell me why you're calling today?'

'I saw the helpline on the news,' she says, confirming she must be in the North West to have seen the piece on TV. 'It's very bad what happened to Megan. Her mother should not have to go through such a thing. No mother should.'

'No, they shouldn't. That's why we set up the helpline,' I reply. I'm trying not to prejudge the situation, but it crosses my mind that I could be dealing with a freelance journalist in search of a scoop after Ruth's revelations, or else a member of the public with a morbid curiosity. I've had my fair share of crank calls but, for the moment, I can't discount the possibility that this girl has recognised herself in Meg's story and needs our help.

'It must be hard for you,' she says.

'Would you like to give me your name?' I ask. Unsurprised by her hesitation, I add, 'It doesn't have to be your real name. What you tell me is confidential unless you say otherwise.'

'What do you mean *otherwise*?'

'We're here to listen and we'll do that for as long as you need us,' I reply. If she is a reporter, she can at least hear the full sales pitch. 'We can't offer practical help but, if you need it and are happy for us to act on your behalf, we can speak to other agencies – people who might be able to give you the extra support you need.'

'You can call me Ellie.'

'And you were affected by the news story about Megan?'

'Yes.'

I leave a pause for Ellie to fill.

'What was she like?'

She was a contradiction, I reply in my head. She was the tomboy and the princess, the captain of the team and the recluse. She was irrepressible and she was repressed. Megan McCoy wasn't only my cousin, she was my best friend and after all this time, I still feel the gaping hole she left in my life. 'I'd rather talk about you,' I say.

'I do not know what to say.'

'Tell me about yourself. What do you like about your life?' I ask as a prompt.

'I like living in Liverpool,' she says.

'And where are you from originally?'

'Romania.'

'But you've settled into the area? You like the people?' I ask as I search for a rhythm in the conversation to keep it flowing.

'I work a lot of the time,' she replies, offering no insight to why she might be calling.

'And what is it that you do?'

There's a pause. She doesn't want to tell me. 'I work in a shop. Not very exciting.'

'Do you live with anyone?' I ask, hoping that I'm edging closer to where the problem lies.

'I shared a house but now I live by myself.'

'You're not in a relationship?'

'It is not important.'

I lean forward in my seat. I want to get closer to her so

that I can work out why she's making me feel so uncomfortable. 'Then what is important, Ellie?'

'The truth,' she says simply. When I don't respond, she adds, 'Megan's boyfriend did not hurt her.'

My jaw clenches. I've been trying to work Ellie out and I think I just have. She's not a reporter, or any other sort of ghoul, but neither is she a genuine caller. 'Has someone asked you to phone?'

'No, it was when I saw the news. Mrs McCoy is wrong.'

'Why is she wrong?' I ask, a little too sharply. 'Do you know Megan's boyfriend? Is that why you're defending him?'

'I do not mean to upset you. And I do not want to upset Mrs McCoy. I thought you should know that Megan had other problems.'

'Really?' I ask. 'Look, I don't know what you've been told but I can't discuss what happened to Megan with you. If you're having difficulties of your own, I'm happy to listen. And if someone's pressurising you or intimidating you in any way, I can help.'

'No, I do not think you can. I am sorry, I should not have phoned. Please, do not say anything to Mrs McCoy. I will go. Goodbye, Jen.'

The phone goes dead and I'm left stunned.

'The bastard,' I hiss as I jump up from my seat and start to pace. 'The utter bastard.'

Lights flicker on, tracing my path through the maze of empty desks as I gather my thoughts. Lewis has to be behind the call. Why else would Ellie phone up to defend him? Is she the girlfriend in the beach photo? How easy would it be to convince her that it was Meg who had the problem?

Whoever this woman is, she doesn't know the real Lewis, and for her sake, I'm glad.

When I return to my pod, the entire office is ablaze with light. I feel exposed to the darkening city and crouch behind the privacy screen as I type up the call sheet. The one thing Ellie and I do agree upon is that Ruth shouldn't know what passed between us, so I keep the note vague – a general enquiry from someone who had seen Ruth's interview.

At eight o'clock, I close down my computer and shrug into my cotton jacket before escaping through the double doors and down the stairs. I don't want to think about Lewis but thoughts of him follow me as I leave the office. It's normally a ten-minute walk home along the Strand but I turn away from the bright lights and the city centre hotels, and head for the waterfront. There's a sharp breeze that tastes of sea salt as I follow the promenade along the curve of the river, past the Albert Dock and the Echo Arena. My path is dimly lit but I prefer the shadows. Ruth was right. We do have his attention and her interview has set a spotlight on us all.

6

Jen

'Did you get the sour cream?'

'The what?' Charlie's question startles me as I stagger into the apartment after assailing the stairs to the seventh floor.

My jacket hangs off my shoulders and I let it drop to the floor with my bag. The gulp of air I take is spiced with cumin and makes me want to heave.

'You forgot it, didn't you?' he asks as curls of steam rise up from the pan he's stirring, wrapping around his face so I can't read his expression.

'Sorry, it went straight out my head.'

'Too busy checking Facebook, by any chance?'

'What?' I ask, glancing longingly at the bedroom door which is where I'd been heading. I want to change into my pyjamas and crawl beneath the bedcovers until the storm in my head passes, but from the way Charlie tilts his head to one side, I see the clouds are still gathering.

'I had a message from Jay. He's asking if he should accept your friend request.'

I curse Jay under my breath as I take a step closer to the bedroom door. I should have known this would happen. The tight group of friends we formed at school might have disbanded, but some of those old loyalties managed to survive. Jay thinks he's watching Charlie's back.

'Is there a reason why we shouldn't be friends?' I ask casually.

'Yes there is, and I quote, "Jay's an embarrassment and I don't want any of my friends knowing I associate with morons."'

I ignore the annoying way he mimics my voice, and keep my head held high. 'People change.'

'Last time I said that, you bit my head off,' he reminds me.

'That was different, Charlie.'

'Of course it was. And I'm sure it's pure coincidence that you've decided to contact the one person you know who's in touch with Lewis again. Correction, *two* people. I hear Meathead had a similar request.'

The apartment is silent except for the gentle rattle of a bubbling pot. 'I'm not going to do anything,' I say at last. 'I just wanted to know what Lewis was up to so I can stay one step ahead.'

'I'd rather you didn't steer yourself onto the same path at all.'

'He's the one who came back to Liverpool.'

'It's a big city.'

'But it's a small world,' I tell him as my thoughts turn from Lewis to my last call.

'Don't get involved,' Charlie warns. 'Please, Jen.'

'Fine!' I snap before retreating to the bedroom. I shut

the door firmly but Charlie opens it again as I'm unbuttoning my shirt.

'I don't want you doing something stupid, that's all.'

'I'm not going to do anything stupid,' I reply, my tone abrasive to his soothing words.

Charlie moves closer. 'You look tired.'

'I feel it,' I reply as the last of my strength is carried away with trembling words.

'Need some help?' he asks with warmth in his eyes as he takes over undoing my buttons.

My arms drop to my sides. 'We can live without the sour cream, can't we?'

'It's not a deal breaker.'

His fingers stroke the curve of my breast as he takes hold of my shirt to slip it off my shoulders. When he kisses my neck, he feels my body stiffen and slides his hands to rest comfortably around my back instead.

'Bad day?'

Rather than answer immediately, I rest my hand on Charlie's shoulder and step out of my skirt. 'I feel so helpless sometimes,' I tell him. 'We have no way of knowing who's at the end of the line or what's going to happen to them once they've hung up.'

Charlie sits down on the bed. He's watching me closely as I begin slipping into my Minnie Mouse pyjamas. 'A difficult caller?'

'More like a difficult call,' I correct him. 'And I'm still not sure what to think of the caller herself.'

Charlie purses his lips. He knows I can't talk about the calls we receive so he doesn't ask. He waits for me to straighten my vest top before pulling me into his arms. I straddle him and cup his face, grateful that I have someone I love and trust.

'Ruth said something the other day that's been bugging me,' I tell him. 'What happens if we get a call from someone who's being manipulated the way Meg was?'

'I thought that was the whole point of the helpline?'

I lower my head until our foreheads touch. 'It is, but . . .' I take a breath. Assuming my leap of faith is correct and Ellie is who I think she is, she could be being abused by Lewis, if not now, then in the future. She asked me not to tell anyone and I won't, but I can still theorise without breaking that trust. 'What if one of our calls was from Lewis's girlfriend?'

Charlie draws back so he can look me in the eye. 'For a start, I'd say it would be one huge coincidence.'

'Would it?' I ask. 'What if she saw Ruth's interview? Lewis won't be the only one who worked out she was talking about him. Why wouldn't she phone us?'

'Are you trying to say she *has* phoned?'

'No, I'm talking hypothetically,' I insist. 'But he does have a girlfriend. I saw a picture of her on Facebook. Did you know?'

'So that's what this is about,' he says with a sigh. 'Yes, I had heard. Lewis told Jay he met her a few months back when he was buying a present for his *sick mum*.'

Our eyes lock as he presses the point home. 'Oh, I see. How stupid of me. Lewis can't possibly be a threat to women any more because he buys presents for his poorly mum.'

'I'm not saying that.'

'Then what are you saying?' I ask. 'You think we should turn a blind eye because his mum is sick?'

'Stop it, Jen. I'm on your side,' he reminds me.

'I know,' I say as I slide off Charlie's knee and slump down onto the mattress so I can stare at the ceiling instead of his face.

'All this publicity for the helpline has brought back memories that none of us take pleasure in revisiting,' Charlie continues. 'That's why I didn't want to add to your worries by telling you Lewis was back home. You're bound to be paranoid for a while.'

'Paranoid?' I could laugh. Actually, no, I could cry. I squeeze my eyes shut to stop myself but the urge intensifies as the mattress dips, rocking me slightly as Charlie lies back too. We're shoulder to shoulder; two friends trying to make sense of the world and the people in it.

If I try really hard, I can imagine it's Meg lying next to me. She might not have told me everything but we did talk, and I long to go back to those times in her bedroom when I fretted and she fixed.

'It's so lovely and quiet here,' I'd told her once as we lay sideways across her single bed with our feet dangling over the edge. It was the beginning of summer – our last one before Lewis entered our lives – and we were recharging our batteries after our GCSEs. Unfortunately for me, it had been impossible to find peace at home with one sister back from uni and reclaiming the top bunk in our bedroom, another having practically moved her boyfriend in and the third spending the last months of her pregnancy under Mum's watchful gaze.

'It's *too* quiet,' Meg replied.

I'd noticed a certain frostiness between Ruth and Geoff when I'd arrived. Ruth was complaining about the amount of time her husband spent on the golf course and his response had been to pick up his golf clubs and storm out.

'Is everything OK between Auntie Ruth and Uncle Geoff?'

'It would be if Mum would stop having a go at Dad all the time. Can't she see what she's doing?' Meg said, letting her arm drop across her face to cover her eyes.

'You think they'll get divorced?' I asked with a gasp as I stared at Meg's downturned mouth and willed it to stop trembling.

'They'd have to break up the business if they did that, so no, they'll just carry on making each other miserable.'

'As well as you?'

Meg pulled her arm away to stare up at the ceiling. 'Sean's so lucky, heading off to uni. I can't wait till it's my turn,' she said.

'I can't either. It'll be the two of us against the world,' I said, offering her a smile.

Meg didn't take it. 'Oh, no,' she said extending her arm behind her so she could tug at the brightly coloured scarves she kept hanging over her bedpost. Draping crimson silk across her face, she added, 'You need to find your own way, Jennifer Hunter. We will not be going to the same university. You can't hide behind me for the rest of your life.'

'But I don't want to be on my own.'

She silenced me with her gaze. 'And right now, neither do I. I'm dreading Sean going.'

'I could come over more often. Mum probably wouldn't notice if I never came home at all. Dad definitely wouldn't.'

Meg let the silk fall and pulled herself up onto her elbow, her eyes alight. 'In that case, why don't you move in? Mum wouldn't mind and I can get around Dad easily.'

Her excitement had been infectious but it wasn't Meg's parents who had stood in our way. I never did move in.

When I open my eyes, Meg is gone and it's Charlie who's lifted himself up to look at me. His eyes look as scratchy as mine feel.

'Can you at least find out who Lewis's girlfriend is?' I ask. 'Please, Charlie.'

'And what exactly do you plan on doing with that information? You can't contact her, Jen. Please. You don't know what kind of trouble you might cause.'

I twist onto my side so I can look Charlie in the eye. His frown matches my own. 'Surely Lewis will be too busy caring for his mum to cause us any more trouble,' I suggest innocently.

'Keep away from him, Jen.'

Charlie's tone makes my cheeks warm with guilt. Dismissing the idea that he might be jealous of the attention I'm giving Lewis, I say, 'I know he's dangerous. It's not like I've fallen for the sympathy act.'

'Neither have I.'

Unconvinced, I add, 'That's how men like Lewis get away with what they do. They make you believe they're *nice* because they seem vulnerable, or misunderstood, or in need of a second, third or fourth chance.'

'So being nice is a bad thing?' says the nicest man I know.

'No, your kind of nice is good,' I say, my tone softening as I stroke his cheek.

'Are you sure about that?' he asks. His eyes narrow and his words have an edge to them that I'm not expecting. 'Are you *absolutely* sure?'

'Yes.'

'But not sure enough to marry me.'

I suppress a groan as I roll onto my back again but I don't break eye contact. 'It doesn't mean I love you any less, Charlie. You're one of the good ones. I've never doubted that, not for a minute.'

Charlie turns his face away from me and gets up without a word. Squeezing my eyes shut, tears burn the back of my closed lids as I listen to him padding across the room.

'I might nip out and pick up the sour cream,' he says. 'When I get back, could we just forget about everyone else for at least one night?'

'Yeah, that would be good,' I say. I don't open my eyes until the door clicks shut, and I don't move off the bed until I hear Charlie leave the apartment.

Wrapping myself in Charlie's towelling dressing gown, I return to the living room. I stir the chilli before grabbing my phone and slumping down onto the sofa. I have until Charlie comes back to continue my hunt for Lewis.

Am I being paranoid? A little obsessed perhaps, but isn't that understandable? Lewis hasn't simply returned to Liverpool, he's come back into our lives. The solicitor's letter might have been a knee-jerk reaction to Ruth's accusations, but what about Ellie's call? What if Lewis had been listening in, laughing at me? Ruth was promoting the helpline when she attacked him so it makes sense that it should be his target.

Opening my Facebook app, I see that Jay has refused my friend request and, to my utter humiliation, Meathead has unfriended me too. My sigh of frustration catches in my throat as a new thought strikes. I open a browser and tap in a new search.

Lewis McQueen, the personal trainer, appears on the second page of results with a link to his website. Skimming through the information, I can't see any mention of the hotel where he works, but it would appear that Lewis offers boot camp sessions in the city centre. Judging by the photo on the bookings page, they take place in Chavasse Park, which is on the upper level of the Liverpool One shopping mall, on the opposite side of the Strand to Mann Island. As I scroll down the page, I find a Twitter feed showing comments and conversations from apparently satisfied customers. Most are women.

From what I read, the six-week courses offer high intensity training and provide Lewis with a legitimate excuse to hurl abuse at women, but I'm looking for something that exposes him for the bully I know him to be. It doesn't take long to find tweets about him pushing his victims to their limits but none are genuine complaints. He's actually found a way of turning his cruelty into a business opportunity.

I've scrolled past a comment before I realise its importance. There are a few flirtatious comments about one to one workouts, with other boot camp recruits joining in. One mentions that Lewis has a girlfriend. Another replies that it won't last – she only wants him for his UK citizenship. There follows an argument about the legal status of EU citizens but I've found what I needed from this thread. Ellie *is* his girlfriend.

I'm vaguely aware that the chilli is burning but I can't take my eyes from my phone as I go back up through the latest tweets. There's no further mention of Lewis's girlfriend but one very recent comment catches my attention. A new recruit is begging Lewis to go easy on her when her course starts on Saturday because she'll be hungover that morning. I check the date of her tweet and realise she's talking about this weekend.

It would be foolhardy to go there but it's not like I have to speak to him. Seeing me should be enough to send a message that I can stand up to him. I can't believe I'm contemplating doing this. It's not like me. It's more like Meg and that thought fires me up.

'See you there,' I mutter to myself, then hurry to the kitchen to stir the boiling pot that's been left for far too long.

7

Ruth

The conference room looks like a war zone, with battle plans scattered across the table. Friday afternoon was not the best time to receive another set of queries from the planning department regarding the Whitespace project, not when we have a meeting with them on Monday morning, so action had to be taken and quickly.

McCoy and Pace's reputation will be on the line if we don't secure planning approval but after a quick brainstorming session, I'm quietly confident. Geoff might have a knack for innovation, but whenever we hit a problem with the conceptual boundaries he likes to push, I'm the one who fixes them. And from the look on the faces of the team as they file out of the room, I've found a solution they can work with.

'Geoff looks happier than he did at the beginning of the week,' Jen says as she gathers up the CAD drawings.

The glass partitioning allows me to look out across the office to where Geoff has pulled up a chair next to one of our senior architects, and he's pointing at whatever plan she's opened up on screen. If drinking less is the barometer for my husband's happiness then, yes, he is happier. I have no other means of measurement. 'I suppose,' I reply.

'Has he mentioned any more about retiring?' Jen asks quickly as she sees me reach for the door handle.

I pause. 'Not a word.'

Like me, Geoff has relaxed back into the life we scavenged from the wreckage of Meg's death but there's something not quite right between us. This year's anniversary has caused a ground shift that's unnerving me, and it's not difficult to trace the cause. Geoff and I still haven't sat down and talked about his proposition for our premature retirement; in fact, it's a subject I've been deliberately avoiding, and as a consequence, our conversations at home have stagnated.

Our silences aren't necessarily a bad thing. It's always been difficult finding something new to talk about when we spend so much of the working day together. It's why we maintain our separate interests. Geoff has his golf and he leaves me to the day to day running of the foundation. Ours has never been the perfect marriage but I thought we were settled. I shouldn't have baited Lewis on TV. I should have known I was asking for trouble.

Jen continues to shuffle papers. She's been exceptionally quiet in recent days but I suppose it's natural that the uncertainty Geoff's plans have cast over our future would shake her too. Returning to my seat, I pull out the chair next to me. When Jen joins me, she fidgets with the papers she's set down on the table. She doesn't look up.

'There will come a time when Geoff and I have to think seriously about retirement but I don't want that to worry you, Jen. When it does happen, we're not going to simply abandon you, or the rest of the staff for that matter. There's no harm planning for the future, and that includes yours,' I tell her, willing her to lift her gaze. When she does, I add, 'Are you still serious about becoming a counsellor?'

'Yes.'

'Then you already have your new path to follow, all you have to do is take it.' When Jen squirms in her seat, I catch hold of a half-remembered conversation that had been lost in the fog that descended as Meg's anniversary approached. 'Wasn't there a part-time foundation course you were looking at? Shouldn't you have started it by now?'

'It was only a vague idea and I didn't think the timing was right this year. We've been snowed under with the Whitespace project and the helpline relaunch, and I know you said the foundation could fund me, but there isn't the budget and you know it. It's fine, honestly,' she adds when she sees me raise my eyebrows. 'I'll do it next year.'

'Oh, Jen, you can't keep putting these things off.'

'Yes, Mum,' she says, only for her smile to freeze when I flinch. 'Sorry, stupid thing to say.'

It's hard to predict or avoid the comments that stab at my heart without warning. I love Jen dearly, and there have been times when we treated her more like a daughter than a niece, but she isn't. Meg is my daughter and always will be, and it feels like a betrayal having the kind of conversation with my niece that I can't have with Meg.

Bringing Jen back into my life was always going to be a blessing and a curse. My sister-in-law, Eve, had distanced herself and her daughters from her brother's family as if suicide were contagious and for a time, that suited me because Jen's presence served only to amplify Meg's absence. But I'd been furious when I heard Jen had turned down her place at university, angrier still when I found out she was working as a cleaner for Charlie's fledgling company. I had to do something and I still do. I need to make sure Jen reaches her full potential because I know that's what Meg would be doing if she were here.

But it's not easy, and there are times like this when it bloody hurts.

I brush off Jen's comment with a smile. 'Just promise me you'll do something about it. If you've missed the September intake then find out if there's one that starts in January. At the very least, apply for next year and send *me* the bill. If this is your dream, go for it.'

Jen relaxes. 'It is, and I will.'

'Good, because I don't want you stuck here shuffling papers for the rest of your life.'

'But I love it here and I'll do anything to keep the helpline going,' she says with such conviction that it takes me by surprise.

'You're already doing more than enough. Geoff pulled up the stats and was surprised at the increase in activity . . . although I did have to point out that a good few were put-down calls. You didn't have any on Wednesday night, did you?'

Jen's lips are pressed tightly together. She shakes her head.

I tilt my head, sensing there's more to Jen's unease than I'd first thought. 'Anything else that's making you anxious?'

With a tentative shrug, she says, 'I had a good chat with Gemma. Well, when I say *good*, she's still being hounded by Ryan.'

'We'll need to watch her carefully. She says she doesn't want him back again but he's creeping into her life by stealth.'

'They always do,' Jen replies sadly.

Her anxiety creeps into my bones and I resist gnawing on the acrylic nail I stroke across my lip. 'Is it possible someone's doing that to us?'

Jen's eyes widen. 'Lewis?' she asks.

'I can't help wonder if the put-down calls on Monday were from him. It seems a coincidence for it to happen on the same day we received the solicitor's letter.'

'He wants to intimidate us,' she agrees.

'He can want all he likes. If I get any nuisance calls on my shift tonight, I will be polite and professional and I'll send a note to the others asking that they do the same. We do not quake in fear from dead air at the end of a phone.'

'No, we don't.'

The determination in Jen's voice is a contradiction to the fear in her eyes and I look away before we both lose our nerve. Across the office, Geoff remains absorbed in the designs we'll need to resubmit to the planners. I can't imagine him turning his back on his life's work. He thrives on the glory when our designs are brought to life, but I know my husband: he didn't mention retirement on a whim. The subject hasn't been dropped, and one way or another, I will have to follow the advice I gave Jen and consider my own future.

The foundation isn't the only legacy of Meg's that I'm struggling to keep alive. She loved her family and there was a time, before Lewis, when Meg would have done anything for me and Geoff. She went to great lengths to keep our marriage together and in spite of the horrific odds of parents breaking up after the loss of a child, we kept going after she'd died. We had to, for our business and the staff, for our sanity, and for Meg most of all.

'I've finally built up the courage to watch Meg's videos, or at least the earlier ones that remind me of what mattered to us all back then,' I say. I tip my head towards the window: the red brick and Portland stone striped hotel on the opposite corner of the Strand was once the White Star Line offices. There's a bride and groom out on the balcony, surrounded by guests. 'Remember our twentieth wedding anniversary?'

'I helped Meg organise the party.'

Jen's smile chases away our fears and reminds me how good it is to have her around to share happier memories. Our lives had been peppered with simple moments that I didn't appreciate at the time, but I do now as I think back to the day my caring and thoughtful daughter decided to patch up her parents' failing marriage.

'How many guests were at your wedding, Mum?' she'd asked as she came tumbling downstairs with Jen in tow.

I was in the sitting room leafing through a community newsletter that advertised all kinds of night school classes. I'd found it that morning on the kitchen counter and I was fairly certain it hadn't been Geoff who had turned the corner of the page for ballroom dancing. The summer holidays were drawing to a close, Sean was all set to go to uni and, as Meg kept reminding me, she was old enough to look after herself. Geoff and I needed new challenges.

'We only hired a small function room,' I said. 'So not many.'

'But you would have liked a bigger party?'

'We were busy building up the business at the time and we didn't need the expense. What mattered back then was exchanging vows and committing ourselves to each other. Isn't that right, Geoff?' I added through gritted teeth, pausing until he peeked over the top of his newspaper.

'What was that?' he asked as if he hadn't been listening.

'Mum was saying how she missed out on a big party and we should have one for your anniversary.'

I was about to correct my daughter but she was pulling Jen into the centre of the room so they could present their plans.

'We've been looking at hotels and Thornton Hall looks nice and has a room for a hundred guests, which would be a good number and not that expensive. You said you liked the DJ at Melanie's wedding and Jen can get the number off her, can't you, Jen?' Meg asked, looking to her cousin for confirmation that Jen's older sister would provide the necessary information.

Jen nodded. 'But Meg doesn't want the same buffet.'

'No one likes curled-up sandwiches,' my daughter continued. 'But this hotel does barbeques.'

The sun had been streaming through the window, adding streaks of gold to Meg's dark blonde hair. She had been so sure of herself, as if the future were hers to command.

'A barbeque? In November, Megan?'

She had beamed a smile at her father. 'OK, fair enough, we'll go for a hot buffet instead. So how big a budget can we have?'

If it had been left to me, the budget would have been zero but when Meg asked her father for something, Geoff delivered. The party had been an extravagant event and, as an extra surprise, our children had booked us into the honeymoon suite so we could stay over. Meg had wanted to make us happy but when I'd looked at the video footage, I was reminded how little enjoyment she had taken from the occasion.

She had been dropping hints for weeks about Jen moving in with us after Sean moved out. I wouldn't have minded, Jen was no trouble and our spare room was practically hers anyway. Geoff didn't seem to care either way but it was Eve who put her foot down. Meg had hoped to ply her aunt with drink at the party to get her to agree but Eve wouldn't hear of it.

Meg was distraught but she wasn't the only one struggling to get into the party mood that night. Our marriage wasn't in a state worth celebrating back then, no matter how hard Meg tried to pretend it was. She didn't know the exact details of her father's affair with a barmaid at the golf club but she knew how close he'd come to destroying the family and the business.

Jen had known about the affair too, but if that's what she remembers as we watch the wedding party through the window, she doesn't let it show. 'Whatever happens,' she says, 'I'll keep fighting as long as you want me to. Meg wouldn't have it any other way.'

Whatever happens? Jen makes it sound as if we're going into battle. Perhaps we do have a fight on our hands, I think to myself as I watch an unexpected gust tug at the bride's veil and pull it free. It floats away, out of reach of grasping hands. Not everything can be saved.

8

Jen

It's half past eight in the morning and although there are some early shoppers out and about, few have ventured to the upper level of Liverpool One where the shopping mall gives way to green space. It's mostly restaurants up here and I suspect that the people I can see crossing Chavasse Park are bracing themselves for a gruelling weekend shift.

Keeping some distance from the expanse of damp grass that might cool a tired and exhausted body after an intensive workout, I head towards The Club House which occupies a central position close to the green. There's a section of tall hedging that surrounds an outdoor dining area and offers the perfect vantage point to carry out my undercover operation.

The park grows busier but after half an hour, I wonder if I'm wasting my time. The girl who posted the tweet about the workout didn't specify a time and it's possible I've missed them. I couldn't leave the apartment until Charlie was safely out of the way. He's spending his day checking out his new commercial contracts at New Mersey Retail Park and was too anxious to notice my impatience for him to leave. I haven't spoken to him about Lewis, and even last night, when I mentioned the nuisance calls in passing after Ruth messaged to say there had been more during her shift, I didn't suggest who might be behind them. Charlie would only tell me I shouldn't assume it's Lewis. I don't. There's the possibility it's Ellie acting under instruction.

We've never had this many put-down calls before. Is it a coincidence? No more than it is for me to be in Chavasse Park when Lewis turns up with his boot-campers. *If* he turns up, that is. I could have missed him by minutes, or the session might have been relocated or cancelled all together. It rained overnight and the grass is sodden.

Shuffling from one foot to the other, I press my hands to my cheeks to warm both. I sweep my fingers beneath a fringe that has become slick with moist air and is sticking to my forehead. My hair will be a frizzy mess within the hour, which is annoying because I'd taken particular care with my appearance. If I do manage to spot Lewis or, more to the point, if he spies me, I want him to know that I'm a force of nature, just like Meg had been before he stepped into her path.

'What do you think?' she'd once asked. We were backstage, peeking through the curtain after dress rehearsals for the alternative nativity play Meg's sixth form drama teacher had co-written with her students. I wasn't part of the production but I'd shown up to rehearsals once too often and when one of the cast had dropped out, I'd been commandeered to play a sheep. It was originally a talking part but after an unconvincing performance, the script had been adapted around me.

'What do I think of what?' I asked. I was playing with my hooves rather than eyeing up the group of students who had gathered in the auditorium for a sneak preview, and continued to loiter with intent despite the performance being over.

'Him.'

She pulled me closer and I followed her gaze to the group of boys who had lost interest in heckling the actors for an encore and were kicking at the parquet floor tiles. Charlie was there too but that wasn't where Meg had her sights.

'Lewis Rimmer?' I asked with genuine shock. There was no doubt he was drop-dead gorgeous but there was a rumour he'd stabbed someone in revenge for his cousin's death, and that was why he and his mum had had to run away in the middle of the night with only the clothes on their backs. Clearly it was an exaggeration but I panicked every time he caught me looking at him, and I could never imagine talking to him without stumbling over my words.

'Oh, Meg, you can't,' I whispered.

'You'd be surprised what I can do.'

And that was the thing with Meg: I never could second-guess her. She'd been in a foul mood for weeks as the pressure mounted before opening night but the minute she put on her costume for the dress rehearsal, she was a different person.

'At times like this, Jen, there's only one way to find out if it was meant to be,' she added. 'If my public want an encore, that's what they're going to get.'

And with that, Meg flicked back the curtain and ran onto the stage. The Angel Gabrielle sparkled in her sequinned ballgown, revealing jeans and trainers as she lifted the hem of her dress. She was running fast and her pace didn't slow as she ran out of stage. She leapt over the footlights with her arms held out wide in a swan dive.

I couldn't take my eyes off her, and neither could anyone else. Charlie was one of the first to react but Meg had her own flight plan. She didn't doubt that Lewis would catch her, although it was more of a tumble as she thumped into him, knocking off his glasses as the two of them were sent skittering to the floor. She was sixteen and she thought she was indestructible but the countdown to her death started that day. She had two more Christmases, two summers and only one more birthday.

The sound of shouting pulls me back to the present. I see two blokes on the opposite side of the park look down over the tiered steps that rise up from the ground level. I can't see who they're laughing at but I can hear a man yelling instructions. Bodies clad in Lycra begin to appear one by one, their contorted features burning red and their backs bent.

'Move, move, move!' a man hollers. I'm too far away to hear their weak replies – it's only Lewis's voice that travels.

When he reaches the summit, Lewis is straight-backed as he continues to jog on the spot. I thought I was prepared for seeing him in the flesh but I'm overcome with such a sense of loathing that my damp skin burns. Here is a man who thinks nothing and no one can defeat him. I step away from the hedge so that he can see me if he chooses. That's all I want – for him to look at me and know that I'm not scared. Except, despite my fury, my legs are like jelly and

I flinch each time he yells, recalling how often he had screamed in Meg's face.

Unable to pretend I'm as brave as Meg for a moment longer, I stumble back into the shadows and remain there like a frightened rabbit, caught in the headlights of indecision and fear. I want to stand up to Lewis but what if he takes one look at me and laughs at my frizzy hair and shaking body? He might have reinvented himself with contact lenses and a manbun, but in the last ten years, I've stayed the same. I haven't moved on from Meg's death, I've been swept along by the sheer force of time, and that's how it's always going to be unless I do something.

So do it, I tell myself, although it could be Meg's voice I hear.

When I reappear from behind the hedge, the group have moved onto the grass. If it's too wet to lie down on, none of the prostrate figures are complaining. It's grotesquely symbolic that Lewis should be the only one left standing and I don't think about the consequences as I stride towards him.

Lewis is wearing a vest top and shorts that cling damply to his body, and his arm and leg muscles glisten with perspiration. Veins on the side of his neck bulge and if he would only stop shouting instructions to his class for two seconds, he might turn and notice me fuming from the sidelines. He doesn't stop, however, and the first to note my presence is a young woman who has dared to defy his order for another set of push-ups by resting her chin on her hands.

'EIGHT. NINE. Oh fine, why don't the rest of you give up too?' Lewis yells. He glares at the rebel and she points at me with her eyes.

There are moans and groans from the group as they collapse onto their bellies while their personal trainer forgets they exist. He's looking at me, his eyes darkening from steel-blue to iron, and I don't think either of us has blinked.

'Are we finished?' asks the rebel. When she receives no reply, she raises her voice with what little breath she has left. 'Lewis?'

'Since you're so good at shouting the odds, Shannon, you can take everyone through the cool down and then we'll call it a day,' he says without looking at her.

Shannon stands up with a grunt. 'Right, people, the sooner we do this, the sooner we can all get home and dry.'

Lewis stretches his shoulders as he steps away from the group and walks casually towards me. With time to compose himself, he has a smirk on his face when he says, 'You always did find me irresistible. I don't suppose you're here to join the group, are you, Jen? You look like you could do with a good workout.' Slowly and deliberately, he looks me up and down.

I don't like the shiver that runs down my spine that has nothing to do with fear. I don't need that kind of reminder. 'And you look like you don't give a shit who you hurt. Some things never change.'

'Clearly not,' he says, dropping his voice so we're not overheard. 'You can't leave me alone, can you?'

Rather than answer, I look over his shoulder at the group of supple bodies bending and stretching. 'You enjoy humiliating and controlling people, don't you?'

With his hands on his hips, Lewis swivels around to check on his acolytes. 'I'm not doing anything wrong. These people pay good money for me to shout at them.'

'You need to go back to Newcastle,' I tell him. 'Slither back to whatever life you made up there and leave us alone.'

'Me leave you alone?' he asks, his words crackling with anger. He uses his hand to wipe away the sweat trickling down his face before adding, 'Ruth publicly shamed me and now you're stalking me. If anyone's being victimised here, it's me. Isn't it time we all got on with our lives?'

'Meg's dead.'

His eyes close briefly and I wonder what image of my cousin forms in his mind. I doubt she's smiling. In those two years we all spent in sixth form, I have more memories of Meg's eyes full of tears than I do of them sparkling with laughter, but what is Lewis's enduring memory? Could it be her dead eyes? Hanging is not a pretty or peaceful way to die and that image must surely haunt him.

'How can you live with yourself?' I ask, my voice low with emotion.

'How can any of us?'

His cold stare turns my blood to ice and, frozen to the spot, I couldn't turn away if I wanted. 'Everything was fine until you showed up.'

'I bet it was. How is Charlie?'

'None of your business,' I reply.

There's an imperceptible shake of his head. 'What do you want, Jen?'

'You could start by telling me what you did to Meg that day. What was in the missing section of the note?'

I listen to his breath, exhaled through his nose like a bull that's ready to charge. 'This again? There was no note. I wasn't there.'

I flinch from the force of his words. His anger thickens

80

the air between us and as I breathe it in, my throat constricts. 'You're lying. You hurt Meg and she was going to tell everyone.'

'Why do you all insist on painting this perfect picture of Meg? As much as I loved her, she was a fucked-up bitch who messed with all of our lives. Ask anyone in our group. Ask Charlie.'

'That fucked-up bitch was my best friend and my cousin,' I reply, but it's more of a croak.

'So at least we're agreed she was fucked up,' he says, his smile returning.

'Is that how you live with yourself – by blaming her?' I scoff. 'Take a long look at yourself, Lewis. You need help.' I glance over at the collection of women bending and stretching on the grass. 'You have to find a better way of dealing with your anger than taking it out on women.'

'It would help if they didn't make me so fucking angry. I thought you were better than this, Jen,' he mutters, his eyes softening as he attempts to draw me in.

He's playing with me. I should know by now that my energies would be better served helping the victims, not the perpetrators. 'The solicitor's letter isn't going to make us go away and neither will the nuisance calls. We'll call the police if you don't stop.'

He shakes his head. 'Nuisance calls? Seriously, I don't have time for this. Go away, Jen. Get the fuck away or you might just regret it.'

'You're a bully, Lewis,' I hiss before his warning has a chance to sink in. 'You bullied Meg and I bet you're bullying your new girlfriend too.'

'Iona?'

At last I've wrong-footed him. I know Ellie's real name now. I can't suppress the smile.

'Have you been stalking her too?' he demands.

I'm tempted to break all the rules on confidentiality and mention Ellie's phone call – it's not as if it should come as news – but Lewis's growing agitation stops me. My stomach clenches as I consider the possibility he doesn't know she's spoken to me. His girlfriend might have leapt to his defence of her own volition. Then another thought occurs: what if I'm completely wrong about Ellie being his girlfriend? But who else could it be? 'No, I've not seen or spoken to her,' I say, no longer sure if this is the truth or a lie.

'Well, make sure it stays that way,' Lewis says as he closes the gap between us. His body radiates hatred and I can smell the sweat soaking into his vest top. 'I came back here for my family, not for you, and I'll do whatever's necessary to protect the people I care about. Don't put me to the test, Jen. If you come near Mum or Iona, I *will* retaliate. Take this as your final warning.'

With my chin raised in defiance, I look past Lewis's snarling features. The woman who had been leading the group's cool down is standing directly behind him and our eyes meet briefly. I force myself to smile, hoping my feigned confidence is convincing.

Confused, Lewis looks over his shoulder and I enjoy seeing him recoil. 'What do you want?' he snaps.

Shannon clears her throat. 'We're all done,' she begins.

I don't hear what she says next because I'm already on the move, heading for a set of steps hidden behind The Club House. Not stopping when I reach the bottom, I race out of Liverpool One towards Lord Street. There aren't as many shoppers milling around as I'd like so I rush into a shop. It's an opticians and as soon as I step through the door, I'm accosted by an assistant. I'm out of breath and I can't talk. I feel like an idiot. I am an idiot.

9

Ruth

The book I'd planned to spend a lazy Sunday devouring lies abandoned on the cushion next to me, while my open laptop is balanced on the arm of the sofa. My hands hover over the keyboard as I dare myself to watch the video recordings of Meg I've so far avoided; those last months and years of her life when I was too busy talking at her to listen.

The clips I have indulged in over the last week – the footage of holidays in Cornwall; the birthdays with clowns that enthralled Meg and terrified Jen; the snatched moments of Sean playing pranks on his sister – they tell me nothing I don't already know. Meg had a happy and contented childhood. There were the expected mood swings during her early teenage years but nothing remarkable. I have to search beyond the summer she passed her GCSEs to discover more about the troubled young woman Meg would become.

I scan the thumbnails of the videos Geoff has catalogued in chronological order but I'm scared of what I might find and my courage fails. Distracted by the bottle of wine chilling in the fridge, I get up to pour a glass. I glance at the clock. Geoff will be out for another hour at least and preparations for dinner can wait. Something quick and light will do. I've lost my appetite and Geoff will have eaten at the golf club. He's with our Whitespace clients, sweetening them up in case the meeting with the city planners tomorrow doesn't go our way. It'll be a disaster if planning approval is turned down. I'd like to say I care, but I don't.

There was a time when I took pride in every tender we won and every building we created or restored, but all I see lately are bricks and mortar. I hope this bad humour I've fallen into is a passing phase because the helpline is the only thing I care about these days and, even there, I can feel my strength waning. The call I took from Gemma on Friday evening has affected me more than I would like.

'I've seen him, Ruth,' Gemma had confided in me. 'He's lost so much weight.'

It had taken all my self-control to keep the disappointment out of my voice when I replied, 'What did he say to you?'

'That he loves me and he'd die without me.'

'Wasn't that part of the problem? I remember you saying you found all the attention smothering.'

'I haven't got back with him,' Gemma said. 'Mum would have a fit if I did. It was bad enough when she found out I'd met up with him again.'

'She might not say the right things, but if she's anything like me, it's only because she'll be desperately worried.'

Gemma snorted. 'Believe me, she's nothing like you. Mum does all of the talking and none of the listening. She's got her own life to lead now, and she'd probably be better off without me holding her back.'

'I'm sure that isn't true,' I said, my voice breaking as I catch a glimpse of myself through my daughter's eyes.

Like Gemma's mum, all I'd wanted to do was protect my daughter, but as I return to the sofa, I know the video evidence contained on my laptop will confirm how utterly I failed her. By the time I'd realised what kind of a person Lewis was, Meg was on the wrong side of the drawbridge I was attempting to pull up.

I'm no more equipped to save Gemma, and my growing concern for her welfare has become entangled with memories of my daughter. They both vie for my attention as I set down my glass of wine on the floor and pick up my mobile. As I wait for one of our longest serving volunteers to answer my call, I pull my laptop closer.

'Hi, Ruth. What's up?'

'Hi, Janet, I'm not disturbing you, am I?' I ask as I stare at the computer screen, the cursor hovering over a tiny image of Meg sitting alone at a table with anniversary balloons floating in the background. Her head is bent and she's sulking.

'No, it's fine,' Janet says.

I move the cursor away from the thumbnail. I don't want to be reminded of the Band-Aid Meg slapped over my marriage when I can feel the edges peeling away. The next clip is entitled, 'An Alternative Nativity Play', but I skip this one too. I'm not looking for a performance. I want to see the real Meg.

'I won't keep you long,' I promise as I move on to a recording labelled 'Christmas Morning'. 'I had a message from Alison earlier. She's come down with a virus and can't make her Monday shift. I offered to do it, but right now I don't feel up to it either.'

'Are you sick too?' Janet asks, concern in her voice.

'No, it's not that,' I reply. 'It's just that after my shift on Friday, I don't think I could face another one so soon.'

There's a hiss as Janet exhales. 'Are those nuisance calls bothering you?'

'They are annoying, but no. If there's anything worrying me, it's Gemma. You know how Ryan's been priming her for weeks, causing friction between her and her mum. He's going to keep going till he gets her back and . . .'

My voice trails off as I tap the mousepad and the Christmas video begins to play. I feel a familiar sense of yearning at the sight of my daughter's face in spite of her sour features. She's kneeling in front of a tree bedecked with baubles and twinkling lights, opening presents on what would be her second to last Christmas.

'Ruth?'

As I stare at the flickering screen, I pray that Gemma's mum will realise the danger her daughter is in before it's too late. I don't want her missing the signs that I ignored. The sound is off on the video, but there's nothing to hear anyway. My daughter had been withdrawing into herself at that point and I watch her open her presents without looking up or saying a word. Meg couldn't speak up because I was usually too busy talking over her. Fear that I'll do the same with Gemma rattles my next words.

'If Gemma does call tomorrow, I'm not sure I'm the best person to speak to her,' I continue. 'Is there any chance you could cover Alison's shift?'

'Of course, I will,' Janet says gently. 'She's got to you, hasn't she?'

I could lie but if I'm going to talk to anyone, it might as well be one of our own helpline volunteers. 'It does feel a little too close to home. Ryan has had a difficult life and Gemma sees herself as his saviour, not his victim. If she phones up and says she's seeing him again, I have this horrible feeling my patience will snap. I won't be any good to her.'

'Don't talk rubbish,' Janet tells me, before her training kicks in and she responds like a true helpliner. 'It's only natural for you to feel the way you do – even I can see the similarities with what you went through with Meg. There's no reason for you to put yourself in the firing line if you don't have to, and you *don't* have to.'

'Thanks, Janet.'

'We're a team, Ruth. We'll get through this together and I'm happy to cover your shifts for as long as you need me to.'

'It's a bit of a wobble, it won't last,' I promise.

When the call ends, I drop the phone onto a cushion without taking my eyes from the screen. I will Meg to look up, or better still, for the camera to pan around to me so I can reach through the screen and give myself a good shake. 'Look at her!' I want to yell. 'Ask her what's wrong!'

But Meg doesn't look up and the camera zooms in as she unwraps the ceramic heart-shaped pot I'd made for her. Its edges were lopsided but I was proud of it, and I'd wanted Meg to know that her idea for me to take up a hobby had been inspired. The pottery classes had managed to distract me from picking at the scabs of a marriage that was in the process of healing, but from Meg's glum features, the message doesn't get through. She looks briefly at the bowl before wrapping it up again.

What had I been thinking as I watched her set it to one side? I recall being disappointed, and a little annoyed, but I was too busy enjoying life again to acknowledge there was a problem with my daughter that couldn't be fixed with gentle warnings and stricter house rules. I thought she could be moulded like a piece of clay.

The video goes blank, my chance to save Meg lost long ago, and despair consumes me. I snap the laptop lid shut and bring my fingers to my lips out of habit. I pulled off my acrylic nails this morning and can feel the rough surface of freshly gnawed cuticle. I'll draw blood if I carry on chewing so I reach for my drink on the floor, but in my haste, I knock over the glass. It smashes against the porcelain tiles and I curse under my breath. I leap up to fetch a dustpan and brush but as I hurry into the utility room, it's the memories I'm trying to outrun. They catch me up and I'm no longer thinking about the broken glass as I root out a large box from the back of the store cupboard.

The collection of hand thrown pots and vases I'd amassed during my pottery classes had been wrapped with care before being buried out of sight. My heart flutters like a trapped bird in a cage as I take the box into the kitchen and unpack the contents, lining up the pieces on the breakfast bar. As I glare at them, an ethereal hand tugs at my arm and pulls me back to a memory that wasn't caught on camera.

'Can I have a lift to Jen's?' Meg had asked, grabbing hold of me before I could leave for my evening class.

I looked past Meg to her father, who had appeared in the hallway with his arms folded. 'No, Megan, you're not going out on a school night,' he said.

'Mum, please. I haven't got any homework.'

Geoff raised his eyebrows. We didn't know about Lewis at the time but we knew from our last parents' evening that Meg's first term in sixth form wasn't going as well as it should. It was her form tutor who dropped hints that there might be competing distractions in Meg's life and I'd asked my daughter outright if she had a boyfriend. She'd said no, but the blush rising in her cheeks had told another story.

'You must have some work to do, Meg,' I told her.

'So must you but you're going out!'

'Megan, do not talk to your mother like that!' Geoff's voice boomed. He didn't lose his temper often but Meg was trying us both.

'Please, Mum. I won't stay out late. You can pick me up on your way back.'

I knew she was hiding something. She was a little too desperate to sneak out and I thought how clever I was to be one step ahead of her. 'No, Meg. Do as your father says. I won't be long.'

'Fine, go!' she said. 'You care more about those stupid pots than you do about me!'

'It was your idea for me to get a hobby!' I roared as she stomped upstairs.

After she died, I'd wrapped up the pots with such care because it was Meg who had encouraged me to take up a new interest. Why I've kept them hidden is a little less palatable. Meg had wanted Geoff and I to do something together, but he'd shown polite disinterest when I'd mentioned the ballroom dancing. Far from being upset that Geoff didn't want to come along to the pottery classes either, I'd relished my time alone, escaping my cheating husband and yes, my troublesome teenage daughter.

Picking up a brightly enamelled fruit bowl, I weigh it in the palm of my hand. It has substance. My daughter does not. Meg was right; I cared for these stupid pots far more than I did her. The bowl wobbles slightly as I raise it over my head and when I launch it at the section of wall between the dresser and the bookcase, I release a grunt like a wild animal. The crash as it explodes on impact fires up my belly and the shattering of broken pottery pieces as they hit the floor is especially rewarding.

'You selfish cow!' I yell as I hurl the next pot. 'You couldn't wait to get out of the house!' Smash. 'You didn't want to spend time with her.' Crash. 'You wanted to spend time away from her!'

Thump!

Smash!

'What kind of a mother are you? Why didn't you talk to her? Why didn't you listen?' I ask as another pot shatters, then another, and another. I sob, I yell, I plead but I can't stop. The burning ache in my arms dulls the ache in my heart.

'I'm sorry, Meg. I'm so sorry,' I cry over and over until there's only one vase left. Tall and cylindrical, the green and silver glaze had matched the décor in the hallway and had stood pride of place on a window sill so I could look at it every day while I ignored my daughter. Meg had left her suicide note pinned beneath it so we would find it as soon as we came home.

'I didn't care more about these stupid pots. I didn't!' I cry out, issuing a curse as I grab the vase and let it fly. A shower of green and silver ceramic shards rain down onto the floor but the sheath of paper that had been curled tightly around its inner wall takes its time to settle on top of the wreckage.

I take a deep shuddering breath because I think I might throw up. I recognise the yellow lined paper immediately. It's a page from Meg's notepad. Could this be the missing piece of her suicide note that will prove Lewis's guilt at long last? I don't move. I don't dare. I hear the front door opening and I wait for Geoff.

'Oh, my love,' he whispers as he appears in the doorway. When I don't respond, he follows my gaze and gasps.

He takes a step towards the note but I hold up my hand. 'Let me,' I tell him as I kneel down on the floor. The jagged edges of broken pottery that slice into my flesh barely register as I lift up the folded piece of paper that has retained the shape of the vessel that kept it hidden. I uncurl it with a sense of reverence, opening one fold, and then another.

Geoff releases the breath he's been holding and his voice shakes when he says, 'It's not it.'

The A4 sheet of paper trembling in my hand has no torn edge. It's nothing more than a piece of Meg's schoolwork. It has her name written across the top and the title of the essay on English poets she had started to write, but there's only one paragraph under the Introduction heading and it's been scored through with two lines and the word 'fail' written in capitals between them.

The disappointment is crushing and I let out a sob as my hope collapses. I feel Geoff's hand on my shoulder as he crouches down next to me. He reaches to take the note but my grip on it tightens as I read the first line of Meg's long-abandoned essay. *Do you want to know where the space girl goes?*

'Wait,' I tell him. 'Let me read it.'

We read it together.

Do you want to know where the space girl goes? She travels to a secret universe inside her head where the world is just a tiny speck in the distance. As she floats in space, she screams and screams and screams, but no one hears her. No one's listening. And when the air runs out and she can't breathe, she's not scared, not any more. It's amazing what you can get used to with enough practice. The lungs that burn are in a body she left behind. It's just a shell and he can have her shell if he wants. She's happier where she is, feeling nothing, being nothing, while he breaks her one last time. Except it never is the last time.

10

Ruth

It's a thirty-minute drive to the office and almost every face I see is sombre, including Geoff's. Hunched over the wheel as the Monday morning traffic crawls along Aigburth Road, he huffs loudly when we come to another stop.

'I don't understand why we shouldn't take it to the police,' I say.

Geoff keeps his eyes on the taxi cab in front of us. 'I never suggested we don't,' he replies. 'All I'm saying is don't expect them to reopen the case.'

'But this proves he hurt her. It's her writing, her words, and it was written while she was still at school. It's evidence that she was suffering over a longer period of time. The exam results weren't the reason she killed herself. Lewis is the reason she killed herself.'

I see Geoff's shoulders tense. His thoughts have turned to what we've both spent a sleepless night imagining. What did Lewis do to break her over and over again? What was it she was forced to get used to?

'As obvious as it is to us, she doesn't name him, or herself for that matter. It could have been a creative writing exercise.'

'In an essay on English poets?'

'I'm not arguing with you, my love. Honestly, I'm not,' Geoff says as the traffic moves off again. The car jerks as he crunches the gears. 'But do we have to talk about this now?'

'I'm sorry you think it's so unworthy of your time.'

There's hurt in his bloodshot eyes when he turns to me. 'That's unfair, Ruth. She was my daughter too, and I'm sorry if I'm a coward but I don't want to think about him with her. Not ever. I wish you'd never found the essay, or whatever it is.'

'No, I'm the one who should be sorry. You're right, it's not enough,' I force myself to admit.

We lapse into silence as we head towards Otterspool, and as we follow the contours of the river, we ignore each other's pain. It's what we do. Geoff didn't ask me why there were smashed pots all over the kitchen floor when he came home yesterday, and I haven't mentioned his red-rimmed eyes this morning. It works for us. Ignorance might not be bliss but it could be worse.

'Are you worried about the meeting with the city planners?' I ask as we join a new queue of traffic on the Strand.

'I'm not sure we've done enough with the revised design.'

'If anyone can persuade them to put it through for approval, it's you.'

'I'll need your help.'

'At the meeting? I assumed you'd go on your own and I have other work to do this morning. I want to finish off the extension plans for Selina's refuge. She needs something she can share at the fundraiser on Saturday.'

'But it's only a loft conversion. Can't you get someone else to do it?'

'I want to do it,' I insist. It's the one design job I'm still passionate about and the only thing right now that could help take my mind off my space girl. 'Honestly, Geoff, you don't need me there. I might have come up with the suggestions but you're the one who revised the plans. You know it better than I do, and Jen could always go with you to take notes.'

'This project is important to us,' he reminds me.

'I know,' I say, when what I really want to ask is why he's ready to give it all up if it is that important. As I nibble the torn cuticle on my fingers, a picture forms of my two irrepressible granddaughters.

Geoff catches me chewing my nails and releases a sigh. 'OK, fine. Leave the planners to me. I can manage.'

As we turn into Mann Island and drive across the concourse to the underground car park, I wonder why I'm putting myself through this when Geoff has put an alternative life on the table.

'Is that Jennifer?' asks Geoff.

I follow his gaze and catch sight of a young woman shuffling along the road from the direction of the waterfront. Geoff slows the car but Jen has her head hung low and she doesn't see us.

'She looks like she has the weight of the world on her shoulders as it is,' Geoff says. 'You're not going to tell her about what Meg wrote, are you?'

'Probably not,' I reply. 'She's worried about the helpline,

and the nuisance calls haven't helped. She doesn't need more upset.'

The voice in my head grows louder. Why am I putting us all through this?

11

Jen

The knot in my stomach twists so tightly that it pulls my body into itself. I've been so stupid. I should have known I'd make Lewis angry and I can't stop imagining what actions I've set in train through my recklessness.

'Are you all right, Jennifer?' Geoff asks. 'You seem distracted.'

We're walking down Castle Street with the town hall behind us, weaving our way through a swarm of city workers on the hunt for lunch. I haven't said a word since we left the meeting with the city planners, despite it having gone better than we expected.

'I'm fine,' I say as someone thumps into my shoulder. The man almost knocks me off my feet, although a light gust of wind could have done the same.

As Geoff puts a hand out to steady me, he glares at the man who melds back into the crowd. 'I was going to suggest we grab a bite to eat but you don't look like you could stomach it.'

'Don't you want to get back to the office and share the good news?' I ask.

'We've got time for a celebratory drink, at least. I'll text Ruth from in here,' he says, keeping hold of my arm so he can steer me towards the pub we are passing. There are no free tables so we stand at the bar. 'Can I tempt you with a glass of prosecco?'

I nod politely while my stomach raises an objection. It's not only worry that's caused my queasiness but the two bottles of wine Charlie and I demolished the day before. At my suggestion, we'd made Sunday a duvet day and binged on a Netflix box set. I love Scandi noir dramas but I found no sense of satisfaction at the end when the killer was caught. It wasn't true to life. Sometimes it's the bad guy who gets to live happily ever after.

Thankfully, the plot was enough to keep Charlie preoccupied. He'd already commented on my nerviness when he arrived home from work late on Saturday afternoon and I'd made up some story about my mum phoning and annoying me as usual, which was partly true. Mum always annoys me.

My mobile had been in my hand when she'd called me at lunchtime but I'd let it go to voicemail while I continued to scour the internet for any mention of someone called Iona who was associated with a Lewis McQueen. My efforts drew a blank but I couldn't let it go so I searched for the origins of the name, hoping it would match Ellie's Romanian accent. My heart sank when I discovered the name was Celtic. That was when the landline rang out. Mum wasn't giving up.

'So you do exist,' she'd said. 'I was beginning to think you were a figment of my imagination.'

'Sorry,' I mumbled as I wedged the phone under my chin so I could continue tapping on my mobile.

'Have I done something to upset you, Jen?'

Where do I begin? I'd wanted to ask. Should I start with how you allowed your petty jealousy of your brother's success to come between me and Meg? Would you like to speculate on how different things might have been if I'd been allowed to live under the same roof as my cousin? Could you tell me how you can sit in judgement of how Ruth deals with her grief when you've never tried to understand what she and Geoff have gone through?

'I've been busy, that's all,' I'd said.

'And you'll be too busy to come over tomorrow for Sunday lunch, I suppose. All your sisters will be there.'

'Sorry,' I'd replied as my internet search continued. I tried alternative spellings of Lewis's girlfriend's name.

'I don't suppose you've started your counselling course and that's what's keeping you so busy?' Mum had offered.

'No,' I'd said flatly as I typed the name Ioana.

'Then promise me you'll come over soon,' Mum continued. 'You have a niece and nephew who've forgotten what you look like.' She had waited for a reply but I was too busy punching the air. 'Jen, are you still there?'

I'd found a match. Ioana is a Slavic girls' name popular in Romania. I was right but being right hadn't made things better. If Iona and Ellie are one and the same, her call to the helpline could have been an attempt to calm the situation and it's possible I've only made matters worse, so much worse.

I haven't been able to stop thinking about it ever since and I'm not expecting the prosecco to help ease my worries, but it goes down exceptionally well as I watch Geoff tap out a message to Ruth. 'I needed that,' I say after he slips his phone into his jacket pocket.

Geoff sees my empty glass and, picking up his neat whiskey, downs it in one. 'How about one more for the road?'

'I might even taste it next time,' I say, pushing my glass towards the bartender.

While I watch our drinks being poured, Geoff watches me. Although he's my boss during work hours, it's hard to forget that he's the uncle who would have happily absorbed me into his family if his sister had allowed. It was awkward for a while after Meg died, but we've forged a new kind of relationship, and I respect and admire him as much as I do Ruth.

'You've been looking troubled lately,' my uncle tells me.

This, I realise, is why Geoff has taken me to one side. 'It's been an odd few weeks.'

'You did a good job with the relaunch, although Ruth tells me not all of those extra calls are exactly what we were expecting.'

'We can't let a few nuisance calls get to us,' I say, as if it isn't perfectly apparent that they already have. 'I know you had your doubts about the helpline's future, but the PR campaign was all about creating the springboard we need to extend our services. New beginnings . . .' My words falter. I can't pretend there isn't a problem.

'Except now it feels more like the beginning of the end,' Geoff finishes for me.

'We can't give up, Geoff,' I plead, taking my drink from the bartender before he has a chance to place it on the coaster. 'There have been new callers, the kind that remind us why we need to keep trying. We can see the way their lives are leading and we can do something about it – before they reach the point where they feel trapped in circumstances they can't control.' It sounds like a sales pitch and that's exactly what it is. 'They're girls like Meg.'

'And that's my problem.' Geoff takes a sip of his drink and lets it warm his tongue before swallowing hard. 'As a trustee I have a duty of care to you and the other volunteers, and that includes Ruth. Did you know she'd promised Alison to cover her shift tonight, only to realise she couldn't face it? She's asked Janet instead.'

'No, I didn't know,' I reply, leaning heavily against the bar.

'She can't do it any more, not that she'll ever admit it.'

'It's because the helpline means so much to us.'

'No, it's because Megan means so much to us,' Geoff says. I can see a decade's worth of pain in his eyes and the weight of it is crushing. He puts a hand on my shoulder. 'I know you've tried your best, and no one's doubting your intentions, but you have no idea how much strain Ruth is under at the moment. I'm not sure I do. She hides her pain too well.'

'I think she'd say the same of you,' I suggest as my heart sinks. Despite my best efforts, the future of the helpline is still under threat and the end could be nearer than I'd feared.

Geoff drains his glass. 'There was a time when Ruth couldn't bring herself to look at Megan's videos. I never understood why but now that she is replaying them, I think she was right to avoid them.' He holds up his glass for the bartender to refill while I place my hand over the top of my half-empty glass. 'Yesterday was truly awful.'

'What happened?' I ask. I'd noticed a change in both of them this morning. They looked beaten.

'It's best that you don't know,' he says. 'All I can say is don't let Ruth's act fool you.'

I can see where this is leading and I put Geoff out of his misery. 'Ruth mentioned you were thinking seriously of retiring.'

'I wasn't planning on it being so early but now that the Whitespace project is back on track, it would be an ideal time to bring in new investors,' he says. 'And as for the helpline, I said it before and I'll say it again. It's better to plan its closure than let it fizzle to nothing, and there are other helplines out there to fill the breach.'

'But what about the girls who don't have a label for how they're feeling? They're the ones who talk to us, Geoff. They're at the beginning of a relationship that feels wrong and we help them work out why before they're stripped of their confidence and their identity. We do make a difference.'

'But at what cost?'

I don't know what to think. Am I pushing the foundation for my own selfish reasons and ignoring Ruth's suffering?

'It's ironic that we've lost one child and yet we're missing out on so much of Sean's life,' Geoff continues. 'Megan adored her brother. If she were here, I think she'd be telling her mum to make the move.'

'How is he?' I ask, grasping the opportunity to change the subject.

'Frazzled, as you can imagine with twins. I know new mums don't always appreciate interference from their

103

in-laws but I get the feeling Alice would welcome the extra help too. And I want to be part of my granddaughters' lives, Jennifer. I don't want to be a stranger to them.'

Geoff is looking for an ally but I'm not ready to give him what he wants. I can't let Lewis win again. 'Is it possible that you could move to Stratford and keep things going here?' I ask. 'You could bring in a new partner to run the business, and I don't mind taking on more of the foundation's work.'

'In my view, we'd be surrendering control whilst keeping all of the stress. I don't think our marriage would survive it,' he admits in a low voice.

I'm relieved when Geoff straightens up without waiting for a response. Taking out his wallet, he hands the bartender more than enough to settle our bill. His cheeks are ruddy and I suspect mine are too as we leave the tavern.

The weak sunlight soaking through a haze of grey cloud temporarily blinds me and I feel distinctly woozy. I'm beginning to regret the second glass of prosecco, if not the first, as we resume our journey back to the office. If I'd kept my head clear, I might have been able to persuade Geoff to shelve his plans for retirement but he's made the winning argument and he hasn't finished yet.

'There is another reason I'm trying to persuade Ruth to move away,' he begins. 'I didn't want to tell you but I need you on my side, Jennifer.' He looks about him as if we're being watched. 'And perhaps you could do with being extra vigilant.'

As my hand skims a lamppost, my fingers clamp around it and I come to a stop, much to the irritation of the woman who almost walks into me. Adrenalin floods my body and sets my heart racing. I know what Geoff is about to say. He's carried on walking and it takes him a moment to realise he's left me behind. I don't want him to come back to me but he does. He gives me a curious look and we both weigh up our options. Who's going to say it first?

'Did you know Lewis was back in Liverpool?' he asks.

'Yes.'

'But you haven't told Ruth?' Geoff adds quickly.

'No, and probably for the same reasons you haven't.'

Taking a chance that my legs will carry me, I let go of the lamppost and we continue on our way, albeit hesitantly. 'Doesn't it make you angry that Lewis thinks he can pick up where he left off?' I ask.

'Lots of things make me angry,' Geoff admits, although it's despair I hear in his voice. 'That's why I have to get away.'

'So he's won?'

Geoff's pace quickens and I struggle to match it. 'It's not a matter of winning, it's a matter of surviving,' he says. 'You don't know how hard I try to erase all memory of him from Megan's life. He could be in any city, doing whatever he wants; I don't care as long as I never have to set eyes on him again.'

'Well, lucky you,' I say. I'm gasping for breath and my words are harsher than I intended. Geoff looks back and his eyes narrow. I'm calmer when I add, 'I've seen him.'

'When?'

'He was taking an outdoor exercise class in Liverpool One,' I say, as if I'd come across him by chance.

'Did you speak to him?'

'He's not sorry, Geoff. He's not sorry about anything.'

Geoff puts a hand over his ashen face. 'What does he want, Jen? I knew he'd react after Ruth's interview, but was the solicitor's letter simply a shot across the bow? Are the nuisance calls the start of a more concerted effort to intimidate us?'

'I don't know, but I suspect seeing me didn't help.'

Geoff sees my eyes glistening and his features soften. He places his hand gently on the small of my back as we walk. His voice is gentle too. 'I'm pretty sure you managed better than I would,' he says. 'Don't think there haven't been nights I've lain awake thinking about what I'd like to do to him, but if I were to carry through my fantasies, I'd be the one arrested, not him. He's never going to be punished for the crimes he's committed against us, and while that's been a bitter pill to swallow, that's how it has to be. That bastard doesn't deserve our thoughts or our time. He has no place in our lives, he never did. Help me, Jennifer. Help me persuade Ruth it's time to stop fighting and start living again, far away from here.'

I'm excused from giving Geoff an answer as we take advantage of a break in the traffic and hurry across the Strand. My legs are leaden and I don't know how I'm going to make it up the stairs. I consider taking the lift with Geoff but I'm not that brave, I never was. Antagonising Lewis had been foolhardy. If he can beat Geoff into submission without raising a finger, what chance have the rest of us?

12

Jen

It's Wednesday evening and my palms are slick with sweat as five o'clock finally arrives and the helpline is automatically activated. I'm not sure what I dread more, Lewis hanging up on me, or Ellie phoning to inform me what misery my actions have caused.

As I wait, I tap my fingers on the desk and watch Ruth and Geoff in their office preparing to leave. I didn't agree to help Geoff persuade Ruth to retire, and I don't think I can while there's still a chance that the helpline's fortunes will be reversed, but what worries Geoff, worries me. Since our chat on Monday, I can no longer ignore how run-down my aunt looks. It's not particularly unusual to see her staring off into space as she wrestles with some design issue or other, but at some point her face will light up as she plucks a solution from thin air. It's been a long time since I've seen her eyes alight.

Ruth slips on the raincoat Geoff is holding out for her, but when he puts his hands on her shoulders, she moves away. She and Geoff are pulling in opposite directions and their daughter isn't here this time to push them back together. I can almost hear Meg demanding that I do something about it. Oh, Meg, it's not that simple. Giving up on the foundation that keeps your name in our lives would be like giving up on you all over again.

Before Ruth catches me spying on her, I open up the call log with the intention of getting up to speed with what's been happening with our callers, but my heart sinks when I see that six of the calls listed on Monday were put-downs. Lewis has intensified his hate campaign.

I hear an office door open and Ruth appears next to me. 'We're leaving now,' she says, but before she goes, she taps a ravaged fingernail on the screen. She's pointing to the call Janet took from Gemma. 'Fingers crossed she'll phone again tonight.'

'She's going to be fine,' I promise even though I haven't actually read the latest call sheet.

'If anyone can get through to her, you can,' Ruth says.

'Or you,' I add.

Ruth shakes her head. 'I'd only lecture her like I did with Meg. I wouldn't be able to stop myself.'

I want to remind Ruth that she had good cause to be frustrated with Meg, I felt some of that myself. We were only trying to look out for her, but my dear cousin never viewed it that way.

'Does Auntie Eve nag you like Mum does me?' Meg had asked me once.

'Only if she notices I'm there.'

I was sitting cross-legged on Meg's bed, watching her apply another layer of mascara at her dressing table. I'd

108

got ready before I left the house and although I was wearing some makeup, I wasn't as particular as Meg. We were only going to spend another night with our usual group of friends – plus Lewis – and I had no one to dress up for. I was starting to wonder if I'd ever have a boyfriend – I doubted Charlie would notice if I turned up wearing a tutu and clown makeup. No one would.

'I wish Mum had let me come and live here.'

'You're better off where you are. Being noticed isn't all it's cracked up to be,' Meg said, the mascara wand stilling in her hand as she watched me fall back onto her bed.

'Mothers,' I'd mumbled, as if it were a dirty word.

There were heart-shaped fairy lights woven between the wooden slats of Meg's headboard and it was a relief to see she'd stopped switching them on. I was convinced the scarves hanging on her bedpost would catch a spark and burn the house down but the silk was cool as I tugged at the pastel-green scarf with pictures of galloping horses racing across it. She'd bought it in Cornwall the summer before and recalling our holiday brought with it a pang of sadness. Sean had said it would be his last. Mum had said it should be mine too. She complained it felt like charity, having her brother fund my holidays, and announced I was old enough to conquer my fears of flying and go with them. Not that she was willing to put that theory to the test and our next family holiday – the Hunter family holiday – would involve a ferry across to Ireland.

'Stop messing with my things,' snapped Meg.

'God, you're in such a bad mood. I bet you haven't finished your coursework, have you?' I asked, referring to the cross-examination she'd received from her mum when my arrival gave Ruth the first inkling that her daughter had plans for the night.

Meg had never been good with deadlines, or rules for that matter, but I'd been surprised how difficult she found adapting to life as a sixth former. We had the freedom to plan our own studies but she hadn't made a good start in the first term and the second was even worse. She'd spend weeks prevaricating over a piece of work, followed by intense periods of panic. There wasn't much I could do to help because we didn't take the same subjects and Sean wasn't around to keep an eye on her, or at least divert my aunt and uncle's attention.

'It'll be done by Monday if people will just leave me alone,' Meg replied through gritted teeth. With perfect timing, her phone pinged with a message. It was the fourth alert since I'd arrived and she ignored this one too.

'Does that include Lewis?'

'Do *not* mention his name in this house,' she said, smudging mascara on her upper lid as her hand jerked.

'You can't keep him a secret forever, not with your phone going off every two minutes. Everyone can tell you're up to something. And I bet you've told Sean.'

'No, I haven't breathed a word and that's how it's going to stay. Do not say anything to anyone,' she warned. She grabbed her phone and glanced at the messages. Her features softened as she tapped out a reply, but when she caught me watching, she scowled. 'I'm serious, Jen. If Mum and Dad found out, I'd be grounded forever.'

It would be months before her parents discovered the existence of a boyfriend and I often wonder what might have happened if I'd dropped a subtle hint or two when

Ruth sat us down at the kitchen table to eat before we left that night, or later, when Geoff drove us over to Meathead's house. They might have been able to break the spell Lewis was casting over their daughter. Early intervention, that's what Meg had needed and that's why I'm sitting here at the helpline pod waiting for the phone to ring in the hope that the next call will be from a genuine caller. It's also why Ruth hasn't moved from my side.

'Are you ready, my love?' Geoff asks as he approaches.

His tone is coaxing but Ruth doesn't respond immediately. We wait. She sighs, and only then does she straighten up. 'If there are any problems, you know where I am.'

'You'll be fine, won't you, Jennifer?' Geoff says as we share a look. It feels wrong to have a secret between us but if anything, knowing that Geoff has decided not to inform Ruth about Lewis being in Liverpool justifies my own silence. We're doing this for Ruth's sake.

Once they've left, I do what I've spent most of the week doing, I scour the internet for any shred of information about Lewis. On Twitter, I find a recent tweet from someone called Sha_4893 who describes herself in her profile as a fitness freak from Liverpool. She says she must have been insane to pay someone to shout abuse at her but from the replies received so far, people are interpreting it as a tongue-in-cheek complaint. I don't think it is. I think this is Shannon, and what she overheard on Saturday has made her question her personal trainer's true character.

I enjoy a brief moment of satisfaction, before I remember that Lewis hits back and it won't be me or his boot camp recruits who will bear the brunt of his anger. I look around the office and see that more staff have left for the evening.

Knowing it won't be long until I'm on my own, I tuck myself away in my pod and go in search of a friendly face. I close down Twitter and when I find Ruth's interview online, I mute the sound and fast forward to the video montage.

Despite being less than a minute long, it gives a good flavour of Meg's character. The reporter had wanted to show Meg growing up but it takes a keen eye to see that she hasn't got the chronology quite right. The family holiday in Malta had been before, not after, her sixth birthday, and the wedding anniversary party in Thornton Hall was before the alternative nativity play where she finally caught Lewis's attention by jumping on top of him. The last few seconds are one final glimpse of Meg on her phone in the kitchen. I'd like to believe she was talking to me, but it would have been Lewis. She turns her back on whoever was filming her and the report returns to the interview with Ruth. I rewind to the beginning of the montage and play it again, and again.

I jump when the phone rings and when I pause the video, it freezes on one of Meg's withering looks. It's the anniversary party and the footage was taken not long after I'd seen Meg and my mum arguing. Am I so wrong to blame Mum? Am I fooling myself to think I stood any chance of saving Meg once Lewis had burrowed inside her head? Lewis excels at mind games and my skin crawls as I lift the phone from the receiver.

'Hello?' I ask as I return Meg's scowl. 'You're through to the Lean On Me helpline. How can I help?'

When the line goes dead, I slam it down. 'Bastard!'

My hands are shaking but there's no time to recover

because the phone rings again. I put it to my ear but, this time, I don't speak.

'Hello, is that you, Jen?' comes a familiar voice.

'Yes, it's Jen. You're through to the Lean On Me helpline,' I reply rather than opting for a simple hello because I can't decide whether to call her Ellie or Ioana.

'It's Ellie. I am sorry for hanging up on you.'

'That was you?'

'I've been waiting and waiting for you to answer.'

'Have you been putting the phone down on the other volunteers? On purpose?' I ask. I keep my voice calm despite my rising anger. I'm not going to find out any more about her unless I can keep the lines of communication open.

'I did not mean to. I am sorry,' Ellie says. 'I know I have caused trouble for you.'

'And how do you know that?' I ask. 'You talked about Meg's boyfriend last time. Do you know him?'

'I should not have mentioned him. I did not mean to make you angry,' she says quietly and I can't help wondering how many times she's made that same apology to Lewis.

'I'm not angry,' I tell her as I cradle the phone gently in my hand for fear of losing the call. Despite the distress she's caused with the nuisance calls, Ellie isn't coming across as devious. She sounds genuinely upset. Worse than that, she sounds desperate. 'I'm concerned about you, that's all. I want to understand why you're calling the helpline, and why you want to talk to me in particular. Help me understand.'

'Are you alone?'

A shiver runs down my spine as I peek over the privacy screen to find the office empty. How good are my instincts?

Do I trust Ellie enough to let her know I am alone? 'No one is listening in, if that's what worries you.'

'He cannot find out I am phoning. Promise not to talk to the others about me,' she says. 'You will not tell Mrs McCoy?'

The image of Meg stares out from the screen. The promise I'm about to make is the same one I made to her and I hope that isn't a bad omen. 'I won't say a word, not even to Mrs McCoy. What is it you want to tell me, Ellie? Please, you can trust me.'

'He talks about her,' she says in a whisper. 'He talks about what happened.'

A hundred questions jostle for position in my mind. I have to decide which ones are most pressing. 'What does he say?'

'He says she took over his life . . .'

'Can you tell me who he is?' I ask.

I'm pushing too hard and after a pause, her response is equally blunt. 'John.'

It's a familiar name, one that many of our callers use to protect the identity of their abuser. 'Tell me about John,' I implore her. I hope my apologetic tone makes up for my impatience.

'He was a very kind man when I meet him first time. He would not stop looking at me. He made me feel special but I was the fool. He was only interested because he thinks I look like her,' Ellie explains, her words hesitant as she attempts to find the right words in English.

I think back to the photo of Lewis on the beach. Did that girl look like Meg? With her hair scraped back into a ponytail and a scattering of freckles from too much sun, she didn't strike me as Meg's twin but what I see doesn't count. It's what Lewis perceives. 'Does he hurt you, Ellie?'

'At first we were friends only. He found me a new place to stay and said he wanted to look after me. I believed him until we . . . sleep together. He was very drunk and I did not like it. He called me Megan. It was like she was there and I was not. He cried like a baby when it was over and made me promise not to tell. He said he would not do it again, but he did. He does it again and again, and I cannot escape. He lied about how much is the rent. It is too high for me to pay on my own. I should not have left the house I shared. I wish I had never trusted him.'

'We can stop this,' I promise, knowing from experience that it's never that simple. 'If that's what you want?'

'I cannot tell on him.'

Ellie's fear travels down the line and makes my entire body tingle. 'That's OK,' I say when it feels anything but. 'What would you like to happen, Ellie? How can I help?'

'If only he would keep his promise to be a better—'

'He won't change.' I shouldn't have interrupted, but I can't stop myself. I have to get her away from him. 'I think you've already seen that the more you accept his behaviour, the more he hurts you. Let me help you get away from him. And if you can't name *him*, give me *your* real name. I can get in touch with other agencies and find you a new place to stay. Or I could help you return home to your family.'

'I came to this country for a better life. I have worked hard for four years. I do not want to go back to Romania. I do not want to give up what I have – what I had here. No,' she says, the panic rising in her voice. 'I cannot do this, Jen. Sorry. I should go.'

115

I curse myself. I'm supposed to let Ellie reach her own conclusions and I wouldn't have pushed so quickly if it were any other caller. 'I'm the one who should be sorry. I know this is overwhelming but please, think about what you want and let's see if we can make that happen. I'll do all I can. I'm usually here on Wednesday evenings. If you don't get an answer, it means I'm on another call but please keep trying.'

'Goodbye, Jen.'

When Ellie cuts the call, I have a sinking feeling I've lost her for good. The rest of the office has fallen into darkness and I feel desperately alone. Even Meg's frozen image on screen offers no comfort.

'What hold did he have over you, Meg?' I ask her. 'What did he do that made you think your life wasn't worth living?' My voice is a mixture of anger and pain. 'You should have said something. We would have got through it together. You had dreams, remember? Think of all the amazing adventures you've missed out on, and I've missed out on too because you were the only one who could have dragged me onto a plane. We should have been sitting on a white sandy beach somewhere, sipping cocktails for breakfast because we'd been out clubbing all night. And you'd be thinking, thank God I didn't miss any of this.'

I cover my eyes with the palms of my hands and press hard. 'But you are missing it, Meg. And so am I.'

13

Jen

When the phone rings again, I don't feel that earlier dread: I'd be happy to take a call from our nuisance caller now that I know who it is. In the hour that's passed since my chat with Ellie, we've both had the chance to calm down and consider our options, and I intend to let her do the talking this time. I need to be the friend to her that I wasn't to Meg. I need to atone for my sins so I can get on with the rest of my life.

'Hello, you're through to the Lean On Me helpline,' I say as I strain my ears for the first clues to identify the caller. I can hear the chatter of distant voices and other sounds I can't quite place.

'Hi, it's Gemma.'

I press my lips together as I bring my disappointment under control. 'Hi, Gemma, it's Jen. Where are you?'

'I'm out shopping.'

'Oh, OK. How are things?' I ask as I bring up the call sheet Ruth had pointed out earlier. I still haven't read it.

'Not great,' Gemma replies. 'Mum's furious with me and I haven't been home for a couple of days.'

'So where have you been staying?' I ask, already fearing the answer.

'With Ryan. Mum's made it impossible for me to go back.'

I skim the notes Janet made. There's talk of arguments with her mum and, on face value, that's where Gemma thinks her problems lie.

'You and your mum always struck me as pretty close,' I say, hoping to remind her of a time before Ryan.

'Controlling, you mean.'

'Why do you say that?' I ask, encouraging her to question what I'm guessing Ryan has been telling her.

'She just is.'

'And what about Ryan? How has he been with you?'

'He can't do enough for me,' Gemma says. 'And I know it's early days, but he's been so much more relaxed since I've been staying with him. Do you think I might have been a bit of a drama queen over it all?'

'Like you said, Gemma, it's early days and Ryan will be putting a lot of effort into convincing you to stay with him.'

'He is,' she agrees. 'I think we've both turned a corner.' She stops talking and there's a brief moment when the line goes dead. 'Sorry, I needed to put more money in.'

'You're calling from a public phone? Have you lost your mobile?'

Gemma sounds less certain of herself when she replies, 'No, I've still got it but you know, I don't want this number showing up on my bill.'

'Because Ryan will see it.'

'Maybe.'

'Does he check your account? Have you given him your password?'

'He admits he's insecure, Jen,' she offers. 'But we're dealing with it. Not that Mum sees it like that. She's threatening to wash her hands of me if I stay with him.'

'Why do you think she's reacting that way? Is it possible she's scared for you?'

Before Gemma can reply, the second line starts to ring. If it's not answered, the call will be diverted to a recorded message informing the caller that all lines are busy and encouraging them to phone back. But it's quarter to eight and by the time I've finished with Gemma, there won't be time to take another call before the helpline is deactivated. Even if there's the smallest chance it's Ellie on the other line, I can't ignore the call. I can't wait another week.

'After what happened at the weekend—'

'Sorry, Gemma,' I say, feeling awful that I've cut her off mid-flow. I wish I could split myself in two, but maybe I can. If I could give Ellie my mobile number, we could talk for as long as she wanted, whenever she wanted. I know there are strict rules about non-disclosure and I'd be breaking every one, but to hell with professional standards, this is personal. 'Is it OK if I put you on hold for two seconds? I promise I'll be right back.'

With barely time for Gemma to agree, I mute the phone and dash around to the second pod to pick up the incoming call. 'Hello?' I ask. 'You're through to the Lean On Me helpline.'

There's no background noise this time.

'This is Jen,' I add, in case Ellie is pausing because she wants to be sure it's me.

Still no response.

'I'm here to listen,' I say.

There's the sound of breath being expelled. 'You could have fooled me.'

I recognise the voice immediately and I jerk the phone away from my ear. My impulse is to cut the call straight away but I want to be braver than that. 'Fuck off, Lewis,' I tell him before slamming down the phone.

Standing alone in the darkened office, the pool of light above the helpline pods feels like a spotlight. My legs are weak as I stumble back to my chair. I take a deep breath and, although it's not enough to compose myself, I pick up the muted phone. 'Gemma, are you there?'

The line is dead.

I drop the phone and cover my face with my hands. I can't believe I've just lost Gemma's call for the sake of talking to Lewis. Did he find out Ellie had talked to me earlier? Was he monitoring her calls as Gemma's boyfriend is doing? My fear turns to shame as I imagine what Gemma must be thinking right now. I know it's too little too late, but finally I read the call sheet I should have read earlier.

On Monday, Gemma had told Janet how she'd gone to see Ryan on Saturday. Rather than the reunion he'd been expecting, she had told him to stop messaging her and then she didn't hear from him again until Sunday morning when he texted to say he'd taken an overdose. Gemma's mum had begged her not to go to him – that's what they had been arguing about – but when Gemma had insisted, she had driven her daughter to Ryan's flat and waited outside until it became clear that Gemma wasn't going to come out again. Unsurprisingly, Ryan hadn't needed medical treatment but, by this point, Gemma was furious with her mum for reportedly saying that she should have left him to die.

I'm inclined to agree with Gemma's mum and I want to pick up where Janet left off. Gemma has to realise how dangerous it can be when your boyfriend isolates you from your family and friends, but I can't say any of this because I hung up on her.

I want to go home. Correction, I want to be home because Lewis is out there and I imagine he's laughing at me.

14

Jen

'Here, drink this.'

'Tha— Thank you.' I take the glass from Charlie but my chest is heaving and I don't dare bring the water to my mouth.

I thought I'd be able to hold it together, and I had as I rushed past the security guards and out of the office. The wind had been picking up but being swept along the promenade was preferable to creeping along the Strand. I was scared. I still am. Lewis had done his homework and timed his call perfectly for when the helpline was about to close. He could have been watching me. He knows where to look because he sent his solicitor's letter to the office. Did he know it was my shift or did he just get lucky?

I'd expected to see him at every turn and hadn't relaxed until I was safely in the stairwell. I'd hoped the climb would give me time to compose myself but my exertions had compounded my fear and my heart was punching its way out of my chest when I stumbled into the apartment. I took one look at Charlie's startled expression and burst into tears.

'Are you going to tell me what happened?' he asks when I finally take a sip of water.

I don't know where to start but I've already decided I have to tell him everything, to hell with confidentiality and promises. 'I've messed up,' I say, releasing a heavy sob. It has to be the last one. I need to pull myself together. I take a deep breath. 'I had two callers tonight and I failed them both. I panicked and said all the wrong things but I was only trying to help. I was thinking about what happened to Meg and I pushed too hard, I know I did. I'm supposed to listen, Charlie, but I didn't and then he phoned and mocked me. He wanted to get back at me for Saturday and he has. I put a young girl on hold and then lost the call because I thought . . .' I'm gulping for air. 'But it wasn't . . . It was Lewis. Oh, Charlie, what have I done?'

I'm gasping for air as Charlie sits down beside me. He attempts to pull me towards him but my stiffened limbs refuse to move so he settles for rubbing my back. 'What happened on Saturday?'

He sounds curious rather than angry but I suspect that's about to change. 'I found out where Lewis was going to be and I went to see him,' I say as quickly as I can.

The back rubbing stops. 'You did what?'

'He runs a boot camp and they work out in Liverpool One.'

'Did you talk to him?' Charlie asks, then decides he can answer this one himself. 'Are you mad?'

'I have every right to be,' I snap back. 'He killed Meg.'

'It was suicide.'

123

'And he put the noose around her neck!' I yell. Seeing Charlie's expression, I add, 'What? You don't think he's capable? I do, Charlie. Maybe I wasn't sure before, but I am now.' A shiver runs down my spine as I recall the anger in Lewis's eyes as he pushed his face into mine. Little wonder Ellie sounded so scared of him; I'm scared of him, and despite what I've just said to Charlie, I never had any doubt that he was responsible for Meg's death.

I'm not saying I wasn't fooled for a while. We all fell for the troubled-boy-with-a-good-heart image he projected at school. No one seemed to notice how his arrival coincided with the fractures that appeared in our tight group of friends, but looking back, I can see we all changed during those long evenings spent together in Meathead's dad's shed.

The potent mix of hormones and alcohol in such a confined space had made for an extremely charged atmosphere. We were in that awkward transition phase; no longer children but not yet adults, and some of us took longer to develop than others. I couldn't keep up with Meg, however hard I tried.

Pushed to one side, I'd turned to Charlie and to my surprise, he finally noticed me. It was hardly red hot passion. We were awkward and self-conscious with each other, especially in front of the others, and on one particular night, Meg had started teasing us. Or maybe it was Lewis she was teasing. Either way, she ended up on Charlie's knee and announced he was part of the family now.

I told Meg to stop but she wouldn't listen. Annoyed, I'd escaped to the bathroom and as I came back out of the house, I heard raised voices from within the shed.

'I've had enough of this, we're going!' Lewis yelled.

'Oh, you think so?' Meg snarled back. 'You don't tell me what to do!'

'Someone fucking needs to!'

I crept closer to listen in, although I was hardly eavesdropping. Meg didn't seem to care who witnessed her arguments with Lewis and this wasn't the first.

'You can be a right bitch sometimes, you know that?' continued Lewis. 'I don't know what I ever saw in you.'

'Neither do I!' Meg screamed. 'Well, fine! It was nice while it lasted, now skip on home to Mummy, because I'm staying here.'

'With him?'

'Why not?' she answered petulantly.

'Fine, do what the fuck you like,' Lewis said in a low growl. 'Good luck, Charlie.'

The door swung open and the weak light from the shed trickled along the path to pool around my feet where I stood rooted to the spot. Meg had asked, why not Charlie? The answer should have been obvious. She couldn't do that to me, could she?

'She's only saying that to wind you up,' I told Lewis as he strode towards me.

'You think?' he asked, pushing his glasses up the bridge of his nose as he scrutinised my face. He smiled. 'So how can we wind her up?'

I shrugged. The sudden intimacy with Lewis made me feel uncomfortable but there was a connection too. We were both injured parties. 'Nothing's going on between them. Charlie wouldn't let it happen,' I said weakly, although I was wondering why my boyfriend hadn't spoken up for himself during the argument.

'You sure about that?' Lewis asked. 'You can do better, you know.'

My heart raced when Lewis looked at me like no one else had ever done, not even Charlie. He looked at me as if I was there and his gaze fell on my lips. It wasn't a conscious decision. It just happened. He kissed me and I kissed him back. When he slipped his arms around me, I lifted my hands to his face. I wanted him to pull me into the shadows and keep kissing me. That's all I thought about, that and the heat rising up through my body, but in the next moment, he was pushing me off.

His eyes never left my face as the shed door creaked open. It had been a close call and my heart pounded as I pictured what might have happened if it hadn't been for Lewis's quick action. If we'd been discovered, I wouldn't only have lost Meg and Charlie. I'd have been ostracised by my friends and Meg's family. But we were in the clear. No one had seen us. So why did I still feel unnerved?

I caught a hint of a smile from Lewis as Meg pressed herself against his back and wrapped her arms around him. With his eyes still upon me, he said, 'Why don't you go back and keep Charlie company?' He made it sound like a warning, like I'd been in the wrong and he hadn't. Was that the story he'd tell the next time Meg provoked him?

'And who's going to keep me company?' Meg asked, her words slurred.

I didn't wait for an answer but fled back to the shed. Charlie looked relieved to see me and didn't let go of my hand for the rest of the evening; in fact his grip tightened when Meg and Lewis returned as if nothing had happened. But something *had* happened, and it played on my mind later as Meg and I waited for Geoff to pick us up. Meg was leaning against a wall outside Meathead's house to stop herself from swaying.

'What did Lewis say to you in the garden?' she asked.

'Nothing,' I said, turning away from her.

'Did he talk about me?'

'No.'

Meg's voice wobbled when she asked, 'Then why are you being funny with me?'

'I'm not.'

'Is it because I was sitting on Charlie's knee?'

'Of course not.' I could feel the guilt sitting in my stomach like a lead weight.

'I was only messing around, Jen. You know what I'm like,' she said.

When I didn't respond, I heard Meg's denim jacket scrape against the wall as she slid down to crouch on the pavement.

'I don't blame you for being angry. I'm a horrible person,' she continued. Folding her arms across her body, she slipped a hand into her sleeve to rake her skin.

I sank to the pavement next to her and reached out to still her hand. 'It's OK, Meg.'

When she wrapped her arms around my neck, I could smell the sourness of the strawberry Kopparberg she'd been drinking. 'I love you, Jen. Don't ever think I don't.'

'I love you too.'

'I'm so fucked up,' she sobbed into my shoulder. 'Why can't everyone be happy and normal? Is it me, or is the whole fucking world pretending to be something they're not?'

'It's not you, Meg,' I told her as I thought of Lewis

127

leaning in for the kiss. Had he fancied me, or was it a trick to see if I fancied him? 'You're not the one who's fucked up.'

My assurance was enough to make her smile and she slumped back against the wall. 'I really do love Lewis,' she said, wiping her tears. 'I know he was an arse tonight but that was my fault. I drive him mad.'

'He's the one with the problem,' I'd tried, and there was a fleeting moment when I considered telling her exactly what his problem was, but my courage was chased away by the sweep of headlights from Geoff's car. I kept the secret, hoping that Lewis would never use it against me, never doubting that he would.

'How can you defend him, Charlie?' I ask now, leaning back against the sofa and pushing down the old guilt that threatens to resurface.

'I'm not saying Lewis is completely innocent. I saw what he was like, Jen, but I also saw what Meg was like,' Charlie says, his harsh words knocking against each other as they tumble from his lips. 'OK, he got angry but Meg loved the drama. She brought out the worst in people.'

My jaw drops. I want to tell him that Meg didn't bring out the worst in *me*. If anyone did that, it was Lewis, but my greatest fear is that Charlie already knows this. There's a flash of emotion so intense that it burns my skin – anger or hate, I can't tell which. As I jump up, my glass of water slops over my hand and I'm tempted to throw it in Charlie's face. He needs to wake up.

'What exactly does *that* mean, Charlie?'

'Just that Meg knew what buttons to push with everyone.' Shock forces me back a step. This is the first time Charlie

128

has ever suggested Meg was in any way responsible for what happened, but then he hadn't said that much at all after she died. He'd run off to Warrington and when he came back, he refused to talk about her. Ten years later, I realise why.

'You think Meg was asking for it?' I say, spitting out the words. 'So by the same logic, is it my fault that Lewis threatened me?'

At last I get the reaction I've been looking for. Charlie leaps to his feet. 'He threatened you?'

'Yes, Charlie, he threatened me on Saturday. And before you tell me it was the shock of seeing me again that made him do it and, oh, let's not forget the stress of caring for his sick mum, he's had plenty of time since to calm down and come up with a more considered response. And do you know what that response was? Do you want to know why I was so upset tonight? He phoned the helpline just – as – I – was – about – to – leave,' I tell him, pronouncing each word slowly and carefully in case he still doesn't get it. 'And I'm not talking about a simple put-down call. Oh no, forget about them. He stayed on the line. He wanted me to know he was there and he mocked me. So there I was, in the office on my own, about to walk home on – my – own.'

Charlie wipes a hand across his face. 'You should have phoned.'

'What for?' I ask as I storm over to the kitchen counter and slam down my glass. 'According to you, Lewis is the victim. If he'd attacked me, it would have been my fault. I would have deserved it, just like Meg.'

'No you wouldn't and neither did Meg. I shouldn't have said that. I didn't mean it to come out like it did.'

But it's too late. What he's said can't be unsaid. I press my hand to my forehead. 'You're unbelievable.'

'Jen, please, I've lived with you long enough to know that there's never an excuse if someone's being abused. All I'm saying is that Meg could be self-destructive and dating someone like Lewis was part of the package.'

'Self-destructive?'

'She liked hurting herself,' he says, not meeting my gaze.

'And you don't think maybe there was a reason for her self-harm?' I ask. I want to laugh but my throat constricts and it comes out as a strangled gasp. If Charlie thinks he's defusing the situation, he's wrong. 'Nothing is ever what it seems when you're dealing with someone controlling like Lewis. You don't need a black eye or a broken arm to be the victim of abuse. He intimidated and humiliated her, and right now I know how she felt being played by that man. Lewis hasn't had to touch me tonight to scare the shit out of me.'

'Jen, I didn't—'

'Why can't you see what he did to Meg?'

'Because she was confusing. None of us ever knew where we were with her,' he mutters, his chin pressed against his chest.

'It only got confusing when she met Lewis,' I tell him, although I know I'm being economical with the truth. Meg's lows and highs were *always* lower and higher than the rest of us.

Charlie lifts his head and our eyes meet. 'It got worse, I won't argue with that.'

'So why are you defending him?'

'I'm not defending him, I'm defending us!' Charlie snaps

back. 'Raking up the past won't bring her back. You have to let her go and I'm sorry, but that means letting Lewis go too. Please, don't give him that kind of power over our lives. Keep away from him, Jen.'

The anger is gone and we've both been left a little dazed. I realise I haven't told Charlie about Ellie and how she fits in to everything, and I don't think I can. I feel like something is broken between us and it scares me more than Lewis ever could.

15

Ruth

The nights are drawing in and as I sit alone in Geoff's Audi on Friday evening, New Mersey Retail Park becomes a patchwork of artificial light and lengthening shadows, much like my life. It's exhausting putting on a brave front that doesn't reveal how the darkness has crept back into my soul, but I'm hoping that if I pretend long enough, the light will come back. That was how I survived Meg's death. I told everyone I was strong until I believed it myself, and eventually it had worked. Except now I'm back to faking it.

I keep my hands in my lap, resisting the urge to wreck my latest manicure as I watch Geoff hurrying out of Marks and Spencer laden with more food than we could possibly eat. He's making an extra effort to sweeten me up and my fear is he's planning to raise the subject of retirement again. I wish he wouldn't, and not because I'm refusing to consider it, but because I might be tempted.

I've read Meg's space girl essay so many times that it's burnt into the back of my eyelids. And despite Geoff's protestations, I did contact the police. The officer who had investigated Meg's death has moved on to another force so I had a lengthy conversation with a detective sergeant. I sent him a copy of what Meg had written and his view is that it's not enough on its own to reopen the case. He's asked that I drop off the original but what would be the point? No one's listening to Meg. We never were.

I'm hoping that Selina's fundraiser tomorrow night will put me in a better frame of mind. The speeches and survivors' stories are always inspiring and it's just what I need if I'm to resist the argument my husband is currently raging with kind words and ready meals.

Geoff stows the shopping in the boot before slipping into the passenger seat. He had a few drinks at lunchtime with clients so I'm the nominated driver.

'You don't need anything else while we're here, do you?' he asks.

'No, I'm ready for home,' I tell him, returning his smile before starting the engine.

The text alert makes me jump and my eyes dart to my mobile in its holder. I'm impatient for news from Gill who is on the helpline this evening, but it's Geoff who checks his phone. I'm going to have to wait a little longer. The lines are still open and Gill could be talking to Gemma at this very moment.

Gemma's last call to Jen on Wednesday has left us all frustrated. I'd seen the scant information on the call sheet and immediately cornered Jen in the office but she had very little to add, in fact she didn't want to talk about it at all. It had clearly upset her to have the call cut off mid-conversation. I'm hoping Gemma simply ran out of change but I can't dismiss the possibility that Ryan caught her in the act. If he did, we may never hear from Gemma again and I don't think I could handle that.

'Who's the message from?' I ask Geoff as he holds his phone inches from his nose.

'Just Sean telling us to have a good weekend.'

I can feel my jaw tensing. I want to believe my husband but my mind is already tearing his lie to shreds. Sean rarely texts his father, and if he does, there's usually a motive. I wonder if they're planning something that Geoff doesn't want me to know about. A little retirement cottage perhaps? Or the message might be from someone else entirely. It's been a long while since Geoff's affair and I've learnt to trust him again but it's possible he's looking for someone else to share his retirement plans with, should his wife turn him down. I hate to admit it, but I don't know which of the two scenarios would be worse.

It's not that I don't love Geoff, I do, but it was easier when we wanted the same things – to design buildings that inspire the next generation, to nurture our children, to turn our grief into something positive, to never forget Meg. I hope there's a compromise we can reach that will make us both happy but, until we find it, it's one more thing to fake. I take my eye off the road to offer a smile.

'Send him my love.'

'You can do it yourself,' he says.

It's an odd reply but I think no more of it until we make the final turn home. The extension we added to our Georgian house gives it an imposing double-fronted aspect and it's as if the garage had never existed. Keeping my focus on the present, my eyes narrow as I notice a people carrier parked next to my Ford Focus on the driveway.

It's Sean's car.

'He's here?' I ask as I pull to the kerb and peer at the welcoming lights coming from the house. A face appears at the window. It's my daughter-in-law.

This explains why Geoff bought so much food. I leave him to gather up the bags as I race across the lawn. The front door opens before I reach it and Sean and Alice step out with matching two-year-olds dangling from their hips.

'Oh, my babies,' I cry as I share a bounty of hugs and kisses between two giggling girls. There's a warmth bubbling inside me that makes my heart quicken. It's so much easier to resist the pull of my granddaughters when they're out of sight. The girls are at one end of a tug of war between the present and the past, with my darling Meg at the other, and I'm the ever-tightening knot in the middle.

'Nana, Nana, Nana,' the girls repeat in unison as they attempt to wriggle free from their parents' clutches.

'Let's get inside before one of them escapes,' Sean says.

I'm about to follow when I hear the rustle of shopping bags behind me. I'm smiling as I turn to face Geoff and there's no pretence this time. Happiness is always the most difficult emotion to fake and in the last few weeks I haven't tried. It feels good to feel good, and I don't think about the phone I've left in the car until hours later.

16

Jen

As I step into the brightly lit lobby of the Crowne Plaza, the sparkle of sequins on my black dress is let down slightly by the dirt splatters on the hem I trailed through puddles during my dash from the taxi. The dress is new, or at least it's new to me. I'd bought it on eBay but when it had arrived on Thursday, I'd been in no mood to try it on and realised too late that it wasn't made for my five foot four frame.

Normally, I'd be looking forward to one of Selina's fundraisers but after the week I've had, I'm surprised I'm here at all. I don't relish the prospect of spending an evening talking about domestic violence and sharing success stories when failure is fresh on my mind.

Ruth is the first to spot me, and weaves her way through shoals of women in evening gowns and men in black ties to reach my side. 'Is Charlie parking the car?'

'I'm really sorry but he's not coming. He wasn't feeling too good, whereas you look like a million dollars,' I add quickly before Ruth has the chance to catch me out on my lie.

'Thanks to a good layer of concealer,' she admits. 'I didn't sleep a wink last night.'

'Is everything all right?'

'I need to talk to you about Gemma.'

Now I wish I had stayed at home. It had been excruciating when Ruth had questioned my vague account of the calls I'd received on Wednesday evening. I had considered coming clean about putting Gemma on hold but if I did that, I'd have to explain about Ellie, and then Lewis. Geoff doesn't want Ruth to know he's back in town and I'm deferring to his better judgement. If Gemma is giving her sleepless nights, Ellie will give her waking nightmares.

'Has she phoned back?' I ask.

'Yes, she spoke to Gill. Why didn't you tell me you left Gemma on hold the other day?'

As I cringe, I glance over Ruth's shoulder. Gill has her back to me, but Janet and Alison, our other volunteers, are in my eye line. It could be my imagination but I'd say it's deliberate that they're not looking in my direction. 'I didn't mean to, but another call came through.'

'We never put someone on hold, especially if they're using a pay phone. She ran out of money.'

The disappointment in Ruth's voice makes me shrink with shame. 'I'm sorry. It was a stupid thing to do. And I promise, I didn't put Gemma on hold for long.'

'Was the other call worth it?' she asks, but I look away. 'It was another put-down call, wasn't it?'

'Gemma would have run out of money anyway,' I reply weakly.

'But maybe she wouldn't have felt so abandoned.'

My stomach twists. 'Is she OK?'

'She's still with Ryan, so I'd say not.'

'I was hoping her mum would have persuaded her to come back home by now.'

'I was hoping *we* would have persuaded her,' Ruth says. 'Gemma is refusing to speak to her mum at all. She claims she's happy where she is. Let's hope it stays that way.'

'I'm sorry,' I repeat. 'It was a stupid thing to do.'

She rests a hand on my arm. 'No, it's my fault,' Ruth tells me, releasing her frustrations with a sigh. 'It's the risk we take having only one volunteer on duty but we can only work with what we have. We're still not getting enough calls to tempt new volunteers to sign up. So much for a relaunch, I've let the helpline stall again.'

'We gave out lots of information packs at Fresher's Week. More calls could come in.'

'Let's not worry about that tonight,' Ruth says straightening her back. 'We're here to celebrate our small contribution to another good cause. Selina's really pleased with the designs to extend the refuge, and now that she has a funding target to reach, we're in for a busy night. Come on, there's someone here who's looking forward to seeing you.'

We grab drinks from a waiter on our way to join Geoff and the others, and I'm taking a much-needed gulp of wine when a man turns to greet me.

'Sean, what are you doing here?' I ask, almost choking in surprise.

'The girls have hit the terrible twos, so we thought we'd descend on Mum and Dad and share the pain.'

'They turned up as a surprise last night,' explains Ruth.

She nods to her husband, her eyes shining. 'It was Geoff's idea.'

'Ruth put a lot of effort into doing up their room, it's about time they made use of it,' he replies.

There's a collective smile as we all imagine new life being breathed into what was Meg's bedroom. Ruth had it redecorated shortly after becoming a grandmother, and although I've never had the courage to go in there, I've seen pictures. The duck-egg blue walls that trapped a troubled teenager have been painted a pale shade of pink, her single bed with its fairy lights has been replaced by two miniature princess beds, and her dressing table cleared of its teenage clutter. Ruth didn't completely paper over the past, however. She kept a collection of her daughter's favourite knick-knacks on the bookshelves, along with photos that Meg would have been too embarrassed to have on display if she were alive.

'It's good to see the room being used again,' says Ruth with evident satisfaction.

'Except my little terrors didn't stay put for long,' Sean adds with a grin.

'They ended up in my bed,' Ruth explains. 'Hence the need for matchsticks to keep my eyes open.'

'I take it you've left Alice at home with the kids this evening?' I ask Sean.

'I'm afraid so,' he says without a hint of remorse. 'Dad put aside seats at the table for us, but the girls would have been too much of a handful for an uninitiated babysitter.'

I'm laughing before he's finished. 'It's not to us you need to justify yourself.'

'I know, Alice is bearing the brunt of it at the moment,

and there's only so many times we can ask her parents to give us some respite,' Sean replies. His eyes remain on me but I know he's watching for his mum's response. So am I.

'We've promised her a lie in tomorrow while we take the girls for a ride on the ferry,' Ruth says.

'The ferry?' I ask, checking the half-empty pint glass in Sean's hand. 'I'd love to see you manage a trip across the Mersey with a hangover.'

'If he can't manage it, I'm sure we can,' Ruth says to Geoff.

'Like that isn't Sean's plan all along,' I reply as the maître d' announces that the dining room is open and asks us to make our way to our tables.

Sean offers me the crook of his arm and I accept. Meg wasn't the only one who adored him and although it feels good being close to my second favourite cousin, our looped arms can't quite bridge the gap Meg left.

The dinner, the speeches and the charity auction are over, the lights are up and guests are table hopping. I'm supposed to be circulating but I'm cradling a glass of wine in one hand and my phone in the other. I want to send a message to Charlie but I can't find the words.

I still haven't worked out how I should feel about our argument but Sean has been the perfect distraction. We spent most of the evening sharing memories. At first it was in hushed whispers but Ruth's ears pricked at the sound of her daughter's name and soon we were all recounting stories. Some of my recollections, and I'm guessing Sean's too, had to be sanitised. We concentrated on the happier times and laughter had eased the tension constricting my chest – until the stories ran out, leaving me feeling maudlin.

I miss Meg more than I have for a very long time, and not because Sean is raking up memories, but because Charlie isn't here to do the same.

'So what is this mystery illness of your husband's?' asks Sean. He's the only one left at the table and has been watching me type and retype a text message for the last five minutes.

'A guilty conscience,' I say. 'And you know full well he's not my husband.'

'Ah, is that the problem?'

Charlie was simply one of Meg's annoying friends to Sean, or more recently, my plus one at the occasional family do, and he still doesn't know him especially well. Ruth isn't a gossip so my cousin hasn't heard about my marriage refusals over the years. I try to laugh. 'Only if you ask your Auntie Eve.'

'But something's troubling you,' he continues. 'Not all our memories of Meg are happy ones, are they?'

Despite our shared past, I doubt Sean appreciates how bad the bad times were. He was never there for the tears and tantrums because the dark clouds always lifted when he appeared. I pick up a wine bottle to refill my glass as another memory surfaces.

'Are you going to stare out that window all day?' I'd asked Meg, in an attempt to draw her back into the room.

I hadn't liked the way her eyes had glazed over as if her mind was taking her to some faraway place and besides, we both had AS Level coursework to finish over the Easter holidays. I was ahead of schedule, never one to miss a deadline, but Meg was struggling to make a start.

She was only studying with me now because she'd used

141

me as her alibi one too many times to skive off to see Lewis. Ruth and Geoff had called around to Mum's one Sunday to drop off gifts for her first grandchild, my nephew, James, who had been born the day before, and had been surprised to find me at home and not at the library with Meg. Mum had jumped at the chance to brag about how I'd stayed at home and studied all weekend. I could have warned Meg that she'd been rumbled, but I didn't.

Once my aunt and uncle knew that Meg had a boyfriend, they had found their explanation for their daughter's sliding grades and had grounded her.

'I hate this room, it's like a prison cell,' Meg said.

'At least you're allowed visitors.'

Meg gave a laugh. 'And you're not the only one.'

Her reply made me uneasy. 'Do you sneak Lewis into the house?'

'Maybe . . .'

She returned her gaze to the window but before she could float off into her own world again, I gave a loud sigh. 'I appreciate I'm not Lewis but at least I'm here. Unless you carry on *ignoring* me, that is.'

Meg came back from wherever she had been. 'Sorry, I'm a rubbish friend, aren't I?' she said. 'I'm a rubbish everything.'

'You're a rubbish student,' I told her, tapping my pen against the notepad she had left open on the bed. She had managed to write her name and the title of her essay, but nothing more. 'But you're still my favourite cousin and my best friend.'

Dragging her feet across the floor, Meg slumped down next to me so it looked as if we were kneeling in prayer before bedtime. She was quiet as the sheet of yellow lined paper in front of her began to fill with words but after only a few minutes, the pen stilled in her hand. I knew she was waiting for me to offer help but what did I know about English poets? Meg didn't like being the one who was ignored and when I eventually looked up, she had scored two lines through her work and, in between those lines, was writing the word FAIL.

'Meg, you can't do that!' I said, attempting to grab the pen from her.

'Why not? It's all a waste of time.'

As Meg tore the page from her notepad, I heard the click of the door opening behind us. I turned to find Sean creeping across the room. He pressed his finger to his lips. Home for the holidays, my cousin still had his backpack slung over his shoulder. He was the reason Meg had been looking out of the window and she'd missed his arrival.

'Fail?' he asked as he peered over Meg's head to look at the sheet of paper in her hand.

Meg's books fell to the floor as she scrambled to her feet. 'You're back!' she cried, wrapping her arms around his neck.

'I was supposed to meet Mum and Dad at the office but what's a student loan for if not wasting on taxis?'

'I've missed you!'

'Have the old fogies been giving you a hard time?'

Meg's features darkened and it was left to me to explain. 'She's under house arrest.'

'I'm not surprised if your grades are bombing.'

'Forget that,' Meg said, quickly grabbing the offending page and slipping it beneath her notepad. 'What do you want to do? I can help you spend more of your loan if you'd like?'

Sean took several steps back, shaking his head. 'Oh no, I don't associate with losers. You need to stay here and finish your homework. I'm going to luxuriate in a shower that won't leave my feet dirtier than when I stepped in it and then I'm going to make myself some beans on toast with bread that hasn't gone mouldy.'

Meg scowled at her brother but it was different to the ones I'd come to recognise whenever anyone else upset her. The sparkle had returned to her eyes and she picked up her pen with every intention of proving she was not a loser.

Sean was, and is, the reason I have so many good memories of Meg. He was why she scraped through her first year at sixth form, and if he'd been home more in that second year, she might have passed her A Levels. If he hadn't gone to Camp America that last summer, maybe things wouldn't have turned out the way they did . . .

Guilt makes my ruddy cheeks burn. What about the role I played? 'I wish I could go back and do things differently,' I admit. 'If I'd been a better friend.'

'Or I a better brother,' Sean adds as he drains the pint he's been nursing. He's knocked back quite a few tonight.

In the silence that follows, I consider telling Sean about what's been happening, but he beats me to it.

'I heard about you squaring up to Lewis.'

My brain is sluggish with alcohol and it takes a second to process what he's saying. 'Geoff's told you he's back in Liverpool?'

'It was me who told him. The sister of one of my old school mates was in your year and she found out from a friend of a friend. With you and Mum gearing up to raise publicity for the helpline, I had to warn someone. It's not exactly gone to plan, has it?'

'No, not exactly,' I say, fighting the urge to cry.

'I should have warned you too,' he adds.

'It was Charlie who told me, eventually. He doesn't see Lewis in the same way I do and I'm starting to wonder if I'm overreacting,' I admit.

I've had time to process what Ellie has told me. She didn't exactly say Lewis hurt her and it could simply be that she's upset because he calls her by Meg's name when they have sex. And however shitty that is, it's not abuse.

Am I obsessed? Am I looking for answers that aren't there?

'We had a huge row over it,' I continue. 'Charlie claims part of the problem was that Meg was self-destructive.'

Sean tips his head back to stare at the chandeliers above our heads. 'He's got a point.' When I don't reply, he straightens up to find me staring at him. 'Don't get me wrong, I still think Lewis was the bad blood injected in her veins. You and Meg might not have told me much, but I had my contacts and I kept tabs on who my little sis with knocking around with. Lewis was the problem but Meg . . .' He pauses as he searches for the right words. 'I don't want to say she enjoyed what they did together, but she might have been an active participant, at least in the beginning.'

'She *wanted* Lewis to hurt her?' I ask. It feels uncomfortably like the argument I had with Charlie.

Sean reaches for his drink but it's empty. 'I found stuff on her computer once. I was snooping and Meg had a fit when I asked her about it. She claimed it was a dodgy site she'd been on that had automatically opened up more sites. I didn't believe her, but I was nineteen and I did not want to be having that kind of conversation with my sister. Her internet history was routinely cleared after that – I know, because I checked.'

'What did you find, Sean?'

'Stuff that Meg wouldn't want anyone knowing about, which is why I'm not going to repeat what it was. Let's just say she was into sexual experimentation and my guess is Lewis took it too far.'

'But why didn't you say any of this to the police after she died?'

'Meg said in her note that she wanted her shame burying with her.'

'The part of the note that wasn't destroyed,' I correct him.

'If there was another half, I don't think Meg would have mentioned the bits I know about, and what would it have proved if I had spoken up? That whatever they had been doing had been consensual? How was *that* going to bring Lewis to justice?'

I splay out my fingers on the tablecloth, my fingertips brushing against my mobile. Had I reacted so badly to what Charlie had said because his words chimed with what I'd witnessed myself? I'd seen how confusing Meg could be. She hated Lewis one minute and loved him in the next. If Sean can't make sense of his sister's behaviour, how can I, or Charlie? Have I been too harsh?

Sean waits for me to look back up at him. 'But it doesn't matter whether Meg agreed to what they did or not, Lewis is still responsible for her death,' he continues, derailing my thoughts. 'He trapped her somehow and she thought there

146

was only one way out. Maybe he took videos of what they did together and tried to use them to keep her in check.' He releases a sigh, letting that thought go. 'I don't know. It's just one of many theories I've thought up in the last ten years to explain what happened.'

'Lewis likes having information on people. That's how he gets his thrills,' I tell him.

'One of the ways,' Sean adds sourly. 'He's dangerous, Jen, and I worry about him being this close to you all. I worry about Mum.'

'Your dad wants me to persuade her to retire.'

'Snap.'

'She'd struggle, leaving it all behind.'

'She's struggling now,' Sean replies as he scans the other tables until he finds his mum. Ruth is in mid-conversation with Selina and she tips her head back in laughter. 'The twins aren't completely to blame for her restlessness last night. Dad says she's been replaying Meg's videos every chance she gets.'

'Does that have to be a bad thing?' I ask. 'There are no rules on how to grieve.'

'You're right, and it's for Mum to work through it herself. We can't protect her from everything,' he adds, holding my gaze. 'I know it's not what Dad wants, but she should know why he's so desperate to get her to move.'

'And do you agree with them running away?' I ask as pressure begins to build behind my eyes.

'I'm afraid so. Which makes me wonder what our Jen will do with the rest of her life.'

'You and me both,' I mutter as a hand clasps around my shoulder. I turn to find Geoff, his red cheeks glowing.

'Jen, my love. I've been talking to a lovely lady called . . .' His bloodshot eyes narrow. 'I think she said her name was Sheila and she happens to be a counsellor. I've been telling her all about your plans to get into the profession and she'd love to talk to you.'

Sean raises an eyebrow at me. 'That's serendipitous.'

I don't want to leave. I know Geoff is only trying to help but I've met quite a few counsellors over the years and I already know what I have to do. It's not information I need but courage, or closure, or both. I stand up with more of a wobble than I'd like. I hope I'm not going to make a fool of myself.

17

Jen

Geoff knows exactly what he's doing. He's primed Sheila and, unwittingly, she carves out an alternative career path for me that could take me away from McCoy and Pace, and the helpline, leaving Ruth free to decide her own future without having to worry about mine.

'With your experience,' Sheila tells me, 'there are other support roles in the charity sector you could apply for while you're training to be a counsellor. It might help you decide where you want to specialise. There are many different fields to counselling. Don't limit yourself.'

'New horizons,' Geoff says, lifting his glass. 'For all of us.'

'Can I have a word?' Ruth hisses into his ear, her unexpected arrival making him flinch.

Her jaw is set firm and the tiredness she was fighting earlier has been eviscerated by anger.

Sheila takes a step back, recognising her moment to withdraw. 'I'll leave you to it,' she says as she presses a business card into my hand. 'It was lovely meeting you, Jennifer. Please get in touch if you'd like to talk more.'

I'm tempted to follow Sheila's example but as I edge away, Ruth fixes me with her stare. 'You need to stay.'

'What's wrong, my love?' asks Geoff.

Before she can answer, Sean appears from the dining room. He spots us in the thinning crowd and hurries over. Shock sobers me in an instant. He's told her.

'Mum, hang on,' he says, taking hold of her arm. 'Maybe we should have this conversation at home when you're calmer.'

Ruth looks from Geoff, to me, to Sean, and back again. 'You *all* knew he was back,' she says, the tremor in her voice a warning of the rage to come, 'and not one of you felt the need to tell me?' Her eyes are wide as she stares at her husband. 'You knew, and your only reaction was to start a campaign to force me to leave.'

'I didn't want to upset you,' Geoff replies. 'I knew you'd react like this. I was trying to spare you the pain.'

'Pain?' she repeats, jabbing the word at him. 'I've been living with this pain from the day Meg died and there's nothing Lewis Rimmer can do to make it any worse. Don't you understand? It never goes away, Geoff. I've learnt to live with it, that's all.'

'We both have,' he says.

'Then you should know that you're not protecting me, you're protecting him! Have you forgotten what she wrote about the space girl? That was her, being hurt by him over and over again!'

Sean's expression is one of shock, but I can't tell if it's in response to Ruth's anger, which shows no sign of subsiding, or if he's as confused as I am by the reference to something Meg had written.

'The man who took our daughter from us is living under our very noses,' she continues. 'He's carrying on as if Meg never existed. It's not pain I feel. It's fury!'

'He came back because his mum's ill,' I tell her, only to realise I sound like Charlie.

Ruth rounds on me. 'Are you defending him?'

'No, what I'm saying is, he didn't come back here out of choice. He's scared of us too, Ruth. I saw it in his eyes.' It's a slight exaggeration but maybe Lewis did kick out because he feels threatened.

'You've *seen* him?'

I'm confused as I turn to Sean. 'I thought you'd told her?'

He shakes his head. Not guilty.

'I was chatting to an old friend,' Ruth explains. 'I didn't quite understand why Vanessa was commiserating with me at first. I thought she was talking about how the helpline is struggling.' She laughs to herself. 'I'll be damned if it's going to be mothballed now.'

'Ruth,' Geoff says, in an attempt to get his wife's attention, but she keeps her eyes on me.

'Do you know he has a girlfriend?' she asks. 'I suppose it was ridiculous to think he wasn't going to have other relationships, but . . .' She balls her hand into a tight fist. 'It's so bloody wrong that he gets to come back here and pick up where he left off with another poor girl.'

'That's why I tracked him down,' I explain. 'I had to say something.'

'At least one of you had guts.' Ruth's breathing slows

and she exhales her next breath through pursed lips. 'How did he take it?'

'Shocked more than anything. And then this week, he called the helpline and basically laughed at me.'

'So Lewis *is* our nuisance caller. Oh, let him try phoning again. He won't be laughing when I've finished with him.'

My cheeks burn. Do I tell Ruth the earlier put-downs were from someone else, confessing a fresh secret, or do I keep my promise to Ellie and let Lewis take the blame? The choice is an easy, albeit a cowardly one. 'I think he got what he wanted,' I tell Ruth. 'I doubt he'll call again.'

She closes her eyes briefly to contain the last of her anger before elbowing Geoff out of the way. 'Oh, Jen, is that why things went so wrong on Wednesday?' she asks as her arms encircle me. 'You should have said.'

I don't correct her, making me even less worthy of her sympathy. Tears spring to my eyes but I refuse to burst into tears; our raised voices have attracted enough attention. 'I'm so sorry. I hated myself for not telling you about Lewis. I wanted to protect you.' And I still do, which is why I don't say more.

Ruth pulls away so she can look at me. 'We'll talk properly on Monday, but for now, I think Sean's right. I should go home,' she says, extending her hand in Geoff's direction. 'Car keys.'

'I'll get our coats, my love,' he says as he rummages in his pocket. Placing the key fob in her open palm, he attempts to wrap his hand around hers.

Snapping hers back, Ruth says, 'No, Geoff, I'll make my own way home. Why don't you stay over? That way you don't need to sleep on the sofa two nights running.'

'I was only doing what I thought was best,' Geoff says. He sways ever so slightly from the withering look his wife gives him.

As we say our goodbyes, Sean gives me a peck on the cheek then draws me into a hug. 'Don't worry, I'll get them talking again,' he whispers.

An awkward silence descends as I'm left alone with Geoff. I'm about to leave him to his thoughts when he says, 'I loved Megan too. There isn't a day that goes by that I don't think about her.'

I want to tell him I do too, but this isn't a competition about who misses Meg the most so I keep quiet.

'When I found her suicide note in the hallway, I didn't want to believe what I was reading,' he says as his eyes glaze over. 'Thank goodness Ruth went upstairs to look for her while I ran into the garage. If she had seen what I was faced with, she wouldn't be sipping coffee in that damned kitchen.'

I say nothing. At the inquest, I learnt more about the details surrounding Meg's death than I would have liked, and too often I've imagined what confronted Geoff when he stepped into the garage.

'It was a cry for help. She didn't really mean to do it,' Geoff continues. His mouth is dry and his parched lips stick together as he speaks. 'I could have helped her find a way out of the mess she'd found herself in. I thought we were close but she never told me.'

'She didn't talk to any of us.'

'Or listen to anyone – except Lewis, of course. He turned her against us. I should have done something then. I should be doing something now. It ought to have been me tackling

153

him, not you, Jen. I'm a coward,' Geoff says and something too much like a sob catches in his throat. He hears it too. 'I need a drink.'

I watch Geoff stagger towards the bar but I don't follow. I don't move at all. The foundations of the new life Ruth and Geoff built for us all have been washed away, and we're each marooned on our own individual islands, surrounded by churning waters of grief. I wrap my arms around myself, and as I hug my bag to my chest, I feel it vibrate. I almost drop my phone as I read the text.

Do you want a lift? X

I need to answer the message but as I fumble with the touchscreen, a hand appears to still mine.

'I'm here,' Charlie says.

I don't attempt to hold back the sob this time.

18

Ruth

When Geoff and I stroll into the office on Monday morning, few would guess we've had a falling out. Jen jumps up and offers to make us drinks but I'm in no rush to be locked away with Geoff in our glass cage.

Alone in the kitchen, I press my forehead against the window as I wait for the kettle to boil. I glimpse a ferry making its return trip across the Mersey from Seacombe, bringing forth memories of yesterday's excursion, but thoughts of my cheeky little granddaughters aren't enough to lift my spirits. I shift my gaze from the flowing river to the stagnating waters directly below. The narrow inlet that separates the office from a residential complex next door had originally linked Canning Dock to George's Dock, but the connection was severed when George's Dock was filled in to make way for the Three Graces. The inlet serves no purpose now except to collect floating islands of algae, leaves and litter.

A footbridge spans the inlet where it meets the Canning

Dock and I watch a figure step boldly onto its steel spine. The man stops at the midpoint to pull back his hood and when he looks up, it's as if he's searching me out. The threat is imagined but when the kettle clicks off, it gives me a start. I turn to find Jen has been watching me.

'How was yesterday?' she asks.

'Our trip on the ferry blew away some cobwebs, although Sean remained a delicate shade of green all day.'

'I'm glad you made him go with you.'

'I couldn't have managed on my own,' I mutter. More brightly, I add, 'I've taken tonnes of photos of the girls. Would you like to see?'

Jen makes all the right noises as I skim through the images on my phone. Most are from our seafaring adventures but I pause on one taken of me and the girls cuddled up on the sofa in the kitchen. It's one of the few photos where my granddaughters are both looking at the camera at the same time, and I can see something of Meg in their faces. Although the twins are identical, they have each inherited a slightly different aspect of their aunt.

'Two for the price of one,' I say before I realise the price the fates demanded was Meg.

There's an awkward pause as I grab two mugs from the cupboard. 'Can you thank Charlie for booking Geoff into the hotel? I can't imagine he would have been in a fit state to organise it himself.'

'How are things?'

My smile is stiff and unforgiving. 'He crawled back home while I was out with the girls. Sean made a valiant effort to justify Geoff's actions, and it's only because of him that we're speaking at all. I'm sure Geoff thought he was doing the right thing, but I don't appreciate being manipulated. He was determined that we were going to retire, whether he thought I was ready or not.'

I don't tell Jen how I'd almost fallen for my husband's scheming. When I was greeted by Sean on the doorstep on Friday night with those two precious gifts life has given us, I felt ready to embrace them. Worst still, I thought how insightful it was of Geoff to recognise that I was teetering towards one of the hardest decisions of my life.

'He doesn't think I can stand up to that bastard,' I continue. 'He thinks I'm weak. Well, I'm not. As far as I'm concerned, if Geoff wants to flee, he can go right ahead but I'm staying here. We have a lot of work to do, Jen.'

'OK, good,' she replies cautiously.

'Lewis will not deter us.'

My strong words don't ease the worry lines peeking beneath her fringe. 'But we can't ignore him either,' she says.

'It bothers you having him so close, doesn't it?' I ask, as if it hasn't affected me too.

'Yes.'

'I don't want you worrying, which is why I'm going to join you on your Wednesday shifts. I don't think it's a good idea for you to cover the helpline on your own at the moment.'

I was expecting Jen to be relieved but her eyes widen. 'You don't have to do that, Ruth. I'll be fine. I thought you wanted a break from taking calls for a while.'

'Well, I've had a change of heart. If Gemma won't listen to her mum, she's going to listen to me. I'm taking tonight's shift and I can manage Wednesday too. I'll even drop you off afterwards so you don't have to walk home alone that late at night.'

'At eight o'clock? Honestly, Ruth. If it makes you feel better, I'll get the train home.'

'And why would you do that when you don't live near a station?' I ask, lightly. 'And besides, I wouldn't want him standing behind you on a platform.' I shake my head. 'I can't believe I'm even thinking something like that. We shouldn't have to worry about what he might do next.'

'No, we shouldn't,' she agrees. 'He needs to know he can't intimidate us.'

I like the fire in Jen's eyes. It's a reflection of my own. 'And that's precisely what I intend to show him.'

'How do you mean?'

I briefly consider sharing everything Vanessa had told me at the fundraiser about her daughter bumping into Lewis, but I'm still smarting after being kept in the dark by my family. I can look after myself, and what is more, I can look after others too. I set up the Lean On Me helpline to help young people recognise when they're caught up in a toxic relationship, and there's a young woman who needs to know what kind of man she's involved with.

I know where Lewis's girlfriend works.

'I'm going to poke the tiger,' I say.

19

Jen

As my shift on the helpline begins, I don't know what to expect. There have been no put-down calls since last week but that doesn't mean Lewis won't ring again, nor does it mean that Ellie will.

When the first call comes in at 5.30, my pulse quickens as I pick it up but it's an easy one; a young student who's had one failed relationship too many and wants to know if her current boyfriend is a keeper. There's nothing she tells me about this latest romance that makes my insides twist.

'I hope talking about your feelings has helped put your fears into perspective,' I tell her, bringing the call to a close.

'It really has. I just have to let go of the past and take a chance. We only get one life.'

'Yes, we do,' I reply, wishing I could convince myself as easily.

There's a clean call sheet open on screen and as soon as the call ends, I jot down some notes so that I'm ready for the next caller. From the corner of my eye, I watch Ruth and Geoff in their office. Geoff has shrugged into his coat but Ruth leaves hers draped over her arm, partly concealing the collection of John Lewis bags she's holding, although I doubt she cares what Geoff thinks of her recent shopping spree.

Ruth has been forgoing her usual brisk walk around the Pier Head at lunchtime for trips into Liverpool One, and the department store has been her one-stop shop every day so far. She's bought some gorgeous outfits for the girls as well as a whole range of other goods including perfume and an Apple Mac that she took back yesterday. It would be too much to hope that there isn't a connection between her sudden need for retail therapy and the shock she received at the weekend. She might act cool and collected, but there's tension building inside her that's sharpened her features and her fingernails, and it scares me.

'Goodnight, Jen,' Geoff says, raising a hand.

'Night, Geoff,' I reply as my attention turns to Ruth. She doesn't chase after her husband as he disappears through the double doors but walks over to me.

'You're staying?' I ask with a forced note of curiosity that hides growing dread as I watch her drop her bags next to the second helpline pod. What do I do if Ellie calls again and Ruth picks up? Or worse still, listens in on our conversation?

If Ellie thinks I deserve another chance, I can't blow it a third time. She holds all the answers. I didn't imagine the fear in her voice and I bet it has something to do with whatever Lewis had caught Meg up in, some sexual deviance that Sean couldn't bring himself to tell me about all these years later.

'I thought we talked about this, Ruth. I'll be fine.'

'You're not the only reason I'm staying,' she admits.

'Oh,' I say, realising any further attempt to dissuade her will be futile. 'You think it's a bad sign that Gemma didn't ring on Monday, don't you?'

'She's phoned up on every other shift lately. If something has happened, I can't risk us missing her next call.'

'I'm really sorry about last week.'

Ruth leans forward, raising her chin to look over the privacy screen separating us. 'It's not your fault, Jen. We've spent too many years beating ourselves up over Meg, we can't take responsibility for Gemma's life too. We have to accept there's only so much we can do.'

It's a nice speech but I don't think Ruth believes it either. 'Do you want to be the one to speak to her if she does call?' I ask, glancing at the phone on my desk. Calls will only divert to Ruth's pod if the first line is busy.

'Yes, please. Just transfer her over.'

My cheeks redden. 'But what if I drop the call?'

'OK, how about we swap seats if we need to? We're not going to lose her this time,' Ruth promises, her words as tense as her body.

As we sit back and wait, I'm reminded of the early days when we had enough volunteers to double up for every shift. During the quieter periods – and there weren't as many as there are now – I talked to the other volunteers. Talking to Ruth had been especially therapeutic, for both of us. Talking would help now, and there's been something playing on my mind.

'What was that thing you mentioned about a space girl the other night?' I ask.

161

Ruth straightens up and I hear the gentle taps of a fingernail on her mobile screen as she begins to explain. 'I was having a clear out and found a page from Meg's notepad curled up inside a vase, waiting to be discovered. I didn't mention it because I didn't want to upset you, or raise your hopes. The police aren't interested. I was supposed to pass on the original but I haven't been ready to surrender this last fragment of Meg's life, and they haven't exactly chased me up over it.'

Reaching over the screen, Ruth hands me her mobile. She's opened her photo library, only it's not pictures of her grandchildren this time, but a piece of yellow lined paper, zoomed in so I can read Meg's familiar scrawl.

Blood drains slowly from my face as I read Meg's words, returning to one line in particular.

It's amazing what you can get used to with enough practice.

Enough practice? Is Meg talking about the sexual experimentation Sean mentioned?

'Has Sean seen this?'

'Yes, he asked about my space girl comment too.'

I bite down hard on my lip. Sean was wrong to assume his sister was a willing participant. She's not describing something consensual. Whatever Lewis was doing, it was slowly killing Meg and now he's doing the same to Ellie. Oh, shit.

As I prepare to hand the phone back to Ruth, I zoom out of the image and another secret is revealed. I let out a gasp. 'I was there when she wrote this, Ruth. I remember her scoring across the page, but I took no notice of what she'd written.' I hand the phone back and rub my fingers as if they've been scorched. 'I didn't know.'

162

'When did she write it?'

I scrunch up my nose. It was that day we were waiting for Sean to come home. 'We were getting our coursework out of the way before our AS Level exams, so it was Easter, the year before she died. She'd only been dating Lewis a few months. It didn't take him long, did it?'

'No, it was Meg's suffering that went on,' Ruth says, her eyes rimmed with tears.

I want to get up and give her the hug we both desperately need, but if I do that, I might cry and soon we'll both be a sobbing mess. That simply won't do, I tell myself as I dig deep for the courage to tell Ruth about Ellie. My heart thumps against my chest, only to leap into my throat when the phone on my desk rings.

I recognise Gemma's voice immediately and I'm already standing up as I explain that I'm going to pass the call to Ruth.

'I felt so awful about the other day, Gemma,' I tell her as Ruth circles the desks. 'I shouldn't have put you on hold. It won't happen again.'

'It's OK,' she says. 'There must be girls in worse situations than me that need to talk to you.'

The hum of people going about their grocery shopping in the background emphasises a hollowness I haven't heard in Gemma's voice before. We have to help her. 'Here's Ruth.'

Relegated to the second pod, I have no choice but to sit and listen to the one-sided conversation. Given that we're primarily a listening service, there's not a lot of information to be gleaned, but whatever it is that Gemma is sharing doesn't put Ruth at ease. Resting on one elbow, she uses the palm of her hand to cool her brow and prop up her head. I can't see her mouth and the privacy screen muffles her voice.

Using my heels, I'm edging my chair closer when the second phone rings. I snatch it up. 'Hello?'

'Hi.'

'Hi,' I reply, stopping short of speaking Ellie's name joyously out loud. I have to be careful in case Ruth picks up on my conversation – so much for telling her everything. 'I wasn't sure if you'd phone back.'

'I hoped I would not need to,' Ellie says. 'I thought he would listen.'

Ellie's voice has an unfamiliar rasp to it. Whatever has happened has caused her to cry herself dry. 'But he won't,' I conclude.

'No.'

I push my chair backwards, extending my distance from Ruth before adopting her pose of leaning forward and talking quietly into my sleeve. 'What happened?'

'He was angry. He said it is my fault he cannot keep away. He asks why I do this to him. I try to say I do nothing. I asked him to go but then . . .' Her words trail off as she relives whatever has happened to her. 'He wants to know if I have told someone, a new boyfriend perhaps. I say no but he must see that I am lying.'

'Did you tell him you've spoken to me? Does he check your phone?' I ask, for the first time grateful that Ruth is keeping me company tonight.

'He checks but I delete my calls. I tell him I keep his secret but it does not matter. He does not listen. He is not talking to me, he is talking to Megan.'

'Do you want to talk about it?' I ask.

164

There's a loud sniff and the sound of Ellie struggling to swallow.

'It was worse this time. He forced me to the bedroom. I said I would do what he wanted if he would just love me, be nice to me. He said I do not like nice. I try to stop him, Jen, but that only made him worse. He wanted to know where the scarves were and . . .'

My back goes rigid as a vision flashes across my mind. I'm lying on Meg's bed with the heart-shaped fairy lights above my head. I reach over to play with one of the silk scarves hanging from the bedpost but suddenly they're not there. Meg's taken them into the garage and has tied them into a noose.

My hand sweeps across my face and comes to rest on my throat. 'What scarves?'

'He buys them for me to keep by my bed but I hide them away. He found them in a drawer.'

I've never before made a connection between the scarves Meg treasured and her abusive relationship. Did he tie her up with them? Was her last act a message the rest of us hadn't understood?

'Oh, Ellie,' I say. Realising I've spoken her name, I glance up quickly in case I've drawn attention to the conversation Ruth is better off not hearing. Fortunately, she's absorbed in her own conversation.

'I lie on the bed and I am not allowed to make a sound,' Ellie continues. 'Sometimes he pushes a scarf into my mouth but that was not what he did this time.'

'It's OK. I'm here,' I tell her when she breaks down in tears. I could almost be talking to Meg and not Ellie.

'He put the scarf around my neck and pulled it tight,'

she says, and that's when I realise that the hoarseness of her voice isn't because she's been crying, although she's been doing that too. 'He closed his eyes and he did not care that he was choking me. I thought I was going to die. Everything went dark.'

'Oh, Jesus . . .'

It's like a punch to the stomach and I want to be sick: the old bruising found on Meg's neck during the autopsy hadn't been from a previous suicide attempt – Lewis had done that to her. I'd seen him lash out at Meg but I had no idea what happened to her behind closed doors. This is what Meg described happening to the space girl. The air running out. The lungs that burn. This is what Meg's abuser did to her again and again and again.

Why did I ever think I could stand up to Lewis on my own? If Meg wasn't strong enough to fight back, what chance have I? With a rush of guilt, I realise I'm thinking about me when it's Ellie who's in imminent danger.

'Ellie, listen to me. I know I was rushing you last time but have you thought about what you want to happen so we can get you out of there?'

She continues as if I haven't spoken. 'When I came around, I thought I was alone. Then I heard him crying.'

'He said he was sorry.'

Ellie's sobs rise up again and as I wait for her to compose herself, I'm momentarily distracted by the call taking place on the other side of the privacy screen.

Ruth's voice has risen and her cheeks are flushed as she straightens up. 'I'll phone you straight back, Gemma. I promise. Please, just stay where you are,' she begs. She leans over and presumably cuts the call before dialling the number scrawled on a Post-it note. Gemma must have run out of change for the phone.

'I ask him why he does it,' Ellie is telling me.

'And did he tell you?' I ask, my words coming out as a gasp – I've been holding my breath. I'm still looking at Ruth and I can see the relief washing over her as she gets Gemma back on the line. We still have a chance to save both women.

'He says it is Megan's fault. She made him like this and I am no better.'

My grip on the phone tightens. 'He's going to say a lot of things to justify what he's been doing to you but you must never, ever, think that you deserve to be used in that way.'

'It's because I tell him that I like him and then I act like I don't. He says I do it to confuse him and that Megan was the same,' Ellie continues. 'He loved her but she only made him feel bad. She toyed with him and so do I. We are responsible for everything that happens.'

'And is that what you think? Have you ever felt in control with this relationship?'

Ellie doesn't answer straight away. 'He is a very strong man but I must have some power over him because I am the only one he will talk to about Megan. He wanted me to feel special but he scared me and now he does not try to be kind.'

'Because you know what he did and that scares *him*,' I tell her. 'So in a way, you do have power, Ellie. You know something that could destroy him and he might say he's sorry but it won't stop him.'

'He does not pretend to stop any more. He said I will

get used to it and learn to enjoy our games. He promised he will look after me, but . . . If he knew I was talking to you . . .'

'Remember what I said? He's scared because you have a hold over him.' I'm glancing over at Ruth again. 'Do you have any friends you can confide in, anyone who might help?'

'Not since I moved into this flat. He does not like me to have visitors. I am alone.'

'No, you're not. You have me,' I remind her. 'But I can't do this by myself. I'll need to talk to some people – professionals who can help you—'

'No!' Ellie cries. 'You can't tell anyone. You promised!'

'I know but . . .'

'He will kill me if he finds out. He will,' she says between ragged breaths.

'We can get you to a safe place,' I promise. I'm thinking of Selina's refuge, even though I know there's never enough room. I'd give her my bed if I thought it was safe, but the moment Lewis realises Ellie has been talking to me, he'll come looking for both of us. He knows where I work. How long would it take for him to work out where I live?

'You can trust me, Ellie.'

Over on the other helpline pod, I hear Ruth say the same thing to Gemma.

'I need time,' Ellie says. 'I will phone again next week.'

I'm about to offer her my mobile number but the line goes dead. My hand shakes as I replace the receiver and look at the blank call sheet on screen. How much longer can I keep Ellie's secret? So far, I haven't been able to offer her anything more substantial than weak assurances that she'll be safe. I need to have a plan and I can't do that on my own.

Ruth's telephone rattles as she drops it down onto its receiver. 'I think I need a cuppa after that.'

'I'll get them.'

'Let's both go,' she says. 'As long as you promise to sprint back if we get another call. I don't think my legs would carry me.'

I let Ruth lead the way to the kitchen in case she realises she's not the only one unsteady on her feet.

'Gemma's finally realised that Ryan isn't simply misunderstood,' Ruth says as she picks up the kettle. 'If we don't get her away from him soon, I don't think she'll ever escape. He's already worn her down so much, but we have a fighting chance. She's given me her mum's number so I can let her know what's happening.'

'Tonight?'

Ruth considers her options. 'I should probably sleep on it first. Her relationship with her mum sounds quite volatile at the moment, which has worked in Ryan's favour but will make our job that bit more difficult.'

It isn't easy switching focus away from Ellie, but Ruth has the right idea about sleeping on things. I let Ruth continue talking.

'We know Gemma's mum was the one who got her to phone the helpline in the first place,' Ruth continues, 'but Gemma has been conditioned to do the exact opposite of what her mum says. She doesn't want to be the child who's told what to do. We're going to have to tread very carefully.'

As we wait for the kettle to boil, we each have time to

reflect on this evening's conversations. 'At least Gemma's given us the opportunity to make a difference,' I say.

'I know, but I won't rest until she's safe, and for the moment, that might not be at home with her mum. I might speak to Selina to see if she can offer her a place to stay. She owes me a favour.'

Damn.

20

Jen

I haven't slept for days and I barely have the strength to drag myself home on Friday evening. I would love, just once, to be able to use the lift but my fears defeat me and I'm out of breath by the time I've climbed the stairs. I pause on the landing and look out across the Liverpool skyline. The cooling sun is leaving deep pink and purple gouges in the autumn sky as it begins its descent but I'm too tired to admire the view. I want to be home.

Charlie suggested going out for dinner tonight and although I would much rather crawl straight into bed, I want to make the effort. His perfectly timed appearance last Saturday at the fundraiser has gone some way to heal the rift between us but we're not completely mended. He thinks he's the reason I'm not sleeping. I haven't told him he's not.

My mind has been ricocheting from one problem to another, one person to another, but notably, not one solution to another. I have to remove Ellie from Lewis's influence, but to do that, I'm going to have to draw on support from other agencies. In any other circumstance, Ruth would be the ideal person to source a solution but how can I tell her what I've discovered? I can see what Lewis's return is doing to her by the anxiety on Geoff's face. I wonder if he should be the one I confide in, or possibly Sean. They've both shown they can keep secrets but can I trust them with Ellie's? All I know for certain is that I can't go on like this. I have to tell someone.

With my pulse still racing, I take a lungful of air and stumble through the fire doors and into the corridor. When I reach the door to my apartment, I don't have the strength to turn the key in the lock and, after some fumbling, I give up and rest my forehead against the door – just as Charlie opens it wide with one effortless movement.

'What's this? Too many drinks in the office?' he asks as he catches me in his arms.

As I straighten up, I hear music playing above the thump of my heartbeat. It's the One Direction album Charlie loathes but I love. There's also the smell of fried onions and Chinese five spice.

'What's going on?' I ask as I peer around him to the dining table in the corner of the apartment. There are candles flickering and a bottle of wine poking its neck out of an ice bucket.

'Nothing special,' he says, to give me fair warning that this is not going to be another surprise proposal. 'I know how tired you've been and the last thing you wanted was to go out for a meal, so I thought we'd stay in.'

'You've cooked a meal?' I ask with surprise, although I don't know why. I should have worked out by now that Charlie is my hero.

'I'll even let you eat your dinner in your PJs if you want.'

What I want most of all is to cry so I wrap my arms around Charlie's neck and kiss him. 'I bloody love you,' I tell him before disappearing into the bedroom to change.

When I reappear, I'm wearing my grown-up silk pyjamas and I've touched up my makeup and straightened my sweat-frizzed hair.

Charlie's smiling. 'I expected you to come out wearing your onesie,' he says.

'I thought I'd make the effort,' I reply, hoping he won't notice my Tinkerbell bed socks.

'Sit down while I pour you a glass of wine.'

Charlie is wearing jeans and a grey marl t-shirt that pulls taut across his narrow chest, the perfect spot to rest my weary head later. If only Ellie could see Charlie, she would realise that this was how you make someone feel loved and protected.

'You're not going to nod off and nosedive into your plate, are you?'

I look down to find my dinner has been placed in front of me. The duck breast has a golden, crispy skin and there's a haze of spice-scented steam coming from the noodles. 'It smells delicious.'

'It tastes pretty good too,' says Charlie with his mouth full.

As I begin to eat, I want to think of the food and the man who prepared it for me, but Charlie's thoughtful act is a shining light that intensifies the shadows creeping into our lives. This isn't how Meg, or Ellie, or Gemma were ever treated.

'Is there any more news about that girl?' Charlie asks.

Guilt tightens my chest. Charlie isn't used to me sharing information about our helpline callers and he must think I trust him implicitly to have told him as much as I have about Gemma this week. I do trust him, but talking about Gemma has been nothing more than a diversionary tactic to stop him asking what else has been playing on my mind since my shift on Wednesday.

'Ruth was on the phone for hours with her mum again today,' I reply. 'We can't find a space at any of the refuges so she was checking to see if there's anyone in the wider family, away from Liverpool, who might take her in. Unfortunately, the mum's insisting her daughter comes home. She thinks staying will show the boyfriend that they can stand up to him, but I doubt he'll care.'

'Would he assault her?'

'It doesn't sound like he's ever threatened violence, aside from suggesting he was going to kill himself, but I wouldn't like to predict what he'll do if she breaks up with him again.'

'You make it sound like she'd be better off staying where she is.'

A piece of duck sticks in my throat and I take a sip of wine to dislodge it. 'It's never the better option, and that's why Ruth spent today coaching the mum on how to approach her daughter and convince her to leave. She's going to have to tread very carefully. The boyfriend monitors her calls and takes her to and from work. The only time we're sure she's on her own is when she goes shopping and he waits in the car park. She's been timing her trips for when the helpline's open.'

'You mean now?'

174

I nod. 'With any luck, she'll be too busy to call us tonight. Her mum's waiting for her at the supermarket and if Ruth has worked her magic, she'll take her daughter for a cup of coffee, sit her down and listen while the girl decides for herself what she should do. We're not expecting anything to happen immediately, not with the boyfriend close by, but we're hoping they'll come up with a plan to get her away from him soon.'

'Fingers crossed it works.'

'It's what comes next that worries me but there are precautions they can take, and it's going to be worth it in the long term.'

The music has stopped playing and we lapse into silence. When my pulse quickens, it's as if I'm climbing the stairs again but my body is simply responding to the decision I made when I reached the top.

'I know you're exhausted,' Charlie says before I can speak. 'And I could have picked my moment better, but I wanted us to have a serious conversation.'

'About?' I ask, swallowing back my confession.

He clears his throat. 'I know you don't want to go down the official route,' he begins, waggling the third finger of his left hand, 'but there are other ways we can put down some proper roots.' He coughs again. 'This apartment has been great but our lease is up next year and I'd really like us to buy a place of our own. A house.'

'Oh.' I'm too preoccupied with the present to have energy to spare on the future, but Charlie is waiting for a proper response and I have to say something. 'But it would take ages to save up for a deposit and my job isn't exactly stable. What if we get a mortgage but can't keep up with the

175

repayments? And if there is spare cash, shouldn't you be reinvesting it in the company?'

'Not in us?'

'I'm not saying it's a bad idea. It's a lovely idea.'

'But I could have chosen my moment better,' Charlie adds. He's playing with his food, as am I.

'I want to spend the rest of my life with you, Charlie. You do know that, don't you?'

As I search his face, I catch a glimpse of the scar on the bridge of his nose. He got it during a fight, and although he never told me why he and Lewis came to blows, I don't have to try too hard to imagine the cause. I want Charlie to know that the kiss meant nothing, and I hope the smile returning to his face confirms that he already does.

'Of course,' he says. 'Which is why I can't help picturing us in a little three-bed semi somewhere out of the city but within walking distance of a station.'

'Three bedrooms?' I ask, forcing myself to join in.

'Your mum did suggest four to make room for her next batch of grandkids.'

My fork clatters against my plate. 'You've spoken to Mum?'

Charlie laughs. 'No, I was only teasing, but it's nice to know that what made you baulk was your mum being involved and not the idea of us having kids one day.'

I'm smiling, too. I want to reach out and embrace the new tomorrow he's offering but I know how illusory the future can be. Life isn't a simple matter of making plans and keeping to them. We've tried that before and my mind takes me back to one such conversation.

It was Meg's seventeenth birthday and although none of

us knew it at the time, we were entering what would be her final year. We were gathered around the dining table with Sean sitting next to me and Geoff next to him. Opposite were Ruth and Meg, and directly in front of me was Lewis.

'What are your plans when you leave sixth form, Lewis?' Ruth had asked politely. It was the first time they had met and she had been impressed with the story of how he and his mum had escaped difficult circumstances and were beginning a brave new life without family or friends.

Lewis had been going all out to impress, arriving with a bottle of wine for his host and a gift for Meg which he'd held back. Full of arrogance, he presumed he and Meg would spend time alone in her room before dinner but Geoff had made it clear that Lewis was not allowed upstairs, and I'd had the unenviable task of chaperoning them in the sitting room while her parents prepared dinner. Every time Lewis looked at me, I cringed inwardly as I imagined him recalling that kiss.

'I'm going to study for a sports degree,' he said, looking decidedly studious in his wire-rimmed glasses.

Geoff's eyes narrowed. 'Which university?'

I was expecting Lewis to say Newcastle, which was where Meg wanted to go. 'John Moores, so staying put in Liverpool.'

'And what do you expect to do with a sports degree?' Geoff continued, sounding more suspicious than interested in Lewis's future prospects.

Lewis shrugged. 'Get a good job.'

'So he can buy me more presents,' Meg said, eyeing the gift bag Lewis had left at the side of his chair.

'You think you'll still be together after uni?' Sean asked.

He paused to deflect the glare from his sister before adding, 'I'm just saying. Long distance relationships don't always work.'

'I can always jump on the train and surprise her,' Lewis replied.

'Not too often,' Geoff said, looking to his daughter. 'You don't want to underestimate the amount of study required at university. It would be better if you had no distractions, Megan.'

'The same goes for you, Lewis,' Ruth added.

Meg rolled her eyes. 'Sean manages, and he has *loads* of girlfriends.'

Another staring contest ensued between the siblings.

'What about you, Jen?' asked Ruth. 'Are you going to have Charlie distracting you from your further education?'

Before I could answer, Meg laughed. 'Romance is further education, Mother!'

'If we've all finished, I'll clear away the plates,' Geoff said, rising to his feet at the same time as my aunt.

The moment they had left the room, Meg turned to Lewis. 'Quick, they'll be back in a minute with the cake. Can I have my present now?'

I turned to Sean to make a point of having no interest in the conversation on the other side of the table. 'When are you due back at uni?'

'In a couple of weeks,' he replied. 'I can't wait.'

There was the sound of rustling as Meg pulled the tissue-covered gift from the bag. I had expected a gasp but there was only silence that went on too long. Unable to stop myself, I looked to find Meg clasping a yellow silk scarf printed with splashes of blood-orange, and the horror on her face has come back to haunt me more than a decade later.

I hadn't understood why she would look so terrified, but I do now.

'I didn't mean straight away,' Charlie is telling me. The concern in his voice pulls me back to the present.

It takes me a moment to pick up the thread of the conversation I'd let drop. Children. 'It's fine, I want them too,' I say, but my reassurance sounds weak. My hands are clammy and there's a coldness creeping into my fingers. 'But right now I'd rather not think about bringing children into this shitty world.'

Charlie leans over the table towards me. 'If and when we do have kids, I won't let anyone hurt them, just like I won't let anyone hurt you.'

'You can't always know what's going on inside other people's heads.'

'Why don't you start by telling me what's going on in yours?'

My stomach heaves when I say, 'There's something I need to tell you. Actually, there are a lot of things I need to tell you, but you have to promise to give me the chance to speak this time.'

'This time?'

'It's about Meg, and Lewis and well, everything.'

He sits back. 'Tell me.'

'I know Meg wasn't perfect,' I begin. 'And when I told Sean what you'd said about her being self-destructive, he actually agreed. He'd found something on her computer once to do with sexual experimentation and on the face of it, it looked like what Meg was doing was consensual. The police would have thought so too, which is why he kept quiet after she died. Like most of us, he never doubted that Lewis was the one who made her do things so shameful, she would rather die than carry on.'

Charlie's cheeks redden: I don't need to tell him that he remains alone in thinking Meg brought out the worst in people.

'The thing is, it wasn't consensual, Charlie. Ruth showed me a page from Meg's notepad this week. She only found it recently and it's relatively abstract, but the message is clear. Meg wasn't a willing participant in their games. She only survived her ordeals by withdrawing into herself while he did what he did.'

'Is Ruth going to the police with it?'

'She already has, and apparently they don't think it's enough to reopen the case. I could try to persuade Sean to tell them what he knows, but I'm not sure what that would achieve. And to be honest, I'm more concerned with what's happening now than what happened ten years ago.'

Charlie's expression is a mixture of shock, guilt and confusion. He wipes glistening sweat from his upper lip before he asks, 'What do you mean?'

'What I'm about to tell you cannot go any further,' I warn. 'It's about someone I've been talking to on the help-line.'

'It's not like I've said anything about that other girl, and I wouldn't.'

'This is different. This is the caller I've been dreading and she begged me not to tell anyone, not even Ruth. Especially not Ruth. It would break her if she knew he's doing it again.'

'Wait, are you saying you're talking to someone connected to Lewis?' Charlie asks, his mouth agape.

This is no hypothetical scenario this time and I have to take it slowly, because I need Charlie's reaction to be the right one. 'I didn't trust anything she said the first time she called. She'd seen Ruth's interview and made a point of telling me Lewis was innocent. She knew who I was and that I'd been close to Meg, so I thought maybe he'd coerced her into calling the helpline. It was only when she phoned again that I realised she was terrified of him, by which point I'd made things worse by approaching Lewis when all she'd been trying to do was defuse the situation. That's when I panicked and messed up the call with Gemma.'

'Gemma?'

I'm too tired to pick my way through the conversation without naming names. If I can't trust Charlie, I shouldn't be talking to him at all. 'Gemma is the other caller, the one Ruth's been dealing with this week,' I explain. 'Ellie is Lewis's girlfriend, or at least that's the name she uses. Her real name is Ioana.'

'Tell me about her.'

'Apparently Lewis thinks she looks like Meg and he likes to pretend she is her when they're having sex, hurting her in exactly the same way,' I say. 'She says he's full of apologies afterwards but that doesn't stop him doing it again, and again.'

Charlie falls quiet, his lips pressed firmly together until he's ready to speak. 'You should have told me what's been going on, Jen. I know I've been saying all the wrong things lately but you should have told me.'

I drop my gaze. 'I wasn't ready to face those questions

I know you're trying not to ask, like how do I know for certain that she is who she says she is. And the truth is, I can't prove a thing because she hasn't actually named him. She's too scared.'

'Is it possible her boyfriend is completely unconnected to us?' Charlie asks when I dare to look up. 'He might be some nutter re-enacting fantasies he created in his head after seeing Meg in the news.'

I can't read Charlie's stony expression but from his tone, he's willing to hear me out. 'After her last call on Wednesday, I have absolutely no doubt it's Lewis. The man Ellie talks about gave her some special gifts – silk scarves – and insisted she keep them by the bed. Now, any weirdo could have picked up from the inquest records that Meg used her scarves to hang herself but only someone who had been close to her would know that she kept her collection on her bedpost. I bet if I ask Sean, he'll confirm that what Lewis likes to do with the scarves fits with what he found on Meg's computer. It's him, Charlie.'

Charlie stares at me for the longest time, shock obliterating every other emotion he's shown tonight. It's like he's seeing something else instead of my face until his eyes snap back into focus. 'I believe you.'

As I let his words sink in, the colour draining from Charlie's face rises in my cheeks. 'Do you want to know what he did with the scarves?' I ask as my fingers begin to tingle with the soft touch of silk.

I want Charlie to say no and stop me there but he remains stock still.

'He forced them into her mouth so he wouldn't have to hear her begging for him to stop,' I say. I can feel the food

182

I ate earlier rise up in my throat when I add, 'And – and when that wasn't enough to satisfy him, he tied a scarf around Ellie's neck and pulled on it until she passed out, just like he did to Meg. It's called autoerotic asphyxiation. He tells her she'll learn to enjoy it.'

I stop to clear my throat but the lump obstructing my airway refuses to budge and my words are jagged. 'That's where the faded bruising on Meg's neck came from, Charlie. He was choking her with her own scarves. There were no previous suicide attempts. Her last act wasn't a cry for help that went wrong. Meg knew exactly what she was doing and the method she chose was a message to Lewis that he'd gone too far.'

The smell from our forsaken meal makes me want to gag and it has the same effect on Charlie. He swallows hard and in the next moment, his hand flies to his mouth. He's retching as he jumps up and rushes to the bathroom. The door slams behind him.

Numbly, I clear away the dishes and wait for him to reappear.

'Sorry, I don't know what happened there,' he says when he picks up the glass of water waiting for him.

'It's like a punch to the stomach,' I tell him, knowing exactly how he feels. 'I didn't think the shock of Meg's death could hit me again so hard, but when I listen to Ellie, I'm hearing Meg's story. We have to do something, Charlie.'

'You can't go near Lewis,' he warns. 'Please, Jen. Promise me you'll keep away from him.'

'Ellie is my only concern,' I tell him. 'We can argue about Lewis once I know she's safe.'

Charlie seems satisfied with my answer and says no more

as he helps me load the dishwasher. There's something comforting about doing ordinary, everyday chores as the nightmare we've been running from for the last decade catches up with us.

'Should I tell Ruth and Geoff?' I ask at last. Having witnessed Charlie's reaction, I'm not sure I'm that brave.

'Do you think we can handle it on our own?'

I close the dishwasher. I'm relieved he said *we*. 'I'd like to try.'

'So what exactly do you know about her?'

'Not as much as I'd like. She's from Romania but she's been living in Liverpool for a few years. It doesn't sound like she has any friends who can help, Lewis has managed to isolate her, and she doesn't want to go home to her family. The good thing is she's not living with Lewis.'

'He'll need to stay with his mum for now.'

'Yes, he wouldn't want his mum finding out what he gets up to with Ellie,' I add. 'The problem is, Lewis pays Ellie's rent and she can't afford it on her own. She works in a shop but I don't like the idea of her working in a frontline service. If she's going to get away from him, she'll have to give up her job and her home, which means she faces an all-too-familiar dilemma. How can she afford to start a new life somewhere else if she's not working?'

'How about a refuge?'

'She's in the same position as Gemma. The refuges that haven't closed down after the withdrawal of local authority funding are full to capacity, and women with children have to take priority. Even Ruth couldn't pull a favour from Selina. It had crossed my mind that Ellie could stay here if we clear out the spare room, but we're too easy for Lewis to find.'

'Yes, we are,' Charlie replies soberly. He leans against the kitchen counter, deep in thought. 'What if she came to work for me?'

'You'd find her a job, just like that?'

'For you, yes. I have a group of Eastern European girls who share a house and they might be able to put her up. I think we can sort this, Jen.'

I'm shocked, but in a nice way. 'You're sure?'

'You're not the only one who wishes you could go back and change things. Yes, I'm sure about this. If she phones again, tell her you can help. Tell her we can help.'

21

Ruth

The cream leather armchair squeaks as I lean forward to take the cup of tea Gemma's mum offers. Annabelle is a petite lady in her forties, nothing like the snarling tigress I'd conjured when we first talked on the phone last week. She appears as incredulous as I when she turns to the young girl sitting on the sofa. Taking a sip of my tea, my eyes never leave Gemma as I attempt to identify some of the other emotions bubbling up inside me. There's a mixture of relief, hope and victory. We did it. Gemma is home.

When I arrived at Annabelle's house this morning, she'd been waiting at the door. It was only a short drive to the council offices where Gemma works and we were early. Half an hour later we spotted Gemma being dropped off outside the main entrance by Ryan.

Gemma was expecting us but she didn't give herself away as she waved Ryan goodbye. She kept her head low, letting her long hair cover her face in the same way Meg often did when she wanted to cut herself off from the world.

In the plan she had agreed with Annabelle on Friday night, Gemma was to go straight to her line manager on Monday morning to explain the situation, but when she disappeared into the grey municipal building, I was afraid she wouldn't come out again. The wait had been excruciating and I'd almost lost hope when she stumbled out of the door and lifted her head to the watery sun in an ocean of sky. Annabelle was out of the car before I could stop her, racing over to her daughter to sweep her into her arms, and that's when I felt it. That one emotion I'm pretending isn't there. Envy.

'I can't thank you enough,' Annabelle says as she sets down two more cups on a side table before taking a seat next to Gemma. She clasps her daughter's hand tightly.

'There's a long way to go yet,' I warn, glancing at Gemma whose eyes are red and muddy with mascara. 'When Ryan finds out, you need to make it clear that the break-up is non-negotiable. Keep the conversation short. Don't engage in bargaining. He'll be expecting to win you back again.'

'He's not going to,' Gemma whispers.

'What if he threatens to top himself like last time?' asks Annabelle.

'Even then,' Gemma promises. 'I hated it there, Mum. Everything I did made him angry.'

'Did he hit you?' Annabelle asks, not for the first time.

'No, he's not like that. He takes it out on things instead of me. He smashed up my phone.'

'Even if he's not violent, he could find other ways to disrupt your life,' I tell her. 'It would be a good idea to delete your social media accounts and change all your passwords, especially for things like your bank and your phone accounts.

And you definitely need to talk to the police so they're aware of the situation.'

Gemma's eyes widen. 'Honestly, he's not that bad.'

'We're being cautious, that's all,' Annabelle tells her.

'It's better to be prepared in case things do turn nasty,' I add. 'The most important thing is not to let your guard down.'

It's advice I wish someone had given me but Lewis had been charming on first appearances. I told myself that my unease was natural because he was Meg's first serious boyfriend but after another long weekend sifting through the video evidence, I can see what went wrong. Geoff and I had been watching him when we should have been watching Meg.

That mistake was never more apparent than in the video of Meg's birthday – the last one to be celebrated by lighting candles on a cake rather than in a church. The camera had panned around the table as we all sang 'Happy Birthday', but Meg's head remained bowed. When Lewis elbowed her, she finally looked up and stared straight at the camera, her face lit up by seventeen flickering candles rather than the false smile on her trembling lips.

I set down my cup. 'I should go,' I tell Annabelle but as I stand, the house phone resting on the side table begins to ring.

'Is it him?' Gemma asks as her mum reaches for the phone.

'The number's withheld. Should I answer?'

Annabelle directs the question to me but before I can say no, Gemma holds out her hand to her mum. 'Let me speak to him.'

My heart aches every time I hear Gemma's lisp but there's something else about her voice that feels familiar. It's a steeliness that disappeared from Meg's voice but it's there in Gemma's. 'Remember what I said, no bargaining.'

As Gemma sits up straight, she takes ownership of her life again. 'Hello?' she asks casually.

After a pause, she says, 'Yes, I have gone home sick. Home to Mum's . . . Sorry, Ryan, let me stop you there. I'm not coming back. It's over . . . No, you don't love me. According to you, I make you miserable so really, I'm doing us both a favour.'

Her expression changes as she listens to the bellowed response that's loud enough for us all to hear. I can't make out the exact words but I don't imagine they're pleasant.

'I don't want to be with you any more. Please, don't phone again. It'll be easier that way. Goodbye,' Gemma says quickly before the tremble that has appeared in her voice makes it impossible to speak. She cuts the call and looks to me with trusting eyes. 'Did I do all right, Ruth?'

'You were amazing,' I tell her as the phone starts up again.

Annabelle leaps to her feet. 'I'll disconnect the line until we can get the number changed,' she says as she disappears into the hall. A moment later, the phone stops.

'What did he say?' I ask.

'He phoned the office and someone told him I'd gone home.'

'You need to warn all your friends and colleagues not to give out any information about you, no matter how mundane it might seem.'

'I will,' Gemma says. 'Do you really have to go?'

'You have your mum,' I reply.

Annabelle is standing by the door. 'And I promise, no more Tinder or girls' nights out for me. I'm here for you for as long as you need me, love.'

'You don't have to give up your social life for me, Mum.'

'I want to. And, it won't be like this forever.'

My chest tightens and the walls begin to close in as I grab my handbag. 'I've left you some leaflets to read through and there's a couple of personal alarms for you both. You've done the hardest part, Gemma.'

'We couldn't have done it without you,' Annabelle says, following in my wake as I hurry to the front door.

'No, Gemma couldn't have done it without you,' I reply, my words choking me. 'Just promise me you'll keep her safe.'

As I leave the underground car park and head across the Mann Island concourse, the low sun reflects off the glass shell of our offices. I check my watch. It's ten past eleven, a little early for someone to be taking her lunch break when she hasn't technically started work yet, but my feet take me past the main entrance and along a well-worn route to John Lewis.

There's a small café on the first floor and I buy myself a coffee and slice of cake. I have no intention of eating it but it gives me the opportunity to talk to the girl behind the counter. I don't know Lewis's girlfriend's name or what she looks like – Vanessa only knew where she worked – but I've chatted to enough staff in the last week to have perfected my method of interrogation. I open our conversation with a remark about needing to replenish my strength before resuming my search for a present for my son-in-law. We compare notes with men she knows of a similar age. Her boyfriend is a twenty-six-year-old medical student. I cross another potential suspect off my list.

I choose a window seat that has a good view of the pedestrianised thoroughfare below and the wall of steps rising up to Chavasse Park. As I sip my coffee, I ask myself what I'll do if I manage to find her. I can't expect to swoop in like I did this morning and remove her from harm's way. She might not realise yet that she needs saving.

My phone buzzes. It was only a matter of time before someone lost patience and I'm not surprised when I see Jen's name. I'd phoned around all the volunteers at the weekend to tell them about Gemma's escape mission and they'll all be waiting for news.

'Is she safe?' she asks.

'She's at home,' I reply, which isn't necessarily the same thing but at least her situation is improving. 'I've persuaded her to take a couple of weeks off work and she knows not to leave the house unaccompanied until things have calmed down.'

'She will be OK, won't she, Ruth?'

'I've given Gemma and her mum personal alarms just in case, and Annabelle's managed to get hold of some pepper spray too. I've told her she needs to be careful or she'll be the one charged with assault but, to be honest, if it gets to the point where Gemma feels threatened, I'd rather she worry about the consequences afterwards.'

Jen is quiet for a moment and I imagine she's listening to the hum of conversation and the clatter of cutlery around me. 'So if you've left them, where are you now?'

191

'I fancied a walk and a quiet cup of coffee to clear my head.'

'Are you all right, Ruth?'

I could offer a lie but, as the sun warms my face, today feels like a day for telling the truth. 'How different things could have been if Meg had talked to someone instead of hiding cryptic messages,' I say. I don't need to see Jen to know she flinches. We both bear the guilt of believing we could have been that someone and my thoughts return to Meg's last birthday, only this time it's something the camera didn't see.

While the rest of us were eating cake, Meg had left the dining room on the pretext of making a drink and had been gone long enough for the conversation around the table to become stilted. When I found her in the kitchen, she had her back to me. At first glance she looked statue-still with her hand clasped around her drink, but the water inside the glass had trembled.

'There were times when we were alone together,' I tell Jen. 'Moments of calm between the arguments and the sulks when she might have told me what was going on inside her head – if only I'd had the courage to ask. The silences we used to avoid difficult conversations might not have caused her death, but they represent the lost chances I had to save her.' Goosebumps prick my arms. 'I should have learnt my lesson. I've been keeping something from you, Jen. I've been looking for Lewis's girlfriend.'

22

Jen

There had been the briefest moment during my call to Ruth when I thought everything was going to work out, and not just for Gemma, but for Ellie too. Charlie was going to help me, and all I had to do next was persuade Ellie to leave. It was going to be that simple – except now it's not.

I have no idea how Ruth thinks she can track Ellie down, but I have to stop her, or else Ellie will assume I've betrayed her trust. I suppose I have already. I've told Charlie and as I head off to meet Ruth, I have a sinking feeling it's not going to stop there.

I'm panting when I reach the café. Running my fingers beneath my fringe to mop up the sweat, I spot Ruth and weave my way over to her table.

'What's going on?'

She waits for me to take off my heavy houndstooth jacket and sit down. My shirt is sticking to my damp skin, suggesting I've been a bit too eager bringing out my winter wardrobe.

'I thought setting up the foundation would give me a purpose and stop me obsessing over what Lewis was actually doing, and to who. But it was never going to be enough. Now that he's chosen to come back here, I need to fight him and I need to win.'

'By stalking his girlfriend?' I ask, using the accusation Lewis had directed at me not that long ago.

'Why not?'

I give Ruth a look that says, 'Isn't it obvious?' but I'm playing for time. There's a long list of reasons why she shouldn't be doing this but I can't decide if that list should be edited or not. How would Ruth cope, hearing the things I've told Charlie? I can still hear him throwing up in the toilet.

'Vanessa was a bit short on details and all I have to go on is that she works here.'

'Here?' I ask, almost jumping out of my seat. I check the faces swarming into view, expecting to freeze when I set eyes on a Meg lookalike. There's more chance, I realise, of Ellie seeing us first. She could easily recognise Ruth from the TV interview and, given all the work I do promoting the foundation, I wouldn't be surprised if she's come across an image online of me too.

'I haven't found her yet,' Ruth continues, 'but I'm being methodical and working my way through all the departments.'

'And when you do find her?'

'I'll talk to her and, if she'll let me, I'll listen.' There's a desperation in Ruth's voice that I haven't heard since the aftermath of Meg's death, when she and Geoff had questioned me over and over again. I didn't have the answers back then. I do now.

'You can't do this, Ruth. You don't know what you're stepping into.'

'I understand why you want to talk me out of it but I can't stand by and do nothing,' she says. 'I appreciate there's every possibility that this girl isn't in danger, but in good conscience, I can't take that risk. I watch the videos of Meg and I see her change before my eyes. I don't know what he did to her, I just know I can't let it happen again.'

I can hear whooshing as my blood pressure rises. My mouth is dry and my tongue sticks to the roof of my mouth when I say, 'Do you want to know?'

If there's a moment when Ruth thinks it's a rhetorical question, I don't see it. Her body tenses. 'Yes.'

'I've spoken to her, Ruth. I've spoken to Lewis's girlfriend. She's been phoning the helpline for weeks.'

Before I can talk myself out of it, I lay out the facts. I'm repeating much of what I'd said to Charlie on Friday night but it's by no means the same version of Ellie's story. I explain how the calls started soon after Ruth's interview, and that the put-down calls she had assumed were from Lewis were probably Ellie as she waited for me to pick up. I admit I'd been economical with the truth when it came to the call sheets, and I tell her how and why I messed up the call with Gemma.

The most difficult part is when I have to explain how Lewis calls her Meg when he uses and abuses her. I mention there's physical assault but I don't say exactly what he does. I don't mention the scarves. I can spare her some of the pain, but clearly not all of it. By the time I've finished, Ruth is bent forward in her seat, her head in her hands. She hasn't said a word and I give her the time she needs.

'You're *sure* it's him?' she asks without looking up.

'Yes.'

There's another long pause before Ruth straightens up. She pats her face dry with a serviette. 'She will phone again, won't she?'

'Yes, she trusts me, which is why it's important that you don't approach her, not yet. Charlie and I have come up with a possible solution. She can't carry on working here,' I tell Ruth, my eyes darting around the café again as I'm reminded how close we might be. 'But Charlie's said she can work for him, and he's asking around to see if he can find her a place to stay too.'

'Is there no family who could help?'

'Not in this country – she's from Romania. And there are no close friends either.'

'So Lewis isolates her and moves her into an apartment she can't afford – how perfect for him. He thinks he's trapped her but we're going to prove him wrong, Jen.'

'Yes, we are.'

'Is Ellie her real name?' Ruth asks, glancing furtively to the exit that opens onto the beauty department and all the other floors she's become familiar with in the last week.

'No, it's Ioana, but I still think of her as Ellie.'

'Could you get me a copy of that photo you found on Facebook?'

'Please, Ruth,' I reply, drawing her gaze back to me. 'You can't keep looking for her. Ellie isn't like Meg. She'll bolt as soon as she sees you and if that happens, we'll lose her for good.'

Ruth chews her lip. She wants to take action and I understand why. To my relief, she relaxes back into her chair. 'You're right,' she says. 'But I want you to keep me fully involved from now on.'

'I will,' I promise. 'What about Geoff? Should we tell him?'

Ruth had been about to get up but the question stalls her. 'He needs to know,' she says, 'but let me deal with that. These days I have no way of second-guessing how he'll react.'

'The important thing is that no one does anything rash,' I warn.

'We won't,' Ruth promises. 'I can't imagine it's been easy telling me what you have, but you did the right thing.'

'Ellie might not see it that way.'

'We'll convince her, together,' Ruth says. She stands up and holds out her arm to me. 'Come on, let's go.'

I keep my head down as we leave the department store but I catch Ruth looking around one last time. It's clear she doesn't want to abandon her search and I just hope she's true to her promise about not doing anything rash.

23

Jen

Despite an agreed plan of action, waiting for Ellie to make the next move isn't easy. From my experience on the helpline, there have been too many callers who were ready to make the break, only to go off the radar for months. Some phone back with stories of how their lives have been rebuilt, or fallen apart, but far worse are those we never hear from again. I can't let Ellie be one of them.

I had considered re-sending Jay and Meathead friend requests on Facebook – with Charlie's endorsement this time – but it smacks of desperation and might trigger an online comment from one of his idiot friends that could alert Lewis. Besides, Charlie is happy to spy on my behalf.

This morning, I'm trying to remain positive. Ellie will call again tonight and I am going to persuade her to leave. Unfortunately, that might be more difficult than I anticipated because Ruth is insisting on doubling up with me again. When she had said she wanted me to keep her involved, I hadn't realised how much.

'You do know Ellie will only speak to me, don't you?' I ask when Ruth finds me alone in the kitchen.

'I understand that, but if you explain that I'm right there and I know what's been happening, if she knows she doesn't have to worry about upsetting me, she might be persuaded.'

I turn away to put the milk back in the fridge so I can hide my reaction. I don't know what would be worse, Ellie discovering my betrayal or Ruth hearing in graphic detail what Lewis does to her. 'Perhaps she will want to speak to you, but not yet. We can't risk frightening her off.'

'It's your call, but will you at least suggest that she brings me into her circle of trust?'

It isn't like Ruth to be so insistent but I understand why. She sees this as a chance to redeem herself, but it's mine too. It might have been Lewis who stole Meg away from me but I didn't stand in his way. Our drunken kiss had made me too afraid to speak out against him for fear of him telling Charlie, and I can still remember how utterly powerless I felt every time he smiled at me.

'What's up, Jen?' he'd asked, surprising me one time as I was heading out of the sixth form block.

I swallowed back the gasp. 'Nothing.'

When I tried to keep walking, Lewis stepped in front of me, blocking my way. 'Have you seen Meg?'

'We don't see much of each other these days,' I muttered.

'I suppose you think that's my fault,' he replied.

Holding my nerve, I looked Lewis in the eye. 'Isn't it?'

'Meg does what Meg wants, you know that,' he said. I thought he'd let me go, but he held his ground. 'Does she ever talk to you, Jen? I mean *really* talk to you.'

There had been a time when I would have said yes straight

away, but Lewis knew this was no longer the case. Anger bloomed in my chest. He hadn't needed to ask. He was driving home the point that I was no longer in her life – and he was.

'It's probably better that you don't know what's going on her head,' he continued, his eyes darkening until he realised he was staring at me. He forced a smile. 'Judging by that look, I don't think she'd want to know what's going on inside yours either.'

'Whatever I'm thinking, it's got nothing to do with you,' I told him with a sniff.

Lewis's smile widened. 'Protective as always. I knew there was a reason I liked you, Jen.'

'And what are you two smiling about?' Meg asked as she came up behind me. Her voice was croaky and she was out of breath as if she'd sprinted over to break up our tête-à-tête.

'We were talking about the old times,' Lewis replied, suggesting an intimacy I didn't like.

'Old times? You've only known each other two minutes.'

'I was just saying it's been ages since you've been out with the gang,' I dared to add. 'We're starting to think you've forgotten us.'

'Sorry,' Meg replied, her uncharacteristic apology coming as a surprise to us both. Something was wrong. She looked pale and twitchy. I hadn't seen much of her since the start of our last year at sixth form, but there were times I'd glimpsed her staring out the window in the common room and I'd swear she wanted to jump right through it.

'We're all going to the firework display at Sefton Park at the weekend. Why don't you come with us?' I asked.

'Meg has coursework to finish,' Lewis answered for her.

She rolled her eyes at him. 'Aren't you the hard taskmaster?'

'I'm only thinking of you,' he replied.

'You deserve a break,' I tried but Meg couldn't pull her gaze from Lewis who had slung an arm around her.

'Are you trying to lead her astray?' Lewis asked. 'I thought you were a better friend than that, Jen.'

There had been that smile again; the snake always ready to strike.

'Why don't you come back to mine now?' Meg offered. 'I could power through my essay and then we could all go out at the weekend.'

Lewis's silence unnerved me.

'I'd better not. I've got deadlines too and I could do with the peace and quiet,' I said, not only backing down but backing away.

If only I had gone back to Meg's house, we might have talked. I might have built up the courage to make a pre-emptive strike and tell my version of events before Lewis turned it into something it wasn't. She might have forgiven me and we could have avoided the arguments to come. I missed my opportunity with Meg, but I won't miss it with Ellie.

Ruth is waiting for an answer about bringing her into the circle of trust. She doesn't think I can convince Ellie on my own, and given my most recent memory, she might have a point. 'I don't know,' I say honestly. 'Shall we see how it goes tonight? She might not even phone.'

My comment was meant to field any more helpful suggestions but as my heart clenches in dread that Ellie won't ring, it's Ruth who grimaces.

*   *   *

I'm standing perilously close to one of the floor-to-ceiling windows that looks out over the concourse and when my forehead touches the glass, it isn't because I've overcome my fear of it caving in at any moment, it's simply that I've been sucked into a far more terrifying nightmare. I'm directly above the main entrance watching all the comings and goings, and in the last fifteen minutes there have been a few stragglers late back from lunch, but not one of them was Ruth.

'Should you be doing that?' Geoff asks as he appears next to me.

I raise my head but my eyes are slow to follow, and when I do look at Geoff, he's rested his hands on the window to join me in my search. His gaze leads him to the pedestrian crossing on the corner of the Strand.

'She might use the crossing down by the Albert Dock,' I tell him.

'Have you tried phoning her?'

'Yeah, but I didn't leave a message. Did you?'

'Several,' Geoff confirms. He looks at the clock on the Liver Building. It's twenty-five past two. 'This isn't like her, Jennifer.'

'I could take a walk over to Liverpool One,' I suggest.

Geoff makes a noise that might have been a chuckle if his nerves had allowed. 'I'd say my wife knows the shops far too well to get lost in one,' he replies. The sigh he releases knocks the wind out of me. 'Something's wrong.'

I step back from the window and, as I straighten up, all hope leaves me. There isn't a simple explanation for Ruth's extended lunch break. She's ignored my warning and gone in search of Ellie again, and judging by her delay in returning, she's found her. 'She hasn't told you, has she?'

'Has this got something to do with Gemma again?'

'No, not Gemma,' I reply as adrenalin surges through my body.

'Then who?'

'Who do you think?'

Geoff closes his eyes briefly. 'I think you'd better come into my office and tell me everything.'

'Could we go for a walk instead?' I suggest. 'It isn't the kind of conversation we should be having in here, and with any luck, we'll catch Ruth walking back.'

I'm buttoning up my jacket as we begin our descent. Geoff knows me too well to insist we take the lift and the deserted stairwell gives us some privacy. This is the third time I've told Ellie's secret and it's getting easier.

'Ruth found out that Lewis's new girlfriend works in John Lewis and she's been trying to track her down.'

'She's been doing what?' Geoff asks. He's behind me but I don't need to see his expression to know that his anxiety has given way to anger. 'Jennifer, this is insane. What on earth does she think she's doing? The solicitor's letter was bad enough but God knows what he'll do when he finds out she's harassing his girlfriend.'

My guess is he'll wear Ellie down until there's nothing left, just like he did with Meg. He'll erase her and everything he did to her. He thinks no one can stop him but he's wrong.

'What else do we know about this girl?' Geoff asks.

'Apparently she looks a bit like Meg,' I reply as we make our way past reception. 'She's called Ioana.'

There are two sets of large automatic doors and the glass rattles loudly as a strong gust of wind crashes into the building. I hear Geoff repeat Ioana's name and have to raise my voice when I say, 'She's originally from Romania.'

We keep our heads down as we step outside and are buffeted by the gales. There are people waiting for the lights to change at the pedestrian crossing but we choose to keep moving and walk further along the Strand.

'And how do you know all of this?' Geoff asks eventually.

'Ruth hasn't spoken to her but I have. She's been phoning the helpline for a while. She's one of the reasons I went to see Lewis. I knew he hadn't changed.'

'What do you mean? What has this girl been saying?'

'Lewis made the mistake of telling her exactly what he did to Meg,' I explain. I want my words to be gentle but I have to talk above the howl of the wind and rumble of traffic. I doubt it matters. There's no easy way to break the news, I should know that by now.

'And what did he do?'

I take a breath only to release it with a sigh. 'I know how Meg got the partly healed bruises that were found on her neck. It wasn't an earlier suicide attempt.'

Geoff's pace slows and I'm tempted to race ahead but he reaches out and grabs my arm. 'You need to tell me what you know. I promise, I can take it.'

I'm not sure he can but I continue anyway. 'Lewis has a thing for silk scarves, like the ones Meg had. He likes to force them into Ellie's mouth to keep her quiet. But that's not all he does . . . He uses them to choke her, Geoff. Ellie says he doesn't hide the fact that he's imagining she's Meg when he does it.'

204

Geoff lets go of my arm. 'Ellie? I thought you said her name was Ioana?'

'When she phones the helpline, Ellie is the name she uses,' I explain, thankful that Geoff has focused on the inconsistencies of my story. Neither of us want to dwell on the horrifying picture I've painted of Meg's bright scarves and the equally colourful marks they left on her neck. 'I didn't know her real name until Lewis blurted it out, and it was Ruth's friend who mentioned she worked at John Lewis. We had pieces of the same jigsaw and we've only recently put them together.'

'So Ruth knows all of this?'

'No, not everything. I couldn't tell her about the scarves and – you know.'

Yes, Geoff knows and he remains tight-lipped as we walk towards the pedestrian crossing that links the Albert Dock to Liverpool One. Whether it's deliberate or not, we're heading towards John Lewis. The more I talk, the more I'm convinced that's where Ruth is now.

The lights change, bringing the traffic to a halt, but Geoff doesn't move. When I put my hand on his back, I can feel his body shaking. As difficult as it was for me and Charlie to visualise the sick games Lewis played, I can't begin to imagine how tortuous it is for Geoff. He had been Meg's protector. I know this better than most because the care and love he showered on his daughter, he extended to me.

'I wish Ruth had never given that stupid interview,' he says at last. 'People keep telling us how strong we are but we're not. We're really not.'

'You have to be,' I tell him. I know it's not what he

wants to hear, but for Ellie's sake, now is not the time for resignation.

When Geoff remains immobilised, I feel panic swelling up inside me.

'Geoff?'

The lights change again and as a lorry thunders past, he turns to face me. I want to look away but I can't pull my gaze from the tears slipping down his cheeks. I've never seen him cry before. I doubt anyone has.

When my mobile vibrates in my pocket, it gives me a start. Geoff has obviously received a message too and checks his phone at the same time. It's a text from Ruth.

I'm with Annabelle at the Royal. Gemma is in theatre and we don't know if she'll make it. I'll keep you posted x

The ice in my veins freezes my body. It's not a bad feeling, it's not a feeling at all. I'm numb and that's how I want to stay.

Geoff releases a strangled cry and jabs a finger at his phone. 'Is this what we have to look forward to for the rest of our lives? This is precisely why I wanted to give Ruth a fresh start in Stratford. This is no way to live, Jennifer. No way at all!'

Geoff storms off through the sandstone turrets that mark the entrance to the Albert Dock. He stumbles on the cobbles and I think he's going to fall, and although he doesn't, he's broken nonetheless. He slumps down on a nearby bench, holding his head in his hands.

I don't know how to respond or even if I can. It's wrong

seeing Geoff like this, and I'm pretty sure he doesn't want me here. I should slope back to the office where I can reply to Ruth's text because, despite being an unwitting spectator to Geoff's anguish, it's Gemma that occupies my mind. Is this something Ryan did to her? If my mistakes, or Ruth's interventions have led to this, then it's not only Gemma's life in the balance but Meg's legacy.

As I continue to watch Geoff, he lifts his gaze to the choppy waters of the docks. He doesn't acknowledge me when I take a seat next to him. I don't say a word. He knows he's not alone, and I hope that's enough.

24

Ruth

The crowded waiting room is filled with the chatter, thumps and crashes of hospital life but it's completely drowned out by the noise in my head. There are so many questions.

I hold onto Annabelle's hand but it's a while since we've spoken. It seems only minutes ago that I'd listened to her phone her ex-husband, Evan, but when a shadow looms over us, I know it's him.

'What's happening?'

'We should be allowed to see her soon,' Annabelle says as she lets go of my hand. We rise to our feet but if she's expecting a comforting embrace from her ex, she's left wanting.

'Why the hell didn't you warn me about him?' he asks through gritted teeth. 'I met him, for Christ's sake. I bought him a pint and we chatted about the footie match like he was normal. Why didn't you tell me he was a psycho, Annabelle?'

'If you were so pally with him, why didn't you work it out?' she snaps back, but her anger is short-lived. 'I didn't want to go behind Gemma's back. She had enough reason to blame me for interfering and I'd just got her back. I thought she was safe.' Her hand flies to her mouth to stifle a sob.

'I should have been told,' insists Evan. 'I would have sorted him out. He'd be the one in hospital right now, not our Gem.'

My mind searches for some shred of comfort to offer but Annabelle's next response to Evan stabs at my heart. 'I thought we were doing the right thing,' she says, her shoulders shaking as she begins to weep.

I'm not sure if Evan puts his arms around his ex-wife to offer comfort or to hide his own tears, but it gives me the excuse to escape before he asks who in their right mind told her any of this was right.

Stumbling through the hospital, I find the exit and hurry outside. Light is fading and sheets of rain blur the edges of a day that's more than ready to submit to the night. Sheltering beneath the narrow roof space where the upper floors overhang the front of the building, I take my first lungful of fresh air for hours, only to find it laced with cigarette smoke. Visitors and patients alike are ignoring the no-smoking signs, so I keep moving.

Taking my mobile from my pocket, I ignore the missed calls and text messages and dial Geoff's number. When it goes to voicemail, I cut the call and stare at the photo of Meg that's set as my wallpaper. It's one of the last photos taken of her laughing and that was only because her brother was tickling her. I blink away the tears and take a breath. It's ten past five and I'm supposed to be on the helpline with Jen.

I was determined to speak to Ellie tonight, whether Jen

approved or not, and I might be interfering in her life right now if fate hadn't intervened. I'd been in John Lewis again when I found out that my recklessness might have cost another mother her daughter's life. And if that isn't a message, I don't know what is. Why did I think I could help any of these girls when I couldn't save my own child?

I can't do this any more.

I try Geoff's number one more time but he's still not picking up, so I try someone else.

'Is she all right?' Jen asks before I have a chance to speak.

'She's in critical care,' I tell her, raising my voice above the sound of rain bouncing off the tarmac. 'The operation went well but she'll need to go back into theatre tomorrow, if she's . . . If she makes it through the night.'

'What happened, Ruth?'

From the brief texts we've exchanged, all Jen knows so far is that Gemma was in a road traffic accident and that it was deliberate. It won't prepare her for what I'm about to say and I can't say it with others close by. I follow the curve of the hospital until it gives up its shelter. I'm soaked within seconds.

'Ryan followed Gemma and her mum to the supermarket and waited in his car for them to come out with their shopping.' I lift my face to the storm but the rain can't wash away the intense hatred I feel for Ryan, and all men like him. 'When Gemma was returning the trolley . . .' I take a breath, but my next words are little more than a whisper. 'He mowed her down, Jen.'

'Shit.'

'The only reason she's still alive is that he chose to do it in a congested car park and he couldn't pick up speed.'

210

'Have the police got him?'

'Yes, thank God. There was a group of workmen close by and one of them smashed the driver's window so he could drag Ryan out before he had a chance to reverse back over her.'

'Oh, Ruth. That's awful,' Jen says. 'How are you coping?'

Her kindness is too much and I squeeze my eyes shut while pinching my nose between a finger and thumb. I press hard until the pain distracts me from deeper agonies. 'It's Gemma's family who are struggling and I'd like to stay here with them, if that's OK with you?'

'Of course it is. Don't worry about anything else. There haven't been any calls yet and I'm fine here on my own.'

'Better than fine,' I correct her. 'You were right to tell me to butt out over Ellie. I've messed up so badly with Gemma. We should have been better prepared. She shouldn't have gone home where he could find her. If I'd taken my time with Gemma and her mum, if I'd been more patient, we wouldn't be in this position.'

'How many times do we tell victims and their families not to blame themselves?'

As many times as those words fail to lessen the guilt, I want to say, but don't. 'I should go,' I tell her after a long pause that neither of us knows how to fill. 'Annabelle's ex has arrived and I should probably go back inside before they start taking out their anger on each other.'

'Is Geoff not with you? I thought he'd be there by now.'

'He must be on his way. I tried phoning him a minute ago but he didn't answer.'

'Oh, OK,' Jen says. There's a pause. 'Ruth, there's something I need to tell you.'

211

From Jen's voice, I know it's not going to be good news. I could hang up, or claim the phone reception is failing, but that isn't who I am, not even the part of me who wants to run away and hide. 'What is it?'

'When you didn't come back from lunch, I panicked and told Geoff you might be in John Lewis. I had to tell him why.'

'Oh God, I'm sorry. I shouldn't have left that to you,' I reply, clocking up another mistake that may or may not be fixable.

Geoff and I have been obstacles in each other's lives for too long and I was beginning to think it was inevitable that we would end up in different places. But I don't want to be alone, and I pray that Meg still holds the power to bind us. We do this together, or not at all. I rub my forehead, pinching the skin above my eyebrows.

'How did he take it?' I dare to ask.

'OK,' Jen says but I can hear the grimace. 'It was a lot to take in.'

I could tell her that Geoff has suffered worse shocks but I dare say Jen knows this already. The hardest by far was the day he walked into our garage but there were others that tested him as a father. Meg punished us both, as if she knew we were going to fail her.

'Why did you marry such a fucking bastard!' Meg had screamed at me once.

I'd only just stepped through the door and it had been a rather pleasant evening up until that point. I'd gone to my pottery class straight from work, anxious to see if the pot I'd been glazing the week before had cracked in the final firing. It hadn't, and the colour of the enamels had come out better than I could have hoped. I'd been looking forward to bringing it home to show it off.

Holding the pot under my arm, I asked, 'What's been going on?'

Meg snorted in response. 'Ask him,' she said, tipping her head towards Geoff who had appeared from the sitting room. Judging by his crossed arms and furrowed brow, my hard-to-rile husband had clearly gone a few rounds in the ring with Meg already.

'Lewis was here when I got home.'

'And?' I asked as I tried to picture them sitting quietly watching TV, but I could tell by Geoff's face that I was being optimistic.

'Nothing! What we do is no one else's business!' Meg yelled. I flinched at the volume.

I told myself not to overreact. She and Lewis had been dating for the best part of a year – if not longer – and it was unrealistic to assume they weren't sleeping together. He hadn't made a return visit to the house since her birthday, despite several invitations, and I'd been hoping their relationship was on the wane. How wrong I'd been.

Although I hadn't seen enough of Lewis to form a proper opinion, it was more than apparent that his influence on our daughter wasn't a good one. As well as the challenges we faced at home, her teachers were concerned Meg wouldn't achieve her target grades unless she made significant improvement. I might have been more supportive, or more forgiving, if Meg's attitude to us – and me in particular – hadn't been so hostile.

Her eyes were ablaze. 'Dad almost killed him.'

'He might as well be dead,' Geoff warned, widening his

213

stance in the sitting room doorway and rocking back on his heels. 'You will not be seeing that miscreant again, Megan.'

Meg had rounded on her father. 'You do not tell me what to do, not any more! Lewis won't let you. You're lucky he didn't have a knife!'

'So he carries knives? That's one more reason to keep him away from you!'

'I said he didn't have one!' Meg yelled back but the fury in her voice had given way to fear. She turned back to me, her angry tears washed away with fresh sobs. 'You can't let him do this. Tell him, Mum.'

When Meg rushed into my arms, I opened them wide. Forgetting about the pot tucked under my arm, it slipped from my grasp as I hugged my girl close. There was a loud crack as it hit the floor, if Meg whispered an apology, I didn't hear it above Geoff's roar.

'Get to your room, Megan! Now!'

As she raced upstairs, I had to decide whether to follow Meg or stay with my husband. I chose to stay, hoping to calm Geoff down and find out exactly what had happened, but he refused to discuss it any further and Meg closed me out completely after that. In her eyes, I'd taken Geoff's side and the frightened little girl I'd glimpsed would never reveal herself to me again. I wish I'd chosen differently. I wish Geoff hadn't reacted as badly, but I suspect he regrets not doing more. My husband reacts on impulse and that's why I hadn't told him about Ellie.

'I'll talk it through with Geoff,' I promise Jen as I look up to find my path along the front of the hospital blocked by a collection of industrial bins. With no way forward, I turn back. 'And I'll make sure you're given the time and space you need to help Ellie in your own way, with no interference from us.'

'I don't know . . .' Jen begins, her faith in herself no match for what I know she can achieve. It makes me so angry sometimes.

I would love to have words with my sister-in-law one day and tell her to stop comparing her youngest daughter to the elder three. If Jen is in a competition, it's with herself. It's the fear of the future versus all those untapped possibilities. She is not a failure by any measure, except her mother's.

'I trust your judgement, Jen.'

'Thank you,' she says quietly.

'You know what to do and I'll leave you to decide whether or not you mention you've spoken to me. Just let her know that she's not alone.'

'I will do.'

'I'd better let you go, but keep me updated.'

'Same goes for you.'

I don't try to phone Geoff again. I'm not sure how much longer my rain-sodden mobile will work, or my cold, numb fingers for that matter. I slip the phone into my pocket and am heading back inside the hospital when ahead of me, I spy a golf umbrella emblazoned with the McCoy and Pace logo floating through the murk of a dying day. Hurrying forward, I catch up with Geoff inside the lobby where he's turning in circles as he tries to work out how to get to the critical care unit. I call his name and it takes a moment for him to recognise me.

'Jesus, Ruth, you're soaked.'

I open my mouth to reply but my words catch and I hug him close before he can see my features dissolve. He doesn't recoil from my wet, limp body and I breathe in the smell of coffee on his breath. He feels deliciously safe and warm.

'It's all gone horribly wrong,' I tell him as I feel myself drowning in despair. Closing my eyes, the photo of Meg from my phone rises in my mind only to morph into an image of two little girls who are offering me a lifeline.

Not everything in my life is going wrong, not if I don't want it to.

Geoff pulls back, his features stoic as he uses the end of his scarf to pat my face dry. 'Let me look after you,' he says.

'I don't want to be looked after.'

'Then perhaps I do.'

As we stare at each other, I cup his face in my hands. I don't offer a smile to hide my pain and neither does he. At long last, it feels like we've fallen into step. 'Maybe it is time to start somewhere new,' I admit.

25

Jen

The news of Ruth's dash to the hospital had trickled through the office during the afternoon, and the staff who are working late talk in hushed whispers. They haven't been told that the 'friend' of Ruth's is one of our callers but they've made the connection and glance over occasionally to offer me sympathetic smiles. I'm reminded of the day of Meg's funeral – lots of uncomfortable silences and half-finished sentences – and it's a comparison I could do without. I refuse to acknowledge the possibility that Gemma won't make it.

So why do I feel like I'm already in mourning? It's as if the spirit of McCoy and Pace is slipping away and it's taking the Lean On Me helpline with it. Geoff had warned me that the stress of running the business and the foundation had become too much for them but I'd refused to listen.

It had never crossed my mind that I'd been worrying about the wrong person. Geoff's warning might have been packaged as concern for his wife but the cries for help were his, and today I finally heard them; not when he yelled at me, but in the silence that followed as we sat at the dock-side being rocked back and forth by the unrelenting storm.

It was a relief when he'd told me to go back to the office. I'd presumed he would go straight to the hospital but he'd been gone over two hours before Ruth rang me. I can only presume he used the time to compose himself so Ruth didn't see the broken man I'd glimpsed earlier. I find myself with another secret to keep.

I sit motionless at the helpline pod, with my mobile propped up next to the landline so that I have both in my sights. Will Ruth phone back to tell me Gemma's condition has deteriorated? Will Ellie phone? I'm not sure I want the responsibility of either of their lives. Geoff was right. This is no way to live.

The business card Sheila gave me at the fundraiser is languishing at the bottom of my bag and I consider sending her an email to arrange that chat. She'd told me I had transferable skills but for all those people I can claim to have helped over the years, there are some notable excep-tions: Meg, now Gemma and, judging by the silent phone, Ellie too. Wouldn't I be better off working for Charlie? The risks of a cleaner destroying lives must be negligible.

As time crawls, the stragglers in the office leave and I'm left marooned in a small island of light with only two lifeless phones for company. No one needs my services tonight; no regular callers; no nervous first-timers looking for someone to validate their fears; no nuisance calls, and no Ellie.

When my mobile vibrates, I snatch it up and answer the call before I've registered who it is.

'Hello, love.'

'I'm on the helpline tonight, Mum,' I warn, but I don't try to end the call. It's an odd sensation and one I haven't felt for a while. I need my mum.

'Is it busy?'

'It can be,' I reply, not willing to admit that I haven't had so much as a wrong number in the last two hours. I don't want Mum to know that the relaunch I'd been hanging all my hopes on has failed to meet our expectations. I don't need that kind of judgement.

'Then I won't keep you,' she says. 'I was worried about you, that's all. I was watching the news about some poor girl being run down in a Tesco's car park – *deliberately*. They didn't say who did it but it's bound to be the husband. You must hear things like that all the time. I don't know how you do it.'

'Me neither.'

'You sound exhausted. Are you pushing yourself too hard? Why don't you and Charlie come over this weekend and let me take care of you for once.'

'Things are a bit up in the air at the moment, Mum, and Charlie's working all hours too. But we will come over soon, I promise.'

'Don't leave it too long,' Mum says. 'Oh, well, I suppose I'd better let you get back to it, but you know where I am if you need me.'

'Thanks, Mum.'

It's only when I've returned my mobile to its position next to the landline that I realise Mum didn't mention my sisters once. I shouldn't be so hard on her. She does try.

As the hands on the Liver Building's clock creep closer to eight o'clock, my throat tightens and I struggle to swallow back the growing lump of fear in my throat. I tell myself Ellie is simply too busy to ring, or she might have discovered a real friend who can give her more than a three-hour slot once a week to hear her problems. Her new confidante might have had better luck persuading her to leave Lewis, and I try to imagine her unpacking her suitcase in a new bedroom that doesn't have silk scarves hanging from the bedpost.

Or she might be with Lewis right now.

He might be forcing her down onto the bed and wrapping a scarf around her neck. As I picture him pulling it tighter, it makes me gag and suddenly I'm choking. As I race across the office, lights flicker on. A combination of streaming eyes and the sudden brightness blinds me and I feel my way into the kitchen. I grab a glass from the drainer and fill it with water. The first mouthful is immediately coughed up but I manage the second and my spluttering eases. I'm refilling the glass when I hear a phone ringing.

The explosion of broken glass in the sink barely registers as I race back to the helpline pods. With my hand extended, I don't slow as I pick up the phone and my body slams into the edge of the desk. I topple forward and I don't have time to straighten up as I press the phone to my ear.

'Hel—' My voice breaks before I can finish the greeting. My weakness angers me and I try again. 'Hello?'

There's no response but I know it's Ellie. I know, because as I take a deep, raspy breath, I can hear its echo on the other end of the line.

'It's Jen,' I tell her in case she hasn't recognised my voice.

As I wait for her to say something, I lift myself off the desk. I've written a checklist of all the things I need to tell her. I want to sound confident despite my plan being very much a

220

work in progress. It includes the job that doesn't actually exist, the shared house Charlie mentioned that he's discovered is full to capacity, and the safety measures that will be useless if Ellie doesn't have a place to stay. She'll be taking huge risks, but she doesn't need to know any of this because there's nothing that could be worse than staying where she is. Dropping into my chair, I wonder if Gemma would agree but I push that thought away. There will be no more mistakes.

I'm about to encourage my silent caller to speak when she finds her voice.

'You told him.'

My thoughts race ahead, faster than I can catch them, but it's not hard to work out what she thinks I've told to who. 'I – I didn't.'

There's a sob and this time the hoarseness in Ellie's voice is undeniable. 'He knows I talked to you. I have never seen him so angry.'

My skin tingles as I recall the anger radiating off Lewis when he promised he would retaliate if I didn't leave him alone. 'No, oh no. We have to get you away from him, Ellie, right now,' I tell her. 'I've found you a job and a place to stay where he won't be able to find you.' My throat is closing up again but I keep going. 'He can't be allowed to touch you again. We can stop this and we will. All you have to do is trust me.'

'Trust you? How can I ever trust you again? You – told – him!'

'I don't know how he found out, truly I don't, but it doesn't matter any more.' There's a panic rising through me that makes the phone slippery in my grasp. I have to keep talking because if I don't, she's going to hang up. She'll never phone again and I don't know what I'll do if that happens. 'At least take my mobile number so that you don't have to wait so long between calls. Do you want to write it down? Have you got a pen?'

'I do not want your number, Jen. I should not talk to you at all!'

'OK, I understand why you feel like that now but I swear, I haven't spoken to him. I can explain everything.'

'I do not think you understand what I say,' Ellie replies, her voice cold enough that icicles form down my spine. 'You could not help Megan and you cannot help me. He said you were a bad friend to her and you are to me too. I never want to speak to you again.'

'Don't go! Please, I can help you. You have to let me try.'

The line goes dead.

Refusing to accept she's gone, I keep the phone pressed to my ear. Yes I was a bad friend to Meg and I've had to live with that but I can do better. I close my eyes. I know it's white noise I hear but my memory resurrects the voice I haven't heard for ten years.

'What do you want?' Meg demanded.

She had answered her mobile on the first ring, which wasn't what I'd been expecting. I'd fallen out of the habit of phoning my cousin, and the only reason I'd broken my resolve to wait for her to ring me was because I knew how worried everyone had become. Plus it was Christmas, which meant my sisters had descended en masse and I was back to sharing a room with Hayley. The McCoys' house would normally be my refuge, but not this year.

'Oh, hi. It's me,' I said.

'Obviously. I saw your name come up.'

'I wasn't sure you'd answer. I thought you might be out with Lewis.'

'I wish.'

I left a pause in the hope that Meg would say more. I didn't want to make it obvious that I was digging for information. 'So, what have you been up to?'

'Not half the things I've been accused of doing,' Meg replied. As an afterthought, she added, 'And a few things you couldn't imagine.'

'Try me.'

The conversation stalled and I couldn't help but wonder where my best friend had gone. There was a time when I'd need to remind Meg to breathe because she talked so fast but I doubted the rasp in her voice was the only thing preventing her from yapping away. The dead air was punctuated by her heavy sigh, adding to my frustration.

'Fine, I'm sure you've got better things to do,' I told her as my patience snapped. 'I only wanted to say hello. I'll see you back in school in a couple of weeks then.'

Despite my threat, I didn't hang up. I didn't need to.

'God, when did you get so snarky? If you must know, I've been nowhere and done nothing since before Christmas. I've been grounded, which is ridiculous. Who grounds a seventeen-year-old? It's embarrassing.'

I tried to sound shocked but I was smiling. At last she was talking to me. 'What have you done now?'

'Oh, this and that,' Meg said brightly, her embarrassment over her punishments replaced by a pride for her crimes.

'Meg, what have you done?' I asked again, in my best impersonation of Ruth.

'I sneaked Lewis into the house while Mum was at her pottery class. I thought Dad would go for a quick round of golf after work but I was wrong. We didn't hear him come in and he had a fit.'

'Please say you weren't having sex?'

'And why would you assume me and Lewis are sleeping together? Are you and Charlie?'

'Erm, no,' I replied, blushing at my own embarrassment instead of finding out more about hers. 'We're taking it slowly because Charlie's a gentleman.'

'And Lewis isn't?'

My heart skipped a guilty beat. 'Is he?'

'He has some restraint, yes.'

'So what made your dad so mad?'

'We were in their bedroom.'

'What? And you seriously expect me to believe you weren't up to something?'

'That's what Dad said,' Meg replied with a half laugh that turned into a cough. 'Oh, Jen, you should have seen his face. It was the exact same shade of purple as Mr Barber's nose, but all over!'

'I bet you weren't laughing at the time,' I said, picturing our old chemistry teacher's nose rather than Geoff's face, or worse still, what he'd seen. 'What did Lewis say?'

'Can't remember. He was mostly a blur as he grabbed his stuff and ran.'

'And your dad let him go?'

'Oh, Dad made a grab for him and I thought for a minute there'd be this big fight but Lewis wasn't stopping for anyone, not even me.'

'What happened then?'

Meg's laughter ebbed away. 'Dad made all kinds of threats, said we couldn't see each other again and that Lewis was a bad influence. I said he couldn't be that bad because he'd stopped himself from thumping an old man who should have had better things to do than walk in on his daughter and her boyfriend. I wish Lewis had thumped him. I'm sick of him. I'm sick of them all.'

'Have you thought that maybe it's for the best? If you're not allowed to go out, you can crack on with your revision. You need to pass your exams if you want to escape to Newcastle,' I reminded her. 'You do still want to escape, don't you, Meg?'

'More than ever,' she said with a sigh that deflated her. 'Would you start coming over again to help?'

'Maybe, if you stop seeing Lewis. You don't have to break up with him,' I added quickly, 'just put things on hold for a while so you can get yourself sorted.'

'I can't stop,' she replied. 'It would kill me.'

'Would it?' I asked. 'You haven't been happy for such a long time, Meg. What goes on between you two? Are you doing drugs?'

Meg cackled loudly. 'Just because Lewis messed around with gangs doesn't mean he's a drug dealer who's got me hooked on crack cocaine or something.'

'Are you sure?'

'Christ, Jen, have you been talking to Mum? I've had this from her and Dad, and even Sean was—' Meg stopped mid-sentence and I could feel her eyes boring into the phone clasped in her hand. 'You have been talking to them. That's why you called. You've been recruited as a spy.'

'I haven't spoken to your mum or your dad,' I answered truthfully. 'And whatever you did want to tell me, it wouldn't go any further. You can trust me, Meg.'

'What about Sean? Have you spoken to him?'

'Only a quick hello the other day.'

'Don't tell me, he just happened to drop by your house.'

It was closer to the truth than I would have liked. 'I'm not spying on you, Meg. I'm worried.'

'Well, don't be. For the record, I might be fucked up but I'm not a junkie.'

The phone had cut off and I was left with a useless piece of plastic pressed against my ear, as I am now.

I replace the helpline phone on the receiver in the faint hope that Ellie will call back, but the minutes slip away and only my shallow breaths break the silence until my mobile begins to vibrate again. It's two minutes past eight and I'm not the only one who's been clock-watching.

Did she phone? X

Ruth doesn't deserve another piece of bad news today, so I craft my reply carefully.

Not for long. Don't worry, I'm going to look after her. Will explain tomorrow x

Won't be in tomorrow. Will catch up FIRST THING Friday x

It's impossible to tell from Ruth's reply if she suspects a problem, but I doubt she could imagine the magnitude.

226

She'll be too distracted by Gemma's fight for life to worry about Ellie's plight. That worry is mine alone.

I return to the kitchen to clean up another mess I've made. As I pick shards of broken glass from the sink, I can't help but wonder how Lewis manages to stop anyone speaking out against him, and not just the women he controls. Someone had warned him that Ellie was talking to me, but who?

I've assumed Ellie doesn't have close friends but she has plenty of colleagues, and perhaps she has confided in someone. Or did she let something slip to a customer? She might have heard a sob story and recommended the helpline. But how would it get back to Lewis? Besides, Ellie was convinced it was me who had opened my big mouth, and the truth is, it was.

I told three people and of those, I can't imagine Ruth or Geoff telling anyone else, or certainly not anyone who would pass on that information to Lewis. Gripping a shard of glass in my hand, I'm only vaguely aware of the drops of blood splashing onto stainless steel to form crimson rivulets in the sink. Have I left myself with only one suspect?

26

'Charlie!'

I yell his name at the top of my voice as the front door closes behind me. What little light had followed me in from the communal corridor retreats, and with a soft click, silence and darkness envelope me.

My body aches and my lungs burn after racing home through pelting rain but the pain doesn't register. And it's only as I'm rummaging through my bag that I realise I'm so cold and wet that I've lost all sense of touch. I pull out the umbrella that I was in too much of a hurry to use and grab my phone, but the touchscreen refuses to respond to my white-tipped fingers. My rain-soaked hair drips into my eyes as I feel my way towards the kitchen where I rub my hands vigorously on a tea towel to bring them back to life.

Trying the phone again, I see I've missed a message from Charlie. He's made a detour to the Baltic Market on his way home to pick up some street food for dinner. I'm

228

tempted to hunt him down before my anger has a chance to cool, but he doesn't say how long he'll be and, chances are, I'll be hurrying downstairs while he's travelling up in the lift.

I have no choice except to wait, but I don't turn on the lights or slip out of my wet, woollen jacket. The rainwater running off me hits the tiles, the drips turning to splashes as a puddle forms around my feet. Leaning forward to rest my elbows on the counter, I drop my head into my hands. I'm shivering as well as shaking by the time the door opens and borrowed light floods the room.

The light intensifies as the kitchen spotlights come on and I'm momentarily blinded. When I straighten up and my vision adjusts, I see that Charlie had made it halfway across the apartment before stopping in his tracks. He's carrying a collection of brown paper bags that are sodden and, much like me, threaten to disintegrate at any moment.

'You told him.' Despite my shaking voice, my anger sharpens my words to lethal points.

'Told who, what?'

'Your mate, Lewis.'

The shoulders of Charlie's puffer jacket sag. 'Are we back to this again?' he says. 'I thought something bad had happened. I was expecting you to say that girl in hospital had died.'

'You mean the girl who was mowed down by the man who'd been telling everyone he couldn't live without her? The one who said he was a victim?' I haven't spoken to Charlie since Ruth updated me and I see him flinch.

'People like that don't care about anyone else, Charlie,' I continue. 'There's no room in their hearts for anyone except themselves; not the women they claim to love, or their sick mothers for that matter.'

Charlie's features harden. 'Ellie phoned again.'

'Yes, even though she'd been warned not to. Thankfully Lewis hadn't quite choked the voice from her, though it sounded like he'd come pretty close.'

'Jesus.'

'I promised Ellie I wouldn't tell a soul and now that she knows I have, she isn't going to call again. And do you know what? I don't blame her!'

Charlie drops his head and stares at the takeaway bags hanging limply at his side. 'This food is going to get cold,' he says eventually. 'I'll put it in the oven.'

'Fuck the food! I'm talking about a young woman who's being systematically abused by our old friend. He's going to destroy her one way or another, and unless I can stop him, he's going to walk away again. And do you know why that is?' I ask. 'Because there are enough idiots out there who think boys will be boys. Apparently some concerned citizen warned Lewis that Ellie has been phoning the help-line. I can't imagine how they justified it to themselves, but perhaps you can tell me.'

Charlie places the paper bags carefully on the kitchen counter that marks the boundary between us. I step back and as I do, my sopping wet ballet shoes slip on the puddle I've made. I grab hold of the handle on the fridge door to save myself but as I straighten up, I'm still not sure of my footing.

'Why do you always have to assume that I'm going to let you down?' Charlie asks. 'Sometimes it feels like you believe there's an inherent evil in *all* men.'

230

'Maybe it's an occupational hazard,' I snap back.

'So you think I've been up to something behind your back?'

'We all have our secrets, Charlie.'

For a fleeting moment, I want him to ask what secrets I've been keeping. I want him to admit we both know why Meg died hating me. I'm tired of holding onto my shame and Charlie looks exhausted too.

The anger that had kept me warm burns itself out and my teeth chatter. 'I'm not suggesting you told Lewis deliberately,' I continue. 'Maybe you said something to Jay or Meathead and they mentioned it to him. I don't know. That's why I'm asking.'

'But you're not asking, are you?' Charlie says. 'And as I recall, you *told* me I was the one who warned Lewis – the minute I stepped through the door.'

He waits for me to pose my accusation as a question this time, but I'm not sure I can. I don't want it to be Charlie, but if I don't ask, he can avoid answering. What if he's counting on that? What if he is hiding something? Why can't I trust him? I take a deep breath.

'Did you?'

Charlie's jaw twitches. He's pulling the scarf from around his neck as he turns away. 'No, Jen, I didn't,' he says. He sits down on the armchair so he's facing me. He hasn't taken off his jacket. He hasn't decided if he's staying. 'Next question.'

'Have you spoken to Jay or Meathead about Ellie?'

'You asked me to find out all I could about her, so yes, I've talked to them. If you're asking if I said anything that would link Ellie to you or to the helpline, then no, I haven't,' he says. 'But of course, they won't have forgotten your little trick of sending friend requests, so I don't suppose it's beyond the realms of possibility that they've made a connection, although God knows why they'd want to share that information with Lewis. Other than liking an occasional post, I don't think either of them have had any further contact with him.' Charlie has twisted his scarf into a ball and lets it drop to the floor before pressing his back against the chair. 'Satisfied?'

'I had to ask.'

'No, Jen, you didn't. You really didn't,' Charlie replies, his voice hollow.

The fight has left me too and I feel foolish. I creep out of the kitchen and head for the sofa so we can start this conversation over, except as I sit down, he stands up. My heartbeat skitters: is he going to walk out?

'Is it too late to say I'm sorry?'

Rather than answer, Charlie shakes out of his jacket and disappears into the bathroom. He's gone a while and I'm grateful for the space he gives both of us. I can't get my head around everything that's happened today. I'd gone to work this morning feeling positive. There were problems to tackle but I thought we were on our way to solving them, and then Ruth had gone missing, and like a stack of dominoes, we had been toppled one by one. There's no one left standing to pick the others up.

When Charlie reappears, he's carrying a fluffy white bath towel and his damp hair is sticking up where he's rubbed it. 'You need to dry off,' he says.

From his tone, I'm expecting him to drop it into my lap but he holds out his hand and invites me to stand. I close my eyes as he strokes the towel across my face and I lean into his hand. 'I am sorry,' I repeat.

'I know,' he says. 'I expect I'm at the tail end of what has been an exceptionally shitty day.'

'It's no excuse.'

'No, it's not,' he replies as he unbuttons my jacket to reveal sodden clothes where the rain has trickled down the collar. There's only a small section around the waistband of my grey work trousers that isn't wet. He attempts a smile as he sizes up the problem, looking from me to the towel. 'I'll get your bathrobe.'

I stop him before he can move. 'No, let's work with what we have,' I tell him: I don't want him to leave my sight again.

While Charlie hangs my houndstooth jacket over the desk chair, I peel off my damp clothes down to my underwear, then rub the towel over my wet skin until it's sodden. I'm staring at the rusted smears of blood on the towelling when Charlie returns to me.

'You're hurt,' he says, taking a step back so he can work out where the blood has come from.

I show him my injured hand from the broken glass at work. It's the first time I've taken a proper look and the gash running down my index finger looks nasty. My hands have been too wet to let it scab over but it's stopped bleeding.

'It's not as bad as it looks,' I tell him as I tuck the towel around me and sit on the sofa, pulling Charlie down next to me. 'I'll clean myself up later. I don't want to do anything else until I've worked out what went wrong today, and how I can fix it.'

'With my help, assuming you still trust me,' Charlie replies as he puts both his arms around me.

I feel him tense as he draws my ice-cold body towards him, while in contrast, I soak up his warmth. With my head on his chest and Charlie's chin resting on my damp hair, my shivers subside.

'It wasn't me, Jen.'

I'm tempted to ask Charlie to repeat exactly what he's said about Ellie and to who but it's time to follow my instincts, which should have exonerated Charlie from the start. 'I know, I believe you.'

'But?'

'How did he find out? The only other people who knew about Ellie were Ruth and Geoff.'

'No,' Charlie corrects me. 'The only people you told, other than me, were Ruth and Geoff. You were quick to assume that I'd mentioned it to someone. What if they had? Have you asked?'

'No, I came straight home,' I say, pressing my head against his chest. I can hear Charlie's heart thumping as he relives the moment he walked through the door and I let the accusations fly, but his breathing remains steady, giving me hope that he will forgive me. 'They were hardly going to tell Lewis, and who do they know who might have passed it on?'

'Sean?'

'If they'd told Sean, the first person he'd speak to was me, not someone who'd snitch to Lewis. It doesn't make sense.'

'No, it doesn't,' Charlie agrees. 'But you might want to ask all of them.'

'I will, but not tonight. Ruth was still at the hospital when I spoke to her last, and I'm dreading telling her what's happened with Ellie. I can't say I'm looking forward to speaking to Geoff either,' I add as my mind flicks back to the last time I'd seen him. 'Ruth hadn't got around to telling him about Ellie, so it was left to me to do it after she went missing at lunchtime. He took it really badly.'

'Bad enough to do something on impulse?'

I'm about to dismiss the possibility but then I remember the hours Geoff was missing. Was there time for him to hunt Lewis down, and for Lewis to take it out on Ellie? It might explain why she didn't phone until very late. I lift my head but it's a struggle to meet Charlie's gaze. I should have trusted him. 'But how would he know where to find Lewis?'

Charlie shrugs. 'You did it, and Geoff's known for a while that he's in Liverpool. If I was him, I'd want to know where he was.'

'But if we're right, he's the one who's put Ellie in more danger,' I say, shaking my head. 'How do I tell him that?'

Charlie's body stiffens only this time it's not because of the cold. 'You could try storming into his office and accusing him.'

Like my anger before it, a wave of self-pity washes over me and I'm powerless to hold it back. Tears burn my frozen cheeks. 'I hate myself sometimes,' I mumble. 'I can't get anything right. I messed up with Meg, then Ellie, and now you.'

'You haven't messed up with me,' Charlie whispers, tightening his arms around me. 'And whatever's going on with Ellie will sort itself out.'

235

As I wipe my nose, I note that he doesn't correct me about Meg. There's no second chance to save her and that thought brings a fresh wave of sobs. 'I don't know what to do,' I cry.

'Why don't you start by having a hot shower to warm yourself up? And in the meantime, I'll heat up the food. We have halloumi fries, katsu curry and gyoza dumplings for supper, plus Daim Bar cheesecake for afters,' Charlie says a little too brightly as he wriggles free and leaves me to wipe away my tears with the damp towel.

Deprived of his body heat, I'm shivering again as I watch Charlie scoop up the scarf he had left on the floor. As it unfurls, my mind plays tricks and the heavy wool becomes flowing silk. Ellie could barely speak tonight and I think of all those times Meg complained of a sore throat. I missed the signs then but I see them now.

'I have to find Ellie. One of these days he's going to go too far.'

Charlie sees the fear in my eyes as I stare at the scarf so he throws it out of sight onto the desk. He's rubbing his palms on his jeans as he comes back to me. 'What do you mean, you'll find her?' he asks.

'I should have done it earlier but I'd wanted Ellie to come to me. That's not going to happen now. She said she won't phone the helpline again and I believe her.' I can see from Charlie's furrowed expression that he wants to talk me out of the decision I'm reaching but my mind is made up. 'I'm going to take up Ruth's search.'

27

Jen

My head throbs and my eyelids have acquired a sandpaper backing that scratches my eyes each time I blink. I couldn't sleep last night because I was too busy rehearsing multiple conversations in my head. I want to tell Lewis that I won't run away this time; I want to convince Ellie that I can help her escape; and I need to apologise to Charlie over and over until he forgives me. There's also the news I have to break to Ruth about Ellie, but first I have to confront Geoff – and that's the conversation I haven't been able to get quite right. My stomach is in knots as I knock on his office door.

'I wasn't sure if you'd be in today,' I tell him, keeping hold of the door handle.

Geoff rearranges the scattered papers on his desk rather than look up at me. 'I'd be a spare part at the hospital.'

'Has there been any news on Gemma?'

'The surgeon's reviewing her condition this morning. Ruth said she'll text you as soon as they know something.

Sorry, I should have told you,' he says as if he's just remembered the message and hadn't been avoiding me since his arrival half an hour ago.

I step quietly into his office and when the door closes, Geoff lifts his head. He was hoping I'd left. 'Can I have a word?' I ask.

Twirling a pen in his fingers, Geoff nods towards the chair at the side of his desk. I sit down and fold my hands in my lap. I cast my gaze out the window as if captivated by the view, and it is impressive. Although I have my back to the rising sun, I know the eastern sky is on fire because I see its reflection. The Three Graces have a pink blush that matches Geoff's cheeks.

'I'm sorry about shouting at you yesterday,' he says. 'It was quite a day.'

'And I'm sorry for upsetting you. It can't have been easy for you to hear something like that.' I spare us both by not repeating what that something was, but I can't avoid the subject completely. 'Actually, it's because of Ellie that I'm here.'

'Oh.'

I notice beads of sweat appearing on Geoff's brow. It would be so much easier talking to Ruth but I can't have this conversation with her – I can barely bring myself to discuss it with Geoff.

'How is she?' he continues brightly, in an attempt to fool us both that this is a normal conversation. 'Ruth said she phoned again last night.'

'Things didn't exactly go to plan,' I tell him as I pull at the edges of the plaster on my injured finger.

'But you did speak to her?'

'Only long enough for her to tell me that Lewis found out she's been talking to me, and that she won't be calling again. I need to work out how he knew, Geoff.'

I leave a pause, hoping for an admission, but Geoff's first concern is for Ellie's welfare. 'Did she say how Lewis reacted? Does she think she's in danger?'

'She was too angry to talk,' I reply. I don't mention her rasping voice. 'She trusted me, Geoff. She expected me to keep our calls confidential, but I didn't. One of my first thoughts was that Charlie had said something to one of his old school friends and they'd passed it on, but he's adamant he didn't, and I believe him.'

Again there's a pause that Geoff could fill. I taste bile at the back of my throat. I'm scared that I've got it wrong again but I can't back out of this now. 'Whatever happened, I'm sure it was done with the best intentions,' I begin, 'but if Lewis has a way of finding out what we're doing, I need to know how. I was wondering if perhaps you'd spoken to him. You were upset yesterday, and I wouldn't blame you for wanting to hunt him down . . .'

Geoff's grip on his pen becomes a stranglehold. 'I couldn't possibly tell you what I've wanted to do to Lewis for a very long time,' he says at last. He swivels his chair so he can share in the beauty of the sunrise but the skyline has dulled to grey and only his complexion remains ablaze. 'He took my daughter from me and I let him. My precious girl would still be here today if I'd fought harder.'

'So you did do something yesterday.'

Geoff's laugh is as bitter as the taste in my mouth. 'I had to, Jen.' His shoulders slump as he turns to face me again. 'I've made things worse, haven't I?'

I want to tell him that he's not the only one but I leave Geoff to do the talking.

'We both know there's no point talking reason with Lewis but I wouldn't be human if I hadn't reacted.'

'How did you know where to find him?'

Geoff resumes twirling the pen between his fingers. 'When Sean told me he was back here living with his mother, I got in touch with someone I know at the council. I didn't think through what I might do once I had his address, but there you have it. I went to his flat and I had it out with him,' he says, straightening up.

'What did you say to him?'

'It doesn't matter now,' Geoff replies, and whatever he's recalling makes him squirm. 'Believe me when I say I feel sorry for this girl, Jennifer, but there are other people I have to put first. I see the damage all of this is doing to Ruth.'

'I know,' I'm forced to admit.

His features soften. 'And it's taken its toll on you too.'

I feel self-conscious as he scrutinises my face. I know my eyes are puffy but there could be worse battle scars. 'Imagine what it's doing to Ellie.'

Geoff winces. 'I know. But look at what happened to Gemma. You can't make Ellie's choices for her because if you do, you'll find yourself taking responsibility for the consequences, and it won't end well. With any luck, this girl will come to her senses and move away.'

'She doesn't have the means to do that. He's made sure she's dependent on him. He's trapped her.'

Geoff holds up his hands to silence me. 'Then she can find another helpline and another charity to come to her aid, because we can't. She's said she doesn't want your

240

help and you have to accept that. Please don't repeat my mistake and do something stupid. I know it's hard to step away but that's what we have to do – all of us.'

I can't look at him. 'Fine.'

'Promise me, Jennifer.'

I lift my chin and my eyes follow. 'If she phones the helpline again, I'm not going to turn her away.'

Geoff's eyes soften. 'I wouldn't expect you to.'

'Well, I know you're busy so I'll leave you to it,' I tell him. He doesn't object when I stand.

As I leave Geoff's office, I take a cleansing breath and allow myself to relax. I'd been dreading talking to him but it's done now. I don't want to defy Geoff but I won't be stepping away. I will find Ellie.

28

Ruth

My return to work on the Friday after Gemma's assault is excruciating for many reasons. The covert stares from the staff. The pods in the corner of the office that remind me of my failures. The conversation I'm putting off with Jen.

'Are you going to tell her?' asks Geoff as Jen walks quickly past our office without looking up.

'When I get a moment,' I reply. It takes a lot of effort to keep my tone light.

'She's better off hearing it today. At least she'll have the weekend to mull things over.'

I scrape my nails against my lips. I don't know how I've managed to stop myself from ripping off the false nails to get to the raw flesh but I take it as a good sign. I've made my decision and all I need to do now is put it into action. I'd promised Jen we'd have a chat first thing this morning but I haven't seen her sit down at her desk for more than five minutes. I suspect she knows what's coming.

'Oscar's going to be here within the hour,' Geoff persists.

'We need to speak to him together, my love, and I'd rather you had everything clear in your mind before we do so.'

'Fine,' I hiss, pushing back my chair and standing so fast that Geoff flinches.

My husband stands too, cutting me off before I reach the door. 'I know this is hard but you're doing the right thing.' He places his hand gently on the small of my back in what he thinks is a show of support. It feels more like a shove and I bristle.

This must be how Meg felt because she often reacted to my gentle encouragements in the same way. I'd take time out of my day for us to be together, hoping she'd open up to me, but she misinterpreted my every move.

'I know you're only doing this because you're convinced I'll sag off school,' she'd said to me when I'd given her a lift one morning.

'And there I was thinking I was doing something nice for you. Why are you so angry with me all the time, Meg? What have I done?'

She laughed at the stupidity of my question, as if my crimes were obvious, but I honestly didn't know. Was it unreasonable to push her to keep up with her studies? She was the one desperate to go to university, and in spite of all our difficulties, I wanted her to achieve that dream. OK, perhaps I was partly motivated by the prospect of her moving away while Lewis stayed in Liverpool but still, I didn't understand what I was doing wrong.

As I drove up to the school, I watched a swell of students pouring down the road and through the gates. Their uniforms looked tired and tattered after a year of academia but not so the children whose exuberance would continue to grow as the summer holidays approached. Only the sixth formers remained aloof and uninterested. Excused from wearing uniforms, they set themselves apart and I wondered if they confused their parents as much as Meg confused me.

I parked the car but, not ready to lose my daughter to the masses, I grabbed her arm. 'Talk to me, sweetheart. I know you're having night terrors. What scares you so much?'

She shrugged. 'My final exams are coming up. Everyone's freaking out.'

I chose not to remind her that she wouldn't be panicking so much if Lewis had left her alone long enough to revise properly. 'It's more than that,' I said.

Meg responded by pressing her chin to her chest, hiding her mouth behind the folds of her cowl-necked jumper. She made a move for the door handle but I pulled her back, my grip on her arm fierce.

'I want to help. Please, tell me what to do!'

Panic made the air thick around us and her voice was husky when she yelled, 'Let me go!'

'Please, Meg. We can't go on like this. I know you're not happy, and I'm willing to do whatever it takes to make things right. So is your dad,' I told her quickly before she could wrestle free. 'You might think you love Lewis but look what he's doing to you. It's no relationship, Meg.'

'Like you'd know,' she said, spitting the words back at me. 'You never made Dad happy and look what happened there! Oh, on second thoughts, let's not look. Let's pull my relationship apart.'

'Please, Megan,' I said but she had flung open the door and I was talking to the back of her head.

Ugly curses filled the air in her stead – some from Meg, but one or two came from the poor boy she almost knocked to the ground as she pushed through the throng. I jumped out of the car and tried to call her back but my heart wasn't in it. She wasn't going to listen. Meg did things her way.

Now it's me setting my own course and, like Meg, I'm about to knock someone down in the process. I shrug off my husband as my daughter had done to me. 'Don't, Geoff.'

He looks at me, hurt. 'I'm only trying to help.'

'Then let me go.'

Geoff goes to say something else but thinks better of it, and I leave the office without any more words of encouragement. Jen is coming from the photocopier with a stack of papers in her arms. I catch a glimpse of the Lean On Me strapline.

'Busy?' I ask.

'I thought I'd replenish our stocks. We need more information packs ready for Christmas.'

'They can wait,' I say. 'Do you fancy that chat now?'

I keep my expression neutral but Jen tenses nevertheless. She follows me into the conference room and we choose seats on opposite sides of the table. I should have suggested we make a drink first, my lips are parched, but I can't keep putting this off.

'Do you want me to arrange some flowers for Gemma?' she asks.

'Not while she's in critical care. Maybe later on.'

The word 'maybe' sticks in my throat. The latest operation was successful but Gemma's injuries are extensive and she remains in a drug-induced coma. I'm praying she'll survive but it's too much to hope that she'll make a full recovery. I would love to talk more to Jen about my guilt and my regrets but this conversation isn't about what I've done, it's about what I need to do going forward. There have been too many mistakes and it's time to cut my losses.

'Geoff told me about going to see Lewis and what happened with Ellie,' I begin.

'I thought he might,' Jen says. 'Do you know exactly what he said to Lewis? He didn't want to talk much about it yesterday.'

'I'm pretty sure Geoff wouldn't have mentioned it at all if you hadn't asked,' I say. 'And no, he didn't go into the details but he's mortified about Ellie.' I stop and shake my head. 'What's happening, Jen? Why is it all going wrong?'

She leans forward. 'We will make it right again, Ruth. I know what Geoff thinks and I'm sure he's been bending your ear about retiring again but we can't give up now. Especially now.'

'Geoff hasn't pushed me into this decision,' I tell her, my tone growing firm. 'It's not been an easy one to take but I hope you'll respect my wishes.'

'So it is a decision? You're going to retire?' Jen says slowly.

'When I said Lewis couldn't cause me any more pain, I was wrong. I'm tired of fighting to keep other people's children safe. I was never as good at my job as I claimed to be, you only have to ask Annabelle.'

'She said that?'

'No, she's too busy blaming herself right now, but I'm angry at me on her behalf. It's time to admit defeat before the killer blow. Geoff and I are looking for an investor to buy out McCoy and Pace, and in the meantime, we're going to wind down the foundation and close the helpline.'

'When?'

'Soon. Our success with the Whitespace project has put us in a strong position to sell the company, and it would be better if we didn't have loose ends like the helpline getting in the way of closing a deal. I'm not suggesting we do it overnight but it will be a matter of weeks. I don't see the point in drawing this out.'

I have to stop. There's only so long I can ignore the tears welling in Jen's eyes. I have tissues in my pocket at the ready and I hand one to Jen, keeping the other for myself.

'I know it looks like I'm abandoning you,' I continue, 'but Geoff and I are going to make sure your position in the company is secured. With less of your time taken up with the foundation, we could establish a new role for you and I'll make sure that, whoever the buyer is, they recognise your potential. Or if that's not what you want, I can phone around our contacts and help you find the perfect job that will lead to you being a counsellor one day. I haven't forgotten about my promise to pay for your studies.'

Jen shreds the tissue clutched in her hands. 'I'm not bothered about what happens to me,' she says angrily. 'It's Ellie I care about: we can't turn our backs on her.'

'I'm not turning my back on her. We'll send out a press release to local news announcing the closure of the helpline. It'll give people fair warning and it might prompt Ellie to call back. There's still time.'

Jen looks over my shoulder and through to the office. 'Are you sure about that?'

I follow her gaze and watch Geoff greeting Oscar Armitage with an enthusiastic handshake.

'Isn't that one of our competitors?' Jen asks. 'Or is it my new boss?'

'We're only sounding him out.' As I turn back to Jen, I can see she's disappointed in me. I don't blame her. I'm disappointed in myself. 'I know it must seem like we're moving fast but what else can I do? I've been ignoring two beautiful granddaughters because I'd rather immerse myself in other people's pain than confront my own. I've been too scared of losing them to love them as I should.'

Jen doesn't respond. The worst is over, and I feel myself relaxing for the first time since telling Geoff of my decision. It's time to feel some of the excitement I see in my husband's face as he passes the conference room and gives me a nod. I should go and greet our visitor but I don't want to leave Jen. With a twist of my stomach, I realise I'll be leaving her soon anyway and I force myself to stand. I wish Jen would get up too so I can give her a hug but she remains seated as I move to the door.

'You should have heard her the other night, Ruth,' Jen says before I can escape. 'She's terrified of him and OK, maybe he's already made a start at stripping away her soul like he did to Meg, but she's not dead yet. The fight isn't over.'

'We can't—'

'Yes, we can,' Jen corrects me. Her chin is up, her tears dried and I envy her composure. 'I've no intention of counting down to the last gasps of the helpline. Ellie won't phone back but it doesn't matter because I'm meeting Charlie at lunchtime outside John Lewis and we're going

248

to search until we find her. If you meant what you said about not turning your back on her, you could come too.'

I hesitate before I reply. 'Geoff and I are taking Oscar out to lunch.'

Jen hears the regret in my voice. 'But you do want to.'

The thrill of anticipation I'd been hoping for earlier arrives as a flutter in my chest but I do my best to smother it. I have to stop protecting others and protect myself. 'I can't, Jen.'

29

Jen

I could tell by the way Ruth avoided looking at me all morning that she was going to pull the plug on the helpline. I'm not angry. If anything, I admire her for having the courage to know when it's time to quit. Who'd have thought I'd be the one to keep fighting? Not me, that's for sure.

I don't look like a warrior as I check my reflection in the harsh light of the Ladies. The whites of my eyes are bright pink and the makeup I'd hoped would brighten my pallid complexion this morning has been washed away by my tears. How am I going to convince Ellie that I can still help her?

By the time I've dabbed concealer beneath my eyes and smeared colour across my lips, I'm running late. I hold my nerve and choose the shortest route to John Lewis along the Strand and I'm sweaty and flustered by the time I find Charlie waiting at the foot of the steps that lead to Chavasse Park.

'Sorry I'm late,' I say as I rise on tiptoe to kiss his cheek.

He pulls away and squints at my bleary eyes. 'Has something happened?'

'Not with Gemma,' I tell him quickly. 'But she might be our last official client.'

'Ah. They're closing the helpline?'

Charlie and I had had a long conversation last night. After Geoff's confession, it mostly involved me grovelling for forgiveness again, but we had spent some time speculating about what would happen next. I suppose it was about time I was right about something. 'Can we not talk about it now?' I ask, glancing at the yawning mouth of the store's main entrance.

'I can't say I'm looking forward to this,' Charlie says. His eyes are as bloodshot as mine.

'You don't have to come with me.'

'Yes, I do.'

I link his arm gratefully and we step out of the bleak October afternoon and into the sparkling department store. We stop close to the escalators and check the list of departments spread over four floors. I know which one I'm heading for first. Charlie reminded me last night how Lewis had met his girlfriend when buying a gift for his mum.

'I'll make a start in the beauty department. We need to think presents for a middle-aged mum in poor health.' I stop to bite my lip. 'Although there's always the possibility that Ellie, or should I say Ioana, has moved departments.'

'So basically we need to check every floor.'

I scrunch my nose. 'I'm afraid so.'

Charlie scans the list again. He's not a seasoned shopper

and hadn't realised how much ground we have to cover. 'In an hour?'

'Yes.'

'Don't build your hopes up, Jen,' he says in a way that doesn't inspire confidence.

'We can do this,' I promise. 'And if you do spot her, call me. We have to take this slowly, Charlie. I don't want Ellie to feel like she's being ambushed.'

We agree to take alternate floors and, leaving Charlie on the ground floor, I step onto the escalator. I look over my shoulder to see which direction he's taken but Charlie is exactly where I left him. I want to tell him to get on with it, but I smile. I like the idea of him watching over me.

Growing up in a household where I was often overlooked, there was a time when nobody noticed me at all. Meg would tell me I didn't know how lucky I was but I don't think she ever appreciated how much her parents cared about her. Whenever they tried to intervene, Meg saw it as interference, and it was Ruth who bore the brunt of her daughter's anger.

I'd spotted them once when I was on the bus. I was standing at the front with an annoying group of Year 7s and I'd had the perfect view. Ruth had dropped Meg off close to the school but then jumped out of the car to call after her daughter. I could tell by the way Meg crashed through everyone that they'd been arguing.

When the bus came to a halt and the doors opened, I was swept along by the hordes. I would have to pass Ruth's car to get to the main gates and schoolbags thumped into me as my pace slowed. I didn't want to be drawn into their latest argument. I could see a few of the kids ahead of me rubbernecking as they waited for Meg to react to her mum's calls. Meg didn't disappoint. She held her head high as she turned to face Ruth one last time.

'If you really want to help then leave me the fuck alone!'

I flinched but Ruth didn't. She'd received worse from her daughter by this point. 'Your father will be here to pick you up later so you'd better be waiting!'

Meg lifted her arm to give her mum the finger. I'm not sure that Ruth saw her because she had covered her face with her hands and slumped back against the open car door. I could hear her sobs as I crept past, and thought I'd got away without her seeing me, but Ruth gave a sniff and lifted her head.

'Jen?' she called out. 'Have you got a minute?'

'Sure,' I replied as I glanced up the road to check if Meg had spotted me too. She was gone.

Ruth gestured for me to get into the car but I took my time sliding into the passenger seat. Once the doors were closed, Ruth wiped her eyes again and gave me a watery smile.

'Thanks for stopping, Jen. I just . . . I don't know what to do. I try to reach out but Meg only hates me all the more,' Ruth said, her voice catching. Her mascara was running but she didn't seem to care. 'We tried accepting Lewis but he deliberately avoiding us. It's obvious he isn't making her happy. I don't understand. What does she see in him?'

I explored the corded edges of my backpack resting on my lap. 'We don't see much of them these days. If Meg's out, she'd rather spend time alone with him than with us,' I replied as if it were a simple choice my cousin had made, when in reality we all had our reasons for letting the distance widen.

Ruth picked at the ragged edge of a fingernail. 'She's under the illusion she'll scrape through her exams with some last minute cramming, but I wouldn't be surprised if Lewis is deliberately sabotaging her studies so she doesn't leave for Newcastle. Geoff's grounded her more times than I care to count but she always manages to escape,' Ruth said. Looking towards the school gates, she added, 'She needs someone with a calming influence. You should come around more, Jen. We miss you.'

Tears had stung my eyes and even now, all these years later, I find myself sniffing them back as I step off the escalator.

I start scanning faces immediately, hoping for that sudden rush of recognition, although I'm not sure if it's Meg or Ellie I'm hoping to see. Charlie and I had looked again at the photo Lewis had posted on Facebook, and even with the benefit of a bottle of wine, neither of us could see the resemblance that has Lewis fixated.

There was a time when I would see Meg everywhere. My heart would leap whenever I glimpsed the back of her head and I'd have to stop myself from racing up and hugging a complete stranger. In my heart I knew she was dead. There was no last chance to tell her I was still her friend.

I'm here as Ellie's friend now and I weave my way through womenswear to begin a systematic search of the cosmetic counters. I start with Dior.

There's a blonde woman behind the counter and she smiles as I pick up a sample bottle of Poison and squirt my wrists.

'It's quite a provocative fragrance,' the shop assistant tells me. 'One of our most popular.'

'Yes,' I say as I breathe in the familiar scent and wonder if it had drawn Lewis to the counter too. 'A friend of mine wore it all the time.'

'Are you shopping for a gift?'

I set down the scent bottle and chew my lip as I consider my next move. I'm not supposed to draw attention to our search but the clock is ticking in more ways than one, and the subtle approach didn't work for Ruth. 'Sort of,' I reply. 'I was here the other day and the young woman I talked to was really helpful. I promised her I'd call back.'

'And she worked on this counter?'

I give the sales assistant a broad smile that neither denies nor confirms her supposition. 'I think her name was Ioana.'

The woman's brow furrows. 'If it's who I'm thinking of, she doesn't work on this floor. She's downstairs in the gift department.'

'Of course she is!' I say as I turn on my heels. Remembering my manners, I shout a thank you as I race back the way I'd come, my heart pounding.

Weaving dangerously between shoppers, I clatter down the escalators. Any remaining thoughts of being inconspicuous have been swept away by my excitement, along with my nerves regarding what I should say to Ellie. I don't care how illogical it sounds, this is as close as I'll get to redeeming myself with Meg.

My eyes dart left to right as I zigzag through the aisles in search of anyone in the black John Lewis uniform. I spy a shop assistant, a man this time, and I rush towards him.

'Do you know Ioana?'

He almost drops a heavy paperweight onto the glass shelf he was rearranging. 'What the—' He recovers quickly and straightens up to greet me with a fixed smile. 'Sorry, do I know . . . ?'

'Ioana,' I repeat.

He's taller than I am and looks over the shelves. 'I think I saw her over by the scented candles. Would you like me to—?'

'No, thanks. I'm fine.'

I can't believe I'm heading back over to where Charlie and I first entered the shop. We could have walked straight past her and not realised. Remembering we're supposed to let each other know if we pick up her trail, I check my phone. There's no message to say Charlie has moved on to another floor so he must be here somewhere. I send him a message to meet me by the candles but when I look up, I can see the top of his head over by the cookware. I guess he's reading my message because a moment later he peeks over the display of bright orange Le Creuset pots. When he spots me, he beckons me over.

Choosing a circuitous route, I skirt close to the scented candle displays. There isn't a shop assistant in sight so I carry on towards Charlie.

'She's on this floor,' I say in a hushed tone.

'I know,' he whispers back. 'I've seen her.'

'What? Why didn't you tell me? Where is she?' I ask as I spin around.

'She went into the back a minute ago.'

He points to a set of double doors marked staff only, and we begin an anxious wait that gives my nerves a chance to make a reappearance.

'Are you sure about this, Jen?' Charlie tries one last time.

I don't take my eyes off the doors. 'Yes.'

I'd prefer to continue our wait in silence but Charlie fidgets with nerves. 'You smell nice, by the way.'

'What does that mean?' I snap.

He raises an eyebrow. 'It means, you smell nice,' he says slowly.

'As nice as Meg?'

With his hands shoved in his pockets, Charlie wafts his open jacket to create a cooling breeze while a blush burns his cheeks. 'I don't remember.'

I let the comment slide and we resume our stakeout. With my full concentration on the sealed doors, I don't notice as someone approaches from behind.

'Did you find her?' asks the shop assistant I'd spoken to earlier. He's polite but his voice is louder than entirely necessary and he doesn't appear concerned that he's given us both a start.

'Not yet,' I mutter, feeling Charlie's eyes boring into me. 'But it's fine. Thanks for your help.'

'No problem. Let me know if you need anything else.'

When he's wandered off, Charlie continues to glare at me. 'You've been asking for her? I thought we were undercover?'

'I know, but . . .' My voice trails off as I see our quarry emerge from the staff doors. I watch in horror as our annoyingly helpful shop assistant walks over to her and points in our direction. 'No, no, no.'

Even if Ioana doesn't know what I look like, my eyes widening in panic will give me away. I turn my back on her and Charlie does the same. For now, she'll presume we're normal customers. 'Is she coming over?' I whisper.

'I don't know, I think so,' Charlie replies. 'What do we do?'

I give his hand a quick squeeze before pulling away. 'It might be better if you're not here. She won't want to talk with someone listening in.'

When a figure appears in my peripheral vision, I give Charlie a sharp nod and he walks away without looking back. I'm left to face Ellie alone.

My heart pounds and I feel dizzy as I turn. I'm expecting to see Meg's ghost and although my vision wobbles, the woman's features are clear enough. Her brown hair has more copper than Meg's gold and her bright, friendly eyes are green, not grey.

'My colleague says you were looking for me,' she says in a soft, Irish brogue.

The breath I was holding is forced out by a rush of relief. 'No, sorry, it wasn't you,' I say as I glance at her name badge. She's called Iona and the Celtic spelling matches her accent, but it's not Ellie. *Except*, my brain screams at me, this is the woman in the photo cuddling up to Lewis. I'm frozen to the spot, my eyes flicking between her face and her badge.

Iona's green eyes dim. 'What's this about?'

As I take a step back, my hip knocks into a shelf. I hear crockery rattle above the beating of my heart. 'No, nothing, it's a mistake,' I tell her. I look around for Charlie and find him loitering over by the glassware. Iona follows my gaze.

'Did you go to school with my boyfriend by any chance?' she asks, but not in that curious, delightful way you might when you discover a new connection with someone.

My voice wavers. 'Well. I – Who exactly is your boyfriend?'

258

'Lewis Rimmer, but I think you know that.'

'Oh, shit.'

'Oh, shit exactly,' Iona says. Her lip curls as she takes a step closer. 'I don't know what it is you people have against him but it stops here and now. I feel sorry for that girl's mum, honestly I do, but I've seen her snooping around in here. She was looking for me, wasn't she? I bloody knew it!'

'We're only trying to protect the people he hurts,' I reply weakly. 'And if that isn't you right now, don't think it won't be one day.'

Iona shakes her head. 'You're sick. The whole bunch of you are sick. Do you have any idea what this is doing to him? His mum's dying, for pity's sake. Can't you leave him in peace?'

'No, I can't.' The full implications of what's happening hits me: if Iona isn't the terrified young girl I've been speaking to, then who is Ellie, and how am I going to find her?

'This is harassment and if you don't leave this minute, I'm phoning the police.'

I might not have found Ellie but, I remind myself the man Iona is defending is still Lewis. 'Try suggesting that to your boyfriend,' I say. 'He won't want them involved. He has too much to hide and, by the look of it, he's hiding it pretty well from you – for now.'

I don't wait for a response. I have no argument with this woman and if I wasn't so angry and confused, I'd feel sorry for her. She doesn't know what Lewis is capable of, and while I don't wish it upon her, there will surely come a time when she wants to talk to me.

'How did it go?' Charlie asks, catching me up at the exit.

'I need some fresh air.'

I walk straight out of John Lewis and keep going. I don't want Iona to look out of a window and see me unravelling. Charlie keeps a hand on the small of my back and follows where I lead. I head towards the Albert Dock and slump down on the bench I'd shared with Geoff two days ago.

I hide my face behind my hands. 'It wasn't her, Charlie.'

'Then why are you so upset? What did she say to you? Does she know the girl we're looking for?'

Letting my hands drop, I look at Charlie. He's confused and I'm not sure if what I'm about to say will help. 'She *was* the girl we were looking for. That *was* Lewis's girlfriend,' I say. 'But it turns out she's Irish, not Romanian. She's not Ellie.'

'Oh.'

'Yeah, fucking "oh",' I reply. 'Ellie isn't Lewis's girlfriend.'

After a long pause, it's Charlie who breaks the silence. 'So that's it then,' he says, nodding his head as if we've found a nice, neat solution. 'You tried your best, Jen, but maybe now would be a good time for everyone to accept there's no more to be done and move on.'

'And will Ellie be moving on?'

'You can't help her if she doesn't want you to.'

'Of course she wants help. She phoned the helpline,' I insist. 'She phoned *me*, Charlie. And she didn't make it up that someone's been abusing her. Everything she's said fits in with what we know happened to Meg, from the scarves on her bedpost to the things Meg said about running out of air.' My words speed up as I quickly sift the facts from the fiction. 'Geoff told Lewis that Ellie was phoning the helpline, and the only way Ellie could have found out I'd betrayed her trust was through Lewis. What does it matter if Iona is his official girlfriend? It wouldn't stop him cheating on her. It's not like Lewis ever worried about being faithful to Meg.'

'Didn't he?'

I can't tell if Charlie is trying to prod my conscience or poke holes in my latest theory but, to be safe, I ignore his question. 'He keeps what he does with Ellie a secret while making a show of being a devoted son and boyfriend. It makes perfect sense.'

'Maybe . . . But you know what this means, don't you?'

I lean against Charlie, my energy gone as quickly as it arrived. 'We have no way of finding Ellie unless she phones again, and when the helpline closes, that will be it. He wins. Again.'

30

Ruth

There's a collection of stunned expressions as staff file out of the conference room on Wednesday morning. Geoff and I had been hoping to contain the news of our impending retirement until Oscar had made a firm offer, but the press release I'd sent out on Monday announcing the closure of the helpline in two weeks' time had raised eyebrows, and Oscar's reappearance the day after had fuelled speculation.

I've done my best to pitch the buy-out as a fresh opportunity for all of us, but as I follow Geoff back to our office, I don't think Jen will be the only one with a newly polished CV by the end of the day. She's already sent off her details to some of the contacts we've made through the foundation, and as I pass by her desk and catch her prodding a teetering pile of filing, I'm glad she's setting her sights on a job that will challenge her. She should be helping people find their rightful place in the world, not shuffling bits of paper.

As Geoff and I step into the office and the door closes

behind us, I feel unexpected relief. We can all look to the future now. No good will come of resuming an old war when our most recent battles have been lost, except I still don't know what to make of the latest setback.

After Jen's confrontation with Iona on Friday, she had been waiting at her desk for Geoff and I to return from lunch. She had been shell-shocked, as were we all, but her argument that Lewis has two girlfriends hadn't convinced Geoff, and I have my doubts too. I've never spoken to Ellie so I don't know exactly what she's been saying. I don't doubt she needs help but it's entirely possible that Jen has jumped to one too many conclusions. What if Lewis isn't implicated? Iona was quite feisty by all accounts, not the victim I'd imagined, and she might have a point accusing us of harassment. I have to let this go.

'I've had an email from one of the estate agents,' Geoff says as he settles behind his desk. 'She wants to call around tonight.'

'If she's planning on taking photos, you're going to have to do a quick tidy up before she gets there.'

'Me?'

'I'll be on the helpline tonight with Jen.'

'But I'm supposed to be catching up with Oscar at the golf club later.'

'I thought all the hard work had been done. You must have been working on him for *months* to get him interested in a takeover so quickly.'

Geoff shrugs. 'I might have sounded him out, but it was never a forgone conclusion that you'd agree, my love,' he says. 'And we're still a long way from signing on the dotted line.'

I'm not as annoyed as I might be. I don't particularly mind that Geoff took the initiative in our lives for once but I'm not about to give him full rein. 'If you can't be there, Geoff, you're going to have to rearrange the viewing.'

'She can only do tonight. Please, Ruth. Be reasonable.'

There's a creak as the door opens behind me.

'Sorry, I'll come back,' Jen says, sensing the atmosphere.

Geoff beckons her in. 'No, no, I'm glad you're here. We're having a bit of a domestic and you're the cause of it.'

'Why? What have I done?'

'Nothing,' I reply. 'It's Geoff's fault. We're getting valuations for the house and we've already arranged for two estate agents to call at the weekend. Another wants to visit this evening and Geoff thinks I should do the honours but I'll be here with you.'

'I can do the helpline on my own, Ruth.'

'Not necessarily. It was ridiculously busy on Monday and I wouldn't want you missing any calls.'

It was bittersweet that on the same day I announced that the helpline had reached the end of its useful life, it should be inundated with calls. Most were well-wishers wanting to thank us for the help we'd offered in the past, but a couple were from women who had been hoping for something more than the contact numbers of organisations who weren't about to fold.

Our reversal of fortunes might have tempted me to reconsider if I hadn't gone to see Gemma last night. She remains in a coma and my visit was ostensibly to offer whatever practical support Annabelle might need. I was unpacking the supplies I'd brought when Evan arrived. He'd been too shocked on the day of Gemma's attack to comprehend what part I'd played, but his eyes had darkened the moment he saw me.

'What's she doing here?' he asked Annabelle.

'I wanted her to come. She helped Gemma.'

'Is this what you call helping?' he asked me, pointing at his daughter whose body was held together by metal rods and plaster of Paris. Her eyes didn't as much as flutter at the sound of his raised voice. 'I'm glad that helpline of yours is being closed down before you kill someone.'

I could offer no defence: he was voicing my own worst fears and it was Annabelle who jumped in.

'If Ruth hadn't helped me get Gemma away from Ryan, we'd have lost her anyway. That monster would have stopped her seeing us and then he would have killed her, maybe not overnight but over years and years of abuse. Ruth saved her.'

'Funny how I can't see that,' Evan replied with a bitter laugh.

'I'm sorry,' I whispered as I backed out of the room. 'I'm so sorry.'

'Maybe you should leave it to the professionals next time.'

And that's what I intend to do. But it would be so much easier if I could be sure there was no one left crying out for help.

'Ellie won't phone,' Jen says, reading my thoughts.

'I wasn't suggesting she would.'

'Listen to Jen, my love,' says Geoff. 'She won't phone.'

My husband's intense gaze wears me down. 'Fine, I won't stay if Jen thinks she can manage. But don't think you're spending an evening in the golf club, Geoff. It's a school night.'

'I could do with a drink now,' Geoff mutters, reaching for his empty mug.

'That's why I came in,' Jen replies.

Geoff picks up my cup as he passes my desk then takes Jen's too before she can object. 'I'll make them, Jennifer. You stay here and calm my wife down.'

There's an awkward pause as Jen and I wait for the door to close behind Geoff.

'If you do speak to her again,' I say once we're alone, 'will you ask her directly if it is Lewis? Forget all the rules about not demanding information. I'd rest easier if she would at least confirm that it isn't him.'

'But it is,' Jen insists.

I don't argue. It's going to be a moot point if we never hear from Ellie again. Chances are she'll become another of life's imponderables that will torture me through my retirement. When the helpline closes a week on Friday, I intend to draw a line under the past. I have to for my own sanity.

'Are you sure you should be putting the house on the market so soon?' Jen asks.

'Not entirely but Geoff makes a compelling argument. If we sell the house before the business, we can always rent an apartment here for as long as necessary.'

'And if the business deal falls through?' Jen asks wistfully.

'There are other options on the table. It's possible we could promote from within and become sleeping partners. It's not ideal but there are one or two people out there who would jump at the chance if we put it on the table,' I tell her. With forced cheeriness, I add, 'Meanwhile, Geoff and I have been scouring the internet for properties in Stratford, and Sean's come up with a few possibilities. Chances are we'll end up buying something that's a bit of a project. It'll keep us busy and, more importantly, it'll keep Geoff out of trouble.'

'There's no going back, is there?'

'We can't stand still, Jen. The world changes around us whether we like it or not, and we adapt, whether we realise it or not. It's going to be hard making a home somewhere that doesn't have memories of Meg woven into its fabric, but it's not impossible. I'll carry her with me, wherever I go.'

'Will you tell the girls about Meg?' Jen asks as she follows my gaze to the new photo on my desk. It's the one of the twins sitting on my knee in the kitchen.

I smile. 'She'll be a part of their lives too, I'll make sure of that.'

'I really do hope this works out for you both,' Jen says. 'You deserve to be happy.'

'But I'm going to miss you,' I admit. 'Why don't you and Charlie come over for dinner on Saturday evening? It'll give us a chance to talk through all your exciting plans for the future.'

'That would be lovely,' Jen replies without enthusiasm, leaving me wondering who is trying to fool whom.

31

Jen

Ruth and Geoff leave early to give themselves time to spruce up the house before the estate agent arrives, and as soon as they're out of the door, the level of chatter in the office rises up a notch. Concerns for the future are voiced and it appears that Oscar is not a popular choice. As Ruth predicted, there are a number of senior architects who express disappointment at not being given the opportunity to take the company forward.

There are one or two furtive looks in my direction and I want to reassure everyone that I'm not going to repeat anything I hear, but I'm not the keeper of secrets I once was; you only have to ask Ellie. I make a show of tuning out their conversations by picking up my mobile.

'Are you busy?' I ask when Charlie answers after the third attempt to get through to him and not his voicemail.

'What's wrong?'

'Nothing, I just wanted to say hello.'

'Oh, OK.'

'It's ten to five.'

'Hmm, hmm,' Charlie replies, having switched off now he knows there's no emergency. This is how Mum must feel when I do the same to her.

'The helpline's about to open,' I say with emphasis. 'It's my second to last shift, Charlie, and I have this awful feeling I'm going to spend the next three hours being disappointed every time the phone rings and it's not Ellie.'

'She's not going to call, Jen.'

'I know, I've just said that,' I snap.

There's mumbling as Charlie covers the phone and talks to someone before replying to me. 'Sorry, Jen. What were you saying?'

'Should I go?' I force myself to ask.

'Do you mind? I promise we'll talk later but right now I'm in the middle of something. I'll try to get home before you and cook us a nice meal, or at worst, pick up a take-away. You can tell me all your worries and I'll tell you mine.'

I feel instantly guilty for my self-absorption. 'You've got problems?'

'You could say that,' he replies with a sigh. 'There's a crisis with the rotas but it's nothing I can't handle. Now go and make yourself a drink before the helpline opens. You've got five minutes.'

I put down the phone feeling more anxious than I was before, but I take Charlie's advice and make myself a coffee. The first call comes through as I'm returning to my desk.

'Hello, you're through to the Lean On Me helpline.'

'Is that Gill?'

'No, it's Jen,' I reply, already knowing where this conversation is heading.

'You probably don't remember me,' the caller begins.

She's wrong. I do remember her, and it's the same with the next three callers. I've spoken to each of them in the past and my response to their kind words is a gradual build-up of emotion that has to come out, and it does when the last caller passes the phone to her daughter who insists on saying hello. She's four years old and hadn't been born when her father mentally abused his pregnant girlfriend.

'I'd best let you go,' the girl's mum says when she comes back on the line to find me sobbing.

'I'm so glad you called,' I tell her. 'These are happy tears, honestly.'

There's only a sliver of a lie in what I say. I am happy about what we've achieved in the last seven years, but I'm miserable that it's coming to an end. What am I going to do when Ruth leaves? I don't want to be left behind.

Someone places a hand on my shoulder. It's one of the architects, a middle-aged man who looks distinctly uncomfortable being the only one left in the office to deal with a hysterical member of staff. 'Here,' he says, offering me a tissue. 'I was about to leave. Will you be OK?'

'I'll be fine,' I promise. 'We all will. New opportunities and all that.'

'I've watched you on the helpline over the years,' he says. 'I might not hear what you say but then, you don't say much because you're a good listener, Jen. Don't spend the rest of your life stuck here, listening to us drone on about bricks and mortar. If you'll forgive the pun, be the architect of your own destiny.'

My smile trembles. 'Don't be nice to me, you'll only set me off again,' I warn.

'I'll take that as my cue to leave.'

I'm watching him disappear through the exit doors when the phone rings again. I take a breath and as I prepare myself for another emotional onslaught, my ears are trained for any background noise. There's no chatter, no TV, and no children squabbling.

'Hello, you're through to the Lean On Me helpline. How can I help?'

'Hello, Jen,' Ellie says.

'I – I don't . . . I didn't think you'd call again,' I stutter.

'Neither did I,' she replies quietly.

Something feels different. I thought I'd be able to recognise a call from Ellie without her speaking but not this time. 'How are you?'

'Good.'

'Are you in your apartment?'

'Yes.'

'And you're safe and well?'

There's a pause. 'I am going back home to Romania,' she says. 'My flight is a week on Saturday. He has paid for me to go. I told you, he is a good man.'

I don't believe her, or to be more precise, I don't believe what he's promising. 'Do you have the ticket? Have you seen it?'

There's another time delay, as if we're talking via satellite. 'It will work out. I am happy to go.'

'Because it's what he wants?'

'Yes.'

I'd like to know if it's what she wants but I say nothing. I've worked out what's wrong with the call. There's a tininess to Ellie's voice that shouldn't be there. She's on

271

speakerphone but that doesn't explain the delay . . . not unless someone is listening in to our conversation and vetting her answers.

'I'm sorry for being angry with you last time, Jen. I overreacted.'

'Please don't apologise, you've done nothing wrong,' I reply.

I lean back in my chair as I wonder how I'm going to broach the question Ruth wants me to ask. How likely is it that Ellie will divulge her abuser's identity while he's in the room? I'm not hopeful, so I start with a different question.

'Remember when you first phoned and said that it wasn't Lewis who hurt Meg?'

'I do not know this Lewis,' Ellie says too quickly. These words haven't been fed to her but that doesn't mean the answer is a truthful one. I can hear the fear in her voice.

'He was Meg's boyfriend. Are you sure you don't know who he is?'

Silence.

'So if you don't know him, he's not the one hurting you?'

After a pause, she says, 'I lied. No one is hurting me, Jen.'

'We both know that isn't true,' I tell her, wearily. Ellie's clumsy attempts to defend Lewis simply confirm that it is him and he's there. 'Oh, Ellie, you can't trust him. You know what he did to Meg. She was going to leave him too and look how he stopped her.'

'It is not the same.'

'No, it isn't,' I reply. 'You do know you're not the only woman in his life, don't you?'

'I never meant to hurt . . .' she begins but her voice trails off. Is she being told not to answer the question?

'He keeps you hidden while he puts on a veneer of respectability. He thinks by sending you away, the problem will go away too, but you didn't make him what he is. He'll never rid himself of the need to crush and humiliate, and I doubt he wants to. If it's not you, it'll be someone else. Let me put an end to this.'

'Please, Jen,' Ellie says but pauses again, seeking permission to continue perhaps. 'You must stop this. I only ring to say goodbye. Do not worry about me. I will be OK. It will all be OK but you must stop or else . . .'

'Or else what?' I ask. When she doesn't answer, I add, 'What has he told you to say?'

The silence that follows is broken only when the second helpline phone rings out.

'I should let you get the other call,' she says.

'I don't have to answer it. Did you know the helpline's going to close?'

'Yes. He said. I am sorry.'

'I expect he thought we'd given up but I'm going nowhere. I won't be played and I won't be threatened,' I say, enjoying the opportunity to speak through Ellie to Lewis.

'I will talk to him,' she says urgently. 'You do not need to do anything.'

The second phone stops: soon it will never ring again. 'I'm scared for you, Ellie. I want you to go back home and be safe, I really do, but what happens when the next Meg, or the next you, comes along? There's another young girl out there who's going to find out the hard way that he's never quite sorry enough when he hurts her. That's not your problem, I know that, but don't ask me to stop because I won't. I'd love to meet up with you just once and show you what Meg was like before he got to her. Maybe you have pictures to share of happier times too.'

I'm not surprised when Ellie – or more likely, Lewis – puts the phone down. The person I spoke to today wasn't the real Ellie. She was a puppet and Lewis was pulling the strings. I've seen him in action before.

I recall the time when I'd gone to Sefton Park with Charlie. Our exams were over and everyone was meeting up to celebrate. We were late to the party and arrived to find twenty other sixth form survivors gathered around a collection of disposable barbeques. Meathead was living up to his name by taking charge of the burgers and sausages that would be difficult to discern from the charcoal once we were all drunk.

Meg was sitting on the grass amongst a group of girls. She wore a long floaty dress with a high neckline and bell sleeves, and her hair shone gold as it cascaded over her shoulders. She looked like the old Meg but when she waved at me it was a tentative greeting, as if she wasn't sure I'd wave back.

Leaving Charlie by the barbeques, I made my way over. Glad to find her without Lewis, I wanted the awkwardness between us to be gone. 'Hi,' I said, dropping down next to her. 'I didn't think you'd be here. Isn't it Sean's last day before he goes to Camp America?'

'He won't miss me.'

'But you'll miss him,' I suggested. When Meg simply shrugged, I moved to another topic. 'How did your exams go?'

'No idea. My coursework grades were rubbish so I need high marks,' she said, tugging at blades of grass rather than looking at me. 'I think I've done enough though. I have to have done enough.'

'I can't believe we'll actually be going off to uni soon,' I said, recalling the dreams of escape we'd shared in her bedroom.

When Meg lifted her gaze, her eyes were full of fear. 'Whatever happens, I can't stay here. I'd rather be dead. I'd want to be dead.'

I felt prickles on the back of my neck and I was sure it was Lewis's footsteps I could hear approaching, but when I turned, Charlie was holding out a bottle of cider to me.

Meg tipped her head back, shielding her eyes from the sun as she offered him a confident smile. 'Hey, Charlie. Come and sit down,' she said, commanding him like his queen.

I don't know what shocked me more, Meg's sudden mood change or the sight of the scratches running along her inner arm as her sleeve slipped down to her elbow. She shot me a look as she covered herself up. What she'd said a moment earlier, what I'd seen just now, they were her secrets and I wasn't to tell.

Charlie scanned the crowd around us. 'Where's Lewis?'

'Oh, busy somewhere else, I expect,' she replied. 'Come on, Charlie, sit down. You're hurting my neck.'

Before he could obey, there were more footsteps and this time my fears were realised.

'Why the fuck haven't you been answering your phone?' Lewis demanded. 'I've been looking everywhere for you.' He was out of breath and his nostrils flared as he glared at Meg.

'Must have run out of battery,' she replied as she stretched out her legs and leant back on her arms.

'On purpose?'

'Does it matter? I'm fine. You're fine. We're all fine. Or we were until you got here,' she muttered.

'Stop it, Meg,' he warned. 'I thought—' For a second, his voice had sounded choked with emotion but he set his jaw firm. 'Your message said—'

'He doesn't like me talking to other boys,' she interrupted. 'He thinks I'm going to embarrass him.' Keeping her smile, she held Lewis's gaze when she added, 'Well, if you don't like it, you don't have to watch.'

I couldn't tell if the sparkle in Meg's eyes was defiance or surrender but it disappeared the moment Lewis's shadow loomed over her. He grabbed her arm and pulled her to her feet. She struggled to stand, and that was when I realised how drunk she was.

'I'm up now. Get the fuck off me,' she said, continuing to sway as she attempted to tug free from Lewis's grasp.

'Why can't you leave her alone?' I demanded, haunted by my earlier conversation with Meg when the mask she'd been wearing for the last eighteen months had slipped.

'Me leave her alone?' Lewis asked. 'You're the one who turned your back on her, Jen.'

I stood up, staying close enough to Charlie to feel the warmth of his arm brushing my skin. Emboldened, I said, 'Maybe I didn't like the company she was keeping.'

I locked eyes with Lewis a second too long and he snagged me in his trap. 'Either that, or you liked it too much.'

'No one *likes* you,' I hit back. 'We can all see what you're doing to her.'

'So it's my fault? Are you listening to this, Meg?' he asked. She frowned at him. 'What do you want me to say?'

He let go of her arm with a shove. 'Fuck all, as usual.'

'Come on, mate,' Charlie said as he put out a hand to keep Meg upright until she righted herself. 'We're all trying to chill here. Loosen up.'

Lewis sneered. 'What is this, Charlie? Want to big it up in front of Jen, or is it Meg you're trying to impress? Of course you are. Everyone knows you're only settling for Jen because you couldn't have her cousin,' he said. Checking my reaction, he added, 'I keep telling you, Jen. You deserve better.'

With my cheeks smarting from the look Lewis gave me, I tugged at Charlie's t-shirt. 'Ignore him, he's baiting us. Let's go and get some burgers,' I said. I turned to Meg, who seemed immune to the hurt her boyfriend was inflicting on each of us. 'Come with us.'

'Suit yourselves,' Lewis said, turning on his heels.

I reach my hand out, ready to take back my best friend. 'Please, Meg,' I tried.

'Why does everyone have to be so nasty to him?' she asked. 'Not every couple can be as sickly sweet as you two! Just leave him alone. Leave us both alone.'

'I only wanted—'

Before I could finish, Meg was chasing after Lewis. I watched as she caught up with him beneath the dappled shade of a nearby oak that covered her white dress in dark bruises. With her hands pressed together in supplication, I didn't need to hear what she said to know she was begging forgiveness.

Lewis shook his head as he backed her towards the tree.

When he raised his hand in a fist, I thought he was going to hit her but after a brief exchange, he grabbed her by the shoulders and slammed her against the gnarled trunk. His hand went to her throat.

I took hold of Charlie's arm to hold him back but I needn't have worried. He wasn't about to intervene, and neither was I. Maybe we were expecting what came next, which was that Lewis loosened his grip on Meg's neck as they started to kiss. Or perhaps we were both cowards.

I turned around and didn't look back. I dismissed my cousin's remark about wanting to be dead. I ignored the marks I'd seen on her arm. I even ignored Lewis's suggestion that Charlie had settled for me when he wanted Meg. I knew that anyway. When Meg had leapt off the stage that time, Charlie was the first to have his arms outstretched. Part of me wishes he had caught her. No one else was going to save her.

With the end of my shift approaching, I have three further calls to distract me from my guilt, but when I shrug into my houndstooth jacket, it feels heavier than it should. I'm regretting what I said to Ellie. I was too harsh, but nevertheless, what I said was true. There will be a new victim to replace her if by some chance Lewis keeps his promise and sends her back to Romania.

As I wind my way down the stairwell to the ground floor, I wonder if Iona will be next, or will Lewis have easy pickings from one of his boot camp recruits? Whoever she might be, there will be someone in his sights.

As I leave the office, I'm almost knocked off my feet by the sheer force of the wind that pushes me in the direction of the Strand. Fighting against nature, I head across the concourse towards the waterfront and I'm tucking my hair into a beanie hat as I look across the dark, choppy waters of the docks. The nights are drawing in and the twinkling lights in the distance, guiding visitors to the dockside restaurants, give the illusion of life, but I can't imagine who would be out in this weather.

As my focus returns to the deserted concourse, I realise there is one person I can imagine lurking. Lewis knows I've been on the helpline tonight and I've made it clear that he hasn't scared me off – yet. Will he try a different approach?

My eyes dart from one dark corner of a building to the next, until my gaze settles on the yawning entrance to the underground car park. I'll need to walk past it if I'm to continue on my current course. My jacket becomes a woollen parachute, pulled taut by the relentless wind, and my pace slows.

Deciding the Strand might be the better option, I spin around but I'm not prepared for the wind that's now at my back and propels me forward. I'm almost at a run as I stumble straight into the path of a man who had been walking behind me. He grabs my shoulders and at first I think he's a good Samaritan who's caught my fall, but as I lock eyes with Lewis, I raise my hands to his chest and push him away.

'Get off me!' I scream, balling my hands into fists and raising them up to defend myself.

I'm grateful for the wind this time as it pushes me towards the office, but when I reach the main entrance, the doors don't open automatically. The building has been locked down.

I'm expecting Lewis to grab me at any moment and I hammer on the doors. Catching sight of one of the security guards in reception, I let out a cry of relief. Steve has already seen me and I wait for him to override the locking mechanism. I'm praying for the doors to slide open and when they do, I squeeze myself through the smallest gap. Safely inside reception, I turn back to the entrance. The doors rattle as they continue to open, wider and wider, but no one else appears from the dark world beyond. Lewis has vanished into the night.

Panting for breath, I wait for the doors to close, and only then do I collapse forward and rest my hands on my knees. What do I do now?

'Are you all right, Jen?' Steve asks. 'That wind's deadly tonight. You're not the first to be knocked off your feet, and for a minute there, it looked like you were going to take that bloke with you.'

'You saw him?' I ask, straightening up.

'Yeah, I thought you were mad heading towards the waterfront, to be honest,' Steve says, and despite his concern, his remarks are alarmingly casual. 'Do you want me to call a taxi for you? I can walk you out when it gets here.'

No, I want you to call the police, is what I think, but what good would that do? Steve had Lewis, but he has absolutely no idea of the threat that man poses. He watched a man crossing the concourse and then me being picked up by the wind and flung into his path. He didn't see him grabbing me. He saw him saving me.

32

Jen

Ruth and Geoff's dining table comfortably seats ten, which makes it all the more difficult to ignore the empty chairs as we huddle in the middle. My heart aches for my cousin, but I'm more aware of the tightening I feel around my chest whenever I think of the man who took her from me. It's been three days since I bumped into Lewis outside the office and although the family dinner party is easing my soul, I'm becoming less and less interested in conversations about family, job opportunities and house prices as the night wears on. By the time we take a pause before dessert, my fear is that no one will mention Lewis at all.

'Charlie said he'll pick me up after my last helpline shift next week,' I say to Ruth, edging us into the conversation.

'I should imagine I'll stay behind too, so I can give you a lift home,' she offers.

'Jen's going to bite my head off for saying this,' Charlie says, 'but I'll be breathing a sigh of relief when the helpline closes.'

'I expect Lewis will too,' I mutter.

Geoff stands to top up our wine glasses. 'Charlie's right,' he says. 'The sooner we put an end to this whole saga, the better.'

'And I hope it does bring an end to it,' Charlie says, reaching for his drink. 'After the stunt Lewis pulled turning up at the office, I think we've all realised how dangerous a game we've been playing. I sent him a message, through a friend on Facebook, to let him know this has to stop. With any luck he'll realise there's nothing more to be gained and leave us alone.'

'As long as we leave him alone,' Geoff warns, avoiding eye contact with either me or his wife.

Ruth leans forward in her chair and trails a finger down the side of her glass. 'I'd like to know what he thought he was going to achieve, terrifying Jen like that.'

'Isn't it obvious? It was a final warning,' Charlie says, looking at me with eyes that have developed deeper worry lines of late.

'Then you best make sure Jen heeds it,' Geoff tells him as if I'm not there. He shakes his head solemnly. 'None of us wanted it to end this way, but it has ended. Lewis has a lifetime's experience of wriggling out of trouble, and he's done it again. He can claim bumping into Jen on Wednesday was purely accidental, whereas his list of complaints against us grows longer by the day, from defamation of character to intimidation and harassment of his family.'

Charlie nods. 'Iona did threaten to call the police.'

'It's lucky for us that she didn't,' Geoff adds. He's emptied the dregs from the wine bottle into his glass but remains standing.

'But what about Ellie? Does no one care what happens to her?' I demand.

'This time next week she'll be on a plane home and then we can all rest easier,' says Geoff. 'You should be happy, Jennifer. It's all because of you.'

I fold my arms across my chest as Geoff holds up his glass, toasting my success.

'Geoff has a point,' Charlie offers.

My uncle smiles broadly. 'After all the good work we've achieved with the foundation, it's fitting that you've managed to help one last person, especially after that disaster with the poor girl who was run down by her boyfriend,' he reminds us all. 'The timing couldn't be better. Ruth's doing the right thing.'

We all turn to Ruth for a response. She smiles. 'Cheesecake, anyone?'

'Would you like some help?' I ask, following her out before she has the chance to refuse. Tonight doesn't seem to be the night for asking people what they actually want.

I step into the kitchen as Ruth slams the fridge door shut. The homemade cheesecake is in a springform tin and she has it balanced on the palm of one hand as if she's about to launch it at the wall.

'If I hear one more person telling me I'm making the right decision, I might just scream,' she says.

'You won't hear it from me,' I reply. 'I know Geoff wants us to believe it's over, Ruth, but a sternly worded message from Charlie isn't going to make Lewis change his ways, and there's no guarantee Ellie will make it back to Romania. It's hardly a coincidence that the flight he's allegedly booked her on is after the helpline closes. Her last phone call was a set-up. Lewis was listening in so he could vet her replies. What does that say about him?'

'That he doesn't like giving up control easily,' Ruth says, releasing a sigh that turns into a hiss. There's a snap as she undoes the clasp on the baking tin. She prises out the cheesecake, leaving the hooped tin dangling from her arm. 'I was hoping that it wasn't Lewis she was involved with.'

'I know,' I say as I watch Ruth slide the cheesecake onto a platter and throw the baking tin on top of a stack of washing up. 'But if Ellie's quick denial about not knowing him wasn't enough to convince me once and for all, him turning up at the office an hour later certainly did.'

Ruth plays with the crumbs she'd spilled on the counter. 'I would love nothing more than to bring Lewis to justice, but I've been hoping for that for ten years, Jen,' she says. 'Reluctant as I am, I have to agree with Geoff. When the helpline closes, it has to be the end. No more talk of Lewis, or Ellie.'

'But there's almost a week left before we close down,' I reply. 'A lot can happen between then and now.'

With a swipe of her hand, Ruth scatters the crumbs and looks up. 'You're not giving up, are you?'

'No,' I say simply. I have one more move to make but I'm going to need Ruth's help. She'll need some convincing and, with Geoff and Charlie close by, now might not be the best time to recruit her, but if not now, when?

Ruth's eyes narrow. 'If I can walk away, why can't you? What is it that makes you want to fight on despite the threats from Lewis?' she asks. 'I feel like I'm missing something by not speaking to Ellie myself. What is it, Jen? Is it something she's said, or maybe something in her voice?'

I give a strangled laugh as I recall Ellie's rasping breath. 'Yes, you could say that.'

'Then explain it to me.'

I take a step towards Ruth and rest a hand on the breakfast bar. After an evening sitting at the table being reminded of Meg's absence, it's odd that I should feel her presence here, in the spot where she died. I picture her sitting on a dusty old box scribbling down her last thoughts. She lifts her head to look at me. Does she want me to share her darkest secrets with her mum? Possibly not, but I'm going to anyway.

'When I told you that Lewis hurts Ellie, I didn't say how. If I'd told you that, you would never have doubted that it was Lewis. You would have seen the parallels between now and then,' I begin. I know I'm obfuscating but I'm still trying to justify the pain I'm about to inflict. 'Lewis is reliving in perfect detail what he did to Meg.'

I can see Ruth's body tensing. 'Tell me what he did to my daughter,' she says, her voice no more than a whisper.

'Are you *sure* you want me to tell you?' I ask, offering her one last chance.

Ruth nods, though it might have been a tremor.

'He . . . he used Meg's scarves on her. That's where the bruising around her neck came from. That's why she always sounded like she had a sore throat,' I explain.

I pause to check Ruth's reaction, hoping I've said enough for her to understand because I don't think I can say more. Her expression is frozen as she stares through me to the past but then her hand flies to her mouth as she releases a wail and turns away.

I wait until her shoulders stop shaking before I ask, 'Are you OK, Ruth?'

'Does Geoff know?' she asks, keeping her back to me.

'Yes.'

She takes a moment to gather herself and when she turns, her makeup is smudged but her eyes are sharp and clear. 'So it's down to you and me to rattle Lewis's cage one last time,' she says. 'I presume that's why you've told me? You have a plan?'

'I'd like one last go at disrupting his life, yes.'

'How?'

'I think we should pay Iona another visit. She deserves to know who she's dating.'

'I'm not sure, Jen. We don't know how Lewis will react and I don't want to put Ellie, or you, in more danger.'

'What can be worse for Ellie than leaving her to whatever fate Lewis has planned?' I reply, skimming over any repercussions I might face. 'Lewis isn't going to send her away if he thinks we've stopped looking for her, so let's give him reason to think we haven't. It might be the best chance she has.'

'Iona could report us to the police.'

'Lewis won't press charges, we both know that.'

I can see Ruth weighing up the options, and the flicker of fire that appears in her eyes leaves my skin tingling. For the first time in months, it appears that Ruth and I are moving in the same direction, but to be sure, I ask, 'Will you help me?'

'One last time,' she says. 'And then we take back our lives.'

'Agreed.'

Ruth steps around the breakfast bar and, touching my arm, leads me towards the dresser. I assume she wants help collecting up some side plates but she reaches for her laptop.

'I left this out to show you the videos Geoff took of the twins. Do you mind if we watch a clip? After what you've just told me, I need something to clear my mind.'

'I'd love to,' I reply, standing close to Ruth as she starts up the media player. She taps the mousepad with her long fingernail one too many times and the last video she'd been watching begins to play.

The image is grainy and overexposed, making it difficult to work out what it is I'm looking at, but the sound of music and excited squeals quickly transport me back to happier times. I hear Meg's laughter.

Ruth goes to close the recording but hesitates as the camera pans across the darkened garden and a younger, less troubled Ruth steps forward.

'Megan, come back here!' she yells. 'I know you've taken a bottle.'

Shadows scatter, but one comes forward. Sixteen-year-old me is harbouring a bottle of champagne and a guilty look.

'Sorry, Auntie Ruth,' I tell her, offering up the stolen goods.

'I was only going to give you these,' Ruth replies, handing over plastic cups. 'Happy New Year, Jen.'

I beam a smile at my aunt and uncle. 'It's OK, Meg!' I call out to my missing cousin. 'We're not in trouble.'

'How many of you are hiding out there?' Geoff asks from behind the camera. 'Do you need any more?'

As I recall, there were at least six of us who had been hopping from one New Year's Eve party to the next, and it was past midnight by the time we'd sneaked into Meg's house and grabbed the booze. We thought we hadn't been spotted.

Meg stumbled out of the gloom and held up a second bottle. 'No, we're all sorted,' she says, peering over a pair of thick-rimmed glasses that were too big for her. She doesn't smile and she doesn't wish her parents a happy new year as she takes the plastic cups. 'Come on, Jen.'

Ruth pauses the video before Meg has a chance to return to the shadows. 'Do you think she knew what lay ahead?' she asks as we both scrutinise Meg's guarded expression.

'I don't honestly know,' I reply. 'She was always racing ahead, it was hard to tell when she stopped running to get somewhere and started running away.'

'I've looked through this entire sequence but there's no sign of Lewis.'

'He wasn't there,' I say. 'Meg had invited him to come out with us but he was playing it cool. He let her dangle for a few weeks until he was ready to reel her in.'

'But the glasses she's wearing. They were his.'

I peer at the screen. 'No, they look like Charlie's, or at least the ones he carried around in his pocket. Meg was always teasing him about them, saying they looked better on her, which was probably true.'

'But Lewis wore glasses,' Ruth insists.

'Not ones like that,' I reply. 'Charlie was forever losing his, so his mum only let him have the cheap and nasty ones.'

I offer Ruth a smile but she doesn't take her eyes from the screen. 'My daughter's still a stranger to me,' she whispers before snapping the laptop shut and straightening up, the recording of her granddaughters forgotten. 'If only she'd told me what was happening to her.'

'She was conditioned not to,' I remind her. 'Lewis made

her believe she was safe as long as she didn't speak out. It's the same with Ellie.'

'If we're going to claim her as the success Geoff wants her to be, we have to make sure she's safe,' Ruth says. 'I don't think my conscience could take another failure so soon after the last.'

'Gemma was not a failure – we got her away from Ryan and he's going to be put away for a very long time.'

'Yes, but at best, it's been a questionable success.'

'Is there any news?' I ask, having avoided asking so far this evening. I hadn't wanted to hear anything that might weaken my resolve, but perhaps I do need a reminder of how dangerous these men can be.

'The doctors have started withdrawing sedation and Gemma seems to be responding well,' Ruth says, as she returns to the kitchen counter where she left the cheesecake. 'I've promised Annabelle I'll visit them tomorrow evening when her ex-husband isn't there. Unlike him, she still thinks that I know what I'm doing.'

'You do,' I insist. 'That's why I wanted your help.'

Ruth manages a smile but it doesn't reach her eyes. She hasn't completely cleared her mind of the thoughts I've put in there. 'Come on, let's get back to the others,' she says. 'I'm going to have to sweeten Geoff up before I tell him his retreat from the enemy might not go as smoothly as planned.'

33

Ruth

After waving Jen and Charlie off in their taxi, I return to the dining room to find that Geoff hasn't moved from the table. He's rolling a tumbler of whiskey between his palms and doesn't look up as I begin clearing away the last of the dishes and empty wine bottles.

'Jen seems happier,' he says to the amber liquid sloshing around his glass. 'Whatever you said to her in the kitchen must have worked.'

Wine glasses clink as I pick up the last two. 'I can't say talking to her has made me happier,' I admit. I keep thinking about what that man did to my daughter, and what he's doing to Ellie. 'How did you do it, Geoff?'

Finally, my husband looks up. 'Do what, my love?'

'How did you hunt down Lewis and not squeeze every last breath from him?'

If Geoff has worked out that Jen's told me the intimate details of what Lewis did to Meg, he doesn't let on. 'Because the man's half my age and a body builder,' he says. When

I don't react, he adds, 'This move is for the best, my love, and it must go ahead. Oscar is keen but now that the due diligence process has started, we're both incurring significant costs. If you get cold feet, he won't come back a second time.'

'He won't have to. I haven't changed my mind, not about retiring.'

'And you'll keep away from Lewis?'

Geoff is on the other side of the table but I can feel the pressure of his hand on my back again. It's been the same all week. The whole drama over the house valuation last Wednesday had been a ruse to get me away from the helpline. I wasn't needed at home. The estate agent was done within an hour and Geoff still had time to slope off to meet Oscar. 'What's the worst he can do?'

'Mire us in scandal if he does press charges? Ruin our future with our granddaughters?' he suggests. 'I don't care one jot about him, Ruth. I care about you. Let me take you away from this. Please.'

I circle the table to stand behind my husband. My arms are full so I settle for kissing the top of his head. 'On the condition that we walk away, Geoff. We don't run,' I whisper.

'I do love you.'

'And I love you too,' I reply. I feel taller as I head for the door. 'But you have to let me do what I have to do. I promise, it won't be public but I am going to make sure those closest to Lewis Rimmer see him for what he is.'

'Ruth, don't rush into something you'll regret.'

I shake my head. 'It's been ten years, Geoff. This is hardly rushing.'

'You won't win.'

'No, but neither will he. I'm doing this for Megan,' I say, and the mention of our daughter's name silences him. 'I'm going to bed soon. Are you coming?'

'In a while.'

After stacking the dishwasher, I make my way upstairs. I pause on the landing and hear the clink of a glass as Geoff pours himself another whiskey with unsteady hands. Despite my reluctance to pack up and leave, I am looking forward to a better life and a new health regime for the two of us. There will be no more liquid lunches, only picnics followed by a long walk along the River Avon, or a sandwich in the grounds of one of the many National Trust properties I'd love to explore. We can take the girls to the Butterfly Farm, or we might be a bit more adventurous and go to Alton Towers. We've been searching for peace in all the wrong places. It can't be found in the bottom of a whiskey glass or at the end of a helpline telephone. It's in our grand-daughters' giggles and squeals that will deafen the silence coming from Meg's room as I reach the top of the stairs.

Pausing in front of her door, I wrap my hand around the handle. I take a deep breath as if I'm about to storm in and yell at her for littering the floor with dirty clothes, or burning her duvet cover with her hair straighteners . . . or because I'd just found a foreign object down the side of my bed that didn't belong there.

'What are these?' I'd demanded as I squinted through a cloud of dust motes floating in the dimly lit room. It was the middle of August and the midday sun had heated my daughter's room to noxious levels.

'Megan, will you answer me!' I yelled at the unmoving mound of white cotton sheets. I couldn't see her head but from the arm dangling over the side of the bed, I surmised she was lying on her stomach.

My outburst had been acknowledged with a grunt but no movement, so I made a grab for the sheet and yanked it off her. I hadn't considered that she might be naked beneath. She was, and I'd quickly squeezed my eyes shut, but not before catching sight of the marks on her arms. I wasn't sure what I'd been looking at or what they meant. From an early age, my daughter's irrepressible energy had always got her into scrapes. It never entered my mind that the scratches were self-inflicted.

'What the fuck?' Meg screamed, snatching the sheet back.

I gave her a moment to adjust herself and when I peeled my eyes open, she had the sheet tucked under her chin.

'What?' she asked again, her voice croaky but her eyes blazing.

'These!' I hissed as I dangled a pair of spectacles from my hand. They were dark framed and thick-rimmed. 'What were they doing in my bedroom?'

'They're mine,' she replied, kneeling up to snatch them back.

I let her take them because I certainly didn't want them. 'No, they're not.'

No longer screaming at each other, our fiery rage was reduced to simmering frustration on my part and loathing on my daughter's. I hadn't been looking for an argument that morning. She'd been broken the day before after getting her A Level results, and I'd been waiting patiently for her to get up so we could talk about it. That's why I'd been busying myself with the housework.

'I've taken the day off so we can go through clearing and get you into another university,' I told her.

'Did you not see my grades?' she asked. 'I failed *everything*.'

'In that case, we need to get over to the school and arrange for you to retake your last year, or we could find you a place at another college. Once you have a new plan in place, you'll feel better about things,' I promised.

'I do have a plan.'

'Which is?'

In the sullen silence that followed, I scrolled through possible answers in my head, but all I had to go on was a pair of glasses. I presumed it meant Lewis would continue to be a disruptive presence in our lives now that Meg's plans to move cities had been thwarted. I didn't know then that the glasses belonged to Charlie, and I still don't know what that means.

Did Meg cheat on Lewis with her cousin's boyfriend? Did Lewis find out? Was that why Meg's despair continued to spiral downwards during those last ten days of her life? It's possible, but I can't imagine Lewis keeping that secret from Jen all this time when he could use it to hurt her. The more I know about my daughter, the less I understand.

When I enter Meg's bedroom, there are no shouts of objection. The timbered floor is clear of clutter and Meg's single bed has become two princess beds, like a cell dividing, or an embryo. I want to believe that I'm here to remind myself of the lives I'm moving towards but as I stand in front of the bookshelves, I ignore the finger-paintings my granddaughters made during their last visit, and reach up on tiptoe to take something from the top shelf.

The box is sage green and there are hand-painted daisy chains on the lid that form the letters of my daughter's name. It had taken days to make the memory box and months to select the most precious keepsakes. Geoff is under strict instructions that if ever there's a fire, this is the one thing I want saving.

I kneel down on the floor and open the box. My fingers trail across the different textures of my treasure trove; the roughness of the heart-shaped pot that's now the only remnant of my pottery classes; the scratch of the glittery star Meg made in primary school; the smoothness of her baby-sized hospital wristband; the crinkle of plastic covering the tumbler I found on her bedside table that still has her lip marks; the coldness of a silk scarf.

This was the first scarf Meg owned, although technically it was mine. A friend had given it to me for my birthday and six-year-old Meg had fallen in love with the peacock colours. She kept stealing it from my room, and it became a game until eventually I gave in and said she could keep it. I'd found it discarded and forgotten at the back of a drawer, but I'd been grateful that it played no part in her final act. Meg had used the others in her collection to make a noose.

I recoil from the touch of silk and begin flicking through a pile of envelopes in varying colours and shapes. Some contain the official documents recording the span of Meg's life, from birth to death. There are a collection of greetings cards covered in a child's innocent scrawl, a stack of glowing school reports and even the A Level results that broke her heart, but I pick up the envelope containing the note that broke mine.

I unfold the sheet of yellow lined paper carefully, as if I can wish the missing half of the note into existence. I trail a finger over the neatly torn edge. This is why my daughter continues to remain a mystery to me.

34

Ruth

When our third and final estate agent arrived for an early morning tour of the house on Sunday, the smell of stale whiskey lingered in our bedroom despite the open windows. It had been a close call hauling Geoff out of bed in time, and I'd like to think it was the hangover fogging his brain that made him suggest to the agent that we set the asking price lower for a quick sale, but I suspect it had more to do with wanting me out of Liverpool as quickly as possible. I sent him off to the golf course with a warning that he'd better not offer Oscar our business at a cut-down price too.

I have a dull headache and I'm swallowing back two paracetamol when the doorbell rings. The chimes make my head throb and I'm inclined to ignore the intrusion but the caller is persistent and rings again.

When I open the door, I'm surprised to find Eve on my doorstep. My sister-in-law is older than Geoff and four inches shorter but she has the same hazel eyes as her brother, although none of his laughter lines. 'I'm not disturbing you, am I?' she asks.

'No, not at all. Although, if you're after Geoff, he's at the club,' I say, hopefully.

'I'd be surprised if he wasn't,' Eve replies as she steps inside. 'I was just passing.'

'Can I get you a drink?'

'No, I'm fine for now,' she says, heading for the sitting room.

My sister-in-law has never voiced her disapproval of the way I remodelled the house but she will avoid the kitchen at all costs. She perches herself on one of the armchairs in a way that suggests she won't be staying long, although that might be wishful thinking on my part. I take a seat on the sofa opposite.

'So how is everyone, Eve? Other than Jen, I haven't seen the girls for ages.'

'Whereas I barely see Jennifer at all,' Eve says. 'I phoned her this morning to invite her over for Sunday lunch. She always seems to find an excuse and today it was because of a hangover. Did you all have a good night?'

'It wasn't anything special,' I reply carefully. I'd accepted a long time ago that Eve and I were never going to be best friends like our girls, but we've remained civil with each other despite the odd petty disagreement. If Eve is spoiling for an argument, she's picked the wrong day.

'She tells me you're definitely selling up.'

'Yes, we've had valuations for the house and now we just need to choose an estate agent. The business side will take a bit longer but that's in train too.'

'You're doing the right thing,' Eve says as she looks

about the room for Meg's ghost. 'It can't be easy living here.'

'On the contrary, it's leaving that's going to be tough. For some this might be the house that Meg died in, but for me it's where she lived.'

Eve offers me a tight smile. 'I can understand that,' she says. 'It's only natural to cling onto what you've lost, and I can see how Jen does the same. It's not good for her, Ruth. You must know she can't fill the hole Meg left in your life, no matter how hard you try.'

I blink hard, taken aback by her accusation. 'I didn't realise I was.'

'I'm sure you don't mean to,' Eve says, ignoring my tone. 'But I think it's obvious to all of us that the only reason Jen hasn't been able to find her place in the world is because she's too busy trying to fill her cousin's shoes. They don't fit. Jennifer was never like Meg and no one can pretend she is.'

'You think I want Jen to be a replacement Meg?'

'I wouldn't have put it so bluntly.'

'I think you just did,' I say, anger blooming in my already sore head. 'It's not a numbers game, Eve. You don't take one away, add another, and suddenly you're back at the same number you started with. It doesn't work like that, and I can promise you that if you lost Jen, the pain would be as deep and as cutting, no matter how many daughters you had in reserve.'

Eve closes her eyes. 'I'd prefer not to imagine it.'

'Well, maybe you should,' I reply. 'Because I bet if you asked Jen, she'd say you wouldn't miss her half as much as the others. So if we're giving out advice on parenthood,

I suggest you stop being disappointed that she's not a cardboard cut-out of her sisters and start appreciating her for who she is.' As soon as the words leave my mouth, I know I've gone too far but I've been dreaming of saying this for too long to keep it back.

Eve bristles but she doesn't hit back in the way I'm expecting. 'And how exactly do I do that when she won't speak to me, Ruth?'

She waits for a response but I can't give her one. I've listened to Jen complain about her mum often enough and she has my sympathy. It's never crossed my mind to encourage my niece to build a better relationship with her mum. Jen resents Eve for coming between her and Meg. So do I.

'I appreciate I can be overbearing at times,' Eve continues, 'but I love all my daughters equally. If I try too hard, it's because I made a concerted effort not to be like my mum. Now there was a woman who didn't appreciate her children.'

Geoff's mum had died a year before Meg, and I don't think there was a single tear shed at her funeral. Eve isn't the first mother to overcompensate for the maternal love lacking in her own childhood – and perhaps I did see Jen's preference for my family as an endorsement of my maternal abilities over my sister-in-law's. What do they say about pride coming before a fall?

Guilt cools my anger but it's not completely spent. 'Just so we're clear, Jen is not and never could be a replacement for Meg.'

'I know, I shouldn't have said that,' Eve says as she wrestles with guilt of her own. 'I'm worried about my daughter, that's all. That TV interview of yours raked up the past and she hasn't been the same since. I'm not daft, I know she thinks things would have worked out differently if I'd let her move in here.'

'If we're being honest, and it looks like we are, I often think the same.'

'Different isn't necessarily better, or at least not better for everyone,' Eve says as a shadow crosses her face. 'I stand by the decision I took at the time but I do have some regrets.'

'If we're looking to apportion blame, I'd say there are plenty of other people ahead of you in that particular queue.'

'That's what I've been saying to Jen.' When Eve drops her gaze and fiddles with her fingers, I can only presume it was my name that was mentioned. 'But I did know there was something not right about Meg at that party you had in Thornton Hall. I should have spoken up. You might have handled her better.'

I rub my temples. I don't need Eve telling me where I went wrong, especially not at the moment. I'm wrestling with enough demons from the past. 'It's more important what happens going forward, don't you think?' I ask. 'We both want what's best for Jen, so tell me, what do you want from me, Eve?'

'Will you speak to her? Remind her that I'm still her mum?'

35

Ruth

As Jen and I walk shoulder to shoulder along the Strand, I could mention her mother's visit yesterday but it's a distraction neither of us need. Our minds are crowded enough with last minute doubts about what we're about to do.

'Are you feeling OK?' Jen asks as we turn into Liverpool One and John Lewis's store front comes into view.

'Not really,' I admit. 'How about you?'

'I'm much calmer than I was last time I did this,' she says with a smile that I can't attempt to match.

Jen continues to astound me. For a child who once refused to walk on the stepping stones in Sefton Park for fear of falling in the lake and being swept out to sea, she has shown more grit than the rest of us. She has been the one to face Lewis's wrath time and again and I can only presume he picks on her because he thinks I'm beaten. He'll think differently after today.

'It might be a good idea to split up once we get inside,'

Jen continues. 'Iona will run for cover when she sees us so we'll need to trap her in a pincer movement.'

'And then what?'

None of this is rehearsed. The last time Jen did this, we were all under the misapprehension that Iona was the one being abused. In some ways, the reality is more disturbing. We're not about to help a young woman recognise that her boyfriend's behaviour is unacceptable; we have to convince an unsuspecting girlfriend that the man she loves is a monster, and we're going to attempt to do that in a very public place.

'We can only speak to her,' Jen says. 'And if she doesn't want to listen, at least she takes away a very clear message to Lewis that we haven't gone away. He doesn't need to know this is our parting shot.'

I unbutton my coat and take a deep breath. 'For Meg,' I whisper.

'For Meg,' Jen repeats as we step through the doors. She nods for me to take the left-hand side of the store while she keeps to the right.

As I circle the outer limits of the gift section, I try to keep Jen in my sights but the escalators block my view. I pass the paperweights and glassware and begin weaving my way through Halloween displays with pumpkin-shaped chocolates and bottles of gin wrapped in spider web. I almost overlook the shop assistant crouching down to restock shelves. She has her back to me but Jen has shared the photo from Facebook and this girl has the right shade of hair. As I enter the narrow aisle, Jen appears at the opposite end.

We glance briefly at each other as we wait for Iona to

finish what's she's doing. When she straightens up, she sees Jen first and takes a step back only to bump into me. She turns and her hand flies to her throat. 'Oh, Jesus, what is this?'

'I don't . . . I really am sorry,' I stammer. We've convinced ourselves that there's nothing left for us to lose but what if we're wrong? Iona is young and, despite her blazing green eyes, she's fragile. Lewis could break her.

'We need to talk properly this time,' Jen says, resting a hand on a shelf so her arm is extended, blocking one exit should Iona decides to bolt.

I choose a less aggressive stance and open my arms. 'Please, if we don't do this now, we'll only come back again.'

Iona presses her back against the display unit so she can keep both of us in her sights. 'Not if I get an injunction,' she threatens. 'Lewis has already checked what we need to do.'

'He's spoken to the police?' asks Jen.

'He's spoken to his solicitor.'

Jen raises an eyebrow. 'You mean his friend. I told you he wouldn't go to the police. You might not see it yet but he's hiding what he is from you,' she says. 'You won't see the real Lewis until he has you trapped.'

'Do you ever stop to listen to yourself?' Iona asks. 'Your cousin died and you'd rather blame anyone except yourselves. After ten years, it's getting a bit tedious.'

'Is that what Lewis told you?' I ask, pulling Iona's attention back to me. 'Of course I blame myself. I should have seen what was happening and if I'm being honest, I did, but I ignored all the signs because I didn't want to believe it. My daughter was a fiery ball of energy from the minute she was born and I didn't think anyone could contain her, not even Lewis.'

'Exactly,' Iona says as if she knows Meg intimately. 'She was out of control when he met her. He didn't hurt her, she was already damaged.'

'You're wrong,' Jen says. 'He did things to her that changed her into someone I didn't recognise. I saw some of what he did, but like Ruth, I thought Meg could fight back.'

'It's prejudice, that's what it is,' Iona says, looking to me. 'You knew he had a tough upbringing and you didn't want your precious daughter associating with a thug. He's no thug, Mrs McCoy.'

'I wanted to believe that too. I admired his mum for what she did for him, but Lewis must have had it in him from the start. It was too late.'

'If you had any respect for his mum, you wouldn't be doing this. We had to move her into a hospice last week, did you know that?' Iona asks. 'She doesn't know what's been going on since that interview you gave, and that was bad enough. God knows what it would do to her if she knew the rest. She's proud of her boy, as am I, and nothing you can say will convince us otherwise.' She turns to Jen. 'He hasn't gone to the police because he actually feels sorry for you. So if you want to have a word with anyone, have one with yourself. I've heard enough.'

'No, you haven't,' Jen replies. 'He hasn't stopped preying on women, Iona. He's just got better at hiding it. When I came looking for you the other day, I thought you were someone else.'

'Oh, really. And who exactly did you think I was?'

Jen glances around before she begins. The store is busy but thankfully no one is particularly interested in the Halloween displays at the moment. 'I thought you were the vulnerable young woman I've been talking to on the helpline. She believed, like you, that she'd met someone who would look after her, until he started abusing her.'

Jen leaves a pause so that Iona can digest the information before dismissing it, and she will dismiss it.

'He says it's her own fault,' Jen continues. 'She reminds him too much of Meg and he's compelled to do to her what he did to Meg. Afterwards, he begs forgiveness and makes her promise not to tell, but she did tell. She told me *exactly* what Lewis has been doing to her.'

Iona shakes her head. 'If you claim to know so much about her, why did you mistake me for her? What's her name? Where does she live? When and where did Lewis meet her – allegedly?' she asks, firing off each question when she sees Jen can't answer the one before. 'Is that it? Can I go now?'

'We're only trying to protect you,' I say.

'No, you're out for revenge.'

'Revenge for what?' Jen asks quickly. 'Do you think he's guilty of something?'

There's a flicker of something in Iona's eyes. She's uncomfortable.

'I bet you've seen his temper,' Jen says. 'He might not take his anger out on you but that could be because he's taking it out on someone else.'

'He goes to the gym.'

'Oh, Iona,' I say. 'You know what we're saying is true, don't you?'

305

Iona looks to me and Jen in turn, sizing us up as she works out which of us she should shove past. 'This is ridiculous,' she says, her voice wobbling.

'He chokes her,' Jen says in a hushed whisper that's almost lost in the hustle and bustle of the store. 'He used Meg's scarves as gags at first but when she wouldn't keep quiet, he started choking her with them. I know this because it's what he does to Ellie.'

'I don't know who this Ellie is, but she has nothing to do with me, or Lewis.'

'Ellie is the girl he's been abusing,' Jen says. 'And one way or another she's going to get away from him, which begs the question, who will he turn to next? I'm sorry about his mum but how do you think your relationship will change when she's gone? Who's going to be around to see your bruises? Who's going to speak up for you when Lewis takes away your voice?'

'This isn't fair.' Iona's lips are trembling now, and I feel utterly wretched.

'No, it isn't,' Jen agrees. She dares to look at me before she asks Iona one final question. 'Has he ever bought you silk scarves?'

'Stop it,' Iona pleads before turning to me. 'He loves me, Mrs McCoy. We've talked about getting married. There's no one else for him. There never was.'

'There was Meg,' I remind her as I slip my hand into my bag. I've brought along a collection of leaflets from Women's Aid and Refuge that give details of all the support they can offer, plus information sheets from the Lean On Me website that include a checklist so Iona can work out for herself if she's in a healthy relationship or not, but I leave them in my bag. There's only one voice left that might be able to get through to Iona and it's Meg's.

I pull out an envelope that contains photocopies of two yellow lined pages from Meg's notepad. 'In here are the only clues we have as to why Meg took her life,' I explain as I offer the envelope to Iona. 'One is the remnant of the suicide note we found on the day she died. It doesn't say much because whoever was there with her destroyed the rest.'

Iona puts her hands behind her back, refusing to take the envelope. 'I've looked up her inquest on Google. There was no proof that happened.'

'That's why there's another sheet of paper in here. I only found it recently but I think it's quite telling, more so when you consider what we've told you about Ellie. These are my daughter's words. Please, take them.'

'If I do, will you go away?'

'If you promise to read them, yes, we will.'

I step aside when Iona takes the envelope and she slips past with her head down. I carry on looking, long after she disappears from sight.

'We've done all we can,' Jen says, putting her hand on my arm.

'I know,' I reply. 'But we may never find out if it's been enough.'

36

Jen

I know there's nothing more to be done. Time ran out for my best friend and I feel it trickling away from Ellie too. Today will be my last ever shift on the helpline and I don't know how I'm going to feel when it's over. There's talk of going out for a meal on Friday when the lines close for good but nothing has been arranged. None of the volunteers share the relief Charlie spoke of and there's no appetite for celebration.

As I flick through the morning mail, I search for a thick cream envelope to match the one Ruth received after her TV interview, but if Lewis is planning fresh legal action, he's taking his time. My legs are jiggling under the desk. I've geared myself up for a fight and I need something to happen.

To counter my frustration, I've been using my present state of restlessness to forge on with plans for a new career. I have no intention of staying here when Ruth and Geoff retire, which could be soon, judging by the way Oscar

Armitage has made himself at home in their office. I watch as he leans back in a visitor's chair with his legs spread wide and his hands behind his head. I do not want to work for that man.

One of the jobs I've applied for is an admin post in a hospice. It's only part time but that's ideal if I'm going to study to be a counsellor. There's a foundation course that starts in January and I've accepted Ruth's generous offer to fund my training. All I have to do now is convince Charlie to put his plans for a house and kids on hold so we can afford my drop in salary. The more I think about becoming a counsellor, the more I want it.

What I don't want is to be doing *this*, I tell myself, as I slice open an envelope and pull out an invoice. My mind is made up further when Geoff catches my eye. He's lifting up his mug and pointing to Oscar.

I take Oscar's order with a sweet smile but when I return five minutes later with his coffee, he's hunched over his seat with his phone pressed to his ear. Ruth and Geoff are doing their best not to listen in but it can't be easy.

'In my view, your client's overreacting. There's no need—' Oscar says loudly. There's a pause. 'No, no, I understand. Would it help if I came to your offices? I'm in a meeting at the moment, but—' He looks at his watch and nods. 'Certainly. I'll be there within the hour.'

He's careful to readjust his features into a smile before he looks up. 'I'm afraid I have a minor emergency with a major project. You know how it is,' he says to Geoff. 'Could we pick this up later? Why don't I take you both out to dinner tonight?'

'I'm afraid I have other plans,' says Ruth.

'Tomorrow would be better,' agrees Geoff.

Oscar pulls a face. 'My diary's pretty full,' he says, rubbing a temple. 'It could be next week at this rate.'

'Why don't you two go ahead without me?' Ruth suggests.

If Geoff were about to refuse, Oscar doesn't give him a chance. He stands up and extends his hand. 'I'll get my PA to book a table and email you the details. Sorry, but I do have to dash.'

He shakes hands with Ruth and Geoff and manages a quick nod to me as he hurries out of the office.

'Anyone want this coffee?' I ask.

Geoff waves it away without taking his eyes from his wife, and I'm about to make my escape when he holds up his palm to stop me. His hand gestures are irritating and if it wasn't Geoff, I'd give him one of my own.

'You don't need to stay back tonight,' he tells Ruth. 'Jen's told you before she can manage on her own.'

My annoyance at Geoff immediately thaws. I haven't lost hope that Ellie will ring tonight. She can't want our last conversation to consist of the words Lewis put in her mouth and this will be our last opportunity to make peace with each other. I'm going to have to make every word count and I'd feel less pressured if Ruth wasn't there.

'I am not changing my plans, Geoff,' Ruth tells him. 'It's our last week on the helpline.'

'But isn't that the point? You'll only be passing the callers on to someone else, and I don't know about you, but I didn't like the sound of Oscar's conversation. I'd rather you were with me.'

'You managed to sell Oscar the idea long before you included me in your plans,' she reminds him. 'I'm sure you're more than capable of closing the deal without me too.'

'We could put it back to next week, I suppose.'

'No, you were the one in such a hurry to get things moving and if Oscar has problems back at the ranch, you need to find out what they are pretty sharpish,' Ruth snaps back at him. Catching me backing away again, she adds, 'I am not going to miss your last shift, Jen.'

I'm not the only one hoping for one last chance with Ellie.

As five o'clock approaches, it's time to move over to the helpline pods, but I make myself a coffee first. I'm hoping Ruth will stay in her office until Geoff leaves to meet Oscar but when I return from the kitchen, she's already commandeered the first pod.

'You're eager.'

'You don't mind, do you?' she asks as I slump into the chair opposite.

I want to be mad at her but I can't. 'The helpline was your baby. It's only fair that you take the last calls.'

Ruth's quiet for a moment. 'I suppose it has been my baby, not that it was a replacement for Meg,' she adds quickly as if countering an argument she would never hear from me. 'But it did make me feel like she was still a part of our lives. I can't believe I'm letting it go.'

'Me neither.'

The office chatter floats around us as we still our thoughts. The digital clock on my computer screen appears stuck on 16:59, and when it does change, my eyes dart to the phone. I don't know why, because it's Ruth's phone that will ring first, and what then? What if the first call is from Ellie? What if she hangs up? Will that be it?

'I think she's going to ring tonight,' Ruth says, her thoughts turning in the same circles as mine.

'So do I.'

'I thought Lewis would have showed his hand by now.'

'I'm worried there's a reason he hasn't.'

Ruth closes her eyes. 'I keep thinking about the awful things he did to Meg. That's going to haunt me forever, more so if the helpline closes and we never find out if Ellie does manage to catch that flight on Saturday. She has to phone.'

'If she does, will you pass the call to me, Ruth? This is our last chance to get it right.'

'I'm not sure I know what right looks like any more,' Ruth replies. 'After visiting Gemma last night, the only thing I can tell you is what wrong looks like. Her injuries are life-altering and time alone will tell how she deals with it all.'

Unlike Ruth, I haven't been asked along to visit Gemma since she regained consciousness, and I'm not sure I'd want to go. I'll never know if she would have fared better if I hadn't hung up on her that night, but my guilt isn't the only reason I keep away. I don't want to see what happens when you upset someone who knows how to hurt women.

I cover my face with my hands. 'Oh, God, I can't bear this.'

My head jerks up when the phone on Ruth's desk rings. Our eyes lock as she puts the receiver to her ear and greets the caller with a trembling voice. In the pause that follows, we both hold our breath.

'Oh, hello. How lovely to hear from you again,' Ruth says.

My relief lasts until my gaze settles on the silent phone on my desk. Lulled by the sound of Ruth's chatter, I picture Ellie in her apartment staring at her mobile. As I will her to reach out and dial the helpline, someone whispers in my ear and I jump out of my skin.

'I'm off to meet Oscar,' Geoff says.

I slow my breathing and offer a smile. 'OK, have a nice time.'

He puts a hand on my shoulder and squeezes. 'I hope tonight goes well,' he says, the smell of whiskey on his breath. 'Could you tell Ruth to phone me after the shift?'

'Will do.'

When he leaves, Geoff doesn't look like a man about to close a lucrative deal to bankroll a comfortable retirement. His trench coat hangs from his arm and the belt trails along the floor. Is he expecting the deal to fall through? Have Ruth and Geoff been too hasty putting their house on the market and closing down the helpline? Before I can consider the answers, the phone rings.

It's one of our regulars, a woman who has left her boyfriend several times before. I hope this time will be the last, but I realise I'm never going to find out. I spend most of the call giving her the numbers of alternative helplines and assuring her that she will find new people to support her. My words are choked when we say goodbye and as I replace the receiver, I notice Ruth watching me. She's finished her call too.

'I can't believe how emotional I'm getting,' I tell her. 'And if Ellie doesn't ring, I'm going to be in bits come eight o'clock.'

Tears well in Ruth's eyes. 'I am doing the right thing, aren't I?'

I recall Geoff's slumped shoulders as he left the office. 'However things turn out, you'll make the best of it,' I tell her. 'You always do.'

'I'm not as strong as you think I am.'

'No, but you're as strong as you have to be.'

'It would be nice not to be tested quite so often,' she says with a rueful smile. She sighs loudly then stands up. 'I've been thinking about what you said. This may very well be our last chance to talk to Ellie and as much as I would love it to be me she speaks to, it should be you. It can only be you.'

Ruth takes longer than I to settle after we swap places. I watch as she leans to the side and there's a hiss as she pulls the lever to raise her chair, giving herself a better view over the privacy screen. 'You could put her on speakerphone if she does call,' she suggests.

'I won't break her trust again, Ruth.'

'I know.'

Our wait for Ellie's call resumes and it isn't long before the familiar trill of the phone sets our hearts racing.

'If it's not Ellie, transfer the call to me, Jen.'

I nod as I pick up the phone. 'Hello, you're through to the Lean On Me helpline.'

'Hi.'

I'm looking directly at Ruth when I say, 'Hi, Ellie. How are you?'

There's a snuffling sound as she blows her nose. She takes a deep, jagged breath but can manage only one word. 'Confused.'

'And what exactly are you confused about?' I say, repeating what Ellie has said for Ruth's benefit.

'I do not know what will happen next.'

'Are you still planning to go home on Saturday?'

'It is not up to me. I have not seen the tickets or confirmation of a flight.'

'Was he listening in on our conversation last week?'

She takes another breath that ends with a hiccup. 'Yes.'

I nod to let Ruth know that she's confirmed my suspicions.

'I had no choice,' continues Ellie. 'I promised it would be the last call but he does not believe me. He says he will come over later.'

'You don't have to let him in.'

'I have to. He has my passport.'

'He has your passport? Oh, Ellie, let me help you. It doesn't matter that the helpline's closing, you can take my mobile number and phone me whenever you want. I'll help you find a place to stay and my boyfriend, Charlie, will give you a job if you don't mind cleaning. We'll make sure you can't be found and, if you still want to go home, we can help you apply for a replacement passport. We can pay for your flights,' I tell her, watching Ruth as she nods energetically.

I reel off my mobile number, repeating it slowly because I don't know for sure that Ellie's writing it down. She hasn't said anything. All I can hear are her stifled sobs.

'Please, Ellie. Let me help.'

'You are too kind to me. I was horrible to you. I should not have told you that you were a bad friend to Megan. It is what he believes so he can blame someone else, but it is not what I think.'

'You didn't say anything I haven't thought myself.'

'He forgets he told me once how Megan loved you. You could have helped her if he had let you. That was why I phoned the helpline. It was you I wanted to speak to, Jen.'

The second phone rings, giving me time to process my feelings. Could I have saved Meg, or was Lewis right to say I was a bad friend? The answer is probably a mixture of the two. I could have saved Meg if I hadn't been such a bad friend.

Realising I can still hear a phone ringing, I give Ruth a curious look. She shakes her head. She isn't going to answer.

'I should go,' Ellie says.

'Please tell me that you've written down my number and you're going to ring back.'

'I was wrong to involve you, Jen. I worried about Mrs McCoy finding out what he did, but I should have thought about you too. I am sorry for bringing you my problems.'

'Don't be sorry. Ruth and I have spent ten years imagining what Meg went through,' I tell her, holding Ruth's gaze. 'Nothing was worse than the not knowing. Help us make this right, Ellie. Help us by letting us help you.'

The second caller rings off but that won't be enough to keep Ellie on the line. Ruth scribbles a note and shows it to me.

TELL HER I'M HERE

'Ellie, please don't disappear and leave us with more unknowns. If you care about my feelings, and Ruth's, you have to keep talking to us. You don't have to be afraid any more. You matter to us more than you could possibly know. We'll make sure you're safe.'

'You keep saying we,' Ellie says. There's a pause. 'Is she there?'

'Yes, Ruth's here.'

Ruth springs to her feet and comes to stand next to me.

'Will you speak with her, Ellie?' I ask as Ruth reaches across me and switches the call to speakerphone.

'Tell her I am sorry,' Ellie replies. 'Say goodbye to her, and Charlie too.'

'Ellie, this is Ruth. Please don't hang up, I'm begging you,' she says, her voice rising in panic. 'Jen has told me what he's been doing to you, and I know he did the same to Meg. I won't deny it's been unbearable to hear but the truth has to come out, no matter how painful.'

'I am not so sure.'

Ruth freezes and I'm about to speak up when she finds her voice again. 'Don't let him get away with this. Please! I'll be home alone this evening and we can talk for as long as you like.'

There's a gulp as Ellie takes a breath. 'I am sorry, Mrs McCoy.'

The line goes dead.

Neither Ruth nor I move. The lifeless phone remains clutched in my hand.

'Do you want a drink?' Ruth asks, her voice disjointed, as if her mind is still processing what just happened.

When she picks up my cup, cold liquid slops over the sides, leaving a trail of coffee stains as she walks around to her desk and grabs her mobile. I watch Ruth disappear into the kitchen and, a minute later, I hear her on the phone.

Her voice is too low to pick up what she might be saying, not that I care. There are too many unanswerable questions buzzing around my head.

When Ruth returns with our drinks, we don't make eye contact. I wrap my hands around the steaming mug and breathe in the warm, coffee aroma. It coaxes me from my stupor.

'Did you speak to Geoff?' I ask.

The surface of her mug tremors slightly. 'I don't know why I bothered,' she says, fresh pain in her voice.

'If you want to go home, Ruth, I don't mind finishing the shift on my own.'

'You don't need me to stay?'

I presume she's asking if I'm ready to talk about what just happened – because it's clear that she isn't. Tears sting my eyes but I blink them away. 'I can manage.'

Ruth leaves her drink untouched and slips on her coat, tying the belt around her waist to avoid fumbling with the buttons. I stand and go to her. Her cheek is cold as she presses it to mine.

'I'll see you tomorrow, Ruth.'

'Oh, but I was meant to give you a lift home . . .' she says, suddenly remembering. 'Maybe I should stay.'

'It's fine, I'll be safe enough.'

'I hope so,' Ruth replies, turning away from me before the frown has fully formed on her brow. She holds her head higher than Geoff had earlier, but her steps are as unsure as her husband's as she crosses the office and disappears through the double doors.

Taking out my mobile, I stare at Charlie's name. I can

hear it being spoken in my head by someone with a distinct Romanian accent.

'What's up?' he asks when he answers my call. There's traffic noise in the background and the sound of wind scraping against the microphone.

'Ruth's gone home.'

'Oh, right. Where are you?'

I check the time. There's another hour to kill. 'I'm in the office.'

'Does that mean you need me to pick you up?' Charlie asks in a way that makes it clear it will be a huge inconvenience if I say yes.

'No, I'll get a taxi. Are you on your way somewhere?'

'I'm in the New Mersey Retail Park. I'm just stocking up supplies for the new cleaner, and about – to – drop – everything,' he says in panic. There's rustling as he adjusts his grip on whatever he's holding. 'So what's happened? Did Ellie ring?'

'We can talk when I get home,' I say. 'You'd better go.'

Charlie doesn't respond immediately. It wouldn't take a genius to work out from my lifeless tone that my last shift on the helpline has me beaten. 'Are you sure, Jen?'

'I'll see you later. Bye.'

After only a few moments, the helpline rings out. It's another regular caller but I struggle to resurrect the emotion I'd felt with all the other farewell messages. The conversation is brief and when the call ends, I wait for the next. It doesn't come and at 8 p.m. the helpline switches to the answering service. That's it. It's over.

As I tidy up, I convince myself that slicing envelopes

open for a living isn't such a hard life. I'm not destined for the caring profession. I've knocked up too many failures and it's time to put it all behind me. At least I know how Oscar likes his coffee.

I don't order a taxi and as I leave the building, I face the simple choice of turning left or right. Sneaking along the waterfront or parading down the Strand offer equal risks of coming face to face with Lewis again, so I opt for the city lights. No one follows me and I tell myself I'm safe when I reach my apartment block, but I feel no relief as I climb the stairs to the seventh floor.

37

Jen

'Don't turn around,' he'd said and I'm doing as instructed, keeping one eye on our reflections in the window. We're in a deserted stairwell and Lewis Rimmer sits on the stairs leading to the floor above. I can't see his face but his feet are planted on the small section of landing that separates us. He's been waiting for me, but not as long as I've been waiting for him.

I feel exposed with my back turned but in spite of the fear that crawls down my spine on spidery legs, I have no desire to run. I imagine Lewis's eyes boring into the back of my head but it's the woman's face staring back at me from the window that keeps me fixed to the spot. The apparition floating in limbo above the city looks a little like me, but feels a lot like Meg and I'm ready to pit myself against the man who came between us.

In the reflected glass, Lewis's hands hang loosely over bent knees. He's relaxed, having assumed I'm the timid creature he remembers, but he's got that wrong, hasn't he, Meg?

'Ten years on and Meg's still tormenting us,' Lewis says. 'You have to admit, she'd enjoy this.'

'Only if you have a fucked-up view of what enjoyment is.'

'That was our Meg.'

My jaw twitches. 'Couldn't you see how unhappy you made her?'

'Did anyone see how unhappy she made me?' he asks. When I don't respond, he adds, 'I know you want to remember Meg as funny, energetic and just a little bit crazy, but she had a darker side too.'

'If you're here to rewrite Meg's story and make this her fault, forget it. Do you seriously expect me to fall for something so crass?'

'Of course not. Nothing ever gets past Jennifer Hunter.'

'Except you apparently,' I reply. 'Why couldn't you leave her alone?'

'Because as hard as you find this to believe, I loved her. I thought I could fix her.'

'Fix her? My God, Lewis, you were the one who broke her. She was desperate to escape and when she failed her exams and realised she'd be stuck in Liverpool with you, it was too much for her.'

'Wrong. We'd both applied to go to Newcastle uni.'

My brow furrows. 'No, you were going to John Moores.'

'That was nothing more than a story we made up to keep her parents off her back. Think about it, Jen. Did you seriously think I snapped my fingers and got a place in Newcastle overnight?'

'So what if you did apply to go there?' I answer with a shrug. 'It doesn't mean Meg knew. I can imagine you thought it would be a nice surprise turning up in Fresher's Week. You were playing games then and you're playing them now.'

'Meg's games, Meg's lies,' he says.

'And were there more of Meg's lies in the note you prised from her dead fingers?' I reply. 'What happened, Lewis? Had you grown bored of her? Was it a relief when she killed herself? Did you help her along the way?'

'I was the only one trying to stop her,' he says, with a sigh that sounds remarkably sad. 'Where was everyone else? Where were you? You must have known, Jen. She talked about it all the time.'

'Not to me, she didn't!' I tell him as I shoot an accusing look at his reflection.

'Oh, come on! I can't have been the only one to see how much pain she was in. You must have known she was self-harming.'

'I saw the marks . . . I didn't know what they meant at the time.'

'Neither did I. And I still don't get where all that self-hate came from.'

'You can't work it out? Seriously?' I ask. 'You abused her and humiliated her until she couldn't take any more. She hurt herself to take back control. The marks made the abuse visible in the hope that someone would ask what was wrong, but no one ever did. We were too afraid of the answers.' My eyes sting with tears but I blink them away. 'She was alone, trying to work it out for herself, trying to work you out, and what did you do? You tied the noose around her neck.'

'No! It wasn't like that. I was too late . . .'

'My God, so you *were* there,' I gasp. I want to turn

around but my hand tightens around the door's safety bar to keep me in place. I have to keep my back to Lewis if I want to hear more, and I do.

'She'd been texting me all morning but I'd had enough of her games by that point. I'd lost count of the times she'd send a message that sent me into a panic. Then she'd forget about it, or ignore my calls until I was convinced something bad had happened, only for her to pop back up again and say, "Oh, I'm sorry, I didn't mean to scare you." Except that last time, she never did get back to me. The one time she was serious, I'd ignored her.'

'If you're going to spin the same old story, why are you here, Lewis?' I demand.

I hear him sigh behind me. 'I'm here because it was never the full story, was it? There was a lot more going on back then that none of us wanted to share.'

Shame scorches my cheeks. 'If this is about that stupid fucking kiss we had, don't bother. I already know you told Meg,' I say, my words punctuated by a gulp to hold back the sob. 'That isn't why she killed herself. I don't believe it.'

Except I do believe it. I only have to think back to the last time I saw my cousin.

'You really shouldn't be here,' Meg had snarled when I'd showed up at her door uninvited. Despite the midday heat, she had a heavy towelling bathrobe wrapped around her and was holding the collar beneath her chin. Her hair was unwashed and her eyes hollow.

I hadn't seen Meg since the day we'd received our A Level results. The tension between us had become unbearable, providing the ideal opportunity for Lewis to cut the final threads of our friendship before I disappeared to uni, and I'd known what weapon he would use. It didn't take much imagination to work out how he'd explained that kiss last summer to Meg. He'd probably told her I made the first move and that I'd been jealous of Meg ever since. I should have confessed straight away but I hadn't had the guts to face Meg and I was still a coward.

'I was sort of hoping you wouldn't answer the door,' I replied honestly. 'But I thought you should know that Lewis beat up Charlie and broke his nose. Charlie's refusing to say what it was about.'

'And you want me to tell you? You're the clever one who passed all her exams, Jen. You work it out.'

Meg's hostility told me all I needed to know – Lewis had definitely told her, and one or the other had told Charlie. 'Whatever went on,' I said, 'Lewis didn't have to beat him up like that.'

'It's not all Lewis's fault,' Meg replied curtly. 'Do I seriously need to spell it out, Jen? Haven't I been humiliated enough?'

Those words haunt me to this day, and as angry as I am at myself, I'm angrier at Lewis. He would have known she couldn't take much more after failing her exams, and yet he had chosen then to tell her about us.

'But I didn't tell her, Jen,' Lewis says, jolting me back to the present.

'Don't lie!' I yell at his reflection in the window. 'You and Charlie had a fight over it. Meg said—'

'Meg said what?' he interrupts. 'Even if she had known, you're right, it was only a kiss. Hardly a betrayal when you look at what she did to you.'

'And what's that supposed to mean?'

325

When Lewis doesn't reply, I find myself replaying that last conversation on Meg's doorstep. She'd said she didn't want to be humiliated so I hadn't pressed home the point about what Lewis and I had done, but I couldn't leave without trying to make it right between us.

As I'd stood my ground on her doorstep that day, tears had sprung in Meg's eyes. 'Why are you even pretending you care?' she asked. 'We're not family any more, Jen! Families don't go around chasing after their cousin's boyfriend, do they?'

'It was an accident.'

'No, Jen,' Meg snarled. 'It was deliberate.'

I shook my head, no, not deliberate. I'd been a bit tipsy that night in Meathead's garden and the kiss had happened so fast that I hadn't had time to react. Except I had reacted. When Lewis kissed me, I'd kissed him back. 'Can't we just pretend it never happened?'

'I spend too much of my life pretending and I've had enough. Please,' she said, closing her eyes so she didn't have to look at me. 'Go away, Jen. This hurts too much.'

'I don't—'

'Go away, Jen!' she screamed at me.

'Why do you have to be like this, Meg?' I asked. When she didn't answer, I felt my heart wrench. I should have been begging for forgiveness but I was too angry at her for shutting me out over one stupid mistake. 'I'm so glad I didn't end up living with you!'

Meg's features fell. 'Not as much as I am.'

When she closed the door in my face, I had four more days of being angry at Meg, followed by ten years of being angry with myself.

Lewis releases a sigh of frustration that echoes down the stairwell. 'Do I need to spell it out for you, Jen?' he asks.

Meg had said the same thing right before her remark about someone chasing after their cousin's boyfriend. She thought I was clever enough to work it out for myself, but I wasn't. I was stupid.

38

Ruth

As I step into the unlit house, there's something comforting about remaining in the dark. I pause amongst the shadows in the hallway, tip back my head, and listen. There was a time when the best I could hope for was the sound of shuffling feet or the bang of Meg's bedroom door. It used to hurt, but not as much as the silence that greets me tonight. I want to tell my daughter that I'm pulling down the barricades she hid behind. I'm uncovering what once was hidden and my pulse quickens as I feel my way through the darkness to the kitchen.

'Stay with me a while,' I say, speaking to my daughter as if she has never left. 'Let's do this together.'

I fumble around in a cupboard for the bottle of whiskey Geoff opened last night. It feels half full and I pour a generous measure into a tumbler. The smoky liquid burns the back of my throat before flooding the hole in my chest with warmth. I can understand how it helps my husband trudge through days mired by grief.

It was meant to get better by now, and there have been good times through the years when I could laugh without guilt and look back without trepidation. I hadn't realised how much Meg's tenth anniversary would upset our equilibrium. I wish we'd treated it like any other date on the calendar. The day she died doesn't deserve to be noted. It's the other six and a half thousand days of her life that are important – those treasured times when our family of four was complete.

As I grab my laptop from the dresser and collapse onto the sofa, I prepare to revisit those years. My eyes sting from the brightness of the computer screen as I open the media player and I browse the selection of memories I have at my disposal. I start with the New Year's Eve party I'd watched with Jen at the weekend.

I'd been looking for Lewis amongst the shadows that scattered the moment Geoff and I appeared in the garden but, according to Jen, I'd been searching in vain. Lewis wasn't there. He hadn't started dating my daughter until she returned to school in the new year.

I lean forward as Geoff's camera focuses on Jen holding a bottle of champagne. When Meg appears behind her, our daughter refuses to look at the camera. What was she hiding back then if it wasn't Lewis? I stare at the glasses she's wearing and watch her push them up the bridge of her nose for fear of her mask slipping. It would be two summers later before I'd see those glasses again, caught in the narrow gap between the mattress and my bedside table. These two moments in time are connected by one item, and one person. Charlie.

Returning to the list of videos, I work back to Christmas morning the week before. I watch Meg open the heart-shaped pot and cast it to one side. Her head remains bowed as again she avoids the camera – she's hiding here too.

My hands tremble as I go back a month to our anniversary party at Thornton Hall. There are a dozen videos of the party but I choose the one the local reporter had used in the video montage. I remember noticing at the time that the clips she used had been placed out of sequence, showing our anniversary as post-dating Christmas. It was an easy enough mistake because the reporter had wanted to show Meg's slow decline.

As I watch the video again, I see Meg look up and recoil as her dad points the camera at her. I'd presumed she was upset because Eve had refused to allow Jen to move in with us, but I'm not looking at a child who's sulking. Was that why Eve mentioned the party the other day? Had she seen what I'm only registering now? Meg's eyes are hollow. There's no doubt this time. Meg had been damaged back then – *before* Lewis.

Not liking where my thoughts are taking me, I swallow a mouthful of whiskey before grabbing up my mobile. Sean whispers, 'Hello?' when he picks up.

'Sorry, have I woken up the girls?'

I hear shuffling footsteps until the noise of a TV fades into the background. 'No, but Alice and I might have been dozing,' he admits with a yawn. 'The girls are in bed but they've decided in the last few days that sleep is so last season. Roll on the days when we can dump them on Granny and Grandpa and do something crazy, like sleep in till seven.'

Fearful of speaking my fears aloud, I let the silence stretch out.

'Mum? What's wrong?'

I can't answer. My gaze is fixed on the image frozen on screen. The recording of Meg at the anniversary party has stopped at the point where she turns her head from the camera. The image of the back of my daughter's head is painfully familiar and long-felt fear and frustration sends a rush of adrenalin through my body as I picture myself storming into her room on that last morning.

I'd opened my mouth ready to scream her name and raise her from the bed she hadn't moved from for days, but Meg was sitting at her dressing table with her back to me. Her bed was made and if the silk scarves that hung from her bedpost had been taken down in preparation for what she was about to do, I didn't notice.

'Oh, you're up.'

'I've got lots to do today,' she replied, her eyes meeting mine as I drew closer to her reflection.

The makeup she'd applied lifted her complexion but her hair fell lank at the sides, and her perfume didn't quite conceal the stale smell of body odour. I wanted to suggest she take a shower but progress was progress. Or so I thought.

'What are going to do with yourself, sweetheart? Would you like to meet me at lunchtime and go shopping in town? You could pick out a new outfit for your birthday.'

'Sorry, I have plans.'

I placed my hands on her shoulders and my heart skipped a beat when she didn't reject me as she had so many times before. 'Care to share?'

The smile she gave me is etched in my memory. It was full of sadness and regret and yet offered such hope. I thought I was getting my daughter back, and maybe, *maybe* if I'd held her a second longer, or wrapped my arms around her body and held her tightly, I might have kept her safe. I might have made a difference. I didn't know . . . I couldn't know that our bittersweet connection would be the last.

'Later,' she said.

'Things will get better, Meg,' I promised. 'You know we love you.'

When I felt her body tensing, I chastised myself for being too pushy. I told myself that my baby girl had this, and I should trust her.

'I don't want you worrying about me,' she said. 'I'm going to be fine, Mum. I'm untouchable.'

And I never touched her again.

39

Jen

'Jen, Meg didn't kill herself because of what we did. She killed herself because of what she and Charlie did.'

Lewis's tone is flat and even. He wants me to think he's taking no pleasure in breaking the news, but the Lewis I know thrives on causing emotional as well as physical pain.

'Meg and Charlie slept together the day we got our A Level results,' he continues. 'That's what Charlie and I were fighting over. Not you.'

My toes dig into the floor as I prepare for flight, but if I run now, it would look like I'm running away from the truth when I know that's not the case. It can't be. I was aware that Charlie fancied Meg but she'd never shown any interest in him. No, Meg was angry that day because of what *I'd* done.

So why was she so defensive? I ask myself.

Because she thought I was there to attack her, not apologise. My next words scratch like sandpaper over my vocal chords. 'If what you say is true, why wait until now to tell me?'

'The last thing I wanted was everyone knowing that Meg had cheated on me with Charlie, of all people.'

'Even after she died?' I ask, desperately searching for reasons to discredit what he's saying, but it's futile. I can feel my knees ready to buckle and my grip on the door tightens.

'Everyone had already made their minds up about what I did or didn't do,' Lewis explains. 'And I could tell by the questions the police asked that they were looking to pin Meg's death on me. I didn't want to give them another motive so I kept quiet. And so did Charlie, but I suppose he had his own reasons. You really need to speak to him about what happened between them.'

Lewis waits for my reaction but I'm not going to give him one. Even if I can accept that Meg slept with Charlie, it doesn't explain or excuse the abuse Meg suffered at Lewis's hands.

'I never thought I'd ever move back to Liverpool. I never wanted to revisit that part of my life,' he continues, 'but when Mum got sick, I had no choice. I thought if I used her maiden name I'd be able to keep under the radar. I did it out of respect for Meg's family, and for what? So you and Ruth could attack *my* family? This has gone too far and I've had enough. Sorry, Jen.'

No, he's not. If Lewis were that remorseful, he wouldn't be hurting Ellie the way he is. Lewis didn't change his name out of respect, he did it so he would go undetected, but we found him anyway. We've messed up his life and now he wants to screw around with ours. 'I don't believe you.'

Lewis digs a hand into his jacket pocket and my heart leaps into my mouth when I see a snatch of something yellow. Could it be the missing half to Meg's suicide note? I don't get the chance to find out because Lewis shoves it back out of sight once he's found his phone.

'Charlie sent me a message. Do you want to hear what it said?' he asks. Giving me no time to answer, he clears his throat. '"I don't know what your game is but you've gone too far. Leave Jen out of this. The past needs to stay in the past for everyone's sake."' Lewis laughs. 'I presume that's his version of a threat.'

'He told me he'd sent you a message.'

'Yeah, well, he didn't tell you everything, did he?' Lewis continues. 'Meg said that what happened between them was a one-off, but Iona showed me that page from Meg's notepad, the one with the cryptic message about her being hurt over and over again, and it got me thinking. How much of the past does Charlie want buried? Could it have been going on for longer?'

'No,' I say firmly.

'So what Meg wrote was just another of her stupid games?'

I'm staring at the window but my focus has moved past the reflections to the darkness beyond. I don't know what or who to believe any more.

'It was no game,' I say. 'She was describing her inner-most thoughts and she hid what she'd written. The only thing I think we can agree upon, Lewis, is that Meg was hurting. She was describing something that was happening to her *months* before the thing with Charlie.' I pause, realising I've stated Meg and Charlie's liaison as fact. So be it. 'Now you might believe that what you did to Meg was normal, but it wasn't. That page from her notepad tells you it wasn't.'

'I don't claim that what we had together was normal but I don't recognise what she described, not at all. I never forced Meg to do anything she didn't want. She was the one who took the lead, just ask Charlie,' he says. The sound of Lewis taking a deep breath draws me back to his reflection. His phone is back in his pocket and he has his fingertips pressed together as if he's in prayer, or about to make a confession. 'I never knew where I was with Meg from one minute to the next. There were times when she wanted me to hold her and take things slowly but I'd make one wrong move and that would be it. Sometimes she'd go completely still and it was like having sex with a mannequin, so after a while, I stopped trying. For most of our relationship, it wasn't even sexual.'

'Oh, so I suppose Geoff caught you that time in their bedroom playing Monopoly.'

'I did what Meg wanted,' he insists. 'And when Geoff caught us, we were lying on the bed but that was all. I was glad you all thought otherwise. I didn't want anyone knowing we were happy enough just cuddling. Except, Meg was never happy. She tried to get me interested again but the stuff she wanted me to do . . . I couldn't do it, Jen. And I didn't.'

'I saw you, remember?' I reply. 'I saw you choking her that day we had the barbeque in Sefton Park.'

'You mean the day she told me she wished she was dead and stopped answering my messages? I was shit scared she'd done something stupid, and yes, I was angry when I tracked her down to the park. I know I shouldn't have grabbed her by the throat. It was a stupid taunt, that's all.'

'And was it a stupid taunt that gave her the bruises on

her neck they found in her autopsy? When did you start using the scarves?'

'That wasn't me! For God's sake, Jen. In case you haven't figured it out, she found someone who would,' he says as he shoves his hands in his pockets. 'Do you know how hard it is to sit here and admit that I couldn't satisfy my girlfriend? That I was celibate for most of our relationship when I'd gone around school playing the big I Am? You've got me wrong and this campaign of hate has to stop. I've told you as much as I can. I've been carrying Meg's secrets around with me for too fucking long and I'm beaten. Mum hasn't got long left and you're turning her last weeks into a nightmare. She knows something's wrong and I don't know how long I can keep pretending it isn't.'

If I'm not mistaken, there's a tremor in Lewis's voice. 'I'm sorry about that.'

'Are you? Isn't this what you wanted?'

'What I want is for you to stop twisting the facts,' I say, with a little too much desperation, because I find Lewis's version of events compelling. 'You're the one who hurt Meg and you're the one who's been doing it again to someone else.'

'You mean Ellie?'

'Yes, Ellie.'

'I don't have a clue who this girl is, other than the fact that you told Iona I've been hurting her.'

'Ellie isn't necessarily her real name. You might know her by another—'

'I don't give a fuck what her name is. I've never met her and whatever she's been telling you about me is pure fabrication. She's a crank, Jen,' Lewis says as he pulls something

337

from his jacket pocket. The object I'd glimpsed earlier isn't a page from Meg's notepad at all. The yellow of the silk reflected in the window merges with the city lights beyond, but the splashes of blood orange are hauntingly familiar. The silk scarf Lewis gave Meg on her birthday winds around his knuckles.

My body tenses so that I'm poised to act if Lewis dares stand, but I doubt my reactions would be fast enough, or my legs steady enough for me to fling open the fire door and reach the safety of the apartment in time. I try for distraction.

'She isn't a crank, nor is she another of Meg's games. Ellie is very real and her accounts of what you did to her, and to Meg, are by no means cryptic,' I say, forcing my voice not to waver. I can't take my eyes from the scarf Lewis holds taut in both hands like a garrotte. 'You thought choking the breath out of them would silence them but you were wrong.'

'No, you're the one who's wrong. Those scarves terrified me and if I'd known what Meg liked doing with them, I would never have bought her this one,' he says, pulling it tighter. 'She threw it back at me, you know. She said it didn't belong in her collection.'

'But it belongs in yours,' I reply, staring at the scarf. 'A souvenir?'

'Iona found out I still had it and it freaked her out.'

'I'm not surprised.'

'When did you get to be such a heartless bitch, Jen?' Lewis asks as he stands up to reveal his full reflection. His dark clothes and baseball hat blur his outline but the profile of his face as he glares at the back of my head makes the hairs on my neck prickle.

I'm gripping the safety bar tightly and my palm is slick with sweat. I slip my free hand into my jacket pocket and find the personal alarm I've carried with me since my last encounter with Lewis. I hope to God Charlie is home to hear it when I set it off.

'You're not going to listen to reason, are you?' Lewis continues, turning his head and catching my reflection in the window. Our eyes lock. 'You won't consider anything I have to say about Meg, or me, or Charlie for that matter, because it's not what you want to hear.'

'Not when there's evidence to the contrary,' I tell him. 'Ellie knows too much to be making it up.'

'Unless I'm suffering from some weird form of amnesia, I'm not the Lewis she's talking about,' he says. He catches me blinking one too many times and his grip on Meg's scarf loosens. 'Shit, Jen. She hasn't mentioned me by name, has she? You've assumed it's me.'

'With good reason. When you found out Ellie was phoning the helpline and attacked her, you made your first mistake. You see, there were only a very small number of people who knew about her calls, and one of them was you.'

'Setting aside the fact that I *didn't* know,' he says, 'who else did you tell?'

'People I trust.'

'People like Charlie?' he asks. 'Funny how our conversation keeps coming back to him.'

I want to respond with a clever retort but I can't. I can hear Ellie's voice echoing through my mind. Say goodbye to Charlie, she'd said.

40

Ruth

'Mum, are you OK?' Sean asks. 'Is there a problem with selling up?'

'There could be a setback but your dad's having dinner with Oscar tonight,' I say, wishing that was our only problem. 'I'll know more when he's home.'

I don't mention how angry Geoff had been when he told me there was a real possibility we might have to look for a new buyer and I'd failed to share his frustration. I'd phoned to tell him about the latest call from Ellie but the mention of her name had sent him apoplectic. She's a living reminder of what Meg had been forced to endure, and while I can understand his distress, this isn't going away. In fact, if what I'm thinking is right, it's moved closer to home.

'Then what's wrong?' Sean asks, all traces of sleep gone from his voice.

'I've been thinking a lot about Meg, or should I say, more than usual,' I admit.

'Has this got something to do with that girl who phoned the helpline? Do you really think Lewis is involved?'

I haven't mentioned Ellie to Sean and I'm left wondering how much Geoff has told him. 'I honestly don't know,' I reply. 'We were all so sure that Lewis was the one hurting Meg. It was never questioned.'

'Because he was a thug and that's what thugs do.'

'But what if we were wrong?' I ask, and as I talk, my finger circles the whiskey tumbler. The glass rim is dry and tugs at my skin, heeding my progress. 'I keep looking at the videos. According to Jen, Meg didn't start dating Lewis until months after they'd started sixth form and yet I can see a difference in her before then. You must remember how upset she was at our anniversary party. We assumed it was because your Auntie Eve wouldn't let Jen move in with us, but what if there was something else bothering her?' Or someone, a voice in my head adds.

'I was pretty drunk that night. All I remember is Meg being in her element when all the guests started to arrive at the hotel. She got me to order the bottle of champagne we left in the honeymoon suite for you and Dad.'

'You mean the one your dad polished off before I'd even got to the room,' I remind him. 'But you're right. Meg put so much effort into it all and she was happy for us, and happier still to have you home from uni. Her change in behaviour later on doesn't make sense.'

'Jen and Charlie were there. Have you asked them? They might be able to put your mind at ease.'

'I don't think they will.'

'Look, you're not the only one to go back over what

341

happened,' Sean says as the strength in his voice wanes. 'I wish I'd taken more time with Meg to work out what was going on. I knew you and Dad were worried about her but she was the same old annoying sister in front of me, most of the time.'

My ears prick. 'Only most?'

I hear Sean exhale through pursed lips. 'There was some stuff I found on her computer one time. It was when I was home for that last Christmas with Meg – and she was definitely dating Lewis by then. She'd been surfing the net and I thought she was just being curious. I didn't know the significance at the time.'

'What did you find, Sean? I need to know, no matter how unpleasant.'

There's a long pause before he speaks. 'She'd been looking up articles on autoerotic asphyxiation. You know, it's where—'

'Yes, I know what it is, Sean,' I say, my voice strangled. I let my head fall back and stretch my neck, conscious of the air travelling into my airways unheeded.

'Right, well, I told Meg she needed to find a new boyfriend if he was mixing her up in that crap but she claimed she'd come across the site by accident.'

'Why didn't you tell me, or your dad?'

'I ask myself the same thing every day,' Sean says. 'I suppose I was too embarrassed to talk to you about it. I thought, at worst, she was experimenting. I only realised she was being forced into it when I read that space story she'd written about not being able to breathe and having to get used to it. If you'd known, you might have got through to her before it was too late.'

342

What I'd actually meant was why Sean didn't tell us after Meg's death, but the point Sean raises is far more important, to him at least. Straightening up, I say, 'There are a thousand differences we could have made but we have to keep reminding ourselves that we weren't the ones subjecting her to abuse.'

'I hope this takeover goes through soon,' Sean says. 'I want you down here, Mum and before you say it, I'm not being selfish. You can't keep putting yourself through this, and maybe you should stop looking at those videos. Isn't it bad enough that you have to deal with Lewis coming back, plus all those stories that girl's been spinning? No wonder you're feeling down.'

'She's not spinning stories, Sean.'

'Dad seems to think she is.'

'She's not,' I insist. I couldn't defend Meg but I can and I will help Ellie – now that I know who she is. It had taken a second or two to place the voice I'd heard tonight on the helpline, but once I had, I could connect Ellie with everyone except the one person we thought had been abusing her.

'Mum . . .'

'I should go,' I say. I'm hoping for a visitor tonight. When I told Ellie I'd be home alone this evening, I had no doubt she knew where to find me. 'And don't worry, Sean, we'll work through this, we always do. Leave it with me.'

'Are you sure? I could come up at the weekend if you like. Just me,' he adds. 'We could talk. I miss her too, Mum.'

'I know you do,' I tell him, feeling the tug that will one day help me build a new life once I've finished the painful task of dismantling the old.

41

Jen

'Enough!' I hiss as I let go of my anchor point and turn to face Lewis. There are no reflections, no mirror images, just two people standing feet away from each other with very different views of the world.

Lewis pulls Meg's scarf taut again and I'm close enough to hear the threads snap. He sees my fear and his eyes widen too. 'I'm not . . .' he begins. Shoving the scarf into a pocket, he adds, 'Out of all of us, I never wanted you to get hurt, Jen.'

'No? Have you forgotten when you threatened me in Chavasse Park? Or how you made a grab for me outside the office? And let's not forget that you're here now. You haven't changed, Lewis.'

'No, I haven't. I'm still the same person you're too scared to see,' he says, and as we hold each other's gaze, I catch a glimpse of the boy I wanted to kiss. 'Last week was a mistake. I'd spent the day helping Mum settle into the hospice and I decided then that I should speak to you. I'd had enough – and that was before you'd accosted Iona for the second time.'

'And you couldn't have just called?'

'Last time I phoned you, you slammed down the phone,' he reminds me. 'And fair enough, I was trying to frighten you off so you wouldn't show up at another of my boot camp sessions, but not last week. I genuinely wanted to talk and if I hadn't grabbed you, you would have fallen flat on your face. I didn't realise you'd be so terrified of me.'

'I'm not,' I lie.

Lewis's humourless smile is a stark contrast to the intensity of his stare. 'I know you see me as the enemy, but it wasn't me who brought us to this place, Jen, it was you,' he says. 'Although right now I'm not sure where that leaves us. I thought your friend Ellie was a fraud, albeit a well-informed one, but if you're convinced she's genuine then I have as much of an interest in getting to the truth as you do.'

I lean back and feel the pressure of the bar across the fire door on my back. If I press against it, the door will open but my problems will follow me even if Lewis doesn't. 'The only reason you want to get to the truth is so you can twist it. If by some chance someone else was hurting Meg about, do you seriously expect me to believe you stood back and did nothing for two years?'

'She told me the scratches on her arms were self-inflicted and I assumed the bruises were too. It was what everyone else thought. If someone's twisting the truth, it's not me, I swear. I didn't know of Ellie's existence until Iona told me.'

Lewis's voice holds conviction but at last I spot a flaw in the story he's been weaving. 'Iona didn't tell you about

Ellie. It was Geoff when he confronted you two weeks ago. That's why you crushed her windpipe as a lesson not to talk to me again. You really don't know when to stop, do you? How much further would you have taken it with Meg if she hadn't killed herself? How much further will you take it with Ellie?'

When Lewis takes a step towards me, my instinct should be to push open the door and get out of there but I do the opposite. I press the button on the personal alarm in my pocket and lash out with my free hand, landing a punch on the side of Lewis's face that does more damage to my fingers than his cheek.

'Get away from me!'

Lewis raises his hand but rather than striking back, he grabs my arm. 'I don't want to hurt you!' he shouts above the howl of the alarm bouncing off the walls of the stairwell.

His grip is fierce but I manage to jerk my arm free, turning towards the door at the same time, where my clammy fingers glance off the safety bar. Unbalanced, I stumble forward and my head cracks against the metal rod. The door flies open and I smash onto the hard floor of the corridor.

As I twist over, Lewis looms over me. 'I'm not who you think I am.'

'Get off her!' roars Charlie.

Lewis weaves away from the punch Charlie throws and, this time, he is prepared to hit back. With the poise of a professional boxer, he lands his punch and there's the sickening crunch of bone and cartilage as Charlie staggers back, blood pouring from his nose. I pick myself up from the floor and launch myself at Lewis before he can hit Charlie a second time. Lewis retreats into the stairwell, deflecting my blows with his arms. He still won't raise a hand to me.

There's a brief moment when I think I'm in control but Charlie sweeps past and flails at Lewis. His blows miss their mark and Lewis grabs him by the collar and twists him around so that Charlie is pressed against the rails with his back arching over the stairwell.

'Please, no!' I scream.

Charlie's hands flutter as he searches for purchase on something that isn't Lewis. 'Jen! Phone the police!'

Lewis keeps hold of Charlie as he snaps his head towards me. 'Stay there! You need to hear this,' he says. 'We all need to hear this.'

'Hear what?' Charlie asks, his voice full of panic as he grabs hold of the railing that may or may not prevent him from plunging to his death.

Lewis leans over him, making Charlie's position all the more precarious. 'Tell her what you did to Meg,' he hisses.

'I didn't—'

'Liar!'

'Please, leave him alone,' I beg but there's no conviction in my voice and Lewis doesn't hear me. I reach into my pocket and silence the howling alarm, but that simply allows the questions in my head to grow louder – questions that only Charlie can answer. I could make my plea again but I don't. Lewis is right. I do need to hear this.

'Tell Jen you slept with Meg. Tell her how you humiliated her,' Lewis says, his voice lower but no less menacing. 'Tell her that's why she killed herself.'

'Don't make me do this,' Charlie pleads. He dares to glance in my direction and adds, 'Please, Jen.'

Then keep quiet, I want to tell him. Don't destroy everything I've ever loved about you. I would almost prefer him to disappear over the railing than hear his confession, but when Lewis shoves Charlie hard enough to make him cry out, I rush forward and wrap an arm around Lewis's neck.

'Leave him,' I growl.

To my surprise, Lewis yanks Charlie up straight.

'Tell me what you did, Charlie,' I demand.

His sobs are pitiful. 'What do you want me to say, Jen?'

'The truth!'

The wretched man in front of me with snot and blood sliding down his face is not my Charlie, and I don't reach out to comfort him when, released from Lewis's grip, he staggers to the stairs. He slumps down and covers his face. I want him to cover his mouth too. I believed in you, Charlie. Don't make the last ten years be a lie.

'We were both trying to drown our sorrows,' he begins.

'When?' asks Lewis. 'The first time or the last?'

'There was only one time.'

Lewis looks to me. 'After what I've heard today, I doubt that.'

'Do you want to hear this or what?' Charlie answers back, daring to look at Lewis, if only briefly. 'It was the day of our A Level results. You were all celebrating, planning your futures while I was watching mine go down the pan. I saw Meg storm off and waited for you to follow her, but you didn't.'

'She told me to piss off,' Lewis says. 'And it was always best to do what she said.'

'I went outside for some fresh air and she was leaning

against the wall. She was waiting for you but she decided I was good enough. She asked me back to hers and we opened a bottle of her mum's wine. She didn't say much so I did most of the talking. I told her it was a blessing in disguise; we'd be better off earning a living rather than racking up student debts. I don't think Meg heard a word I said.'

'And then what?' asks Lewis.

Charlie keeps his head down. 'You know what happened.'

'I don't,' I tell him.

Charlie can't look at either of us as he continues. 'Meg came over to sit on my lap. I think she kissed me just to shut me up but eventually she said we should go upstairs. She took me into her parents' room and I should have got out then. Her phone had been ringing – it was Geoff wanting to know her results – and I was scared him or Ruth were about to show up,' he says. Remembering who he's talking to, he adds, 'And I didn't want to hurt you, Jen, but we were never meant to be a permanent thing back then.'

'Funny how I don't remember it like that,' I answer.

'It was hard to say no to Meg,' he continues. 'I told her it wasn't a good idea but she insisted.'

'Like she insisted you strangle her?' Lewis asks.

'It wasn't my idea,' he whispers, leaning over until he's talking to the floor. 'She disappeared to get something from her bedroom. I didn't know what was going on. When she came back, it was like the light in her eyes had gone out and she couldn't see or feel anything. She didn't tell me straight away what she wanted me to do.' He pauses and rakes his hands through his hair. 'I was eighteen years old for Christ's sake, I didn't know how I was meant to react.

I thought she'd laugh at me if I refused to go along with her. She wanted me on top and when she tied the scarf around her neck, she asked me to pull it tight. She kept saying, "Tighter, tighter," until she couldn't speak. It happened so fast and when I saw her face turn this horrible shade of puce, I jumped off the bed. She was furious with me. It was like she actually wanted me to kill her.'

'No, that came later,' Lewis says as he backs away and turns to me. 'I'd left loads of messages for Meg. I was worried about her, but it was days later when she eventually got in touch and we met. She told me what she'd done and I'll admit, I hated her for it, but I hated him more.' He aims an accusing finger at Charlie without looking back. 'Tell Jen what you called her.'

'I didn't mean it, I was in shock, confused,' he moans.

'Answer the question!' I bark at him.

His sobbing erupts again. 'I – I said she was sick in the head.'

'You called her a fucking nutter too,' Lewis says. To me, he adds, 'He made her feel like a piece of dirt. Fair enough, she was mortified that she'd cheated on me and hurt you too, but Charlie humiliated her and there was no coming back from that. I broke up with her, but only because she was going to do it anyway. And then I went to find Charlie so I could knock seven kinds of shite out of that bastard.'

I don't recognise the man dripping bloodied snot onto the linoleum but I have a sick feeling that Ellie would. Whatever had started with Meg has continued with Ellie and I need him to confess all. 'That's only half the story,' I say. 'You're going to have to tell me everything, Charlie, because if you don't, I'll push you over that fucking railing myself.'

Charlie sobs harder than before. 'I was so scared,' he says. 'I knew Meg had told Lewis and it was only a matter of time before you found out. I waited it out for over a week, I didn't want to see Meg again but I'd left my glasses at her house and I needed them.'

I want to stop Charlie there, and explain I was asking about Ellie, but Lewis's mouth falls open and fresh horror dawns on us both.

'I went back to get them, and to talk to her. She'd left the front door open. The note was in the hallway, pinned under some vase. I didn't think . . . I never thought . . .'

Charlie's words become incoherent but I'm not sure how much I would be able to hear above the thumping of my heart. My stomach heaves and as I gulp back air, I hear the final words of his confession.

'I found her.'

42

Jen

I ignore the collection of bloodied tissues lying on the kitchen counter as I pour myself a drink of water. The glass knocks painfully against my teeth as I take a sip.

'Do I need to check what he's doing?' asks Lewis, tipping his head towards the door to the second bedroom.

We can hear Charlie moving around and there's the sound of tape being pulled off one of the many boxes stored in there. I'd assumed it was all business stock, but there's something far more valuable he's been hiding in our apartment.

Before I can reply, Charlie opens the door and emerges with an innocuous looking brown envelope. He offers it to me but I back away.

'I'll take it,' Lewis says, after an awkward pause.

The envelope is torn open and discarded, leaving Lewis with a folded sheet of yellow lined paper. When he begins to unfold it, I glimpse a torn edge that will be the perfect match for the remnant of the note Charlie left for Meg's grieving parents.

'Meg wasn't the one who should have been ashamed,' Charlie says, quoting the part of her note we're all familiar with. 'I humiliated her, I said she was sick.'

'Shut up, Charlie,' I say. 'I don't care about what you said. I want to hear Meg.'

Lewis scans the page, takes a breath and begins. '*This isn't the letter I want to write but I have no choice. Even now, I can't face the shame. I don't want anyone to know what we did. It dies with me because I'm the problem. I'm the one who's SICK. I disgust myself and all I want is for it to go away and take me with it. And as for YOU. You get to live with the guilt for the rest of your life and I hope it eats you up. And if you ever think about treating someone the way you treated me, remember what you did to me.*

I hate this person I've become and I hate the rest of you too. Mum, Sean, Jen, Lewis. I hate you all. You should be glad I'm gone. You're better off without me.'

There's a pause as I wait for Lewis to continue but that's it. Meg didn't leave us with answers, just more questions. 'She was talking about you?' I ask Charlie.

'That's why I couldn't leave the note,' he says. 'I panicked, Jen. I was sure it was going to come out that Meg and I had slept together and I didn't want everyone knowing she'd killed herself because of me. Look at the list of names. My name isn't there.'

'Why would it be?' asks Lewis incredulously. 'You were nothing to her, you never were.' He shakes his head. 'I thought everyone was mad to think there was another part to the note, but it was you who took it and you let me take the blame.'

'Why, Charlie?' I ask. 'Was it really worth putting Ruth and Geoff through ten years of torment?'

Charlie sniffs but his nose is blocked and crusted with blood. He looks like he might start crying again. 'It was a spur of the moment decision and once it was done, it couldn't be undone. I convinced myself you were all better off not knowing what it said. Look at that last line, Jen. What parent wants to read that they were hated?'

Lewis's face twists in disgust. 'So it wasn't your own back you were covering? You were doing it for the greater good?'

'I don't know what I thought. There wasn't time to think.'

'But there was,' I correct him as I picture the scene. It's one I've imagined before but it's the first time that I've had to place Charlie there. 'You read the note and you took great care tearing it into two neat parts. And all the time, Meg's body was hanging in the garage and you did nothing for her. How could you do that, Charlie? How could you live with yourself?'

'I couldn't. That's why I went away, why I left Liverpool. Meg was right. The guilt was eating away at me. I only came back for you, Jen,' he whimpers. 'Our time apart made me realise how much you meant to me. It was wrong what I did, all of it, but I thought, if I could make you happy again, it would make things right somehow.'

'By living a lie?' I ask. 'At least now I know why you reacted so badly when I told you about Ellie.'

'It was because he'd been caught,' Lewis adds.

'No, because I realised that Meg hadn't been experimenting, she'd been experimented *on*,' Charlie counters as he pulls back his shoulders. 'I might have been the one to tell Meg that what she wanted me to do was sick, but that sickness came from you. It's why you're still doing it to this poor Ellie.'

Lewis hisses under his breath and shakes his head in response.

'According to Lewis, he's never met her,' I explain, trying to put the image of Charlie with Meg, or worse still, Charlie with Meg's dead body, out of my mind.

'And you believe him?'

Of the two men, I find myself trusting the word of my old adversary more than I do Charlie, but I need to be sure. I look from Lewis to Charlie. 'Did you know I kissed Lewis?'

'Wh— What?' Charlie's jaw drops. 'When? Why?'

'Ages ago. Before Meg died, long before. All this time I thought you knew. I was wrong, but I've been wrong about so many things, haven't I? I don't know who you are any more.'

'I do,' Lewis chips in. 'Someone damaged Meg long before I met her, and whoever messed her up was the kind of person who'd be callous enough to leave a seventeen-year-old girl swinging from a noose.'

Charlie flinches at the image. 'Meg told me what she wanted. I assumed it was something you were both into until I read that thing she wrote about the space girl. Have you read it?'

'Yeah, and the finger points right at you.'

'Stop it!' I cry out. 'For one minute, will you both shut the fuck up!' I take a deep breath. Sometimes the truth isn't what we hear, it's what we feel in our hearts. 'I don't think it is Charlie who's hurting Ellie. He doesn't have the stomach for it.'

'You've just said you don't know him any more,' Lewis reminds me.

'Maybe not,' I admit. 'But when he helped me search for Iona, he thought we were going to find Ellie too.'

'So you're back to blaming me?' Lewis asks as he thrusts Meg's note into my hand.

I suspect he's about to storm out so I choose my words carefully. 'I keep going back to who knew Ellie was phoning the helpline. Did you tell anyone else after Geoff had a go at you?'

'I told you before, I haven't seen Geoff.'

'But he went to your flat.'

'For a start, I live in a house,' Lewis corrects me.

I could be wrong but I thought Geoff said he went to a flat. I rub my forehead but it doesn't help. 'Geoff went there . . . he told you about Ellie.'

Lewis looks blank. 'No, Iona told me about Ellie,' he says slowly as if I'm hard of hearing.

'But that would have been *after* Ellie was attacked for speaking to me. Why would Geoff lie about knowing where you live? Why would he say he told you, if he didn't?' I ask, but I'm dragging my words through quicksand and they disappear.

'To blame me, obviously.'

'But why?' I ask one last time as I pick up the threads of Ellie's life and attempt to weave them into a new story. I look down at the note Meg left. I read the names of the people she claimed to hate. There's one notable omission on the list, and it's not Charlie. My sob is a precursor to the conclusion I don't want to reach.

Charlie gets there at the same time and takes a stumbling

step back. 'Shit. SHIT. Are we saying he was covering for himself?' he asks. Shaking his head, he adds, 'No, that can't be right. What Ellie described . . . he would have had to be doing the same thing to his *own daughter*. It can't be Geoff. We've got it wrong.'

'No,' Lewis says slowly. 'No, we haven't. It was Geoff. He was the one doing those disgusting things to Meg and now he's doing the same to someone else. I'm going to kill the sick fucking bastard.'

43

Ruth

Sitting on the sofa in the darkened kitchen with my arms wrapped around my body, I rock myself slowly. I listen out for a sign, any sign, that I'm not alone, and recall how often I'd heard our cleaner moving around upstairs and pretended it was Meg. It helped that Helena looked like my daughter, or at least how Meg might have looked if she'd reached her twenties. I shouldn't have let Helena go. Another regret to add to my tally.

Shaking my head to loosen my thoughts, I concentrate on what I do know, and what assumptions I need to dismiss. Ellie is being abused. She hasn't named her abuser. Her abuser hurts her in the same way he hurt Meg. He knows the family, and through him, Ellie has come to know us. She's Romanian. So is Helena. Their voices sound exactly the same.

They are the same.

Which leads me to the questions I've yet to answer. Would it be too much of a coincidence that a young woman who is employed by Charlie, and has worked for me and Geoff, could also cross paths with Lewis? It's not implausible but it is unlikely. And if Helena doesn't know Lewis, then he's not the one abusing her, which means he's not the one who abused Meg.

My thoughts wrap around me like silken strands of a spider's web, making it impossible to separate the truth from lies. What if Jen was wrong and Meg had been dating Lewis earlier than she thought? Were there other lies my niece had failed to detect? Could Ellie have pulled off the greatest deceit? She's been in my house and had time to learn about Meg. Is Geoff right to accuse her of spinning stories? Or what if Charlie lied about . . . about everything? What if I'm lying to myself?

I reach for the tumbler balanced on the armrest but the alcohol doesn't thaw me in the way it had earlier and I can't finish it. Fear has frozen me but when the doorbell rings, I jump up. It has to be Helena.

The half measure of whiskey churning my stomach isn't enough to have made me drunk but I'm unsteady as I cross the kitchen and abandon my drink on the breakfast bar. I flick on a light switch and as my eyes adjust to the spotlights above me, my mobile starts to ring. When I realise it's Jen, I'm tempted to ignore the call. My head hurts and I don't want to speak to her until I know what to say, and perhaps not even then. But Jen of all people needs to know the truth if my worst fears are about to realised and Helena has come to tell me how Charlie is as cruel as he is duplicitous.

When I accept the call, there's the drone of a car engine in the background. 'You're not leaving the office this late, are you?' I ask as I move towards the door.

'No, I left a while ago,' Jen says. She's breathless and her voice shakes.

The hallway is washed in the sickly, yellow light of the streetlamps outside and I hesitate before stepping over the threshold. 'Is Charlie with you?'

'Yes, and we're on our way over to you.'

Before I can ask why, the doorbell chimes again and this time the caller shows their impatience by ringing several times in quick succession. I've revealed someone is home by switching on the kitchen lights.

'Don't answer the door, Ruth!' yelps Jen.

'Why not? What's going on, Jen?' I ask as I stare at the silhouette framed in the front door.

'I don't want you to be alarmed but it'll be Lewis. I'll explain when I get there. We're ten minutes away at the mo—' Her words are cut off by a car horn blaring. 'Maybe less than ten, the way Charlie's driving.'

I rest my hand on my chest to feel my heart punching hard against my ribcage. I don't know what terrifies me more; the urgency and fear in Jen's voice; the possibility that the man who hurt my daughter is sitting next to her in the car; the news that I might be confronted by Lewis very soon; the familiar frame of the young woman standing on my doorstep; or the way the spider's silk tightens around me, bringing everything together.

'Please, Ruth,' Jen says when the next round of door-chimes fades away. 'Is Geoff with you?'

'No.'

'OK, good. We'll be with you in a minute. Don't do anything till we get there.'

I slip my mobile into the pocket of my trousers without

taking my eyes from the ghostly form of the woman who's come to pay me a visit. I don't fool myself that it's Meg but it is someone who can bring me closer to my daughter. My palm is clammy but my grip is fierce as I pull the door open wide.

'Mrs McCoy,' Helena says. 'I do not know if you remember—'

'I know who you are,' I tell her. The muscles on my face work hard to form a smile while dread pulls down the corners of my mouth. 'You'd better come in.'

'You are alone?' she asks, her eyes darting to the empty space on the drive where Geoff normally parks his car.

'Yes.'

Helena follows me into the kitchen but comes to a stumbling stop when she sees the whiskey glass. Her fear is palpable. 'I promise you, we're alone,' I say. 'Would you like a drink?'

'Some water, please.'

I pour two glasses. Neither of us sit but we find comfortable stances on opposite sides of the breakfast bar. I sip my water before I speak. 'We spoke earlier this evening, didn't we?'

'Yes,' she replies, her grey eyes wide. Her hair is pulled back in a messy ponytail and shines gold beneath the spotlights. Her face is rounder than Meg's, her nose not quite as narrow but still . . .

As tears blur their differences, my longing for Meg is all-consuming and I'm tempted to draw Helena into a hug. I want to remember what it felt like to hold my child but that's why I've kept the counter as a barrier between us. I need to hear what she has to say first.

'Did you phone Jen back after I'd left?' I ask as I try to make sense of my niece's desperate race to get here. Is it a good sign that she's bringing Charlie with her? Is Lewis on his way to see me, or is he hunting down Helena? As much as that last thought terrifies me, I want to believe it's true. So why don't I?

'I should have spoken to you first, I realise that now.' Helen says, biting her lip. 'I hear you on the phone tonight and I know I could not leave without explaining. You deserve to know what happened.'

Do I deserve this? I ask myself. I'd told Ellie earlier that I wanted to hear what she had to say, no matter how painful, but I don't know if that still holds true. Despite my grave doubts, I manage a nod.

'And you will believe me? You will give me back my passport?'

'I'll make sure that whoever has it returns it to you,' I reply, not comforted by the idea that Helena thinks it's within my gift. 'I can see you're scared and so am I, but I promise to help you no matter what you say. Don't be afraid of the consequences.' I'm aware that time is against us. Once other people start arriving, Helena is going to clam up. 'Helena, I need to know who it is that's been hurting you.'

'I know.'

I was expecting a name but she's not ready yet. It's more in desperation than hope when I ask, 'Is your boyfriend the same man who was involved with my daughter?'

'Boyfriend is not the right word, Mrs McCoy,' she replies as a fat tear rolls down her cheek. 'He should not have touched Megan in that way. It was not natural.'

The mention of my daughter's name sends a warning jolt zapping through my body. I don't often refer to Meg by her proper name, in fact there's only one person I know who persists in using it. Could Helena have picked it up from Geoff during her brief time here? Had he talked to our cleaner about his daughter? I can't imagine why and tell myself it's an affectation of Helena's, no more. Her English is good but her speech is quite formal.

'Who is he, Helena?'

'I am sorry. I am so sorry,' Helena says, pressing her hand to her mouth.

Before she can build the courage to speak his name, our attention is caught by the rumble of an engine: Geoff's Audi is pulling onto the drive. I'd expected him to abandon his car in the car park so he and Oscar could drown their sorrows. 'It's my husband but don't worry, I'll keep him out of the kitchen so we can carry on talking.'

Helena is backing away, searching for a way out. She eyes the door to the utility room and I'm not sure if she remembers the house well enough to know it leads out to the garden. 'Please, stay,' I ask as keys jangle in the front door.

'He cannot know I am here,' she whispers, her lips trembling.

'That might be a little difficult but I'll see what I can do.'

Helena shakes her head, her hand reaching for the utility room door.

'OK, OK,' I say softly but her fear is unnerving me. 'You can hide in there until the coast is clear. I said I'll keep you safe and I meant it.'

Hoping she'll still be there when I get back, I hurry out of the kitchen to waylay my husband. I enter the hallway as the front door is flung open hard enough to rebound off a wall. Geoff staggers over the threshold. 'You drove home in that state?' I ask.

His eyes are bleary and bloodshot. 'I'm fine,' he says as he puts a hand against the open door to steady himself. The door moves and he almost topples over.

'You're not fine. You could have killed someone.'

He starts to laugh but I don't get the joke. I simply glare at him until his laughter transforms into a sob. 'It's all falling apart, Ruth. Why does it keep happening to me? Am I such a bad person?'

'Go into the sitting room and I'll make you some strong coffee,' I order as I look over his shoulder and glimpse a set of car headlights sweeping the road. I'm relieved to see a cab drive past but time is running out. I wonder if I could slip out of the house with Helena and drive to some place where we won't be interrupted.

'The deal's fallen through so we're going to be stuck here,' Geoff says, his lower lip protruding into a pout. 'Don't know why I thought it would work.'

I'm more interested in getting Geoff moving so that I can close the front door, but as I prepare to bundle him towards the sitting room, a shadow moves behind him. Lewis's shoulders are broader than I remember and the look on his face makes me quake to my bones. He has come for Helena. He is the one.

'What do you want?' I ask, shoving my drunken husband out of the way to grab the door. As I try to close it, Lewis slams it open again.

'I want that,' he snarls, pointing his finger over my shoulder.

When I hear a whimper behind me, I think it's Helena, drawn out of the kitchen by the commotion, but as Lewis sweeps past me, there's only Geoff. He cries out as Lewis grabs him by the throat.

'You evil, stinking piece of shit. I know what you did.'

Geoff's eyes bulge as Lewis's grip tightens. 'Leave me alone,' he rasps.

'Stop!' I yell, wishing I could pause the scene like one of Meg's videos to give me time to think. I yank Lewis's shoulder and although I'm no match for his strength, he lets go.

My husband splutters as he catches his breath. 'I don't know what this is about but if you don't leave this minute, I'm calling the police.' He cowers as Lewis raises his fist.

'I could smash your face to a pulp and I don't think anyone would care.'

Car doors slam and the sound of hurried footsteps grows louder. Jen is panting when she reaches the open door. 'Oh, shit,' she says.

Charlie stands behind her. His face is grey except for the dried blood crusted around his swollen nose. 'Leave him alone, mate,' he says to Lewis.

When Charlie slips past Jen to stand next to me, Geoff makes a pathetic, drunken attempt to puff out his chest. 'Lewis, I want you out of my house now!'

Lewis smiles a terrifying smile. 'Too late, Geoff. They know.'

As the blood drains from Geoff's cheeks, my fingers begin to tingle. Spots of darkness pock the faces of the three men standing in my hallway but I'm determined not to pass out. A decade of questions is about to be swept away by two words. Am I ready? Yes, Meg. I'm ready to listen now.

'Helena's here,' I say, checking to see who reacts first. When Geoff begins to cry, my world implodes.

44

Jen

I'd spent the fraught journey to Ruth's trying to catch up with thoughts that were unthinkable. Geoff wasn't capable of hurting anyone; not Ellie, and certainly not Meg. My cousin had worshipped her dad and he could do no wrong. Even when he'd had that affair with a young barmaid, it was her mum who Meg blamed. Except the barmaid had been very young . . .

I'd run up to the house prepared to be convinced of any other explanation, but as Geoff begins to howl at the mention of a woman's name, I see a guilty man. So does Ruth, and she charges at him with her fists raised.

Geoff staggers back against the wall and cowers beneath the punches raining down on him while Lewis and Charlie look on impassively. Realising that they won't intervene until Ruth's killed him, I'm the one who has to step in.

Ruth claws at Geoff's face and as I pull her off him, one of her iridescent acrylic nails slides down his cheek and onto his torn shirt. 'You bastard!' she cries, spittle flying from her mouth. 'How could you do that? Why?'

Geoff sinks to the floor and covers his head with his arms. His words are a mixture of sobs and splutters and make no sense. None of it makes sense.

Ruth shakes violently in my arms and I don't know if I'll get much sense from her either. 'Who's Helena?'

I follow Ruth's gaze and my breath catches in my throat. The young woman who has appeared in the doorway is as pale as a ghost; Meg's ghost.

'Hello, Jen.'

I recognise the voice immediately. I've spent weeks longing for this moment and I don't know how I hold back the sob. 'Ellie!'

'You're Ellie?' Charlie asks. 'Shit.'

'This is why I wanted to go home, Charlie,' she says.

The confusion on my face is mirrored on Lewis's. 'Who is she?' he asks.

'Helena was the cleaner they let go,' Charlie says above Geoff's sobs. 'So much for finding a job for Ellie; she's been working for me all along.'

'I thought you worked in a shop?' I ask Helena.

'Yes, cleaning,' she says.

'In the retail park,' Charlie adds. 'But she handed her notice in last week and I thought Ellie could fill the vacancy.' He shakes his head in disbelief as he looks back at Helena. 'I can't believe you were one and the same.'

Ruth takes a deep breath. 'It wasn't the biggest thing we missed,' she says. 'Lewis, Charlie, get *him* into the kitchen, please. He needs to stop crying and, God help us, start talking.'

No longer needing my support, Ruth steps across Geoff's prostrate legs and puts her arms around Helena. 'It's going to be all right, sweetheart. We'll get through this together.'

Ruth's calmness is as unsettling as her attack on her husband was frightening. We all follow her into the kitchen, Geoff needing to be dragged, but it's Lewis who stumbles as the three men cross the threshold. He's familiar enough with the house to know where this door led in another incarnation.

'Prop him up on that bar stool,' Ruth says.

As he's pushed towards the breakfast bar, Geoff writhes in protest but eventually crawls onto a stool. Lewis remains standing guard but Charlie comes around to the rest of us on the opposite side of the counter. I step away from him as he approaches and slip my hand into Helena's. She squeezes back and I can't tell if the tremble I feel runs through her body or mine – or both.

'This is all a mistake,' Geoff mumbles as he lifts his head and spies an unfinished glass of whiskey on the counter. He reaches out for it but Ruth gets to it first. She hurls it over Geoff's head and we all flinch as it hits the wall opposite and shards of glass rain down onto the floor.

As whiskey runs down the wall, Ruth picks up a glass of water and weighs it carefully in her hand before taking a sip. When she sets it back on the counter, she leaves rusted impressions of her fingerprints. Many of her false nails have been ripped off but Ruth is oblivious to the blood trickling down her hand as she turns her back on her husband to face us.

'Helena, I'm sorry, but I need to hear it. Was it my husband who was abusing you?'

'No, my love,' Geoff says. 'Please, stop this.'

Ruth doesn't move an inch but her voice reaches out like a whip. 'Keep quiet. You'll get your chance.'

We wait for Helena to answer, which she does with a slow nod of the head.

'And he told you he'd done the same to Meg?'

Above a moan from Geoff, Helena whispers, 'Yes.'

What she's telling us, what Geoff has confessed simply by his response to her presence, is implausible and yet I know it's true. In this room where Meg took her life, there are two victims, speaking with one voice.

Ruth sucks air into her lungs and releases it with a hiss. On the second try, her voice breaks but she manages to ask, 'He forced her to have sex with him?'

Helena clears her throat. 'He raped her.'

45

Ruth

The smell of whiskey from the shattered glass makes me want to gag as I turn to face my daughter's abuser. One glance at Geoff disgusts me and I look away, catching Lewis's eye instead. He gives me a nod of encouragement. His glasses have gone and age has smoothed the sharp features that set him up to play the villain. There's a nervousness about him that he would have disguised with over-confidence in his youth. He knows he's arrived ten years too late to save Meg, but he's not the only one.

I can think of only one reason Meg didn't turn to me for protection: she didn't expect me to believe her. She presumed I'd be swayed by whatever arguments Geoff might have conjured up to discredit her accusations, and I hate to say it, but back then I don't know what I would have thought. The idea of Geoff touching our daughter is so abhorrent that it's unimaginable – unbelievable. I would have resisted the idea, I might have said the wrong thing or asked the wrong question, but I'd hope that I would have believed her. There's only one way to prove it. I have to believe Helena now.

'Send them home,' Geoff slurs. 'They don't need to be here. Go home, Helena. Go away, all of you.' He swings out his arm and almost topples off the stool.

'Everyone stay where you are,' I tell them as I force myself to look at my husband. His face dissolves and he presses his palms into his eyes.

'Those are tears that should have been spent on our daughter. You're crying for yourself now so you can damn well stop.'

'It's not what you think,' Geoff says, sniffing back the trails of snot dripping from his nose. 'What I did with Helena was unforgiveable, I know that.' He waits for me to respond but I hold myself taut. One move and I might just crack.

'You've got it all wrong,' he continues. 'It was a sick fantasy. I was playing out what someone else did with Megan, not me,' he says, not daring to look at Lewis. 'I never touched her, Ruth. You have to believe that.'

'You're lying,' I say through gritted teeth. 'It was *you*. And it was your abuse that made Meg hate herself, hurt herself and then kill herself.'

'No, that's not true,' Geoff insists. He lowers his voice, and adds, 'It was Lewis who turned her against us. She'd be alive today if it wasn't for him.'

'She'd be alive today if you hadn't raped her,' I say, my mouth left gaping open in a silent scream as the full horror of what he did hits me.

Geoff's eyes widen and the gouges I scraped down his face glow red. 'Don't listen to Helena. It wasn't rape! How can you think that?'

372

I take a gulp of air but it's difficult to breathe the same air as my husband. 'Tell me what you did to her!'

'We loved each other, it's as simple as that. What we had was *special*.'

My stomach clenches as if from an invisible blow, and I hear Jen gasp behind me.

'Give me ten minutes alone with him,' Lewis mutters.

'That's not how this is going to be done,' I say firmly. 'Geoff's punishment is going to be long and drawn out.'

There's the crunch of glass against porcelain tiles as Lewis begins pacing the floor. He threads his hands together on top of his baseball cap, presumably to stop him using them on Geoff.

'What do you want me to say?' Geoff asks as I turn my attention back to him. 'That I hurt her? No I didn't. I never, and I mean *never*, did anything Megan wasn't happy to go along with.'

'Happy?' I ask, my resolve beginning to crumble. 'She stopped being happy the day you forgot she was your daughter. When did it start? How long did you make her suffer?'

Geoff squirms in his seat, his movements uncoordinated. The shock of being unmasked hasn't been enough to sober him up. 'I tried for so long to fight against it, and you didn't make it easy for any of us. You didn't want me, that's why I had the affair with that girl at the club. Megan knew all I wanted was to be loved and she was happy for me.'

'And why was that? Had you been grooming her? Did she know you'd prey on her if you weren't being distracted elsewhere?'

'See what you're like? You were the same back then. All

you did was snarl at me after our little falling out. I had no one to turn to except Megan. She was the only one who cared about *me*,' he says, jabbing a finger at his chest. 'Sean had left and you went off to do your own thing. You left me alone with her.'

'Because I trusted you! But Meg didn't, did she? That's why she wanted Jen to move in. She knew she needed protection from her own fucking father!'

'That had nothing to do with it,' Geoff says. 'She knew what she was doing when she encouraged you to take up those stupid pottery classes.'

'No, she didn't – stop rewriting the past to fit your broken narrative. She encouraged us *both* to take up ballroom dancing. She wasn't trying to get you alone, you fucking psycho,' I shout. This was why Meg resented me finding a lone pastime. When I'd smashed the pots against the kitchen wall, I'd been consumed by the shame of my guilty pleasure, but this is something else. I am well and truly broken.

'Stop this. Please, Ruth. Let's move to Stratford. It's going to be fine if you just – stop – talking.'

My mind turns in circles. 'Something happened around the time of our anniversary party, didn't it? Was that when you first raped her?'

Geoff's hands clamp around his ears. 'Stop calling it rape,' he moans. 'It wasn't.'

'Then what the fuck was it?' I scream.

He pulls at his hair and moans. 'It was something neither of us could fight. It was beautiful. Megan had booked the honeymoon suite and I found her waiting for me with champagne.'

'She wasn't waiting for you,' Jen says. 'She was going to

374

sneak into the room to leave it for you and Ruth as a surprise. When I saw her later, she'd been crying. I thought it was because of Mum.'

'I don't expect you to understand,' Geoff says, dismissing Jen's words. 'We didn't understand it ourselves.'

'Try me,' I hiss. Lewis isn't the only one fighting the urge to strike Geoff. I fold my arms across my chest and grip my upper arms tight enough to cut off the circulation. 'Tell me about the scarves.'

The hands Geoff used to inflict pain and violate our daughter cover his eyes. 'It wasn't meant to be what it was,' he says. 'She needed to stay quiet.'

Pins and needles run down my arms like the tips of a thousand spears piercing my skin. 'Why? Was I there?'

'You came back early one day. But we did stop. I wouldn't have . . . Not with you downstairs,' he says as if the idea of having sex with his daughter was only abhorrent if I was in the house. 'But the next time, she pushed it in her mouth herself. I told her not to but you know what she was like. She knew how to press our buttons. That's why she dated Lewis.'

The sound of glass being crushed underfoot stops as Lewis turns to the nearest wall and smashes his fist through the plasterboard.

Geoff flinches, his eyes darting to the side in case the next strike is aimed at him but Lewis stays where he is, and the lack of action emboldens my husband. 'She did it to goad me,' he hisses. Drunk or not, his words are sharpened by his anger. 'That's why she invited him into our bedroom.'

'And then you took it out on her.'

'No, Ruth. I told . . .' He flaps a hand towards Helena. 'I told her all about it. It's a thing. It's auto-asphyx-something.'

'You choked our daughter with one of her own scarves because you thought she'd enjoy it?'

He closes his eyes and shakes his head. I don't know if he intends me to hear when he whispers, 'The things she said . . . *She* was hurting *me*.'

'So you shut her up because what she told you didn't fit with your reality. Did she beg you to stop?' I ask. 'Did she tell you it was wrong? Did she tell you what a sick, twisted bastard you are?'

'That's not who I am,' he replies. 'You know it's not. You've been married to me for over thirty years, Ruth. I'm not a monster.'

'Except you slipped into that skin every time you sneaked into Meg's room.'

Geoff's sobs are pathetic. 'My only crime is that I loved her too much. If I'd known how she felt, I would have stopped,' he wails. 'I didn't want Megan to kill herself. It should have been me.'

'But you left it to our daughter,' I say as I consider how different my life would be if the suicide letter had been Geoff's. The damage had already been done to Meg, but she might have come out from behind those barricades I refused to peer over, and together we might have been able to rebuild our lives. *Might*. What a feeble word.

'She should have told me,' he insists.

'She did tell you. You did not listen,' Helena says, her hesitant words gathering strength as they rise up to strike Geoff with enough force to make his body jerk.

'Shut up,' he hisses. 'You were supposed to wait for me at the flat. You shouldn't be here. This is all your fault.'

I can feel the tears sliding down my face. There will come a time – very soon, I imagine – when I will want to wail and scream and cry and sob and wrench every emotion out of my chest, but it's not now, and it's not here. Geoff and I are not going to cry together, because we're crying for different things. 'Meg asked us to bury her shame with her,' I say. 'What else did she say in the note, Geoff?'

'That was all it said,' he says with a shake of the head. 'You were there, Ruth.'

Lewis steps closer and glances over my shoulder to the group huddled behind me. As I turn, Charlie puts his head down and my eyes settle on Jen who is giving Lewis a warning glare. I wait for her to look at me.

'There's something you should know, but not here, not in front of Geoff,' she says.

I don't like the painful look Jen gives me when there's so much pain already. I don't want another secret to blind-side me and I'm about to insist she explain but Geoff draws me back to him.

'You were never meant to know, Ruth,' he whispers. 'Megan didn't want that.'

'I don't think you're in any position to say what our daughter did and didn't want,' I reply. 'Were there other girls?'

He shakes his head but I'm not satisfied with the answer. If he could abuse his teenage daughter, who else would he prey on? I'd assumed his affair was a symptom of a midlife crisis but was it something more insidious? He was grooming Meg but had sex with someone else. Why? Our little girl would have been only fifteen at the time. Could it be that she was that bit too young for him?

'Waiting until Meg turned sixteen was important, wasn't it?'

'It's important to any girl.'

I press my chin to my chest. I can't bear to look at the monster being revealed one vile layer at a time. How did I not know what he was like? Not only did I believe we provided our children with the perfect family home, I'd offered it up to Jen. My head snaps up. I don't think my pounding heart can take any more strain but I force myself to look back at her. 'Did he ever touch you?'

Jen's eyes widen and fear is about to swallow me up but she shakes her head.

Geoff raises his voice. 'Jesus, Ruth. I'm not some kind of paedophile! I told you, I loved Megan. I couldn't feel that way about simply anyone.'

I round on him. 'No, just your fucking daughter!'

'Yes, my daughter. *Mine,*' he hits back with sudden fury. 'She belonged to me!'

46

Jen

A stunned silence descends. There's so much more Ruth could ask Geoff but he's said it all in that last crushing outburst. Meg was his property to do with as he wished. That was his justification. That was how he lived with what he did to her.

Ruth releases a sob that sounds like the end of her world. White knuckles grip the counter as she squeezes her eyes tight shut. Geoff lifts his chin and watches her. He thinks the worst is over but when Ruth rears up, her eyes are on fire.

'Why Helena? Why now?'

I feel Helena's grip on my hand tighten as the focus turns to her.

'Helena was a mistake. And you were the one who put the idea in my head, going on about how much she reminded you of Megan. We got talking, I said I knew someone with an apartment so she could have a place of her own. And then you sacked her, Ruth! I couldn't just abandon her.'

'So it's *my* fault?'

'You were the one who did all those media interviews, raking up the past and splashing *my* daughter's beautiful face across the news. Do you have any idea what that was like for me? I loved Megan more than anyone on this earth, but the lasting memory I have of her is what she looked like when I found her,' he says, his words catching at the back of his throat.

From the corner of my eye, I see Charlie's body swaying. I wish I could justify his actions but I simply can't. Neither will Ruth when I tell her, and I will once we're out of earshot of Geoff. He doesn't deserve to have anyone else sharing the blame.

'Where's Helena's passport?' asks Ruth.

'What?'

'You took her passport. Where is it?'

'In work. In my desk.'

'Fine.'

'The drawer's locked.'

'I'll break it open.'

'You don't have to. She can have it back. I'll do whatever you ask, my love. It's good that you know the truth. I've carried this guilt for so long but it's done now and we can put it behind us.' Fear has finally sobered Geoff up, and although his eyes are bloodshot, they shine as he looks beadily at each of us before returning his gaze to Ruth. 'No one else needs to know any of this. Imagine what it would do to Sean. And if it became public, the business would fold. All the staff would lose their jobs, including Jen, and we'd lose everything. *Everything*. No one wants that.'

'So we keep quiet for the sake of everyone else?' Ruth

says, as if she might be warming to the idea. My heart sinks, and I see Lewis's jaw twitch.

'Exactly, my love,' Geoff says. 'You know it's for the best.'

'Is that what you told Meg I'd do? Put the business and our name before my own daughter?' Ruth asks. 'Look up, Geoff. Find that spot above your head where Meg hung the noose. If it was made for anyone, it was made for you, so fuck your bargaining.'

Geoff lurches off the bar stool but Lewis grabs him by the shirt collar. Spluttering, Geoff claws at the material digging into his neck but he doesn't fight off Lewis.

Turning her back on them, Ruth steps towards Helena and sweeps a lock of hair gently from her face. 'This is not a man you need to fear any more. We'll look after you,' she promises. 'Will you tell the police what you've told us?'

'Yes,' Helena whispers, keeping her eyes fixed on Ruth and not the man wailing in the background. 'I will tell them everything.'

'Come on then. Let's go into the sitting room and we can make the call together.'

When Helena goes to follow Ruth, she's still holding my hand and takes me with her. It's Charlie who pulls me back. 'Should I come too?' he asks.

'No,' Ruth says before I have a chance to tell Charlie where to go. 'I want you and Lewis to make sure he stays where he is.'

'You're leaving him with me?' Lewis demands as he continues to dangle Geoff by the shirt collar.

What she says next flies against everything we believed just a few short hours ago. 'I trust you, Lewis.'

* * *

381

When Ruth puts the phone down, the sitting room falls silent. A police car is on its way but there's no hurry. We've waited ten years. We can wait a little longer.

'I can't take it all in,' I say.

'I'd thought of every possible scenario except this one,' Ruth admits. 'And I hate to say it, Jen, but when I recognised Helena's voice on the helpline, I thought it was Charlie who was hurting her.'

'He is a good man,' Helena offers.

'Not that good,' I reply as my stomach does a somersault.

Ruth gives me a curious look, but I'm given a reprieve from breaking her that little bit more when she turns back to Helena. 'I know you were planning on going home on Saturday, but it's inevitable that this will go to court. Would you consider staying? I can make sure your rent is covered and I'm sure Charlie would give you your job back. If that's what you want?'

'I did not want to go home. I would like to stay.'

'Then I'll do everything in my power to help you re-establish the life you had before my husband set about dismantling it.'

'You are very kind. You did not deserve this,' she says. 'And neither did Megan.'

Ruth presses her fingers to her mouth but she doesn't cry. She swallows hard and says, 'It's going to take me a long time to process what happened, and I'm not sure I know where to begin.'

'I do,' I answer.

Ruth searches my face. 'You said there was something I needed to know.'

382

'It's about Meg's suicide note,' I say and as we hold each other's gaze, I feel the air being sucked from the room.

Helena shifts in her seat. 'Could I use the bathroom, please?'

Ruth blinks. 'Sorry,' she says, as if she'd completely forgotten Helena was there. 'Of course. You can use the one upstairs so you don't need to go back into the kitchen.'

I wait for Helena to close the door behind her. 'I have the missing piece, Ruth.'

47

Ruth

I can't quite believe that the torn brown envelope Jen hands me contains the missing half of Meg's note. Not ready to look inside, I hold it with a mixture of fear and reverence, exploring its corners with torn fingernails. 'How?' I ask simply.

Jen stares at the envelope rather than my face. 'Charlie had it.'

My body stiffens. I shake my head but it's tiny, painful movements. 'He was there?'

'I'm not going to defend what he did,' Jen begins.

As I listen to her explain, the heat of her anger washes over me until I can feel my skin blistering. When she pauses for my response, I turn the envelope over in my hand. 'What does it say?'

'You should probably read it for yourself, Ruth,' Jen says with a kindness that fills me with terror.

'I will,' I reply, placing the envelope in my lap. 'But not yet.'

There are footsteps on the stairs. 'What should we do?' Jen asks before Helena returns.

I take a breath as my focus shifts from the past to the future. 'I need to pack a bag. Once the police are done with me, I'm going to book myself into a hotel. I can't stay here,' I reply. It's not the answer Jen was looking for. She wants to know what we should do about Charlie's obstruction of justice. The truth is, I don't know.

'Would it be OK if I came with you to the hotel?' she asks. 'I can't face going back to the apartment.'

The door opens and Helena looks cautiously at us both.

'Come and sit back down,' I tell her as I rise from my chair. The interruption has given me time to decide how to reply to Jen. I don't want to hide out in a faceless hotel on my own, but I'm certain it won't be for long once I've phoned Sean. I need to be with my family, and so does my niece. Eve wants her daughter back and, whether Jen realises it or not, she needs her mum, not me.

'If you can't go home, you should go back to your mum and dad's. They need to know what's happening and if it's not too selfish of me, I'd prefer you to do it.'

'I dread to think what Mum will have to say. And she'll do the talking.'

'Give her a chance, Jen,' I say. 'For my sake.'

When I leave the room, my intention is to head straight upstairs but a figure appears in the kitchen doorway. Charlie sees the envelope in my hand and opens his mouth but he doesn't get the chance to speak. The palm of my hand as it strikes his cheek is hard and unforgiving.

My hand stings as I hurry upstairs. I'll have to pack some

essentials but there's only one item I'm concerned about taking with me. I go into Meg's room.

Pulling the memory box from the top shelf, I sit down on one of the princess beds and place the box on the bed opposite. Next to it, I set down the envelope Jen gave me before removing the box lid to find a second envelope. It's in my hand when there's a gentle tap on the door.

Lewis steps into the room and removes his baseball cap. 'Sorry, I had to get out of the kitchen, and I wanted to see if you were OK.'

'Shouldn't you be watching Geoff?'

'I think Charlie can handle him. Geoff's busy nursing a bottle of whiskey and blaming everyone but himself.'

'That man's conscience is bulletproof,' I say, setting down the envelope I'd taken from the box and lining it up next to its other half.

'I'd be happy to put it to the test,' mutters Lewis.

'No, you wouldn't.'

Lewis sighs. 'You're right. I grew out of playing the gangster a long time ago, although my behaviour since I came back here hasn't exactly been exemplary.'

'That was our fault. I imagine you've been going through a very tough time, and we made it impossible for you. How is your mum?'

'Not good. Iona's gone to the hospice tonight to sit with her. Fortunately, she cares a lot about Mum so we're putting up a united front for her sake,' he says. When he sees my brow furrow, he adds, 'She broke up with me.'

'I'm so sorry,' I say as I squeeze my eyes shut. I can feel my body shaking with the effort of holding back the first sob. I can't let it go because I'm scared that I won't be able to stop. The bed dips as Lewis sits down beside me and I lean against him.

'Jen mentioned you haven't read it yet,' he says. 'I'm not sure it's something you should read on your own.'

I peel my eyes open. 'Is it that bad?'

When Lewis doesn't reply, my broken heart rends and the pain I've carried for Meg all these years floods my body. This is her pain, and there's nothing I can do to make her better. The last thing she said to me was that she was untouchable. Why didn't I ask her what she meant? Why couldn't I offer her an escape from the clutches of her father?

'Would you mind talking to me a while?' I ask. 'I need to fill my head with images of Meg that don't involve her father.'

'What do you want to know?'

'Did you love her?'

'I must have done, to put up with all those mood swings,' he says with a wry smile.

'Sounds familiar.'

'My best memories of Meg are when we were together in Mum's old flat. That's when I saw the real her, not the act she was overplaying in front of Jen and the others. That's why I didn't like her hanging out with them. I wasn't trying to keep her to myself, I was . . .' His voice trails off. 'I thought I was helping her to be her best.'

'And what was she like in those moments?'

'Oh, she'd turn up with a dark cloud hanging over her and I'd have to dodge the odd bolt of lightning, but mostly, we'd end up chilling.' He squirms when he adds, 'It wasn't about sex, and with hindsight, I understand why that was.

We fooled around like we were still kids. She had the weirdest laugh.'

Clinging to the shreds of Meg's life that weren't tainted by Geoff, I force myself to smile. 'She was always being accused of putting it on, and maybe she did a bit,' I say as I recall how her cheeks would turn crimson red as she rocked with hysteria. 'She wouldn't stop until every last one of us was creased up. I'm glad she felt able to laugh with you, I don't recall much of that in those last two years. Did she hate me?'

I don't like the way Lewis glances at the envelope I've yet to open. 'Meg definitely moaned a lot about you, but her feelings were way more complex. There were definitely times when she forgot she was meant to hate you and talked about things you did together – all that family stuff she missed.'

'After what I've heard tonight, it's hard to remember that there were good times. In that box are all the mementoes I wanted to keep of her but I'm not sure now that I've picked the right ones.'

'Can I?'

Lewis reaches over and looks into the box. When he picks up the heart-shaped pot, I catch a glimpse of the silken colours of Meg's peacock scarf hiding beneath. I should take both of them out, along with the little silver voile bag containing the party favours Meg and Jen made for the anniversary party.

'I found the scarf discarded at the back of a drawer,' I explain. 'It was the first one I gave Meg. I never knew . . .' My words fail me as tears blur my vision.

'Me neither,' Lewis says as he pulls another of Meg's

scarves from his pocket. 'I gave her this on her birthday and she threw it back at me. I didn't understand at the time but it makes sense now. She was keeping these ones out of reach of Geoff because they were special. As were the people who gave them to her.'

'I wish I could believe you,' I whisper as I lean over and pick up the two envelopes. After ten tortuous years, it takes no time at all to bring the two torn edges together. I read Meg's final message. And then I cry.

Once I start, I can't stop. It wasn't Charlie who stole my daughter's final words, it was Geoff. To the very end, she couldn't bring herself to tell on him and that literally killed her.

'She couldn't hate me more than I hate myself,' I sob.

Lewis puts an arm around me and pulls me to him. 'She didn't hate us.'

'Oh, but she did. Read it.'

'I have, Ruth,' he says softly. 'Look at it again.'

Through bleary eyes, I force myself to reread two paragraphs that have been separated for ten years.

I hate this person I've become and I hate the rest of you too. Mum, Sean, Jen, Lewis. I hate you all! You should be glad I'm gone. You're better off without me.
   I'm doing this because of you.

'Meg hated that she cared about us so much,' Lewis says. 'She couldn't tell on Geoff because she knew it would destroy her family. She loved you, Ruth. That's the weapon Geoff used to keep his secret safe.'

'Well, it's not safe any more,' I reply as the sound of an

argument rises up from the sitting room directly below us. It's Jen and Charlie, which means Charlie isn't in the kitchen. Before I can question the wisdom of leaving Geoff alone, I hear a car door slam. I want to believe the police have arrived but I jump up the moment I hear an engine roar into life. 'That's Geoff's car.'

Lewis is ahead of me as we race down the stairs. Helena is emerging from the sitting room and I follow her gaze to the front door, which is wide open. As a car screeches out of the drive and down the road, headlights briefly pick out the figures of Jen and Charlie running down the path.

'You just let him walk out the front door!' Lewis yells at Charlie when we catch up to them next to Charlie's car.

'He sneaked out the back,' Charlie says, patting his jeans to find his keys. 'I was gone no more than thirty seconds, that's all. I thought he'd dozed off.'

I watch the taillights of Geoff's Audi flicker briefly red before he turns left and out of sight. He's heading for the junction with Aigburth Road, but then where?

'You shouldn't have left him!' screams Jen, thumping Charlie's chest with the heel of her palm.

Keys jangle in Charlie's hand as he unlocks his car. 'We can still catch him.'

'I'll stay with Helena,' I say quickly as the others prepare for the chase. 'But don't come back without him.'

Lewis gives me a nod as he pulls open the passenger door, only to freeze. We all do. We'd been following the roar of the Audi's engine as Geoff raced towards the nearby junction, too drunk to change up a gear. It's impossible to tell if the squeal of brakes that stopped us in our tracks came from Geoff's car, but I doubt it.

I don't know if the ground actually shook as an earth-shattering crash filled the night with sounds of grinding metal and breaking glass, but I began to sway as if it had. It seemed an age before I heard the wail of sirens.

Epilogue

Jen

When I wake up, the room I've come to think of as home again no longer looks alien to me. The new bedroom furniture Dad picked up from Ikea, which Mum filled with the clothes she'd collected from the apartment, are part of the fabric of my new life.

As I head downstairs, Dad appears from the narrow galley kitchen eating a bacon butty. He doesn't say a word as he kisses the top of my head with warm buttery lips before heading out to work. I never appreciated his quiet presence growing up. He's a good dad. I want to cry.

Mum ushers me into the living room and presses a mug of tea into my hand. 'Did you sleep well, love?' she asks brightly.

'Yeah, fine.'

Her eyes narrow. 'It will get easier and Hayley said she'll call around later. Maybe you could go to the cinema or something, make the most of the weekend.'

'Maybe,' I say. Since that awful night three weeks ago,

all my sisters have flocked around me as they had in the aftermath of Meg's death, only this time I haven't pushed them away. I've learnt to appreciate what I have.

When the doorbell rings, I assume it's Hayley or one of the others but when Mum returns, Ruth's face appears over her shoulder. Her gaunt features are reminiscent of my reflection in the bathroom mirror this morning. Her torn fingernails are yet to heal and it looks like there are new scars where she's chewed away cuticle.

'Shouldn't you be on your way to Stratford by now?'

'I'll be heading down there soon,' she says. 'Did you get the text from Lewis?'

'I haven't checked my phone yet,' I reply, glancing towards the mantelpiece. I've found it safest not to take my phone upstairs. Charlie keeps ringing or leaving messages and it's exhausting ignoring him.

'His mum died.'

Mum motions Ruth to an armchair. 'Here, sit down and I'll make you a cuppa,' she says, heading back out the door before Ruth can object.

Ruth stares after Mum but, with one blink, her knitted brow relaxes and she settles into the chair.

'Lewis must be heartbroken,' I say, pulling my dressing gown across my chest. I have an urge to go to him, to support him in the way that he supported me and Ruth that night. But I know it's not my place. 'Is Iona with him?'

'Yes, and I'll take that as a good sign. I hope they get back together,' Ruth says. 'Lewis is going to need someone now that he's lost such an important influence in his life. His mum was quite a formidable character by the sounds of it. I might have got to know her better if things had been different. I might have got to know Lewis too.'

'There's still time for that,' I offer. 'I hope you'll be coming back to Liverpool to pay us all visits.'

'I am only staying with Sean for a couple of weeks,' she warns. 'Although I'll admit, I'm in no rush to get back to that poky little apartment.'

The apartment Ruth has rented is on a temporary lease. She returned to the house only to pack what she needed and arranged for the rest to go in storage until she decides what, if anything, to take with her on her next move.

'You might not need it much longer if you find a nice little retirement cottage down there,' I say.

'That would be nice,' Ruth replies, but with none of the excitement that house hunting should bring. 'But there's still a lot to sort out this end so I will be back.'

'At least the house is sold,' I say, having been as surprised as Ruth that it had been snapped up days after she put it on the market. The low asking price probably helped.

'Yes, I had a call from my solicitor last night to say the vendors want to complete by Christmas. It's a blessing I suppose. I doubt I'd be able to give it away after the inquest.'

An involuntary shudder runs down my spine. The funeral last week had been bad enough, but I'm dreading the inquest. It's yet to be made public that Geoff McCoy's greatest shame wasn't to cause a fatal road traffic accident while drink-driving, although that is bad enough.

It was entirely good fortune that when Geoff ran a red light, the vehicle that ploughed into him was an articulated lorry and it's driver escaped with relatively minor injuries. There was only one death, and it was the right one.

When the police eventually arrived on Ruth's doorstep that night, there had been some initial confusion. They were there to inform Ruth of Geoff's death, not take statements for a report of alleged abuse. We had all looked to Ruth and waited for her to decide if her husband's dark secrets should be taken to the grave. 'Not again,' she had said.

'We're never going to know if Geoff caused the accident deliberately, are we?' I ask. It's what the media have been speculating but I try not to read the reports of a grief-stricken father racing to join his daughter in the afterlife.

'No, but I can't say I care. All I want is for that poor lorry driver to know his conscience is clear, and for the rest of the world to know that Geoff's isn't.'

'Helena has surprised me,' I say. 'She didn't have to give a statement to the police.'

'I wouldn't have blamed her if she had decided to say nothing, but it seems to have helped her, don't you think? She can set her sights on the future without being afraid of the past.'

'She's been telling me she wants to be a nurse.'

'Then we need to make sure that happens,' Ruth says, but her smile fades as she stares off into space. 'I still wonder if there are more Helenas out there. That night, every sick revelation felt like one punch after another, and I can't shake the feeling that there's more to come – one last ugly secret to be revealed.'

Ruth's gaze drifts to the door just as Mum appears with her tea.

Mum's steps are light as she slips into the room and passes the cup to Ruth. 'I'll leave you to it,' she whispers, but before she can disappear again, Ruth stops her.

'I'd rather you stayed, Eve,' she says.

Hesitantly, Mum takes a seat next to me on the sofa and holds her body tense. She's struggled with the news that her brother is an abuser and, for the first time in my life, she hadn't offered opinions or judgements. She prefers listening to talking these days. 'How are you, Ruth?' she asks. 'Jen says you're changing the name of the business.'

'Yes, it's going to be Pace and Associates,' Ruth says, her chin lifting. 'I thought it was better reverting back to my maiden name under the circumstances. It's been one of my easier decisions, and I've already notified Companies House.'

'You're not going to sell up then?'

'It would have been neater, but the staff did an incredible job filling the breach when Geoff died, and I don't think it will be a difficult transition for me to become a silent partner. My solicitor is drawing up the papers now so that a couple of our senior architects can take over the executive functions.' She looks to me and smiles. 'If some people have their way, I'll be out of there and heading for Stratford by the new year.'

Mum takes my hand and pulls it onto her lap, squeezing tightly. 'Jen won't be there much longer either if her interview goes well.'

It's the part-time admin post I'd applied for when I thought Oscar Armitage was going to be my new boss, and although circumstances have changed, my plans haven't. 'I'm going to spend the weekend preparing for it. I can't believe how much I want this.'

'And I've told her she doesn't need to worry about the money side of things – she can forget about giving me any housekeeping,' Mum adds. 'She needs to invest in the future.

There's a counselling course starting in January and she's going to enrol, aren't you, love?'

'Ruth knows,' I say, sharing a look with my aunt. As always, Ruth is the first person I turn to whenever I need to talk through an important decision, although it's a habit I'm going to have to break. The fact I've involved Mum at all in my plans is a step in the right direction.

'I wouldn't worry so much about the interview if I were you,' Ruth says to me. 'They'd be mad not to offer you the job.'

My eyes narrow. 'Have you spoken to them?'

'I don't know what you're suggesting. It will be a proper interview, but let's just say I don't think it will take long for them to deliberate.'

'It's good of you to still be looking out for her, with everything else that's going on,' Mum says.

'Jen has helped me too. The last few weeks have been a constant cycle of chasing paperwork and making statements. I've hardly had a chance to catch my breath. It's a small mercy that the foundation was already being wound up; not that we could have carried on, given the legacy Geoff has left us with.'

'I hear that girl you helped, the one whose boyfriend ran her down, is out of hospital,' Mum says.

'Yes, she's making amazing progress. The doctors have told her she'll never run a marathon but it sounds like she's taking that as a challenge.'

'And how's Sean doing? He did really well with the eulogy at Geoff's funeral service, all things considered.'

'It wasn't easy for him, but I don't think anyone was expecting us to sing Geoff's praises. They don't know the half of it,' Ruth says. When she sighs, her body folds in on itself. 'But in time, the truth will come out and it needs to be the whole truth.' Pulling back her shoulders, Ruth pins Mum with her stare. 'I need to understand who Geoff was, Eve, because I clearly didn't know the man I married.'

I can feel the shudder running through Mum's body. 'I don't recognise him either.'

'But did you suspect something?' Ruth asks, trying not to make it sound like the accusation it is. 'Was that why you didn't want Jen living with us?'

'No,' Mum answers quickly. 'Do you think I would have let her go on holiday with you if I didn't trust him?'

'But you did stop the holidays when she was sixteen,' Ruth persists. Her words are harsh but she softens the next with a sigh. 'Did you have some doubt at the back of your mind, even if you couldn't quite articulate what the problem was? Perhaps something happened in your childhood, to you or to Geoff? I need to know.'

When Mum drops her gaze, I'm the one to squeeze her hand this time. There is so much of the past that needs to be revisited. So many secrets. So many skewed views that need to be brought into focus. 'It's OK, Mum,' I say.

'If you want me to tell you that we suffered horribly in our childhood, then I'm afraid I can't,' she begins. 'Yes, our mother was short on affection but Geoff wasn't abused, and he didn't abuse me, if that's what you were suggesting. We were pretty close before I married, and in hindsight, maybe he was jealous in a way that a brother shouldn't be, but I'm speculating. I honestly don't know.' Her jaw is set firm and her next words tremble with the anger we all feel. 'All I can say is that nothing happened to Geoff that can excuse what he did to Meg. Abuse is abuse, and it's unjustifiable.'

'I'm sorry,' Ruth says. 'I had to ask.'

'You did, but you're asking the wrong question,' Mum says, raising her head and looking Ruth straight in the eye. 'You were right, there was more to why I stopped Jen moving in with you. The girls had been pestering me for weeks and by the time your anniversary party came around, they had almost worn me down, but . . . something happened that evening.'

I pull my hand from Mum's grasp. 'We know what happened that evening, Geoff told us.'

Mum smooths the creases of her dress where my hand had been. 'I didn't mean *that*. When you told me what Geoff had done at the party, love, I swear I didn't see any of that, nor did I suspect,' she says. 'But . . . I did talk to Meg later on, presumably after it happened. She had a glass of champagne in one hand and her makeup was running. I thought she'd been minesweeping drinks and had made herself sick. I wasn't impressed.' Mum closes her eyes and shakes her head. 'I couldn't have imagined.'

'None of us could,' Ruth says, her words catching.

'Meg was spoiling for an argument and had a go at me for not letting Jen move in. She asked if I thought she was a bad influence but before I could answer, she said she would be. Then she got angrier and asked me if I was afraid Jen would turn into a slut like her, that was the word she used,' Mum says. She swallows hard. 'She told me I'd be saying goodbye to innocent little Jen.'

There's silence that no one knows how to fill. So far, I haven't dwelt on the things my cousin did to hurt me because my hurt doesn't compare to hers, but if Meg's intention was to bring me to that house to take her place with Geoff, I don't think I could bear it.

Mum puts her arm around my shoulder to pull me close. 'She knew what she was doing, Jen, even if we didn't. She wasn't lashing out in one last drunken effort to convince me to change my mind. She was doing the exact opposite.'

'She was protecting Jen,' Ruth offers.

Before I can push it back, the memory of the last time I'd seen Meg rises to the surface. It was when we'd had that horrible fight on her doorstep and I'd said I was glad I didn't move in with her. 'Not as much as I am,' she'd replied. It was the last thing she said to me.

My heart swells with love for my beautiful, brave cousin who thought her silence would protect her family. 'She was protecting us all,' I say.

As we take a moment to gather our thoughts, I sip my tea but it's gone cold. Mum offers to make a fresh brew and disappears into the kitchen.

'I know you're trying to fix everything before you think about retirement, Ruth,' I say gently. 'But you've done as much as you can.'

'Have I?'

In the pause that follows, Ruth doesn't mention the one aspect of our broken lives that neither of us has attempted to fix. Ruth chose not to inform the police of Charlie's actions on the day Meg died, but that doesn't mean she's forgiven him, and the same goes for me. I'll never be able to look at Charlie again without thinking of what he saw that day in the garage. Some things will remain forever broken.

Ruth

I sit at a small kitchen table waiting for the sun to rise on what is my first morning in my new home. I'm surrounded by packing boxes and Sean will be around later to help with the heavy lifting but, for now, all is quiet. Through a set of French doors, I watch the darkness retreating to reveal a hoar frost covering my ramshackle of a garden. I can't wait to cut back the overgrowth to make room for the spring bulbs, the meadow flowers and the autumn fruits, all of which I intend to nurture once winter releases us from its grip. I have plans for every room in the house too. Sean had tried to persuade me to have some of the essential renovations completed before I moved in, but I was impatient. I'm ready for this, or I will be.

There's still one last thing I have to do before I embrace my new life. I look down at the clean sheet of paper in front of me. The pen in my hand feels heavy with the weight of the words I've yet to write so I close my eyes and, as I do, I recall snatches of the dreams that stalk me in my waking hours.

There was a time when I longed to dream of Meg but, for years, I was unable to resurrect the daughter who had become a stranger to me. I didn't know her. I didn't understand her. I do now, and although my nightmares are the kind to rip my beating heart from my chest, they bring me comfort. Meg is there and I reach out to her.

Hello, my darling Meg,

It feels like we're getting to know each other all over again, or at least I'm getting to know you. I've been searching for answers for over ten years and I always imagined that, when I had them, I would feel a sense of closure, but the truth has torn the very fabric of my soul. To say I didn't know isn't good enough. I should have seen more. I should have listened more. I should have been more.

I was so angry at you for throwing away the life I gave to you, but that's part of the problem, isn't it? You were not my possession, and you were certainly not your father's. I don't want to make this letter about him so I will say only this. He died still believing that his love could do no harm. Let us be clear. What he offered you was not love. It was not harmless. It was not your fault.

For a long time, I couldn't understand why you gave no thought to how much you would hurt me and how I would carry that pain through the rest of my life. I have come to realise that any hurt on my part wouldn't have entered your head, because you thought you were protecting us.

It wasn't your job to protect our family, sweetheart. It was mine. You were not the problem. If anything, I was. I wanted to keep you locked up safe at home, not realising that was where the danger lurked. I spent all that time standing on the wrong side of a closed bedroom door. We should have had this talk then, not now.

I know your father blamed my failings as a wife for his actions and I think that's why you were angry with me too. I don't blame you for believing his twisted logic. He fooled us both. I let him convince me that I had no influence over you, that he was the one to keep your confidence, that I was the lesser parent.

I've spent the last decade telling myself that the past can't be changed but I was wrong. The past is being rewritten and I see you now, Meg. I hear you and I hope you hear me. We are not the false images conjured by a sick mind. We are imperfect souls and I'd like to believe we've found each other again.

I love you, sweetheart, with every piece of my broken and splintered heart, and if I can ask one thing, it would be for you to walk with me a while. Be by my side so I can help your little nieces grow up to be in awe of their Auntie Meg; the young woman whose voice grows stronger every day.

Your loving Mum, forever and always xxx

Acknowledgements

My ninth book, *Don't Turn Around*, has been one of the hardest to write. It covers a number of difficult themes ranging from abuse and suicide, to bereavement, and not all my research has been comfortable or pleasant to undertake. If I can take anything away from what I've learnt, it's that there is an army of volunteers and professionals out there who are eager to help those in crisis. The online resources on websites such as Women's Aid, Refuge, and the Samaritans have been invaluable and it's comforting to see so many helplines doing amazing work both locally and nationally.

Not everything I've brought to this novel has been through research, and although I haven't experienced a loss through suicide, I do know the pain of losing a child. I'm also aware of how each parent's journey through their grief is different, having spent some years working on the Child Death Helpline, which is a national helpline for anyone affected by the death of a child of any age. It's operated in partnership with Alder Hey and Great Ormond Street Children's Hospitals, and is staffed by volunteers who are all bereaved parents. Although there's little in common with my fictional helpline, I can recall those long evenings not knowing who might phone that night, and when it was time to go home, hoping that the people I did speak to had felt heard.

I'd like to thank Shelagh Hatton and all the staff and volunteers at the Alder Centre for all their support on both a personal and professional level. The Alder Centre is the only bereavement centre of its kind attached to a paediatric hospital (Alder Hey Children's Hospital) and it's a remarkable place. I cannot praise highly enough the team that quietly gets on with what they do best, offering world-leading bereavement counselling, support and training, and it's a privilege to work with you all.

My heartfelt thanks as always goes to my editor, Martha Ashby, who pushes me to my limits with each book, and then some, but I love her for it. Thanks also to the rest of the wonderful team at HarperCollins, including Kim Young, Jaime Frost and Emma Pickard, who turn the solitary life of an author into an incredibly rewarding partnership.

I would like to thank my agent, Luigi Bonomi, for being my champion and believing in me from the very beginning. If it wasn't for you, I'd still be in 'waste', but instead I'm following my dreams with you pointing the way.

A huge, loving thank you to all my family and friends who are always ready to give me back my sanity once I've pulled myself out of my fictional worlds, and especially to my amazing daughter Jess. This is where I usually write how I couldn't be more proud of you, but you keep proving me wrong by making me prouder.

A special thank you goes to Janet Roberts who has

become a good friend and one-woman promoter of my books ever since our dearly missed friend Donna Hall introduced us.

And finally, a thank you to all my readers, new and old. I couldn't do this without you.

A good mother doesn't forget things.

A good mother isn't a danger to herself.

A good mother isn't a danger to her baby.

You want to be the good mother
you dreamed you could be.

But you're not. You're the bad mother
you were destined to become.

At least, that what he wants you to believe…

OUT NOW

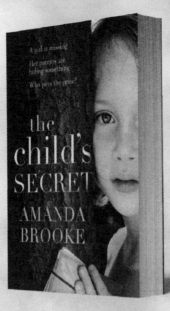

Everyone has secrets…

When eight-year-old Jasmine Peterson goes
missing, the police want to know everything.

What is the local park ranger, Sam McIntyre,
running away from and why did he go out
of his way to befriend a young girl?

Why can't Jasmine's mother and father
stand to be in the same room as each other?

With every passing minute, an unstoppable chain
of events hurtles towards a tragic conclusion.

Everyone has secrets. The question is:
who will pay the price?

OUT NOW